Also by Maureen O'Donoghue

Jedder's Land

WINNER

Maureen O'Donoghue

Simon and Schuster

New York London Toronto
Sydney Tokyo

*Published by Simon and Schuster
A Division of Simon & Schuster Inc.
Simon & Schuster Building
Rockefeller Center
1230 Avenue of the Americas
New York, NY 10020*

*Designed by Mary Beth Kilkelly / Levavi & Levavi
Manufactured in the United States of America*

10 9 8 7 6 5 4 3 2 1

*Library of Congress Cataloging-in-Publication Data
O'Donoghue, Maureen.
Winner.*

*I. Title.
PR6065.D583W56 1988 823'.914 87-36902
ISBN 0-671-53198-0*

Acknowledgments

My special thanks go to David Wright of the National Horseracing Museum in Newmarket for the abundance of information he provided on the Edwardian horseracing scene. During the three years it took to research and write *Winner*, he tracked down the names of the winners of obscure races, stud and groom fees, details of owners, jockeys and personalities of the time and countless other facts with unfailing good humour.

I am greatly indebted to the writers, both present and past, of the many books from which I have received invaluable help, in particular, George Pumptre for *The Fast Set*, John Welcome for *Irish Horseracing*, Vincent Orchard for *Tattersalls*, Dorothy Laird for *Royal Ascot*, and Gerry Cranham for his superlative photography in *The World of Flat Racing* and *The Guinness Guide to Steeplechasing*, which re-created the immediacy, exhilaration and beauty of the Sport of Kings at my desk.

I should also like to thank Susan Watt, my editor, for her patience and care, and Caradoc King of A. P. Watt for always finding the time to listen and encourage, for his comments and criticism (which are always constructive!) and for the shelter of his expertise as my agent.

My husband, Bill, has provided the knowledge of horses and racing gathered from a lifetime's devotion to the Turf. His loving enthusiasm and support for this book have never flagged, and so, above all, I give my thanks to him.

For
my husband, Bill,
with all my love

Chapter ONE

The coffin was lowered, and as the first shovel of earth thudded onto its wooden lid, Macha felt her eyes become bloodshot. The mourners gazed and shook their heads in sympathy, and she clenched her fists. It was a torment, trying not to laugh.

Hugh Mulligan pressed close and squeezed her. Smelling the porther on his breath, she sidestepped out of reach and turned to look straight at him.

"Da's dead," she said, in a low, emphatic voice. "So the wedding's off."

Only the priest's glare stopped his protest, and the sound of his sulky grunt made her cheeks burn again, so that she had to duck her head and hope the kinsmen thought her shoulders were shaking with sobs.

She was free! One week later and she would have been married to Hugh Mulligan, with his pimples and pockmarks, his hair grease and his wrinkled, monkey eyes, and that would have been an end to it. But Da had died just in time.

Macha wanted to sing and catch the fluttering red ribbons decorating the thornbush they were planting on the grave and dance around it, twirling her scarlet cloak. She wanted to gulp down the flagon of liquor they were about to pour on the earth and cause a scandal.

The ocean wind savaged them, flailing at their shoulders and scratching their eyes and sounding pipe and klaxon over the bare, square cemetery as Father Peter hurried through his lines, made the final sign of the cross and averted his eyes from the pagan bush. Tinkers! More heathen than Christian. He wondered why this burial place had to be at least a mile from church and village, and he thought of the dumpling stew heating on the stove. He glanced at the pony and trap waiting to carry him to it and moved to leave.

The girl, Macha, was standing before him, her expression mischievous, reading his thoughts. He blessed her automatically and hurried away.

The company he left behind stood awkwardly around the grave looking at each other. Then Hugh's father pushed a coin into the soft earth and the poteen was poured, a clear, barley-sugar stick of liquid, and they began to disperse.

Macha, reluctant to follow, stared at the oblong mound and sighed. Now she wished she had not been tempted to laugh. She wished he could have been brought here in a fine glass hearse drawn by plumed black horses. He would have liked being carried in style, instead of on the shoulders of the Mulligan men.

"I'm sorry, Da," she muttered. "But everything else was done right."

That was true. His body had lain in its open coffin in a tent on the outskirts of the camp for several days, watched over by relations and visited by others. She herself had eaten only bread and water while he was unburied. He was dressed in his best clothes, and his other clothes, carefully folded inside out to safeguard against ill luck, had been placed beneath him. His drinking mug and fiddle and pocket knife were beside him; a round pebble had been set on his chest and a handful of grain put in his pocket. She checked off each ritual in her mind. Nothing had been forgotten.

They were calling her from the gate, their voices petulant.

"Macha! Will you come!"

Behind them, in the bay, the Aran Islands of Inishmore, Inishmaan and Inisheer sat on high white nests of foam, like three dark birds.

There was trouble coming. Already she could see Hugh Mulligan talking urgently to his father and jerking his head in her direction. They could not be avoided and she wondered what would happen.

"Come here this minute, child, or you'll be left to walk the road yourself."

She looked down at her father's grave for the last time. She would rather have stayed there alone, but instead, picked her way very slowly between the headstones and joined them.

The track was badly made and full of holes. A border of stone-walled swatches of grass separated it from the sea on one side. On the other side, the bog ran like a rust-stained tide all the way to the Twelve Bens in the distance, where clouds, heavily pregnant with rain, had already obscured the peaks and were bowling purposefully downhill.

Five grey donkeys, standing together, swivelled their ears without turning their heads towards the tinkers as they tramped past.

"I've a throat on me as dry as a stone in an ould shoe," Hugh's father complained. "Jack Sheridan, God's mercy on him, weighed worse than a knacker horse in that box. We should have put him on a cart."

"Hush yourself!" His wife cast a look over her shoulder at Macha trailing behind them. "It was a fine burial with a very decent number paying respect. The Holy Father himself, in Rome, couldn't have wished for better."

"I think maybe Queen Boswell's passing had the edge on it," commented a Doran aunt. "The Duffys and Connors and Sheridans and Finneys were all present, and the Gormans. There was a multitude fit for a city procession saw her earthed."

"That was because she was a Boswell, and she passed on at Puck Fair," Oul' Arigho pointed out. "Sure, anyone who snuffs it at Puck Fair could fill Christ Church Cathedral with respect and no mistake."

"Aye, it was a convenient dying. If she'd chosen Derby Day on Epsom Downs, she couldn't have done better."

Macha heard their voices without registering what they were saying. Nervous with a mixture of melancholy and apprehension, she was wishing the day and the night ahead were over and that everything was settled.

The village of Kilkieran came into view at the end of the long, flat road, and the first bunch of mourners had already reached it. Cousins had travelled over from Dublin, and other uncles and nephews and aunts, each with his or her own family, had come up from the south to be at Jack Sheridan's funeral, and having done their duty, all now felt deserving of the succour obtainable at Flynn's bar. The pace of the Mulligan clan quickened. Nan Mulligan took Macha's wrist to hurry her along too, and by the time they arrived, there must have been fifty or sixty travellers crammed into the back of the close, malodorous cave in the main street.

Mugs and tankards were filled, and the local drinkers found themselves squeezed to the door and then out of the place altogether. There was that avid, tender, religious moment when everyone drew and swallowed his first drench, the contented sigh before the rest of the pint followed in a silky glissade and then the rattle of empty vessels slapping against oak.

The mirror over the fireplace reflected their slippery and demanding faces between the curlicues of its frosted lettering, which read "POWER'S WHISKEY. Estabd. AD 1791. 10 years old Extra Special pure pot still." Other, different brands of whiskey lined the shelves on the opposite wall in a display of distilled maturity, and several bar cats sat among the bottles or stalked the edges of the ledges, polishing the glasses to a gleam with their fur. A further notice overhead announced in scarlet, "FLYNN'S FEROCIOUS FEED IS THE FINEST."

The Flynn of this notorious feed, forewarned of the Wake, had removed all other breakables and chairs, congratulating himself on having fixed the tables to the floor after the last local fair. He had shouted his wife and daughter through from the grocery end of the premises, where they filtered and improved the gossip of Kilkieran. Now all three grimly measured and poured, and thought of the profit.

The drinking steadied into an even pace, and the sound of conversation increased from a growl to a smothering stipple.

"The roads of Ireland will seem as empty as a hunger twenty miles from a fat goose without Jack Sheridan travelling them." The panegyric began.

"And him so young! Why, the man was in his prime. It's a mortal tragedy that would not find the like in one of his own fine legends."

"Aye, he could tell a tale fit to break a shaft of sun into drops of tears, or put a smile on the face of a buck ferret. It's Christ's honest truth that there was a man with a gift."

"A prodigious fellow of a man."

Annie Doran stroked Macha's hair in a motherly way. "And here's the angel child left an orphan. Lord forgive me, but it is a bitter and thankless life."

"Our Hugh will mind her," Nan Mulligan said, complacently. "No girl has time for sorrow when she has a man."

Macha sat down on a shadowy bench in the corner as they began to tease the intended bridegroom about his forthcoming marriage and the number of children he was going to manage to sire in the shortest possible time. When he flushed and looked over, she glowered until his eyes slid away.

She stopped listening to them. It was all nonsense anyway. She was no orphan, her mother having run off to England with a Protestant fourteen years previously, sometime after her birth, and, far from being in his prime, her father had been well over sixty, the most unsuccessful horse dealer in all Ireland. He had drunk himself to death, and certainly she would not be marrying Hugh or any other Mulligan. But they were right about one thing. Jack Sheridan could tell wondrous fables.

He had been a large man, with thick grey hair which curved back in a luxuriant shag from his forehead to his shoulders, big hands, broad shoulders, barrel chest, with height to match; a noticeable man. And he had had a special voice, bass and expressive, which could purr of love, or crackle of perfidy, or breathe sadnesses too unbearable to be expressed above a whisper, or rasp with a blaring and unheralded harshness that ambushed his listeners in fear; a hypnotic voice, which she could still hear as though he stood behind her. With education, he would have been an actor. As it was, he had been the best storyteller in the land.

"You were born at midnight on May Eve, when the moon was so bright that scholars were reading books of Latin and Greek in their gardens and the shops of Dublin forgot to close and were full of grand ladies not knowing they should have been sleeping, and there were boats on the river and bees in the air."

When he had first told her, he had dandled her on his knee. Later, as she grew older, he had repeated the history over and over, each time further embellished and polished until it reached the perfection of an ancient ballad as they sat by the fire together, or drove along secret Irish lanes.

"There was to be a great fair that day, and me with the only horse I had to sell lying sickly on the ground, and that creature all there was to save us from a starvation worse than famine. Midnight on the eve of May, the time of the old gods, and as you were born, that dying horse suddenly scrambled to its feet and threw back its head like a warrior and neighed loud enough to be heard in Ulster, and the light came back into its eyes as though struck in a forge. It was a sign. MACHA, the great mare goddess, was speaking and could not be ignored."

And then he would recount the legend from before the time of Christianity, of how MACHA OF THE HORSES had fallen in love with a mortal and turned herself into a woman to wed him. "And she was such a woman, tall and beautiful as no man had ever seen, with silver eyes full of mystery, like your own, and shining black hair and long, slim legs like a true thoroughbred."

It sounded like descriptions the child had heard of her mother, and her father's voice used to deepen and soften, as though talking to himself at this point, and sometimes he would stop and stare into space before taking a deep pull at the whiskey bottle.

"But the man she espoused was an idiot fellow, an ass, and despite warning, he bragged of her grace and speed in front of the King of the Ulaid himself, at the great annual fair, with the result that the King commanded this woman to run against his finest horse.

"She was brought before him and it was seen by all that she was heavy with child, and she begged upon her knees that the race be postponed until after the birth, but the King would have none of it, for his pride was greatly offended."

The funeral faded into the back of the girl's mind, and the crescendo of animated shouting around her in the bar seemed like the accompaniment to that infamous race. She could hear her father recite it again, his hand arcing to outline the gleaming, steaming flanks of the King's stallion and cutting across the air to illustrate the speed of the immortal; telling how the breath of the horse grew so hot that MACHA's streaming black hair was scorched and turned red as she fled before it, and the foam from their bodies was lifted and tossed by the wind into the sea, where it can be seen riding the waves to this day; and how the throng of fairground folk and farmers, hirelings and courtiers, fortune-tellers and Druid priests cheered with joy when the woman won.

"The MACHA fell to the ground in great agony," he would conclude. "And as the birth pangs gripped, she cursed the King and every man hearing her screams that each would suffer the pains of birth for five nights and four days and the men of the Ulaid would suffer these pains and remain as weak as a woman in labour for nine generations; an unendurable curse, which in the end was to cost the King his kingdom and his crown. And before them all, the goddess gave birth to twin horses."

The day his only child was born, Jack Sheridan had sold his unsound horse for a miraculous sum of money, far beyond its value, and he had named her Macha in gratitude.

"Never let yourself be without the horses, daughter. They will run for you and bring you riches," he had often promised. "You will have great power over horses and great power over men."

Then, to her incredulity, he had disregarded all his predictions of her special future and, without word or warning, had traded her one night in the public bar to old Mick Mulligan for his pit-skinned son in return for a couple of nags, to be stolen and delivered by the boy as a sign of his manliness by the day of the wedding.

It was the custom for traveller girls to be married early, sometimes as young as twelve years old. Usually the matches were arranged between families already closely related through blood or marriage, and as a first cousin, Hugh Mulligan was considered a most suitable mate. It was irrelevant that Macha had known and thoroughly despised him all her life.

"Lifting a bag of praties would break his back, and if he falls off another pony, he'll turn into a bag of praties himself. There isn't as much meat on him as would feed a crow," she had protested in vain, adding desperately, "He doesn't talk and he doesn't move his hands. He laughs like a donkey at nothing at all, Da. And doesn't everybody know he's backward. I don't want him."

The horse dealer had slapped his daughter hard with the flat of his hand and promised her a thrashing if she complained again. The deal had been agreed. That was the way it was always done.

Then, only days before the ceremony was due to take place, Jack Sheridan had died.

Macha stared at the kinsfolk, by now more drunk than sober, and wondered with a shiver what they would do that night, how they would react.

The women, their shawls tight about them, were still talking with lugubrious enjoyment of other deaths.

"There was this couple who sailed to America and there they had a babby," one retailed. "And the babby, God bless its little soul, died. And they brought the body all the way back to Connemara to be buried."

Her listeners were impressed.

"Now, was that stupid? Or was it not?"

Cosily bunched in their thick wrappings of wool, they looked like a pen of sheep, but Macha had heard them screaming with fury over slights and jealousies, and watched them attack a girl and shear off all her hair for having broken a taboo by letting that hair down and combing it in front of the men. Macha herself had been beaten not long before by Nan Mulligan for washing her own clothes in with those of her father. Tonight, she knew, they would not be placated.

In the murk of the bar, the men looked dangerous, black eyes like holes, red rising under their dark skins, broken teeth and nails, and the atmosphere of anarchy which marked all meetings between them. Macha felt dread squeeze her breath, and she gulped down the porther.

An argument was developing in the opposite corner between a Cauley and Manni Gorman, who was stabbing his forefinger into the other's chest. Their voices were already louder than the rest, and their bodies tensed, swaying forward to balance on the balls of their feet in readiness, backs arched and buttocks tight.

The landlord lit oil lamps as the short day dimmed, and the shadows of the two men were suddenly flung across the ceiling to dominate the room. A cat, which had seemed asleep in the corner, moved away with swift stealth. The other mourners began to shift position, moving slightly back and apart from each other, as though unsure of their friends. John Flynn sent his women out and began surreptitiously taking bottles from the shelves and placing them in a cupboard.

Manni's wife sidled through to put her hand on his arm and was roughly pushed aside. A cousin from Dublin intervened and was punched in the mouth. The first blood was drawn, and the bonds of the Wake burst with female ululating and a violent smell of sweat. The drinkers backed and bumped, angular with clumsy elbows and feet, then parted, and through the gap, Macha saw the Cauley man clutch his groin and recoil from Manni Gorman. The slim black outline of a knife appeared in his hand.

The crowd collided. Old quarrels and rivalries were resurrected with explosive grunts and the tearing of cloth and women clawing and screeching and male fists and boots pounding flesh, which swelled and blackened and split to smear and mingle blood from victim to attacker in an obscene travesty of brotherhood.

She had watched the scene countless times before; men brawling over women or bets, women fighting over men or money, at fairs and on camp sites and in bars, wherever travelling people met. Her Da had been a superior wrestler, and although she had often washed clean the lesions and cuts of his battles, that was only after his opponents had been left unconscious or crawling away in ignominy.

Usually, at the outbreak of a scrap, she found a good vantage point and took sides, yelling her support and relishing the excitement, but this night, as people blundered and fell into her, she felt invaded and angry, as though they were robbing Jack Sheridan of regard and belittling his memory before he was cold.

She edged along the bench to the door and stood up. A man

catapulted from the melee and smashed the partition into splinters. Macha pushed her way out into the village street.

Local people had already gathered in the dusk. She felt their indignation before she heard their insults.

"Will ye look at the scruff of her!"

"Dirty, filthy tinker."

"Reared like animals, they are."

There was the sound of breaking glass from the interior behind, and the group moved forward, ominously.

"Listen to the dirty, drunken bastards!"

"Aye, drunk on stolen money, you can be sure of that."

"I've lost three fine fowl since they came camping by O'Leary's Dip with their thieving ways."

"They'd steal the button from your belly."

Macha stopped with her back to a shop wall, very still, pretending to look into the distance, but watching from the corners of her eyes. The young men among them were growing restive, roused by the sounds of fighting and keen to join in. Only the thought of tinker knives and known ferocity was holding them back.

A woman at the back of the crowd shouted, "Let's be rid of the rotten dogs! Run them out of Kilkieran!"

Others echoed her.

And the young men looked at Macha, who was easy prey.

The open doorway to Flynn's bar was yards away. A youth walked up and spat in her face, and a woman laughed. They began to close in.

She could see their faces, the tight, right features of settled people, the buffers, who hid from the weather in houses and cabins of stone, who had never seen the castle ruins at Athlone, or the vast stretches of Lough Corrib, yet thought her ignorant. Their expressions were full of hatred, mouths open and eager, noses made grotesque by distended nostrils, necks bulging with blood pressure, the narrow frost of their eyes. Made bold by their number, they wanted vengeance for their own superstitious fears and for the freedom of the travellers. They moved as a pack.

Macha cursed them, "May God make you cough blood and have stillborn children and drive the fish from the bay till you starve, if you cross a gypsy."

They stopped, instinctively, and with profanity and commotion two Doran brothers came battling out of the shebeen. The village gang swivelled to see the action. Macha slipped away, keeping to the shadows, past the two-roomed cottages which lined the street, then running with silent feet out along the coast road towards the heath where the travellers' tents and carts were drawn up.

By the time she slowed to cross the stone bridge about two miles from Kilkieran, the ugly little incident had lost its importance. All her life she had been accustomed to the hostility of the settled people, the mixture of contempt and fear in their eyes and the taunts their children shouted when they saw her.

"Scabby!"

"Slopeen tink!"

"Dirty stroller!"

She had learnt to follow the example of other travellers and pay little heed.

The rain, which had stopped for an hour or so, began again with fine, soundless drops, and beyond the boundary of the shower, a half moon sprayed stars across the sky, and the rippled surface of Kilkieran Bay repeated its reflection infinitely. Macha thought of the coming hours and drew her shawl closer, more as protection against her own imagination than against the damp.

The scrum in the bar would soon be over and the bereaved evicted from the village to make their tipsy way back to the camp. Her thoughts fled ahead of her hurrying feet in her anxiety to reach there well before them.

A shapeless, flapping mass appeared and materialised into a bush draped with clothes, like wet flags. The bender tents humped in a shoal through the night beyond and a motley guard of dogs leapt out, snarling, as the girl arrived, only to fawn with recognition when she swore and kicked them off. Four horses were grazing at the edge of the bog, and grasping their head ropes, two in each hand, she ran them, stumbling in their hobbles, to where the only barrel-top waggon on site was established in ostentatious prominence.

Bartered from an English gypsy, this Bow-top had been Jack Sheridan's display of status. At a time when there were very few such vehicles in the whole of Ireland and most travellers slept in the hedgerows or barns, or under bent hazel rods covered with felts, he would have sacrificed his beasts and starved himself and child, stolen and possibly even murdered to keep it. It was the proof that he was no tinker. It was the mark of his claim to be a half-blood Rom.

She hitched the horses to the rear of the waggon, untied the two lurcher dogs from between its wheels and led them up the steps. The door opened to his familiar smell of tobacco and horses, so powerful it made him seem alive still, and she sighed his name and let the first tears free.

"Da. Oh, Da."

Macha had not been on her own since his death. For the past five days close kinsmen had fasted and kept "vigil" along with her, while others had come to view the body. Her Aunt Nan had fussed over the proprieties, and there had been no time to resolve the feelings which had stormed her.

For weeks before, she had been in a state of rage over the way he had matched her with Hugh Mulligan, and after the shock of his sudden sickness and dying had come a childish sense of having been avenged and the secret conviction that she had outwitted him and that Macha, the immortal, had delivered her namesake. The thrill of escape had persisted to the edge of his grave, when for the first time she had begun to understand that this was no little victory soon to be forgotten. Jack Sheridan would never again pat her cheek, or eat the food she cooked, or shout at her for the sake of it. She would never again hear his fantastic stories, or help him "doctor" old horses for sale, or shoulder him onto the manger-like bed in the end wall of the van. She would never see her father again.

Now, in the womb of the Bow-top, a sensation of isolation overcame her, and she cradled into the hay-lined bed and wept the noisy, gulping sobs of loss and guilt at last.

Their voices, still cantankerous with porther and whiskey, were carried ahead of them on the wind, and Macha dried her eyes and stood up, straightening her skirts and pushing back her braided hair. A last plea for forgiveness was whispered to the soul of the horse dealer. She knew what she had to do and wondered if it would send her to Hell.

The dogs growled and the men grumbled, and there was a shot-sharp cracking as someone threw wood on the fire, and then the shuffling of their gathering outside.

"Well, where in God's name is she then, woman?" Mick Mulligan was heard to ask.

"I've not seen whisker of her since Manni Gorman there set upon my man and near murdered him." The accusation outweighed the reply.

"Me murder him! Would I bother myself with the likes of your puny man, who'd have trouble skinning an egg without your help, ma'am?" The third voice was indignant. "Didn't the whole world see it was himself fancied himself as the fine fellow, leppin' up and down trying to take a poke at me until I was forced to lift him off the ground a little, for fear he would damage me kneecaps."

This reference to the slightness of a Cauley versus the height and tonnage of the Gorman drew incoherent protest from the former and the sounds of renewed scrummage.

"Divide yourselves and shut your mouths, the both of you," commanded Michael Mulligan. "Now, where the divil is Jack Sheridan's daughter?"

"She said there was to be no wedding, Da," Hugh Mulligan said plaintively.

"That was the grief speaking, son," his mother explained. "It would be a hard one that didn't act a bit queer after the death of her own father. She's probably gone off to sorrow a while."

"Well, we'd better get on without her, starting with the van," the senior Mulligan decided. "Have you that torch aflame yet?"

Macha opened the door and saw a blazing brand being raised from the fire.

"Mother of God! Will you look at that? Another instant and the child would have been kindled to death." Nan rushed up the steps and grabbed her arm.

Macha shook her off and looked over her head to the company.

"You will not burn the waggon, nor will the horses and dogs be murdered," she said, shrilly.

"She's drunk, Nan. The girl's ranting drunk!" exclaimed her uncle. "Get her out of there!"

As the woman raised her hand threateningly, Macha jerked out of reach, and the two dogs appeared, snarling, beside her.

"My soul from the devil!" Michael Mulligan strode forward, slamming past his wife, and seized his niece round the waist. The lurchers catapulted into attack, one sinking its teeth into his thigh and the other landing on his chest so that he tumbled, backwards and bellowing, to the ground.

Macha watched impassively as the other travellers beat them off, and when the furor had died down, she spoke again.

"This is my waggon and those are my ponies and hounds now, and I say you will not touch them."

"The Lord's mercy! The child's demented!" Nan crossed herself and then changed her tone to a wheedling plea. "Macha, me babby, the belongings of the dead are destroyed by flame to keep their spirits from returning to haunt us all. You know that."

"Jack Sheridan told me with his last breath that the waggon must not be burnt. It was his dying wish, and he won't ever leave us to rest if it is not carried out."

It might have been true. The horse dealer had been excessively proud of the Bow-top. The mourners murmured angrily, but could not argue.

Mick Mulligan, who had clambered to his feet, was outraged.

"Enough! Take that madwoman away and let's have no more time wasting."

All eyes fixed on the blood soaking through his trouser leg and on the two dogs apparently eager for more, and no-one moved.

"Now, listen you here, you heathen little tramp." He snatched the torch from his son and turned back to Macha. "Your father's dead and you are charged to me as next of kin and you will marry my son tomorrow, so come down out of there this minute, or I'll put fire to the lot, mongrels, nags, yourself and all."

Macha held her breath while he raged. The moment had come and there was no avoiding it. She stared at him, forcing herself to the act, then leant forward and ground out the words.

"You are no next of kin to me. You are no kin at all. And I'd sooner spring over Couragour Falls into the Shannon with a rock as big as a sheep round my neck than marry that half-witted idjiot of yours. You've got no rights over me, Michael Mulligan, because I am not Jack Sheridan's daughter."

There was an indrawn breath from the crowd, and she glared down through the firelight at them.

"Why do you think my mother ran off?" she demanded. "I'm no orphan. I am *his* blood, the Protestant's blood, the child of the *gaujo* she lives with now in England. But she is still Jack Sheridan's rightful widow, and this waggon and the horses and all his goods belong to her, and I am her nearest kin. 'Uncle' Mulligan, you have no rights here, no rights at all."

"That's an infernal lie! You evil harlot!" Michael Mulligan rushed at her, roaring abuse and kicking the first dog, so that it limped away, yelping.

Macha felt her guts churn at his driving wrath; and then he was on her, and the pain, as his fist crashed into her face, lit the night with flat, white light. Involuntarily, she raised her arms for protection, but his blows thumped against her head and her rib cage, collisions which knocked the breath out of her in screams. Then she was falling, and the trampled mud of the enclosure splashed stickily into her mouth and nostrils and filled her eyes to blindness before she was hauled to her feet again.

"Now take back that lie, ye filthy witch, or it's more than mud will choke you."

Macha shook her head and cried, the salt tears diluting the dirt into grit.

"It's God's truth," she swore, weeping. "Jack Sheridan himself told me . . . just last week . . . just before . . ."

"For a dying man, he seems to have done a deal of talking and yet there's only yourself heard it all." His breath smelt sour, like that of his son at the funeral, and it gave her courage. She stopped crying and smeared the mess from her eyes.

"He wanted me to know," she said, quietly. "Just me."

The man released her and put an arresting hand on his wife's shoulder as she was about to go to the girl she'd thought was her niece.

"Leave the bitch alone," he snarled, turning his back. "She has nothing to do with us. She is cursed. She is *mochardi*."

As he walked away, the rest of the travellers began to disperse too, silently and without looking at her, until Macha was quite alone.

Trembling, she climbed back into the waggon and onto the rustling hay again to lie, ice-cold and staring at the direful knowledge that she had condemned her soul to eternal damnation.

For it *had* been a lie, a vile, disgusting lie; and her father in purgatory must have heard her deny him. She had committed a foul sin and knew she was beyond forgiveness and beyond redemption.

It was many hours before sleep came and then only as a disturbance of dreams full of menace and vibrations which made her flinch and moan.

People in row upon row, people with no facial features except holes where their eyes should have been, were all staring at her, and she realised she was naked. Then the ranks broke to allow through a mighty man with knotted fists and a hooked nose like the beak of an eagle and the shoulders of Atlas; Jack Sheridan, her father, was marching upon her, nearer and nearer, making her cower and grow smaller until she could diminish no further. He was there, but he did not stop, or even pause. He strode straight through her, as though she did not exist. And the faceless people came tramping after, row upon row, and in her terror, she screeched and covered her face, and the air shuddered with a hammering of hooves.

When she looked up, the people had gone, and in their place stood an unholy woman with hair so long that it reached the ground in labyrinths and conundrums and mazes and whirlpools, in which men were floundering and drowning and calling for help in fly-small cries. The hair held the owl with the moon in its horns and the open knife. It hid half the woman, so that only one eye, one arm, one hand, one breast, one foot were visible, the invulnerable oneness. And the woman neighed, brassy as a horn, and Macha awoke.

She was wet, her clothes clinging coldly to her back and chest, her ribs sore from Mick Mulligan's fists. It was daylight. The camp would be alert and brisk with men watering and feeding the beasts, and women cooking, and children running between the two. Some families would be preparing to move on, rolling up the covering of their tents and loading the hazel poles onto carts, or onto their donkeys' or even their own backs, if they had no transport.

Macha tried to imagine how they would receive her when she appeared. Would she be upbraided, or ignored? The night before, her uncle had cursed her, called her *mochardi*—unclean. Had it not been so cold, she would have stayed out of the way; but her teeth were chattering, and her fingers were white and bloodless; and she would have to face them sometime. Pulling her shawl over her head, she opened the waggon door.

There was no-one there. The site was deserted, the tents and carts and washing and animals all gone, with no more than a few tins and rags and the black circle of the dead fire to show where the travellers had stopped.

Followed by the lurchers, the girl ran to the back of the waggon, to find only Jack Sheridan's horses still tethered as she had left them. Everyone and everything else had vanished. And then Macha understood that this was the penalty. They had left her behind, deliberately. She was completely alone; an outcast.

Chapter TWO

Macha was frightened. Her life had been spent among other travellers. They had journeyed the roads of Galway and Mayo and Sligo and Roscommon together, gone to horse sales and crowded into bars, eaten and sung together. Mulligan and Doran children had been her playmates from birth, as close as siblings. Even when her father had steered away from the group for a day or two, rarely had more than a few hours passed without their meeting other friends along the way; and besides, he himself had always been there, with his celebrated stories and ballads. She had never been alone.

The grey water dressed the shoulders of the shingle dully, and the road, which trimmed its edge, was deserted. Empty and muddy, both its directions appeared identical, seeming to lead to nowhere. The village was too far off to be seen, and there were no other houses or cabins in sight. The whole area looked like part of the seabed, strewn with rocks and silt and dark brown puddles, as though the tide had just retreated. It was an unsheltered and forbidding place, blocked off to the north by the treeless scars and chilled by the scouring wind. Without the fire and the safe ring of tents, she felt the more bereft, frightened.

Once, as a small child, she had become separated from the others at a fair and had wandered about bumping into the roots of the moving forest of adults, squalling and petrified by the hubbub and by having her distress so completely ignored. She recognised that same feeling again, but this time there was no Jack Sheridan to pluck her up and set her on his shoulders to see that the booming height of the forest was only the harmless laughter of people enjoying themselves. Now the booming was the ocean, and the kinsmen had gone. Only the cobbled pattern of many hooves and the thin, straight wheelmarks betrayed their direction.

They had left no food, and the waggon, having been uninhabited for the past week, contained no supplies. After the trouble at Flynn's bar, no traveller would be welcome that day in Kilkieran, and the nearest town was forty-eight hours away. Macha, with hunger cramping her stomach, imagined herself starving dramatically there by the desolate track.

She thought of trying to catch up with the others and knew they would accept her again if she begged forgiveness, handed over her father's possessions for destruction—and married Hugh Mulligan.

A lone wild swan flew over with eager, outstretched neck and singing wingbeat. The three-year-old whinnied and pawed the ground. Macha turned, guiltily. None of the animals had been watered, and the morning was half over.

O'Leary's Dip, a small inland lough, lay a hundred yards off, and untying the horses, she led them to it. They sank their muzzles into its peat-dyed water and drew long, soundless draughts. When they raised their heads, their mouths dripped over the dogs, which ran into the water up to their bellies and stood there panting. The filly plunged after them, kicking up her heels, while the older horses dropped their noses to drink more.

Their calm presence was comforting. Every day had always been full of the talk and care of horses. In other travelling families, women were never permitted to handle them, but with only one child, Jack Sheridan had been forced to use his daughter's help with his bunch of ponies around the campsites and especially at markets and fairs. Their curving bodies and flowing manes and tails, their elegant shoulders and knowing, bony heads delighted her, and she was forever intrigued by the extraordinary complexity of their movement. In her mind there had formed a blueprint of the perfect horse, and her judgement and eye for good animals had become so acute as to be intuitive. Now she was simply glad of their company.

The sun parted the clouds, unexpectedly, and softened the sharp-edged flaw, and Macha sat on the grass to let the gauzy warmth flutter over her skin. She was an unusually tall girl, flat-chested and still childishly spindly, with long, thin legs which folded awkwardly under her, their joints pronounced and angular. Pale beside the shorter, dark-hued traveller children, her appearance was so different she might have been a stolen child, or a changeling, with her deep red hair and bright grey eyes.

The sun grew more powerful. It turned the lough blue, and the sea began to spit light, like hot oil. It buffed the winter-coated haunches of the horses and coloured the gorse with sudden yellow flowers. The damp rocks and stone walls glistened as though varnished, and the tight thatch of turf covering the bog achieved that aggressive greenness unique to Ireland.

Light and shade hardened, and the land seemed to tumble from mountain to sea in an abandoned scattering of marble boulders and jewelled tarns. The limpid intensity of the west exposed and projected the minutiae of the scene—blades, sprigs and leaves, fibrous peat, the lichen flowers, each reed, each pebble thrown into enamelled relief—and the earlier portents of the day were replaced by citrus-sharp promise under the solar influence.

The horses had begun to crop the sparse growth by the water, and the rhythmic sound reminded Macha of her own hunger. Already, she had accepted her situation, and the initial feeling of panic had receded before the need to make decisions and the first independent moves in her life.

Travelling east would take her to the lodge at Screeb where Jack Sheridan used to stop—to help the widow with outdoor tasks, he said, although it had always seemed to his daughter that he had spent most of his time indoors, while she had been sent off to clean out chicken houses, or milk the cow. But the widow would certainly give her food, perhaps enough to last the journey to Galway.

There the horses could be sold. She looked at them and grimaced. They were all too typical of her father's standard of trade, which had never moved higher than the bottom end of the market and had frequently not reached even that level, with jades no-one would buy and which had been all but given away to the knacker.

The piebald was so ancient that the infundibulum which should have told its age had disappeared years before.

"Nothing wrong with bishoping a good horse," she could almost hear him advise.

But Macha doubted that even if she followed such advice and reproduced the teeth marks of a younger horse perfectly with his hot iron, anyone would have been fooled in this case. Some animals were past bishoping, and this was one.

The grey was almost as old, his coat faded to white. He was lame as well, but there were tricks to make him seem sound, and despite his age, he looked strong, so would probably find a buyer, though at a poor price.

The mare was required to draw the waggon: which left only the three-year-old. The girl looked at her and swore. A better illustration of almost every known equine fault would have been hard to find. Ewe-necked and herring-gutted, with a flat-sided, mean body running to quarters which fell away to a low-set tail and cow hocks: too light to make a decent draught animal and without even the advantage of good colour. A showy black-and-white or well-marked skewbald might have appealed to a gypsy, in spite of other deficiencies, but no-one would be proud to own such a nondescript brown weed of a brute.

The filly, unaware of her shortcomings, wandered up and pushed against the pouch where she knew loose corn was kept. Macha offered a handful, and the soft suede nose fidgeted over her outstretched palm as the grains were delicately removed. The girl ran a hand up the side of the grinding jaws and over the disc-shaped cheekbone to a tapering, flexible ear and pulled it forward affectionately. The filly smelt as redolent as newly sawn timber.

"Who's to say we can't find a blind man with a pot of gold to take you?" said her mistress, optimistically.

She looked all around, carefully, almost surreptitiously. There was still no-one in sight, either on the road or crossing the open bog. Tucking her skirts into their waistband and catching hold of the mare, she vaulted onto her back. The animal moved forward automatically, and with her bare legs dangling against the warm sides, Macha was filled with a delicious sense of delinquency.

Since first she had been able to scramble from a wall onto a donkey's back, she had secretly broken one of the strictest interdictions, that females must never ride, not even sitting sideways, let alone astride, as was her custom. For traveller men believed that women were all *mochardi* from the waist down and contaminated their horses, or anything else they crossed on foot, even water. Yet whenever her father had left her, she had ridden all the hours of his absence, starting with an ass and the quiet mare and gradually progressing to livelier mounts, on which she had learnt to balance while cantering through the screening forest at Lough Rey, or galloping over the strand of Gorteen Bay.

She dug her heels into the ribs of the horse, which broke into a stately trot, to be followed by the other three back to the van.

Usually, washing and pots had to be collected and the fire put out, and the overspill from the parked barrel-top—covers and hammers and baskets and knives and boxes—had to be packed before moving on; but this day there was nothing to do but harness up.

The leather collar was torn, and she stuffed the straw padding back through the gap before slipping it over the mare's head and twisting it round. The bridle was so stiff with dirt that the leather was cracking, and the throat-lash had lost its buckle and had to be precariously secured with string, but the hames were of lovingly polished brass, which looked incongruous against the rest of the rotting tack. Jack Sheridan had obtained them from a butcher in Sligo in exchange for an old cart only a fortnight before, and there had not yet been time for them to blacken with tarnish. They flashed as the horse was backed between the shafts, and Macha checked the turnout with a final glance.

The mare's head was up; the brass licked the collar with two yellow flames; red and green painted decoration showed fresh and shiny; the three-year-old and the other ponies were tied to the back of the waggon; the lurchers were already in their running place between the wheels.

It was then that the girl realised they all truly belonged to her. She could never be forced to leave them to live in a bender tent with any man she did not want. They could not be taken away.

The previous night, she had been goaded to rebel against the kinsmen by the compulsion to avoid being coupled with Hugh Mulligan. She had not thought of more. That morning, alarm at discovering herself alone had blocked all other reflection, so the sense of ownership was unforeseen and exhilarating, and she began to understand just how Jack Sheridan had felt about the waggon. Now it was hers, and in it, she could travel wherever she wished, making up her own mind from day to day, or even from hour to hour, deferring to no-one else. Through this possession, she was exclusive and free.

She rubbed the mare's noseband with her sleeve and resolved to obtain a buckle and repair and clean the bridle as soon as possible. She walked round the outfit with a swagger. There were few in Ireland travelled in such style, and no mere girls.

Bobbing onto the driving ledge, she picked up the reins. The mare leant her weight against the collar, the tug chains rattled and tautened and the Bow-top lurched forward onto the track with a flinty scraping of iron against stone.

She had spent all her life roaming the province of Connacht, from Sligo to the Shannon Waterways, from Achill Island to Athlone, and so she knew every twist and bend of the road and where each stream rippled into the sea and where each shingle leant against the tide.

It was one of the most desolate stretches of the coast, where Nature had defeated even the ingenuity and endurance of the tough people of Connemara, who could somehow grow potatoes and maintain themselves and a cow on a patch of poor soil only inches deep. Here there was no soil, only bare stone and mighty outcrops, a few turf banks and deserted, nameless loughs. Yet pipewort and water lobelia flowered white and pink round the edges of these pools in summer, and the burnet rose clung to fissures in the rock faces, and on the strands where she often paddled, blue butterflies searched for their own images in the flowers of the sea holly. Macha knew them all, and the road was her home.

From her vantage point on the waggon seat, she could see down Kilkieran Bay to Golam Head, across Greatman's and out over Galway Bay. Islands and islets, too many to count, hinted the undulations of underwater lands. Like sirens, they enticed in the noonday brilliance; beryl and olive, russet and sienna, each in its spangled nimbus was a container of secrets, an enigma and a temptation. A fishing boat with a lone man gripping its oars steered sternly between them.

The mare set her own casual pace, and Macha rested against the frame of the Bow-top with half-closed eyes, like an invalid, letting the emotional confusion of the past week fall away and allowing the rocking motion and the briny air and lovely land to do their healing work.

Travellers are fatalists. They accept the events of each day without question or resentment; a sale or a loss, hunger or food, harassment or peace, birth or death, all are absorbed and then forgotten. So the decease of her father and the heinous lie she had told and the rejection by the family, the fighting, fear and tears all became part of the past on that journey along the shore.

At last, a jigsaw of low, stone-walled enclosures invaded the borders of the wilderness and a donkey, a hummock of hay and a cottage came alongside. An old woman stood waiting in the doorway.

"Good afternoon to you, lady. May you live sound and alive," said Macha, pulling up the mare.

"Them others did not stop," grumbled the old woman, without the courtesy of returning the greeting. "And here's meself fit to faint with age and wanting no more than a bit of turf brought in for the fire."

"I'll fetch it," Macha offered eagerly, thinking she might get a bite to eat in exchange. "You'll not know the cold by the time you turn around, for such will be the blaze."

"The ruck's at the back," directed the crone, and screeched as she set off, "Your soul from the devil! Not that way! Keep away from my hens with your thievery!"

The girl changed direction obediently and reaching the high, solid stack, lifted off as many sods as she could carry and returned to the cabin.

"Arrah! You cannot come in here, tinker! You'll not steal from me!" the old woman raged. "And I'll need more to burn than that. Why, that little bundle wouldn't melt candlegrease."

Macha put down her load by the door and went for a second, piling up the blocks to balance under her chin and fill both her arms. When she returned, the hag was within, poking at a dismally smoking heap in the centre of a wide fireplace. She could see a pitcher of milk against the wall, and her belly rumbled.

"Out! Out with you!" crunked the old one, rushing forward with upraised arms. "And you need not expect thanks for such a miserable amount I could have hauled in meself."

Macha spent the next hour at the job, until there were flakes of peat in her hair and ears and up her nose and between her teeth; she could feel them scratching her skin under the belt of her skirt and rubbing inside her boots. The sods she had shifted stretched one width of the cottage and were heaped to the level of the window ledge.

"That'll do," the old woman said reluctantly, eyeing the work with suspicion.

Macha, still panting with the effort, leant against the wall. "Jesus and Mary bless you, lady, for a drink of milk."

"Milk is it?" The crone gave an affronted yawl. "In the name of God, how do you think I have milk to spare for an idle, lazy tink, me with a husband and sons to feed? You will have a bit of loaf and fresh water and praise the Lord for his kindness and mercy."

She thrust a lump of hard bread and a tin mug of water into Macha's hands and disappeared inside.

Macha stared at the reward and shrugged. She was very hungry. Carefully, she poured a little of the water over the bread to soften it and took a large bite.

On the way to the lodge at Screeb, she thought about the settled people with their dim, sooty cabins and grudging ways, many living all their lives in godforsaken, uncharted corners of the country. Even a visit to the nearest village of one street, one shop and a public house was an event to them. What happened when they did not like the locality, or grew tired of seeing the same view and the same folk every day? She could simply set out along the road to somewhere new and stop when she pleased. They were trapped. Small wonder they turned out as mean and peevish as the old woman. She felt sorry for them, and began to sing.

Because of the delay at the cottage, it was almost dusk by the time she reached Screeb. The loughs and sea had turned the colour of weathered slate. Glowing cinders of clouds burned low in the sky behind her, and the old stone lodge in its surrounding trees was draped in mist, like a dream. Leaded windows reflected the last slice of the sun as it dropped into the wide mouth of the horizon.

As was the way of all travellers, she attended the horses first, leading them to drink at the stream before hobbling their forelegs with rope and letting them loose to feed along the "long acre" which borders every country road in Ireland.

By then it was nightfall, and she wondered if it was too late to knock at the widow's door. An oblong of grass brightened at the back of the house, showing that a lamp had just been lit in one of the ground-floor rooms. The hollowness in her gut made her daring, and keeping close to the bushes, she approached stealthily.

The back door was slightly open, and the appetising smell of meat wafted out through the gap as she peered in at the window. The room was a kitchen, its walls running with condensation from the heat of the modern stove. It contained a dresser, several slat-backed chairs, a rag rug and a long, scrubbed table, on which lay a dish of boiled potatoes and a whole leg of steaming mutton.

Macha drooled. Late or not, she would knock at the door. She turned and was hardly aware of the looming black shadow before she collided with it, to be clamped in the vise of its arms.

She squealed and felt herself lifted off the ground, swung, like a feather pillow, over the man's shoulder and carried face down into the house, where she was dumped on the floor and held by her braided red hair.

"Just as I thought; a snivelling little tink." The man's features were obscure in the darkness behind the lamp. "And what were you minded to lift? A lot more than a small fowl, to be sure, coming creeping right up to the place, like a worm on a wet day."

"May God cut out my tongue if I wasn't looking for the good lady, Your Honour." Macha's voice quavered from shock.

"And what lady would that be?" asked her captor.

"The widow lady who lives here. May Jesus and Mary bless her gracious heart for all her past kindnesses to a poor traveller," she gabbled, trying unsuccessfully to free her head. "Tell her it's Macha to see her and she'll know it's me, sir. She'll know I've not come to rob."

"How should I tell her about you when she's been dead this year or more?" the man mocked. "And what would the likes of you be wanting with her anyways?"

He seemed broad and powerful in the gloom, with a gold watch chain curved low across his paunch, and a commanding moustache. He must be the new owner, she thought, and the fat odour of the joint encouraged her.

"I used to work for the lady, Lord rest her soul; fetch and carry, search out eggs, feed the calf and the like. Herself was an angel of goodness and would think nothing of giving meself and me Da a good hot feast of a meal."

"Hungry are you? Always scrounging, you tinkers," the man said contemptuously.

From habit she ignored the insult and wheedled.

"I could do the same work for a gentleman like yourself."

"There's enough turf in to last till summer, and I've no need of a slopeen to find a few eggs," he retorted, and suddenly gave her a shove towards the table and stepped into the light.

She turned and saw a balding head and an unshaven face with a mouth full of discoloured and broken teeth. What had seemed like a watch chain was a twist of straw holding together a torn waistcoat. He was not quality.

He lifted the plate of mutton and waved it in front of her with one hand, the other still holding her hair.

"Want some meat, do you?" he asked, putting his face so close to hers that she felt the heat of his skin.

He smelt of sweat and rotting cabbage. There were thick hairs growing out of his nostrils. He was very drunk.

"Well, a tink like you knows what to do to earn it."

As he put the plate down, some of the gravy spilled. "Living all together the way you do, men and women without shame, boys and girls worse than Turks." His grease-covered hand thrust under her cloak and pushed at her chest.

Macha, whose life had been governed by the strictest of tribal taboos, designed to protect her virginity and value as a bride, was petrified.

The gibes of the *gaujos* were easily deflected with resignation and feigned meekness, and on the rare occasions when local antagonism became menacing, as in Kilkieran, a well-rounded curse usually ended the confrontation. But this lecher, with his bulbous, florid features and prying fingers, was a danger outside her experience. Instinctively, she struggled, and instantly felt her head wrenched back until she was arched across the table and he was pressed against her, fumbling at her skirts.

"My Da'll come," she lied, desperately. "He's outside."

"You'll not trick me, stroller. I saw you pull up, and there's no-one with you." He was growing irritated by her layers of petticoats, and the material tore.

Macha cried out and the ceiling above revolved as he hit her.

"Don't play the shy maiden with me," he snarled. "I've had more than one tink woman to *chavver*. That's what you people call it, isn't it? *Chavvering*. Well, I'll take a bet a big girl like you's been *chavvered* by half the gippos in Ireland, so don't pretend you're some innocent virgin."

His face was mottled and sweating, and he was breathing in hard groans. The edge of the table was cutting into the small of her back as though to break it, and as she made a frantic effort to change position, he overbalanced and pulled her with him to the floor.

The grip on her hair released as he flung out an arm to save himself, and she rolled off and whirled to her feet while he lay struggling, his limbs waving feebly, like a beetle. He was between her and the door.

Macha ran to the window and wrenched at its frame. The sashes were broken and it was covered with cobwebs, and although she banged with her fist and strained with all her strength, it would not open.

With the aid of a chair, the man had hauled himself upright. There was no way past him. He was lurching towards her with crazy eyes. There was spittle in the corners of his mouth, and she saw him with revolted clarity, which replaced her fear with a cold anger.

She put up a warding hand and gazed at him, humbly. "I'm sorry, mister. I was playing. It was just a little game."

There was a bottle of whiskey on the dresser, and she took it and held it out.

"It was a game and I'll do what you like, I swear on my mother's grave, if you'll just let us have a drink first."

He paused in his advance, and she forced herself to smile and even took a hesitant step towards him. "We could have a drop of whiskey together."

Her change of mood had caught him unaware. It had to be gauged. She let her cloak fall open, and with an expression of silly satisfaction, he stretched out his hand and took the bottle.

"You are quite right, tink. We need a drink. A drink is what we need."

She kept smiling and did not move as he wiped the top with his sleeve and returned it to her with an unsteady flourish. She raised it and tilted back her head. The liquid was as drastic as a purge. It bit her lips and tongue and plunged down her gullet like a spike to her hollow maw. She took several large gulps, gave back the bottle and smiled her smile.

He leered and began to swallow. Striking like a snake, Macha seized the end of the bottle with both hands and rammed it hard into his mouth. She heard his teeth break. He reeled back with a throaty gurgle of pain and the bottle smashed to the floor as blood spurted down his chin. She ran past to the safe side of the table. The door was open. She hesitated only long enough to snatch up the leg of mutton before escaping into the night.

Down the slippery cobblestone path and between the clawing bushes she sped, bumping into branches and a gatepost in the moonless black. Already, he was out in the darkness behind her, swearing and bellowing for vengeance. She reached the road, stumbled through a water-filled pothole and dropped the meat into the mud. Picking it up, she raced on towards the sound of the barking lurchers and saw, at last, the solid, arched shape of the Bow-top.

The man was close. Her fingers were shaking, and the knots of the dogs' ropes had tightened in the dew and would not come apart. His studded boots scraped blue flares from the stones. The lurchers were baying uncontrollably. Macha crawled under the waggon, still wrenching at the knot. He was there. The great cross-bred wolfhound was free and pounced. Uncannily, the other tether slid undone as though waxed, and the second dog joined in. The uproar of growling and anguish deafened, and under its cover, Macha scurried inside and bolted the door.

"God will strike you for this, you filthy strumpet! You'll suffer! I'll hunt you down and have you jailed." His threats ended in a yowl which told that the lurchers had renewed their attack.

Macha leant against the door, gasping, and the noise of the fracas outside grew fainter and finally stopped. Within minutes, the patter of feet announced that the dogs had returned.

She lit a candle and, filling a mug of water from the stone crock, poured it over the leg of mutton to wash away the mud before cutting off the worst pieces. Then, very cautiously, she opened the top half of the door. The lurchers were standing at the foot of the steps with tongues lolling and tails wagging. She threw them the dirty scraps one by one and chuckled as they sprang to catch them in the air.

She sat down with the plate on her knee. The meat was now cold and damp, but it did not matter. It was so tender that chunks came away at the touch of the knife. Combined with the whiskey she had drunk at the lodge, it was rich enough to make her feel dizzy, but she was too famished to mind. More than half the joint had been devoured before she felt sated, and by then, she was also exhausted. The past twenty-four hours, so crammed with difficulties and strains, seemed longer than a month. She just had the strength to reach the hay-lined bed.

Macha slept so deeply that the whinnying of the horses and the whining of the dogs went unheard and the cocks crowing behind the cottages at Screeb did not disturb her, and the dawn spread and the sun rose almost to midday before her eyes opened again.

Immediately, she was possessed by an urgent need to move on, to travel as far from this place as possible. The sense of danger was tangible, draped over the waggon like a shroud. Angry with herself for having overslept, she darted outside in bare feet to fetch the animals and be on her way.

The lakes lay on the bog like sunstones, blinding as ovals of glass. About half a mile away, the lodge seemed more intimidating for being invisible within its dark circle of evergreens. A few poor hovels straggled back from Camus Bay.

The horses could be watered later, when miles stretched safely between her and this miserable hamlet. She caught the grey and the piebald and quickly tied them to their following position behind the van, knowing she should have moved on the night before, as soon as the man had gone. There was something wrong, and yet she could not pinpoint what it was. The day was Sabbath-silent.

Then she realised that it was the very quietness which was wrong.

Her attacker had promised reprisals. Knowing no-one would believe her word against his, by now he would have told the people in the surrounding crofts how she had stolen the meat and probably the whiskey as well. They should have been there at the Bow-top, accusing her, and yet there was no-one in sight: no men round the fishing boats, no women hanging washing, no children staring curiously at her, no-one working in the few stone-bound fields.

The filly was some distance down the track, and as Macha hurried towards her, she snorted and backed away, stumbling in her hobbles. The mare was stretched out, basking, and the girl whistled to her. At the sound, the filly reared, her eyes rolling, mud-encrusted forelegs flailing. The mare too was covered in mud and was lying very still. Too still.

The girl's heart thumped and her mouth went dry. She took a few swift steps forward, then stopped. The mud was red. The mare's head was flung back at an unnatural angle. Then she saw that a massive gash had almost hacked it from the body, and the blood which had fountained and dried over the chest and shoulders after the assault had gushed on to form a wide pool on the ground. The horse's sight was glazed and its teeth bared in the hideous last rictus.

Macha closed her eyes to shut out the sight, and wailed a harsh, keening note, like a gull. Dropping to her knees, she put out a hand to touch. The winter-thick fur was hot from the sun, but the skin beneath was cold and stiff. The man had taken his revenge many hours before.

The three-year-old was whimpering and shuddering, and her owner, twisting in added alarm, ran over, grasping the halter before it had time to shy and tracing the blood-covered legs with anxious fingers. There were no wounds. The blood must have come from the mare. As relief followed so closely after shock, Macha felt nauseated. Slowly, she led the terrified creature back to the waggon and secured it close to the grey gelding.

Already, the dogs were nosing around the dead mare. She called them off, furiously, and felt her stomach heave. Without further warning, she was violently sick down the decorated wall of the Bow-top.

Although the vehicle was too heavy for the ancient black-and-white pony to draw, there was no alternative but to put him between the traces. The girl's shivering reaction, together with the smell of blood, was transmitted to all three horses, which jerked and sidled, refusing to stand still, while the lurchers made repeated charges towards the carcass. But with forced pace to carry them speedily out of the area, they were on their way at last.

The coast rolled by, but she hardly saw it and was unaware that her face was wet with tears. The mare had been stocky and sure, with a broad chest and strong hindquarters and the coarse head of carthorse descent; a very ordinary animal, but she had faithfully pulled the Sheridans around the West of Ireland in all weathers and had taught the girl to ride upon her patient back. Macha felt she had lost a friend.

Depression, like a soporific gas, affected the little group, so that the dogs lagged dispiritedly and the gait of the piebald soon slowed to a trudge. It was a reaction Macha had never endured before and did not understand. It seemed to drag the flow of her blood and make her lethargic and subdue the colours of land and sea and even make the sun's rays oppressive. Her head was heavy with thoughts of despair.

After only twenty-four hours of independence from the other travellers, she had already failed. The old woman at the cottage had tricked her, the man at the lodge had assaulted her and she had lost her best horse. Freedom was not as she had imagined. Without the protection of the kinsmen, she was defenceless, and she began to believe she was being punished. The unforgivable denial of her own father and the breaking of sacred customs had caused her misfortunes.

Already, in retrospect, life on the encampment had taken on a romantic ambience; the communal fire grew bigger and hotter, the food more abundant, the accordion and songs more musical; her aunts and uncles and cousins seemed to have been uncritically loving, their backbiting and rivalries fading behind a conjured screen of gratifying safeness.

The quietness, as she travelled, became intolerable. The previous day, thankful for the opportunity to recover from Jack Sheridan's death and burial, she had been unaware of it, but now she longed for their chatter and shouting, for the clatter of many hooves and the acrobatic daring of the boys as they galloped past in spontaneous races, for the companionship of the women and the secrets of the other girls. They would all be nearing Galway City by now, and she knew she would find them at the market.

Subconsciously, she had begun to picture how she would tell them of the misfortunes she had experienced and how the initial aloofness of their disapproval would give way to welcome and a return to the old, snug way. Perhaps she might even grow to like Hugh Mulligan.

She tried to imagine married life with him. He was not a horse dealer, only a maker of clothes pegs and panniers, which it would be her job to peddle from door to door. She would tell fortunes and go begging in the streets, like other traveller wives, and hand him the money she made, and take a beating if it was not enough. She would find food and take it to him. While he sat smoking and whittling wood, she would struggle against the wind and rain to pull the felts over the frame of the bender tent at each new camp. When he was ready, he would come to her with his foul breath and runt's body.

She could not do it. The acceptance and fellowship of the clan, her security and the elevated position of being a married woman in the group, the children that would be born to her: none was reward enough. She would not, could not marry such a man.

"You are only a woman, so you can't go your own way," she had once heard Michael Mulligan say to her Aunt Nancy.

Well, she, Macha, would go her own way. In fact, had she not done so already? She had left the travellers, for good or ill. The first day had been beset with problems because of her inexperience, but she would learn, fast, and if she had to tell fortunes and beg, she might as well do it for herself as for a man she despised.

Screeb was now far behind, and she reined in the pony by a pond and loosened its girth. As all the animals drank, she fetched the remains of the mutton, sat on the waggon steps and began to eat. Her mind was finally made up. She would definitely not rejoin the clan. Whatever the future held, she would go on alone.

The road wound through the afternoon round Camus and Cashla Bays, which lay scaled with silver, like two sinuously weaving fish, through the little settlements of Kinvarra and Costelloe and Rossaveel, each leading to the next with a straggle of thatched two-roomed cabins. The Twelve Bens and the grim mountains of Joyce Country became distant blue brushstrokes.

Early bogbean was flowering like white-fringed orchids in the marsh. An Irish hare skittered madly over the turf, its coat beginning to turn red. Colonies of razorbills and guillemots were starting their noisy pairing, and the first corncrakes rasped their arrival over the turloughs with harsh repetitive call. A raft of barnacle geese rested on the water before heading north. It was the spring equinox.

The mildness of the weather sweetened the coastal people after the relentless, storm-blasted winter. Isolated boys pulling the ridges in the lazy beds waved at her. At Keeraunnagark, the only shopkeeper responded to her sad grey eyes and orphan plea with a pint of porther, some salt and a bag of old potatoes. A burdened girl of about her own age promised milk and three eggs in return for a lift from outside that village to near Inveran.

"If you'll put me down at the Crumlin bridge, there won't be a one the wiser," she giggled, and then perched precariously on the shaft, ready to jump off and pretend to be walking should anyone come into view.

By the time they reached the river, feathery clouds, lit faintly from behind by the pale white light of evening, were floating above Galway Bay.

Macha gazed at the girl's hand and promised her a husband within the year and five fine sons to follow. The girl added a cabbage to her fare.

"I'll tell Ma the basket dropped from the weight of itself and the eggs got broke and the milk spilt and the cabbage rolled into the sea and was lost," she said, delighted with her future.

"Good luck and health," replied Macha. "Wealth and happiness to you."

She camped on the riverbank where the horses could eat the first of the spring grass. Over the fire, the potatoes in their skins boiled with the greens, and when she threw some of the resulting mash to the dogs, they bolted it down without chewing, or caring that it was still scalding hot.

Refreshed and fed, she felt contented, and when an unbidden memory of the slaughtered brown mare flickered into her consciousness, she put it from her, firmly. That had happened in the morning, and the morning was over.

Palm trees and large houses marked the approach to Galway, and from the hill, she could see over the whole city. A tall, square church tower rose from its centre, like an obelisk, and gaily coloured cottages decorated the banks of the river Corrib, and a line of ships, some with masts, was anchored against the quay.

It was a prosperous and attractive town, and the roads leading to it rumbled and rang with carts and carriages, iron-shod horses and soft-footed donkeys, as the farmers and country folk crowded in for the two-day market and races. Many, like Macha, who had taken only a couple of hours' sleep, had started their journey through the night. They drove small flocks of sheep, or gaggles of geese, or led a single cow and calf. Cottiers' wives toted live hens, hung upside down with wings outstretched, and baskets of eggs and butter and cheese. They were excited and jostled, calling out to each other, pink-faced from the long walk and the adventure of being propelled so rapidly into such a multitude from their quiet, lonely lives.

Macha enjoyed herself, too. Everyone was in good spirits. They admired her Bow-top with its intricate scrolls in scarlet and green and its brilliant yellow-and-red-painted wheels and shafts. The young bachelors, hoping to be hired as farmworkers, sidled alongside with daring compliments and invitations.

"Sure, you look like a queen up there upon your carriage. Will you be at the dancing tonight?"

"What lovely girl would want to miss the chance of being accompanied by a fine fellow like meself this day?"

Men with small strings of Connemara ponies were good-humouredly rude about her horses.

"You must have broken the spring on that one when you wound it up this morning."

"Are they dressing up barreners in horse skins this year?"

For the last few miles, she carried an ancient, toothless woman, who squawked and mopped at all the passers-by over a sackful of seed corn. They parted with an exchange of incomprehensible cackles and wishes of good fortune and God's grace.

Knowing that the Mulligans, along with most travellers, always camped to the north of the town, Macha drove downhill to the fishing quarter of the Claddagh and found a patch of waste ground between two buildings behind the harbour. The horses were dirty from the journey, and she brushed the caked mud from the coats of the two she planned to sell, then washed them down with seawater and combed out their tangled manes and tails.

Lifting a foreleg of the limping grey, she drove a rusty nail between the wall and the shoe of the sound hoof with a stone, then tugged the animal across the plot. Being tender now in both feet, he appeared to walk sound. Jack Sheridan had always done that with a lame horse, and it rarely failed.

Forced to keep the piebald to draw the waggon, she left him tethered and led the other two over the Claddagh Bridge to the market.

There must have been five hundred horses and ponies around the Lynch stone. They rattled by, pulling dangerously swaying carts, or were galloped by tinker boys up and down the street, scattering the crowd. Young, unbroken ponies straight off the mountains milled about, neighing in terror, and worn-out nags were provoked into a semblance of action before prospective buyers by the heartily delivered sticks of their owners. Rows waited patiently for old masters already in the bars, or for collection by new masters sealing their deals in whiskey. They sagged with boredom, resting their hindquarters alternately and half-heartedly sniffing at their neighbours. Occasionally, an argument broke out in squeals and kicks. Then men would run up, swearing, to separate and clout the offenders.

The grey was walking gingerly on his sore feet, picking them quickly off the ground after each step. It gave him a sprightly appearance, and Macha was well pleased with her ruse.

"If you've a nag to sell that looks like a mule, stand it next to a donkey, so that it looks more like a horse," her father used to say.

So she searched until she found a group of broken-down screws and stood her two animals next to them, though even that did not help the filly, whose goose rump and slab sides earned only stares of contempt.

"Ten pounds for him," said a voice.

A very drunk farmer was standing in front of her.

"What?" She had been there only a few minutes and thought she had misheard.

"Fifteen pounds, then."

Fifteen pounds! It was a fortune. The grey was not worth half that.

"Will you take what I offer?" the man was asking.

Macha shook her head regretfully. "No. I couldn't do it."

The farmer ran his hand over the horse's shoulder, and she held her breath. He began to examine a foreleg and overbalanced to cling heavily to the animal, which did not move.

"Safe as your aunty's hat, mister," the girl pointed out, quickly. "He would carry you home twenty miles blindfold and take your whole family to Mass next day."

"There's ten children," confided the man.

"That would be a rest for him, sir, seeing as I bought him off a poor soul newly widowed and left with fourteen." Her tale raced on inventively. "Why, he can even pull a little plough."

The farmer was impressed. "Eighteen pounds and ten shillings."

Macha gambled. "No. No."

"Twenty pounds, then. 'Tis the best I could do."

She held up her hand for his slap before he had finished the sentence, then slapped his smartly in return to confirm the deal. He counted out the notes at once. It was impossible to keep the grin off her face.

As soon as the man and the unsound grey had disappeared into the throng, Macha moved her own position. It would not be long before he realised he had bought a jade. Even if he was too drunk to notice, his friends would certainly point it out, and he would come looking for her.

Leading the three-year-old to the most congested part of Market Street, she tied it between a hunter and an exquisite Connemara, the contrast making it appear weedier than ever, but she was unconcerned. With money in her hand, she itched to go spending, and the whole town was full of temptations.

To compensate for the fasts of the past fortnight, she promised herself a feast and bought big, bright pink candies shaped like farm animals—pigs, horses, cows, dogs and sheep—and gobbled down the first few, then slowed to bite off the heads and nibble the legs and crunch the bodies of the rest. Their sweetness coated the inside of her mouth thickly and lingered even after she had drunk two pints of porther and eaten a bag of apples, some gingerbread and three thrush pies full of little bones.

Only then did she think about supplies and purchased two bottles of whiskey, some tea and sugar, paraffin for the lamp, ten loaves of soda bread, onions, carrots, a hare and a cast-iron cooking pot in which she carried everything back to the filly, which she rewarded with the apple cores.

An Englishman stopped to appraise the hunter.

"Here's a nice pony," she touted. "She would suit Your Honour's little girl, or boy."

The dapple grey Connemara next to her raised its beautiful head and stamped a slim leg. The Englishman glanced from it to the filly and walked away without a word.

Macha swore to herself. That was the way of the English, stalking about and never passing the time of day. Her Aunt Nan had explained that they were slow, none of them being able to talk at all before they were ten years old. It was God's punishment on them, she said, for being Protestants.

A small group of men was approaching down the row, eyeing every mount. Macha swung the three-year-old round in an attempt to hide the Connemara.

"What the devil's father would that be?" One of the men stopped and pointed.

"Arrah! If it's a horse, it must be the cattle we're buying," another laughed.

"She's a fine pony," Macha said stoutly.

"Give them no heed, girl," said the third man. "Now, do you want to sell the pony?"

"I do," she replied, surprised and hopeful.

"Well, there's a man around the corner." He winked at his friends. "He deals in secondhand furniture and, if you drape a rug over that thing, it'll pass as an ould settee."

There was a guffaw of laughter, and the men slapped him on the back and staggered over the road under the weight of the joke, and other onlookers joined in, repeating it to each other.

Macha felt a moment's annoyance, then looked at the filly and flung back her head and burst out laughing too. The laughter brought tears to her eyes and shook her whole body worse than weeping. One of the men took off his overcoat and put it over the filly's back, and the mob screeched, and Macha fell against her, helplessly.

"It's the truth. She's got the bones of a broken armchair," she gasped, then added loyally, "but she's as fine a tit as would lep over a goat, in spite of it."

And that set them all off again.

She had lost the will to sell. The afternoon was late and there was too much money in her pocket and she had had enough of the crowds.

The fishing boats were putting out from the Claddagh under the moon when she returned. The air was fresh and keen off the bay, a relief after the closeness of the city. She put the money in the concealed cupboard Jack Sheridan had always used and after feeding herself and the dogs, lay down well pleased.

The races started at midday, but Macha was at the Ballybrit course well before that. Had she not wished to avoid other travellers, she would have driven the waggon there and watched from its roof; but by being early, she had time to visit the parade, place a bet on a powerful-looking bay and secure a prime vantage point.

There was a flutter of anticipation in her stomach. It made her restless, and she found it hard to stay still in her place. The horses had strolled around like gods, their eyes remote, their silk-skinned glamour unattainable. It was impossible to believe they were the same species as her piebald and filly.

Now they cantered down to the start with long, graceful strides as though skating, their jockeys shouting to each other as they went. Macha felt she would choke with excitement. She checked her betting paper over and over, hugging herself as people began to yell, although the race was not yet begun. Frantic last-minute bets were made, and the ring's runners waved wildly to each other, until, to a great whoop, the Thoroughbreds bounded away on the far side of the course.

Everyone pressed forward, straining to see the distant bobbing colours as they cleared the fences. The gabble of cries crescendoed, and she heard her own voice join in. The horses rounded the bend and cleared the great bank and were beating towards the last fence, which came and went like a hiccough, and then they were in the straight, clods of turf at their heels like hornets. Everybody was jumping up and down, and to the accompaniment of an ear-splitting cheer, they passed the post.

There had not been a nostril between Number 14, the big bay, and Number 6, Lord Manners' chestnut. Macha hovered by the ring-man, wishing by magic and prayer and calculating the odds. She had put a whole pound on the bay to win at 25–1. If he had won, she would get her pound back plus £25. A labourer would have to work two and a half years to earn that. She jigged from foot to foot and chewed her nails and felt the tension increase, unbearably.

The second race started and finished, and the winnings on it were paid out, and the horses were leaving for the third race before the word came via a man with a loud-hailer:

"The result of the first race. . . .

"First, Number 14.

"Second, Number 6.

"Third, Number 1."

She let out a yodel of delight and rushed forward waving her receipt. A couple pushed before her, and as she waited impatiently, she saw in the crowd the farmer who had bought the lame grey.

The bookmaker was counting out bank-notes slowly enough to stop a clock, and the couple insisted on recounting them before moving away. She handed up her slip. The farmer turned his head and recognised her. The ring-man was examining the ticket and frowning. The farmer had begun pushing through the crush.

"Have we to wait until the Second Coming to collect?" grumbled an angry voice behind her.

The bookmaker muttered and thrust out a fistful of notes. The farmer was running towards her, his stick raised. Macha snatched the money and fled, zigzagging between the spectators of the third race, bumping into people going in the opposite direction and ignoring their curses. She could hear him bellowing behind her.

"Stop that thief! I've been robbed!"

Out through the gate and between the parked carriages and cars, dashing down the long road with hair shaken loose and skirts impeding her progress, back into the streets of Galway. She looked over her shoulder and saw he was no longer in pursuit; but now that he knew she was still in the city, he would send for the police, so she did not reduce speed.

Breathless to the point of pain, she reached the Claddagh, ran the startled piebald between the shafts with the filly alongside and careered off over the bridge, turning right past the Spanish arch and onto the Lough Atalia road, where the Bow-top would be less noticeable than on a main road from Galway.

It was important not to attract attention to herself for a while. The farmer's was a common complaint, and the police no doubt thought him a fool and would not search too seriously for her. Once safely beyond the city limits, she relaxed, looping the reins over the hook on the frame of the waggon and letting the blown black-and-white pony set its own ambling rhythm as she counted out her winnings in her lap and wriggled with pleasure at the sight of the jumble of coins and notes.

All together, there was enough to buy a string of cheap horses from isolated holdings and villages around the province to trade in the towns. The success of the past two days had completely obliterated the earlier feelings of failure, and she promised to treat herself to a brooch and a pair of earrings at the next stop.

For over two hours the waggon followed the waterline until they came to a grassy semicircle bordering a narrow strip of white sand. By then, the sun was rolling along the horizon and holding vainly to the sky with thin ribbons of gold. Macha, still elated by her good luck, released the tired gelding and watched the dogs hurtle away down the stretch. The filly was jerking her head. The girl put a rope through her mouth, swung onto her bare back and turned her to the inviting strand.

The animal sprang forward with a massive vault which almost unseated her rider. Then, seizing the rope between her teeth, stretching out her neck and flattening her ears, she streaked along the beach. The girl grasped the whipping mane as the wind hit her like a wall. She rolled in her thighs and calves against the ribs and crouched low in an effort to stay on; and the filly incredibly increased speed, the blades of her hooves slicing gasps of sound out of the air, her body streamlining into a living missile, her stride lengthening until she seemed to flash parallel to the ground without touching it.

Sea and sky blurred into a hurricane of colour, and then, miraculously, Macha felt her flesh become one with that of the horse, their heartbeats synchronise, their muscles join. Her breath was the breath of the horse and the blood of the horse pulsed through her arteries and the hair of the horse entangled with her hair and she saw and heard and smelled as the horse, and it was no longer necessary to hold on for they were racing the same joyous race, until at last there was no flesh and no blood and it seemed as though they were galloping over the surface of the sea itself, and had become elemental, part of the air and the water, fire and earth.

As suddenly, the filly's pace shortened and her free action faltered and slowed. The girl automatically gripped and caught at the mane, and discovered herself a separate being once more.

The opalescent dust of sand settled and the waves splashed as they cantered through the shallows. There was a crust of foam on the three-year-old's shoulders, and her own skin was wet with sweat.

The end of the beach rose in a dune before them, and when the rope was pulled, the young horse obediently stopped. They stood together, slightly dazed and breathing hard, returned from a long distance, and Macha knew she had found her purpose.

Chapter THREE

"That horse could run before a train."

A boy who had been sitting on a hump of the sand dune rose and walked towards Macha as he spoke. "I bet she could beat Gallinule."

"She could." Macha looked down at the filly in surprise.

Kept hobbled, and exercised only alongside the waggon, her astonishing speed had never before been displayed.

"She doesn't look much," said the boy. "But that doesn't matter a tinker's jig when she can bolt like that."

"No," Macha agreed emphatically, ignoring the deprecatory reference.

The boy himself did not look much either. He was sandy-haired and skinny, and his nose, which had been broken, had not mended straight, so that his face had a lopsided look. He appeared to be about ten years old.

"What's your name?" He seemed to be asking more to keep the conversation going than out of interest.

"What's yours?"

His attention was fixed on the filly, and he reached out to rub her muzzle. "Declan O'Brien."

"Macha . . ." She waited to see if that meant anything to him, but he did not react. "Macha Sheridan."

"I suppose you race her."

"I do," she claimed loftily, sliding off the hot, damp back.

He walked round behind them and stood watching as she threw the rope over the three-year-old's neck, turning her about.

"Could I have a ride?" he asked, abruptly.

"No." She was adamant. "You're too young."

"I'd be as old as you. I'm fifteen, *and* I'm a racing man," he responded, with the defiance of one used to being teased about his lack of height.

But Macha was unmoved. "You still can't ride her, because she's as tired as an ould bee now."

They returned along the beach towards the Bow-top in silence, the filly scuffing through the edge of the ocean to cool her legs, the boy walking as close to her as possible without wetting his boots, the girl wondering whether the speed of the gallop had been a hap, or just an illusion. The notion of entering a race developed unexpected potential.

"There's sweet water yonder." He reached out and took the rope from her. "I'll lead the way, while you fetch the other."

He walked on without waiting, talking to the young horse so earnestly that Macha grinned.

"Don't let her drink much after that run," she called, and received a withering look in return. By the time she and the piebald caught up, he was rubbing down the filly with a twist of coarse grass.

He was uncommunicative, almost sullen in his answers that he lived and worked on a nearby farm, that it was of fifty acres and tenanted to his father, that he had six brothers and six sisters. It was as though he were being interrupted.

"Where's her next race?"

"Killarney," Macha replied without hesitation. "And have you ridden many a race yourself?"

"A few."

"How many?"

"Not many."

"How few?"

"One or two."

"Which would it be?"

"None, exactly."

She gave him a little push and laughed.

"If you're passing this way and happen to have a pail of milk and a few eggs on you in the morning, you could ride the filly along the strand," she offered.

He was waiting when she opened the top half of the waggon door at dawn, and impatiently, he helped her light a fire and cook a mess of eggs, which he did not share.

With some cruelty, she ate slowly and then deliberately scraped out the pot and put everything away before nodding permission to him to vault onto the filly's back.

Fine, dry sand flicked over her from the striking metal shoes, and by the time she had brushed it from her face, Declan O'Brien and the horse were halfway along the beach, indistinct against the glare of the sea under the rising sun, meteorically diminishing to faint thunder in the distance. Macha ran to a better vantage point and watched them bend into the return gallop without pause.

The familiar approaching image of a coursing horse lit a known rapture. From resembling a far-off, rocking toy, the boy and the filly gathered substance and life, bowling into focus as though windblown, the smack of her feet on the wet shore crescendoed. She drew nearer, grew larger, with sweat-streaked chest and striving, sinew-plaited legs, mighty with fevered eye and red-cored nostril and the lethal weapons of her hooves. Her breath crashed like cymbals, and they passed so close that Macha felt its heat on her skin and the ground shake and a twinge of fear which made her shut her eyes.

When she opened them a blink later, the boy was already dismounting at the Bow-top. It had not been her imagination after all. The three-year-old really was fast, very fast.

She was so distracted by this new conception of her young horse that she almost forgot to wave farewell to Declan O'Brien, left standing forlornly on the side of the road as she set off for the south. The filly looked fleet, seemed like a winner, but without others to run against, there was no proof. The only certainty was that she had to be raced, and as they travelled from sun into rain, the girl pondered over where to begin and who would ride her.

The land had changed from the barren rock and stone of Connemara into a rolling prettiness of wide, fertile fields. Sleek cows grazed in place of the undersized steers of the bogs, and flocks of spherical sheep moved in clouds across the startling green, so different from their long-haired, rangy cousins of the northwest coast, they might have been another species.

A large camp of travellers was set up on heathland beyond Andrahan, and Macha, with stomach muscles clenched, drove past, waving airily and relieved that there were no faces she recognised. Before long, however, word of the girl who had refused to have her dead father's possessions destroyed and had so scandalously broken taboos and marriage tradition would reach every encampment, and even those she did not know would know and spurn her. She shook off the thought physically, flapping the reins to hurry the old gelding away from it.

The ruined tower house of Thoor Ballyle loomed out of the downpour, strange and brooding by its murky water. She, who only days before had scorned the cabin women of the mountains, had rarely been so far from childhood routes and now felt as timid as they on a visit to the city. Arriving at the edge of Gort, she was glad to leave the Bow-top on a clearing and walk in amongst the people.

It was a deceptive place, appearing to be a village with rows of cottages and then expanding, unexpectedly, into a garrison town with a spired church and a square of important buildings. There a couple of soldiers followed her, making suggestions in incomprehensible Cockney accents, and a sergeant marching from a doorway beetled and shouted,

"Clear orf, tinker! We don't want the likes of you round 'ere."

The soldiers had miraculously vanished. Townsfolk turned to stare and mutter. Macha felt her face burn, and she slid down a side road to escape attention.

She felt both restless and aimless, unsure where to go and what to do next. Without Jack Sheridan and having firmly left the Mulligans and Dorans behind forever, it no longer seemed enough simply to meander along the ways of Ireland. She needed a plan.

A lane led to the deserted marketplace, its ground uneven with hardened dung and littered with empty wooden sheep pens. Wind blew in from all directions through the tunnels of the streets so that the hurdles rattled and the doors of the shacks banged and paper and old cabbage leaves and bottles scurried about. There was a board outside the only stone structure. Torn and out-of-date announcements of sales and auctions still clung to it alongside a brash fresh poster. She mouthed each letter and tried to string them all together as Jack Sheridan had forced her to learn:

KILLARNEY BUMPER AND PONY RACES

It had to be a portent. Only the day before, she had told Declan O'Brien that the filly would race at Killarney. Now she was being directed there. You could never be tricked into signing a paper if you could read, her father had said, though she had resented the lessons. Now she felt grateful to him and struggled on, laboriously:

KILLARNEY BUMPER AND PONY RACES
AND HORSE FAIR
1st May, 1895

That was only five weeks away, and the town was no distance at all. If she journeyed there immediately and stayed on the outskirts, the filly could be given a good gallop each morning and extra corn rations until the day.

The image was powerful. The long line of horses, groomed to a fine finish, sidling and prancing, tossing their heads and snatching at their bits in impatience for the off; their riders like warriors on their backs. The flag dropping. The concentrated plunge forward.

It was only after she had returned to the waggon and was on the road again that she began to consider the project with any sense of reality and to realise that it was a practical impossibility.

Apart from the fact that the other horses would be experienced—hunters and well-bred chasers perhaps, against which the scruffy little filly could not stand a chance—there was also the insuperable problem of having no rider. At a time when it was actually said by some (English, it was true) that hurdling was not a sport fit for female eyes, not even the boldest horsewoman in the province would have been permitted to take part in a race.

Macha worried angrily over this complication for some time before finally giving up with a feeling of frustration, though she continued heading in the direction of Killarney anyway.

The rain, which had dripped since she'd left the strand, thickened into a meniscus which distorted the distance, so that the grand new castle appeared to float in a flotilla of misted islands on the loughs of Cutra and Ballynakill, and the rivers of Owendalulleegh and Moyree were changed into trails of steam.

Water poured off the roof of the Bow-top in a glassy curtain, and the overhanging ledge under which she sat was not shelter enough. Her old shawl and dress had already absorbed the dankness of the air and become clammy and cold, and the moisture had seeped through the eyelets of her boots to soak her feet. The dogs had long since sensibly disappeared underneath between the wheels, and the two horses, their coats wet to gleaming, walked with downcast heads in mournful resignation. The beechwood, which ruffled the shore, would have made a good place to stop and light the stove, had there not been bender tents already grouped below its branches. Taking a swig of whiskey from the bottle, she drove on with a shudder and longed for a mug of scalding tea.

To the west, the loughs and streams became enveloped and indistinguishable from the downpour. The vehicle creaked up and down hills and complained over waterlogged marsh, through scrubland and past big barns stuffed with hay, impressive after the little, painfully gathered stacks of Connemara. Nondescript villages came and went, a single row of single-storey cabins at a time, and half the day was gone before the girl emerged from her hunched-up reverie to notice that although the countryside had levelled out, the lurching motion was worse than ever.

The old piebald no longer walked straight, but staggered unsteadily from one side of the road to the other, and as she swore, he stopped and sank to his knees. Jumping from her seat, she hurriedly released the breeching, tug and ridger chains and unbuckled the girth. The shafts swung high, and the pony slumped between them to lie groaning on his side.

"Mother of God forgive me!" Macha was struck with remorse. "It's been the death of you. I should have put you to the knackers and bought a decent animal in Galway."

They were in the middle of a broad, draughty plain, unbroken by hedge or tree, across which the gale was driving the rain horizontally. Its gust of needles stabbed as she put her ear to his rib cage and felt the irregular heartbeat.

"You're worn out as a granny's corset, you poor ould sod."

She stroked the pony's wet head, and he looked back at her through eyes without lustre.

The canvas she had often slept under was roped with a few hazel rods beneath the van. Unrolling it, she constructed a shelter over the piebald, tied up the dogs, collected some money and started out, on foot, along the stony way with a philosophical grimace.

She was not sorry for having taken the precaution of tucking the whiskey bottle into her basket. Frequent gulps from it kept her warm inside, although she was soaked to the skin. Her optimism rose with the spirit level. At any moment she would come to a prosperous farm with fields full of horses, all for sale and none costing more than an old fowl. Besides, by the time she returned, the piebald would undoubtedly be rested and recovered. Apart from that, the filly would run and win at Killarney and be sold to Lady Stamford for eight thousand guineas (the price everyone knew Barcaldine had fetched).

As she marched through the rain, Macha sang, louder and louder, swinging the basket and rejoicing in the freedom of not being overheard.

Had she lowered her voice when the houses of Tulla came into view, all might have been well; but by then, she was hugely enjoying herself skipping and tripping and bawling out the ballad.

'Twas the same old wretched story that for ages
bards have sung;
'Twas a woman weak and wanton and a villain's
tempting tongue;
'Twas a picture deftly painted in a silly
creature's eyes
Of the Babylonian wonders and the joy that in
them lies.
Annie listened and was tempted . . .

An old woman, who should have been walking sedately as befitted her age, literally charged into her like a hurley player, and then a man, who looked like a gentleman but could not have been, gave her a shove that would have knocked a bullock through a boghouse door. It was only after a well-dressed lady deliberately put out a foot and sent her into a puddle the size of Lough Derg that Macha became angry.

"Ruffians and bats, the lot of yis! Damn louts! May pox pepper your nutmegs!"

She crawled out of the water and tried to stand, only to be impeded by crowds of people, who walked into her and over her without so much as an apology. There were more folk in Tulla than fleas on a hedgehog, and it was a relief to reach the solid security of a cottage wall and sit leaning against it, shouting all the insults she could think of at them.

". . . Friday-faced crones, bacon-fed buckeens! May the Devil choke ye, and the curse o' God on every bachelor's son of yis. . . ."

A hand gripped her shoulder, and she turned to look mistily into a face that advanced and receded before being recognisable as that of a man wearing a policeman's helmet.

" 'Tis a fine thing that you've come when you have," she confided as they began to walk down the street together. "I was only after buying a horse and I've been pushed and pulled about worse than a rug in a copper."

He took her basket, rummaged in it and produced the bottle. It was empty.

"Holies! Will ye look at that! They've even drunk my whiskey!" Macha exclaimed.

When she woke up, it was so dark that she was unable to see her surroundings and was aware only of her aching head and of having slept on a cold stone floor in a claustrophobically small room. Groping her way round the wall, she came to a door and hammered on it, wincing.

After a few minutes, a grille slid back and wrinkled eyes peered through. A key turned noisily, and the cell door opened.

"So you've decided to waken yourself at last, ye drunken baggage!"

The sight of his uniform frightened the girl, and she shrank back.

"What's to happen to me, sir?" she asked pathetically.

"You'll appear before the magistrates on Thursday, and if you're lucky, you'll get off with a fine. If not, it'll be the jail."

"Mother of God! It's only Monday today." She let out a sobbing shriek and clutched at her hair. "What'll happen to my Ma? Mary and Jesus, she'll be without a bite or a sup, alone on her sickbed for three days."

The policeman was not a young man. He looked down at her from over a beefy belly and thought wistfully of his ample, sleeping wife and his warm bed. It was after midnight.

"What's wrong with your mother, girl? Where is she?"

Macha sized him up, a tired and fatherly man, and shaped the tale accordingly, letting huge tears gather and spill and twisting her skirt with her hands.

"She's terrible ill, sir, like to die, thinner than a finger of stolen beef on a Friday, and coughing and sweating, and I've had to leave her in the bender fifteen miles back, for the pony dropped dead on the road without more warning than a cowpat."

She punctuated the yarn with a wail before continuing.

"She gave me all the money we have, sir, to buy another poor old nag to pull the cart and fetch a little physic to ease the vicious pain in her chest, which tears her apart day and night. The heart of you would break at the sight of her, your honour, and if she has to lie there without even a drop of broth for three days, 'tis certain she'll be taken . . . just as my Da and babby Sean perished before her, bringing up torrents of blood and weighting no more than rags."

She rocked, weeping, before him.

"How old are you, tinker?"

She crouched even lower, silently cursing the fact that she was taller than average.

"About eleven years, they tell me," she whimpered, widening her grey eyes into round, abject pools. "Don't keep me here, your worship. The Blessed Virgin and yourself save me from being turned into an orphan."

The police sergeant frowned, took a step back and asked sternly, "And what were you about, a girl of your age, being in drink in the public street and screeching like a body coming alive in a hearse?"

Macha thought quickly and gazed up in damp innocence. "It was such a labour of a walk through the rain and the storm, and my Da always said there was no better guard against the cold than the whiskey, so I thought it would do no harm to bring his bottle-een with me, seeing there was no more in it than a few mouthfuls . . ." She checked his expression with a swift, flickering glance. "Oh, it is heathen stuff, sir. I thought it would burn the inside right out of me, the way it clung to the skin of my mouth and sent a fire right through my gut. On the holy hem of Mary's gown, I'll never drink a drop of it again."

She grabbed his hand and sank on her knees to the floor.

"If you let me go to take food back to my Ma and find a horse for the cart, all the angels in heaven will bless you."

The policeman withdrew his hand to lift her by the arm onto the stone bench.

"The magistrates decide such business," he said. "And besides, I can't have a town full of wandering biddies in the middle of the night."

"You can't let my Ma be taken," she pleaded. "I swear, by the good Lord and all His saints in heaven, if you'll just let me go to her, I'll return here in time for their worships."

He sighed and looked at her, skinny and snivelling in old clothes still wet from the rain.

"You can go in the morning . . . provided you return first thing Thursday."

"Oh, I will! I will!" Macha would have dropped to the floor again, had he not turned away. "Dear joy! I'll be waiting at the entrance when your honour himself rises."

He shook his head as he closed the door.

In the morning, he took her a cup of hot water and a lump of soda bread and delivered a lecture on the evils of whiskey while leading her from the cell, which was a specially constructed extension to the back of his house, to the station office, which was a room at the front.

"Mary Fitzgerald," he repeated the name she gave and wrote it in a book. Then he said, "The O'Clery brothers will sell you a good pony. Tell them I sent you and they'll charge a fair price."

At the door, he called out after her, "Now, see and you be here before nine o'clock on Thursday."

"I will! I will!" she replied, trying not to break into a run.

She turned the first corner which would take her out of sight, and he knew he would never see her again.

Following his instructions, she reached the O'Clery house, by the side of which were stable buildings forming three sides of a yard, with direct access to the road through a pair of massive, studded oak carriage gates.

"What are you hanging about here for, girl?" a suspicious old man in breeches and boots and a patched tweed jacket growled as she pushed open one of the gates.

She mentioned the policeman and watched his demeanour change.

"And what would Sergeant MacGrath be doing with the likes of you, if it's not to be locking you up for thieving?" he asked.

"The Peeler is a personal friend of me and my family." Macha drew herself up haughtily. "Now, are you in the business of selling horses? Or would this be just private racing stables to the Lord Lieutenant of Ireland?"

"Let us be seeing your money, tink!" he demanded.

"My name is Miss Fitzgerald, and I'll see the horses first."

Although it was still early in the morning, as they walked through the stables she noticed that all the horses had already been fed and watered. They were now pulling hay from their racks contentedly, and most looked round with curiosity as they passed.

"Here's a fine mare. Wouldn't jib if you threw the serpent of Eden before her."

Macha saw the weak hocks at a glance.

"No," she said, and walked on.

"What about this, then? He could pull a row of gun carriages from Belfast to Dublin without sweating."

"Yes, and need an army's rations to do it," she pointed out. The beast must have been 17 hands high; she could not have reached his withers without a ladder, let alone harnessed him. "He's not wanted for gun carriages, but just to pull a little cart, no bigger than a baby's cradle."

A lean and handsome bay was brought out and put through his paces and away, looking more like a lady's mount than a draught animal. She would have bought the strong brown gelding had he not had such a mean look in his eye.

"Here! She came in yesterday and you can run her for yourself," the man said, leaning against the wall and mopping his face with a rag. "I'm too old for this careening about."

Macha trotted the pony around the yard, then let go her halter and whooped. The mare took a few paces forward and stopped. She was already blowing slightly, but she was also very fat. Less weight and regular exercise would soon harden her up.

"What do you want for her?"

He named a ridiculous sum.

"My personal acquaintance, Sergeant MacGrath, told me you'd be asking a fair price for a fair beast," she protested. "And the way she's gasping, that screw sounds like a saw on a fiddle. There's something far wrong with her wind, whatever."

"Wind is it? Hasn't she the breath that wouldn't cloud a glass and the pull of a locomotive," he retorted. "She's as sound as my own whistle and belongs to my father's old sister. It's not being worked for more than a year has put a wafereen of fat on her, which no more than a week in the shafts would melt. I'll take five pound off my price for you."

Macha handed him the rope and stepped back.

"No, I could not take the gamble of it," she said. "I could not put my own mother's little savings onto a jade that would most likely break down before I could drag her a mile or two down the road." She shook her head at him accusingly. "I understood from the sergeant of the police that you were an honest fellow that would not be expected to cheat a poor girl of her bit of money."

"And what figure did you have in mind yourself, Miss?" He raised his eyebrows with the query.

"Not a penny more than six pounds," she replied. "And that's committing a sin against my sick mother, so it is."

"You're asking me to make a gift of the horse to you, you impudent piece." The man turned, affronted, to lead the fat mare back to the table.

"Eight pounds," the girl said, quickly. "And that's putting in even the few coppers saved for a potion to save my sainted mother's life."

"Done!" agreed the man.

And they spat and slapped hands and she drew the bulging purse of sovereigns from under her shawl and counted out the sum.

He saw the amount left over and grimaced. "The last few pence for a potion, is it? And what kind of cordial would that be? A draught of French champagne and tablets of pearls by the look of it."

Macha tilted her nose in the air and took the pony from him, leaving the yard with a cocky smile, well pleased with herself.

She returned to the Bow-top without more event and there found the piebald recovered enough to have struggled to his feet with the canvas still draped over him. She rubbed his ears with gentle regret as he buried his nose in a feed bag of corn. An animal which could not work was no good to her. He would have to go.

By contrast, the filly bucked and kicked up her heels upon being freed from her hobbles and hardly gave Macha time to swing onto her back before crossing the uneven turf in a series of bounds and then levelling out to smooth, even strides, which outpaced her rider's vision, so that their path became a mist of green and grey dissolved by windstung tears. A bank came at them and disappeared, the filly never faltering; another followed. The filly rolled over it like a billow and churned on. Macha pulled up at last and hugged the dewy neck, burying her head in the coarse mane. Once more, the extraordinary speed was confirmed.

The detour to avoid Tulla added a day to the journey, but was not without advantage. Macha managed to exchange the piebald for a tough, headstrong mule beyond the control of its elderly master. By the time she reached Limerick, she had also sold the mule to a young farmer, as brawny and boneheaded as the animal, and bought from him a good, strong mare with new foal at foot, which slowed them all down still more, but was far better value.

She drove obliquely along the north bank of the Shannon, looking over the widening water at ships anchored by the line of quays. Behind these, the houses of Limerick had been crammed together within ancient city walls, now breached by neglect, beyond which new buildings luxuriated in broad gardens.

She watched the salmon leap the Curragour Falls, fifteen-pounders arcing like dancers out of the opposing current, spurred by a sexual compulsion, insane and irresistible, to leave their cool and silent worlds, to transmute from silver fish into desperate birds drowning in alien air, to take flight through the hot, brash hell of earth over the final peril of their ocean-long struggle to return to the place of their birth, to give birth.

The big, strange city both invited and repelled, and only the need to purchase supplies made Macha cross the Sarsfield Bridge to brave its crush. She, who had so often wished for human company during the friendless hours of her vagrancy, now found herself buffetted and pushed by the congestion and nauseated by the smell of their bodies and the stench from the sewers.

Not caring what she paid, too hot and bothered to waste time bargaining, she snatched up a couple of rabbits from the first butcher she came to and some stale bread from the baker next to him, then groceries from an expensive shop hung with hams where the girl assistant looked at her in disgust and handled her money at arm's length.

The crowd shuffled on, compressed by the narrow route. Macha, wedged in the centre, was unable to turn back or escape and found herself carried through the bottleneck of Balls Bridge before being able to elbow her way into a bar.

"A pot of porther," she gasped.

The man gave her a look of disapproval and poured it reluctantly. It was only as he laid it on the table before her that she discovered her money was missing, along with a bag of sugar and one of the rabbits. Someone in the throng had had nimble fingers.

Seconds later, she was back in the thick of it, still dying of thirst and with the publican shouting insults after her, so that the passersby all looked and then held on to their pockets and chatelaine bags as though she were the thief.

Oh, the sweet relief to be back at the waggon and on the country road again, with only the clopping of her horses' hooves and the panting of the lurchers as living sounds alongside.

It was lucky she had not taken much money with her to lose to the cutpurse, she thought, and then dwelt on the fashionable ladies, envying them their feathers and lace; yet even so, to live in a stone prison next to the same neighbours and to walk down the same streets to the same places for a lifetime on end seemed far too high a price to pay for a gown or two. It was to be the last town she was to see for many days.

* * *

The little party followed the Shannon past castles and abbeys to its estuary, turned south again and left Limerick for Kerry.

At the kitchen entrance to a great house, she was given bread, a bowl of soup and a bundle of clothes by the kindly cook, a leer and a pinch by a man in fancy dress the like of which she had never seen, before being chased away by an Englishman dressed fit for a funeral, whom she took for the master, but who was in fact the butler.

Rumbling along soft, earth paths, lighting dusk fires in woods dangling with catkins, watching the fishing fleets from the shore road, galloping the filly down tracks and strands, over headlands of fields and grassy spreads, all formed the easy pattern of the journey.

Two more horses were bought from outlying farms, which also kept her supplied with milk and eggs, for which she paid; and the occasional fowl, for which she did not.

Evenings with golden skies struck by scattered salvos of early stars deepened into rich, sable nights, through which she slept untroubled, to awake to those lucid mornings of the west coast. Macha had lost her fear of being alone and no longer found the solitude lonely. The lurchers, which on the encampment had been more accustomed to abuse and stones and accurately aimed boots, sensed the change and grovelled to her, fawning their way on flat bellies to her side to be rewarded with caresses as she sat by the fire.

Wildlife was undisturbed by the procession with its unhurried gait. Long-tailed field mice nibbled on new shoots and watched them without alarm. Hares played their mad game around them, through the Silvery Hair and Silky Bent grasses. Harriers in flight exchanged prey, male to female, overhead, and the secretive pine marten merely turned its delicate, round ears towards them as they passed. After dark, Pipistrelle, the smallest bat, darted and swooped about their heads, as though jerked by wires, and hedgehogs rustled almost to their feet.

About a mile short of Killarney, they turned right up a narrow lane, so steep in places that she had to harness one of the new horses in front of the fat mare from Tulla to pull the vehicle up to Aghadoe, where the views suddenly opened over a magnificent lough to a range of awesome peaks, all overhung by one darkly purple mountain.

The turf of the north bank stretched like baize for about two miles. There was a ruined round tower and sheltering church walls. It was the perfect place to camp for the fortnight before the races.

Macha sat staring beyond the lake, with its tree-covered islands, to where she knew the town and racecourse lay. The decision to run her horse here had now become an obsession, the brown study of her days and recurrent dream of every night. The projection of the race was so real that already it seemed like a physical experience. She could feel its pressure against her body, the jarring of its hooves in her head, the heart-stopping finish, the victory.

The three-year-old, already fit from daily work and extra feed, would do her proud; yet there remained the impasse of having no rider. The more she thought of this, the more insoluble it became. News was passed on with the speed of Morse among travelling people, and all would be aware of her disgrace by now. There would be no help forthcoming from any she might meet at the sales, and there was no-one else she could ask, for she knew no-one. Another day closed, and once again she sat impotently before the flames of the fire.

The lurchers, which had chased off after idly thrown chicken bones, returned, snarling over a large rag. Pulling it away from them, she saw it was a garment from the bundle of old clothes given to her at the big house a few days earlier. As she held it out, a slow and beatific smile spread across her face. Here it was, the answer she had searched for. Now the filly would certainly race.

Overnight, the three-year-old was tethered instead of hobbled, and her action was freer as a result. Each morning, her legs were bathed in the ice-cold waters and she was cantered along the lough side. In the thin woods fringing the slopes, she was set to makeshift jumps of fallen tree trunks and then ridden up and down the rocky, sharply angled foothills. She had grown surefooted, strong and supple. Her coat, brushed clean for the first time of loose hair and scurf and dirt, shone a rich brown, and although all her faults were still ludicrously obvious, at least she looked hard and in condition.

In the late afternoon before the fair, the girl attached the folded canvas behind the saddle and tied a hessian nosebag full of oats from the pommel. She changed her clothes, pushed a few necessities into a satchel, mounted and rode down the hill and quietly to Killarney, to follow the signs pointing the way right through the centre of the town and out the other side. No-one took any notice of her.

Some way on, men were erecting marquees and booths in a field; but next to that, the racecourse was deserted under low, fast cloud descending from the mountains, and wind whistled across its emptiness. It did not look hospitable. Macha shivered and rode past.

The road became a wide ride enclosed by trees. A mist was beginning to obscure its surface and trail from the thin branches above. The trees were emaciated and overcrowded, cluttered with ivy and leafless strings of vines, and when she ventured between them to find a clearing, the filly sank to her hocks in quagmire and had to scramble out. The stagnant muck clung to them both and reeked.

It was almost night, that hour of dimpsy tricks when obstacles are conjured up which turn out to be shadows, and ruts and holes are set to trip the traveller. Without warning, the byway ended at a cliff face and a black, shining span.

When her eyes grew more accustomed to the change, Macha realised that the shining was an oval sheet of water covered in countless reflections of the moon, like a compound eye, and the cliff was in fact a massive man-built wall, rising so far above that she had to bend back her head to see it join the sky. This mighty keep dwarfed the round gate tower alongside and reduced the lantern light dappling one small window to the effectiveness of a will-o'-the-wisp.

As the girl gazed, impressed, a door creaked somewhere and a man's voice shouted. Instinctively, she wheeled the filly about and cantered off.

Crashing into the thicket with its spindly saplings, ducking to avoid low branches, feeling the mud splatter up into her already blind eyes, trying to steady the panicking young horse and aware that it had begun to rain, Macha regretted the whole venture and heartily wished herself back in the warm, dry Bow-top.

There was not enough space to erect the bender tent where they were finally forced by overgrown vegetation to stop, so she rolled up in the canvas with her swag of belongings and lay down.

The marsh gave soggily beneath her, like an old mattress, leaving unrelenting lumps in the wrong places. The overlapping boughs scratched each other, and dead timber groaned. Macha, seeing the goblins and little people of her dead father's tales, muttered spells and prayers and closed her eyes tightly. But she did not sleep. The filly squelched about, snorting in irritation, all night; the sound of water in slapping waves on the lake and rattling rush from the many rills and exploding raindrops was worse than whistle and bodran. She grew afraid of her own daring, anticipating the speed and the uproar of the next day, the crowds, imagining the young horse lagging in last and the whole of Munster laughing.

However, by the time weakening darkness told of the approach of dawn, discomfort had outweighed all her fears and she was grateful to crawl from under the leaking cover and be on her way, emerging from the wood onto the tip of a narrow peninsula reaching into the lough.

Macha looked at the filly and then at herself. They were both covered in thick green slime. She was aghast—and yet here was the very excuse she had been half hoping for all night. In such a state, it would be impossible to ride to the fair, let alone enter the filly in a race. She could justifiably return to the waggon without feeling a coward, and they could be out of the district before noon. There were plenty of other times and places for racing.

Wind picked fiercely at the lake, raking open sores and rents in its surface. Macha slowly rinsed the mud off the saddle in the shallows, absently watched her hands go blue and pondered. With a noisy sigh, she took off her jacket and dunked it in the water too, washing it thoroughly and squeezing it as dry as possible before spreading it out on a rock. Then, collecting a can from her bag, she vaulted onto the filly's bare back, clenched her teeth, kicked hard and rode straight in.

Her mount bucked in protest, but was driven on, ruthlessly, until its hooves left the submerged ground and the girl felt it begin to swim. Ignoring the whinnies of anger, she deluged the encrusted head and neck without mercy and swabbed them clean. All sensation had gone from her own legs, and the blast felt like a bistoury against her face. She filled the can with water again and tipped it over her own head.

I'm a lunatic! she thought, and was clearly aware of her entire flesh peeling from her bones like a suit and floating away. Michael Mulligan and Aunt Nancy were right enough. Da's death has turned my brain and left me a madwoman.

"Mother of Jesus! This is worse than any wedding," she said aloud, still scooping the glacial liquid over herself and sluicing the dirt away. "If I'd married Hugh Mulligan, I'd never have needed to wash at all, let alone drown myself like a fly in the milk on a winter's morn."

Now only the filly's head and ears were still abovewater. Macha, mortified beyond feeling, steered her towards the shore at last. The rain had stopped, and the rising sun cast a rosy path across the lake to the gold-tinted castle. The horse and rider emerged like a legend, a silver armour cascading from them, and shimmering ethereally in the clear light. A young servant girl, looking through an arrow loop in the keep wall, believed she had had a vision and had to be shaken out of her hysteria.

In the lee of some bushes, Macha took off the rest of her clothes and wrung them out, tying one end to a stump and twisting the material until it curled around itself and held not a drop more water. The man's trousers from the bundle she had been given were far too large, of course, but she folded them over at the waist and tied them up with string; then plaited her hair and stuffed it under the old cap. Luckily, the tweed jacket had shrunk with the scrubbing, and when she put it on, she did look like a lanky lad in hand-me-downs and was ready to ride in any pony race.

She gave the filly a small ration of corn in the nosebag and brushed her vigorously, making the blood course again and restoring warmth and sensation, and by the time she herself sat down to oatcakes and butter, they were both tolerably improved.

The air was apple-crisp, and they reached the fair in good spirits. Although it was very early, the field and course were full of activity, goods being unloaded from carts and traps in the one, and preoccupied men in bowlers and caps carrying sheaves of papers and pacing the other.

"Get off the course at once!" A tall man in a top hat pointed a stick and bellowed, "The sale is in that field, not here."

"Oh, she's not for sale, mister. She's for the racing," Macha replied.

The gentleman seemed personally insulted, though she did not know why.

"Declarations behind the stand. Now, get off the course and put that brute out of sight somewhere," he rapped, and turned heel.

Humbled, she guided the filly to the far hedge and tied her there before working her own way round to the weighing room, where a number of officials scurried about.

"I want to put a horse in the races," she said, stopping in front of a man seated writing at a table.

"Name of owner?" he asked, not looking up.

"Patrick Sheridan," she replied.

"Name of rider?"

She took a deep breath. "It's myself, Patrick Sheridan, that's the rider."

He entered the information without question.

"Name of horse?"

She had not thought of that and hesitated. The filly had no name.

"Well?" His eyes travelled from the paper over her damp and crumpled appearance, and looked pained.

"Macha's Girl!"

"Which race?"

"All of them, sir." She was enthusiastic.

"All of them? That's quite impossible!" The clerk could scarcely believe such ignorance and showed his annoyance.

Macha looked at her boots and wondered what to do.

"Are you selling the pony?" he asked, crossly.

"No, she's not for sale."

"Then she can't run in races Number 2 today, or 4 tomorrow."

"Age?"

"I'm sixteen," she lied.

"My God!" he glared. "Not you, you young dolt. The age of the horse."

"She's a three-year-old."

"Too old for the third tomorrow, which is for two-year-olds. I don't suppose she's been hunted?"

"No."

"That rules out the third race today and second tomorrow. Never raced before either, I suppose." He was sounding bored.

"No," she whispered.

"Then not in the fourth, or fifth today."

Macha had lost count and began to believe the filly would not be permitted to enter at all.

"She must run, your honour!" she insisted, desperately. "We've come all the way from Galway. She's fleet as a bird. She can canter faster than all the rest can gallop. She's got to race!"

"There's only the qualifier for tomorrow's bumper left. That is the first race, twelve o'clock today. If she's placed in the first six, she can enter the fifth tomorrow." He was scribbling as he spoke. "That will be one guinea."

Unable to speak, she counted the coins silently into his hand.

For half an hour, she groomed the filly mechanically and concentrated on the coming ordeal. The three-year-old had never been tested against others, and she had no idea how it would react, or what her tactics should be. Should she get out in front from the start? Or should she hold back in the early stages and let go in a burst of speed at the end? Her lips were dry and her body perspiring with apprehension, and afraid the animal would become agitated by the smell of her anxiety, she drifted off to stare at the stalls of the fair without seeing and listen to the auctioneer without hearing.

A very long, chalk-written list appeared on a board. She was grateful for the confusion of its scrawl, which she unravelled carefully until she reached the name "Macha's Girl."

There was no nonsense about weighing in, or wearing silks for these races. Each rider was simply allotted a number, walked his mount once around in parade, usually to the shouts and whistles of his friends, and then made for the distant end of the track.

All manner of nags and men congregated there. Underfed ponies ridden by hungry-looking lads, old hacks which should have been retired carrying ancient equestrians who were, coloured ponies belonging to travellers, hunters topped by green jackets, cobs and thoroughbreds nudged and pushed, sidled and backed, while the starter issued impossible orders through a speaking trumpet in a vain attempt to arrange them in one straight line. The girl did not take her eyes off him, and the filly, amazed at the commotion, stood like a rock with only her pricked ears betraying tension.

Eventually, hoarse and frustrated, and with a quarter of the entries still facing the wrong way and several already bolting in the opposite direction, the starter gave up the struggle and dropped the flag.

The filly, taking off by mere instinct, was propelled along in the first scramble. As the others bumped and pushed, Macha herself lost a surprised breath before she pushed her feet home in the stirrups, sat deep in the saddle and drove her mount on.

The response was magical. The little horse eeled through a narrow gap between two others and stretched for the front runners, passing the third and second and drawing level with the leader with smooth, giant strides which did not seem to touch the ground.

The drumming of hooves and snarls of laboured breath, the hissing of sticks and bellowing of the jockeys clamoured at their heels. Macha's throat was choking on her own heartbeats. Unready for the noise, the speed and the sheer hard work entailed in keeping the filly balanced, she could feel the band of tension across her stomach and the muscles in her thighs trembling with the strain.

The two horses ran nose to nose, and the girl, hearing the other jockey shout, turned her head and felt a cutting pain across her neck. Her weight shifted automatically as she realised her rival had grabbed and slashed her with his whip. The sting of pain and rage communicated itself through her body to the filly and Macha's Girl winged ahead in a mighty leap, galloping straight and true for the post.

They sensed all the rest fall behind, further and further, and heard the baying crowd. The rails merged into a white streak alongside. The last furlongs speared to the sky. The girl felt superhuman, in a halo of power as, together, they were borne on the wind of success, blowing effortlessly as thistledown over the turf, the three-year-old so relaxed, she could have raced on to America without sign of stress. The winning post hung in the air like a balloon, spurted by and was gone.

They had won! A huge bubble of excitement broke in sparkling effervescence over them. They had won! Nothing in Macha's life had prepared her for that moment, for the elation it generated. The glory and the masses, the sunlight and the emerald grass, the rich steam rising from the filly's skin, her own thundering heart. It was as though they were whirling in a prism of colour. The winning of that first race on the scrawny little beast was unique and was to inspire all the rest of her days.

People swarmed around. She caught snatches of their comments.

"Won by six lengths at least."

"Put a guinea on Macha's Girl for the bumper."

"I'd have said ten lengths."

". . . looks like a dog."

"It can be a two-headed jackass if it wants, just so long as it goes like a dose of Senna."

"5–4 on Macha's Girl for the last race."

They elbowed each other to catch a better glimpse of the extraordinary animal and put out their hands as though to touch her for luck. Someone took the reins and led them through. The onlookers stopped pushing and made way, quite suddenly. Their voices dropped, so that by the time the girl and her winner arrived at the enclosure, it was remarkably quiet.

Her neck ached where the rider of the runner-up had slashed with his whip. She put up her hand and withdrew it covered in blood and understood why the mob was backing off. What a sight she must be.

A very important person was approaching, beaming at everyone else, without looking at her at all.

"I have great pleasure in presenting the five-pound prize to the winner of . . ." he announced in a fat, carrying voice, then turned. The smile was replaced by a look of disbelief, followed by an expression of disgust. He stepped back, beckoning authoritatively to a clerk.

"Christ Almighty! The sinfulness of it . . . !" she heard a woman say behind her.

"Avert your eyes this instant, Peggy Casey!" a man's voice commanded.

The officials were talking conspiratorially among themselves, casting sidelong glances of indignation in her direction. The man who had been holding the filly's head had disappeared. She could feel the blood trickling and looked down. Her jacket was open and her shirt had been torn half off, baring her breast.

"Be jabus! That's no lad. That's a damn woman!" The exclamation came from the back of the gathering.

The very important person was shouting to a policeman. "Sergeant! Arrest that woman for gross indecency!"

Macha dug her heels hard into the ribs and brought her stick down on the dark brown flank. The filly squealed and catapulted forward, scattering the functionaries congregated in the opening to the paddock and swerving into the entries already parading for the next race. Ignoring the chaos of shying horses and falling riders, she headed for the fence and soared over, as racegoers on the other side ducked to the ground beneath her.

They sped on to the wooded end of the course, and looking over her shoulder, the girl saw that the police sergeant had scrambled onto a big, strong bay and was pounding after them.

"Mary, Blessed Virgin, Mother of God, if you save me now, I'll give up all wickedness for ever. I'll go back to Hugh Mulligan."

The three-year-old pecked. The sound of the policeman's horse thudded into hearing.

"MACHA! MACHA! Look after me! Save your namesake, your child!"

The filly covered the soft earth without leaving a trace, not a hoofprint, not the mark of a shoe. The pursuer and the shrieking multitude shrank and were outstripped. The trees rolled aside like parted waves and received her into their canopied and mysterious obscurity.

At last rider and horse felt safe enough to slow to a jog, and their hammering breath became gradually even and quiet until they moved on like ghosts. South, keeping the lough on the right and putting the town behind them; they were going away from where the Bow-top waited.

By now, the whole of Killarney would be agog at the outrage of the woman who had ridden half naked around the racecourse, and there was no possibility of her returning by the route by which she had come.

On the far side of the water, Purple Mountain ascended aggressively to almost three thousand feet within the dark and gloomy range of Macgillycuddy's Reeks, which seemed impassable, and Macha began to wonder how she was going to reach her home.

They travelled for over an hour and still the lake bordered their path. The filly's head was low and her feet dragged with exhaustion. The girl too was sore and stiff when they stopped to rest on the shore. The animal, with loosened girth, sucked a few gurgling draughts of water through her teeth before dropping her nose to the grass with a thankful sigh. Macha bathed her own cut neck, buttoned the jacket securely over her torn shirt and stretched out in the sun to lie between sleep and consciousness, with a head full of disoriented fantasies of flags and flames, gold cups and truncheons, lines of Thoroughbreds and rows of graves.

Cold and the sound of wheels aroused her in the end. The sierra had blocked the rays, and looking down the expanse of the lough, she saw, with incredulity, a horse pulling a cart across the surface of the water. The illusion persisted as she rode towards it, and only when a few yards off did she realise that a narrow isthmus divided the lake like a belt. The sounds of singing came from the converted jack wain, which had reached the other side as Macha cantered after it.

Three very drunk men were lolling and bawling in the back of the cart without attempting to drive the horse, which walked with the purposeful resignation of one habitually left to find its own way home.

"The luck of the day to you all," said Macha politely.

"Have a drink on that," responded the nearest. "For it's luck we've had indeed."

He held out a stone jar, and after Macha had taken a fiery swallow, it was solemnly passed from one to the next. They were dressed in bowler hats and homespun tweed suits, as inflexibly bristling as boot scrapers. Three farmers on an outing.

There were formalities to be completed: the return of the good wishes and another round drunk to that; the news to be imparted that each had won tidily on the horses.

"A gross of little money spiders couldn't have spun a prettier profit," said the second man and raised the jar again. "It was as though they were buying coppers for gold back there."

The third farmer lay on the floor of the cart, still singing to himself.

"And you'll have been to the fair yourself?" the first assumed.

"Not I." She shook her head, sadly. "My master wanted me for work."

"And what master would that be?"

"The castle," she invented, and decided to approach her business before they grew more curious. "Would you know if there's a way north through the mountains?"

"There's Moll's Gap to the chasm of Dunloe; but although fools have passed into it, there's not a one known to have passed out at the far side." He waved vaguely with his right arm and Macha followed the direction to see, at the top of a spiralling cut, a fissure between two sheer precipices.

"In there, rocks the size of churches tumble from the heavens year in and year out, and there are waterfalls plummeting from the very peaks with the force to drive a man as far again into the ground, to Satan's palace itself." He rolled his eyes and opened another jar. "There are storms of thunder and blizzards and lightnings and tempests worse than at sea trapped to rampage forever in the centre; and even if you escape those, there are the Hidden People waiting to drag you into their unholy world, to dance like an Arab for all eternity."

His companion, who had been watching her through narrowed eyes, reached out and caught the filly's rein.

"The castle, did ye say?" He sounded suspicious. "I've never seen you at the castle, ye young flipe, and don't I deliver praties there every week as regular as the bus."

Before Macha could answer, the third farmer suddenly stopped singing and sat up.

"If the bastards had paid out on the first race, I'd have cleared three guineas this day!" He pointed an accusing finger, as though holding them all responsible, then turned to her, glassily.

His squint focussed. An expression of perplexity was followed by one of angry enlightenment.

"Cock ye up! I know that one like I know me own bum," he roared at his fellows. "That's the winner! That's the Devil's daughter that took the first race—and my five shillings!"

Chapter
FOUR

The second farmer tugged on the rein and shouted. The girth, which had not been tightened, slipped, pulling the saddle sideways and causing Macha to wrench the other rein. In fright and pain, the filly reared and bolted, her rider clinging to her neck and ribs like a Red Indian and trying frantically to struggle back into position.

The stirrups swung loose, catching the terrified animal on the barrel and spurring her the faster. The saddle slid right under her belly and the loose reins flapped dangerously close to her scudding feet. The unfamiliar ground was strewn with shale which rolled beneath her shoes and ricochetted, cracking like pursuing shot. She tripped and swerved, returning Macha violently onto her back once more, then headed blindly up the winding path to Moll's Gap.

Water gushed towards them through the opening. Boulders had been tossed from its course, leaving holes to become swirling pools, through which they splashed and stumbled without reducing speed. Overhead, Carrantuohill and Purple Mountain strained from their whirling heights to topple together in one mighty cataclysm and close the hair's breadth between them as though it had never been. The tsunami of night was mounted in the east. Beyond, the gap looked deeper than space. The filly gave a huge lunge. Macha felt her calf scrape agonisingly along the scar face and they were through, into the ravine of Dunloe. Instantly, it was japan-black.

The young horse floundered. The loose reins whiplashed around a foreleg and brought her down. Macha felt herself propelled upwards, the air rush past and a burst of lights as she hit rock and crashed back to the ground.

She regained her senses briefly once or twice and was dimly conscious of wind and water and stone before gratefully settling back into oblivion.

Night became wan and smeared into grimy grey. It was morning at last. Macha felt the lump on her head and sat up, wincing, to find herself on a floor of algae-covered rocks, walled in by flat, wet slabs. A dense fog curled unmoving about ten feet off the ground, completely obscuring everything above, including the sky. There was no sign of the three-year-old.

She stood up and reeled. The cut in her neck throbbed, and there was a stitch behind her eyes. It was twenty-four hours since she had eaten.

Not far ahead, a small waterfall plashed through the ceiling of mist. Macha made her way to it weakly, bent forward and let its freezing spray numb her sores and clear her brain. Kneeling, she cupped her hands into its pool and drank until her stomach felt full. Then she began walking.

Twice she took off her boots to cross streams, and once, attempting to jump another, she slipped and fell in. About half a mile on, she was relieved to find the saddle lying battered on the ground, for it showed that the filly had come this way and not doubled back on her tracks.

The fog began to lift quite rapidly, revealing overhanging corniches and ledges so delicately poised that it seemed the slightest sound or breeze would bring them hurtling down. Yet the draught echoed through the tunnel and moaning and clamour, and the shrill trilling of water skirled and chorused from the interior ahead. The track plunged down and down and then, surprisingly, opened into a wide and lovely glen, at the northern end of which was a lake, and standing up to her knees near the edge was the brown filly.

She nickered on seeing the girl, who ran to her, delighted.

"What are you standing there for, you gossoon?" Macha scolded affectionately. "I thought you'd have galloped back to Galway by now and I'd lost you."

She put the reins carefully back over the animal's neck and tried to draw her forward, but she did not move.

"Come up! Come up! It's not far," her owner encouraged. "And I want a good feed, even if you don't."

The three-year-old staggered from the shallows on three legs and stood with her offside fore dangling. It was the size of a baby's corpse from knee to fetlock.

"Oh, Jesus! What's happened to you?" Macha stared in dismay and put out an exploratory hand. Although the animal had been standing in sleety water, the skin was burning to the touch and far too swollen to expose how much damage had been done.

Macha wondered fearfully if the cannon bone was broken. Because of the impossibility of keeping its great weight off such an injury, there was no cure for a horse with a fractured leg, and the filly would have to be put down. Helplessly, Macha rubbed the velvet nose.

The fog had gone. Tomies Mountain and Macgillycuddy's Reeks ramped mightily on either side and interlocked like wrestlers at the far end of the fishless lough. The girl tried to remember the distance from Aghadoe to the racecourse in an effort to compare the return, for there was no alternative but to go on. It was as well that the day had just begun, leaving plenty of time before dark. At least, they would be able to see where they were going.

"Come on, mavourneen. Macha will mind you."

With the saddle over one arm and the reins over the other, she set off, the filly faltering behind.

The red sandstone was dangerously slippery, and with both hands full, Macha lost her footing more than once. The young horse paused before every step and often stopped, sweating profusely despite the cold. Numerous becks streamed into the ravine at varying speeds, and at each, she had to be cajoled and persuaded to risk the crossing.

After two hours, they seemed to have covered very little distance. The saddle grew heavier and heavier, and unable to burden the three-year-old, the girl abandoned it in a cave, intending without much hope to return for it later. Another mile and they were both exhausted and distressed when the filly tottered, knocked her damaged leg and screamed. Macha soothed her as best she could, stroking the convulsive muscles and murmuring, then sitting down to wait until she recovered.

Gradually, she began to cry herself, bitter drops of despair at being trapped in this terrible place so far from the waggon, so hungry and hurt and so lonely. She buried her head in her hands and broke down noisily for minutes; and there came a soft breath in her hair. The filly was nudging at her shoulder and gazing at her with wide, kind eyes.

"You're so much worse off than me and still as brave as a badger," Macha said, feeling ashamed of herself. "I'll get you out of here yet, and I'll not let you die, nor sell you neither."

They managed to reach to where the way became so narrow there was barely space to pass. They rounded the bend. The gorge ended and open, wooded country stretched before them. The shores of Lough Leane curved off to the right to the remains of St. Finian's monastery. And there, sheltered by its ruined church and tower, stood the Bow-top. They had come through the Black Peaks of Kerry and were safely home.

Macha gave the filly a big feed of horse bread, a mixture of beans, wheat, yeast and water kneaded together, and while she was eating, pressed a water-soaked pad to the wounded leg and secured it with a bandage of rag strips. Only then did she go inside, change out of her wet clothes and find herself some food.

She was so chilled that even hot tea, laced with whiskey, and peppery colcannon, made from potatoes and cabbage fried in butter, failed to stop her shivering.

Sliding back the door to the hay-filled bed, she climbed in, drew up a threadbare blanket and called the dogs. In the encampment, dogs had never been permitted inside tents or the waggon, but she did not care. They jumped and burrowed down, one on either side, and soon she felt their body heat wrap around her, deliciously, like down.

The sensation of utter contentment and security was relaxing and unexpectedly answered a riddle she had sometimes asked herself. This must be why the settled people stayed on in their suffocating cabins: for this same feeling of peace and protection. A flea worked its way down the inside of her arm, leaving a row of bites. She scratched without concern and fell asleep.

The dogs had gone when she awoke. She could see stars through the doorway, and the night hovered overhead like a hawk. She waited, aware of fine hairs on the back of her neck rising and her skin creeping. Not a whisper. Not a sigh. She reached above the bed for her father's shotgun, inching it from its rack and then swinging with it to the floor. Two steps to the opening, a soundless stoop to the grass and slither along the wall of the Bow-top.

He was there, furtive in silhouette against the moonlit lough.

"Stop where you are, mister, or I'll blow your belly open!"

The noise of the safety catch being released slammed against the quietude, and he started, visibly.

"Don't be rash, now. It's nothing at all. It's nothing." His voice was wheedling and sly, but she heard the tremor, too.

"Come over here!" she ordered, and he came closer, close enough for her to see he was lightly built and not tall. She sensed he was a young man. His eyes glittered, unblinking, but she could not tell their colour.

He had a clearer view of her, for the moon was shining on her face, and this made her feel at a disadvantage. An unlit lantern was hanging from his right hand.

"Light the lamp!" she said, and watched him kneel to do so.

The wick sputtered; the little flame ran across it like a caterpillar and grew into a brilliant butterfly inside the glass. A fan of light opened between them. She saw his bold Rom face looking up without a trace of alarm and felt angered by his confidence.

"What are you doing here?" she demanded harshly.

"You'll not shoot me if I get to my feet before my kneecaps grow roots?" He clambered up without waiting for her answer, but without taking his eyes off the weapon.

She moved her finger on the trigger, and he talked hurriedly. "I've told you it's nothing. I'm stopping a day or two in the wood yonder and thought I'd just come and take a little look at your pony."

The truth dawned.

"May the devil give you a hook for a tongue! You were stealing her! You were stealing my horse! You scrub! You shit sack!" Macha was enraged and the gun twitched dangerously in her hands.

"Will ye put that thing down, in the name of God!" he gasped, suitably nervous at last. "Wouldn't it look most untidy to have the likes of meself spattered all over this lovely spot? I've no appetite for it at all."

His gaze flickered almost imperceptibly, and she swayed out of reach a split second before his fist struck out to seize the weapon. Her heart jerked with anger. His eyes remained expressionless.

"You were stealing my horse!" she repeated, taking an audacious step forward so that the mouth of the gun pressed against his chest. If he tried to snatch it again, he would be a dead man. In her fury, she wanted to kill him.

"I was not going to steal her exactly. I might have borrowed her for a while, that's all," he said, through lips now stiff with apprehension. "I mean, looking the way she does, like an ould coat hung on a tentpole, she's not a horse you could hide. You'd have found her soon enough—but not before she'd won me a few races, Macha Sheridan."

That he knew her name was ominous. It meant he knew all about her—where she came from, her behaviour after her father's death, the scandal of the Killarney race, everything.

He followed up on his gain. "It seemed an indecent shame that a brilliant beast like that could never run again because she hasn't a jockey."

"I'll find a rider," Macha said defensively.

"There's not a man in the land will ride for you, Macha Sheridan, as well you know."

Certain that she would not shoot now, he turned away. The light from the lantern fell on the three-year-old with her injured leg still bulging under the rough bandage.

"What have you done to her?" he shouted.

He strode to the filly's side and stared at the injury, then rounded on the girl, his face contorted.

"You stupid slut! The curse of hell on you!" he swore. "You've wrecked the best capall in Ireland."

"She fell! Her reins caught round her leg and she fell! There was no helping it." Macha was high-pitched in self-vindication. "And I've done what I can."

"There was no helping it!" He was heavily sarcastic. "And what were her reins doing hanging about her fetlocks in the first place? Or do you always gallop her about like that? Mother of God! Look at the mess of her."

He ran a hand tenderly down the filly's shoulder and began talking to her, his voice changing from rasping contempt to a crooning. He began to undo the rags, and the horse recoiled.

"Do some small thing right, girl! Hold her still!" he commanded.

Macha put down the gun automatically and took the rope halter.

"Steady, now. Steady, babby. 'Tis a scratch no worse than a pen stroke. Gently. Gently. Have I not said you'll be right and dancing within the hour?" He no longer noticed Macha, but muttered on and on to the filly, easing the wet pad off and then swearing under his breath at the extent of the damage.

He took the rope and gradually cajoled and petted the young horse into the lough until the water reached to her knees.

"Keep her here till I come back," he ordered her owner, who had not had time to put on shawl or boots and found herself wading in barefoot to do his bidding. He strode off towards the woods without glancing back.

Lough Leane cut a channel along the edge of Macgillycuddy's

Reeks for five miles, and a piercing air ceaselessly cut over its surface. As her bones began to ache and her teeth to chatter again, Macha felt wearily that she would never escape from the cold and wet which seemed to dominate her life.

The stranger was gone for a long time, and only the sensitive but unmistakable expertise with which he had handled the three-year-old induced her to wait on in such acute discomfort. When he returned, it was so quietly that he was almost at her side before she was aware of it. She wondered why the dogs had not barked or attacked, but they were nowhere to be seen.

"Bring her up on the turf," he said.

He poured some liquid from a bottle into his palm, rubbed his hands together and then stroked down the filly's face to her nose. She half-closed her eyes, and her ears drooped, and for the first time she lowered the crippled leg to the ground.

"Now hold her fast as a trap. She's going to like this as much as a hare being jugged."

He opened a jar carved out of horn, and the mordant fumes from it chopped Macha in the throat, so that she turned away, gagging.

"Hold her! Hold her!" snapped the man, and scooped out a dollop of the substance and spread it over the puffy flesh, working it in with quick fingers. There was no doubt he knew what he was doing.

The animal's nostrils flared and her eyes jerked wide open. There was a hesitation before she screeched and reared, running backwards on her hind legs and hauling the girl off the ground.

The stranger moved by reflex. As Macha was sent sprawling in the mud, he caught the rope and tied it to a waggon shaft, humming and hissing to the shocked filly until the snorting and pulling and shuddering finally stopped.

"Have you whiskey?" he asked calmly.

"Will she be all right? Is her leg broken? She won't have to be shot?" Macha, covered in sludge, was on her feet and staring at her horse.

"There's no saying till the swelling goes down, but I'd guess the tendon's torn," he replied.

The girl was abject. "Then she'll never race again."

"Oh, she might. Or she might do something better. There's ways and ways," he hinted cryptically. "Now, have you a drink for a man, or do you not? Poteen will do."

Half an hour earlier, he had been about to rob her, but now, concerned only with the fate of her horse, she realised she needed his knowledge and help.

She led the way to the Bow-top and noticed him hesitate at the foot of the wooden steps. He was afraid of Jack Sheridan's spirit. Deliberately, she stood inside, the full bottle in her hand. He cleared his throat and entered.

As she poured, the bottle clinked against the pot in her quaking hands and she spilt some of the spirit on passing it to him.

He did not take it, but regarded her, unsmiling.

"Drink it yourself, Macha Sheridan, to warm you," he said. "Then get rid of those soaked clothes."

The whiskey, burning and bitter as peat fire, blazed its way to her stomach. She choked and would have put the half-empty mug down.

"Drink it all," he instructed. And she did.

Then he took the bottle, drank directly from it and pointed to the heap of men's clothes she had worn to the races.

"Put those on."

"They're wet too," she protested.

"Then wrap this about you." He pulled the thin blanket from the bed.

She had never undressed in the presence of a male before, not even her own father. Women, she had been taught, were dangerous to the health and strength of men; *mochardi*. It was forbidden to cross a stream from which men drank, to step over food or drink or any utensil, to pass in front of a seated man, to comb or let down her hair where men might see. To remove her clothes must be the ultimate sin.

She waited for him to leave the waggon, but he merely drew a pipe from his pocket, lit it slowly and turned away.

The waterlogged blouse clung and the skirt tangled about her as she endeavoured to remove them modestly, cringing at their rustling sounds and trying to hide herself with the cover, in case the man should look. Short of breath and feeling degraded, she finally pulled the wool tightly around her and sat, with legs compressed together and feet tucked back under the bench.

The stranger was punishing her because she had made him enter the Bow-top and risk the wrath of the dead. Tears began to spill onto her cheeks. He poured some more whiskey into the mug and handed it to her.

"Drink this, and sleep," he said. "I'll be back to see the pony in the morning."

Then he left.

Whiskey and tobacco fumes seasoned the air in the Bow-top, just as they had during her father's time. She breathed them in deeply and was somehow consoled.

The man announced his arrival with tuneful whistling. By the time Macha came out, the dogs were lying near him wearing expressions of stupid adoration and the filly was chewing his hair. The injured leg appeared miraculously improved, the swelling reduced and the lacerations almost closed. He was pasting on more ointment, and this time his patient stood stock-still and unconcerned.

The girl was able to contemplate him without being observed. He was slim, but the shape of his shoulders and biceps curved powerfully under the heavy jersey which he wore over narrow trousers. Thick, black, straight hair kept falling into his eyes and being tossed back impatiently as he worked. It was unusual to see a man without a cap or hat, almost as though he were half-dressed. Macha blushed, remembering the night before. He looked up at that moment, a disconcerting blue glance, and smiled, reading her thoughts.

"What is that stuff?" she asked quickly, pointing to the horn jar.

"Oh, just the feather of a toad and the juice of a dandelion and all my grandmother's beard," he grinned, evasively.

She felt rebuked and cross. The lurchers had worked their way so close to him that their noses were pressed against his boots.

"Fine guard dogs they are," she said resentfully. "They should have gone for you."

"Ah, don't you blame them. Dogs never attack me," he said. "Not after I tell them it would not be courteous."

He talked down to her as though she were a child. She decided she disliked him.

"We will be moving today, anyways." She made the statement as a challenge.

"Yes, I was going to suggest you shift the waggon into the woods by my bender," he responded. "But you will not be going further than that before the little pony here is fit."

He spoke placidly enough, yet as though he expected to be obeyed. But Macha was not to be bullied.

"And why would I move the Bow-top under the trees when a ruby could not be better set in gold than it is in this place?"

"Or slot in snow before guns. It must be visible for twenty miles."

His eyes were full of amusement. "Sure, it's none of my affair, but there was this bit of mild annoyance on the racecourse after you left yesterday. A few punters had lost their money, you will understand, and seemed to feel the blame was on yourself. Of course, if they find you here, they might give you time to explain it was all a joke, but you'll forgive the thought that you'll more likely finish up in jail, or worse."

A cat on a silk cushion with a mouse under each paw and a fish in its mouth could not be more smug, she thought, and flounced off sulkily to harness the mare.

Each day he dressed the filly's wounds. Macha kept out of the way, and he did not seem to notice her absence. By the end of the week, the leg was reduced to its normal size, although still fragile.

Against her will, the girl was impressed. She had seen badly broken-down horses before, and few recovered. Certainly none had ever mended as fast as this. She wondered why he was taking the trouble. The three-year-old would surely not race again, so there seemed to be no motive to it.

Meat was roasting over the fire one evening when he was suddenly there, standing in the dark, observing her through the red smoke.

"Do I get something to eat?" he asked.

She shrugged her permission for him to help himself.

"I knew Jack Sheridan well," he said.

"He never talked about you."

"How would you know that, when you don't even know my name?"

It was true—she had no idea who he was. It was obvious that he was a Rom, perhaps even a pure-blood, but it was peculiar that he travelled alone and not with others. She had deliberately not asked questions and now waited, trying to look indifferent.

"Molloy, I'm called. Coper Molloy."

Molloy the Coper! There was a name! Her father had said Molloy the Coper knew more about horses than any other man living or dead. He could trade flat-catchers as show-worthy, cocktails as Thoroughbreds, blood weeds as studs. No-one could bean or bishop, feague or fake a screw better than Molloy, who could steal a beast one night and sell it back to its rightful owner next day and the buyer would *never* discover he had been tricked.

She gave him a scathing stare. "What would Coper Molloy be doing in an old bender with not one horse of his own?"

"Is it horses you want? Well, the horses aren't far off. I'll take you to them tomorrow, down beyond Kate Kearney's cottage." He tore off a piece of meat and nodded patronising approval of her cooking. "And I'm in the bender because, as you well mind, it was my intention that the little pony should join them.

"As for knowing your father, didn't he buy every broken-down tit I ever traded! There couldn't have been a jade west of Dublin City that did not pass through his hands."

He laughed uproariously.

"That's a dirty lie!" Macha, roused by this slight on her father's reputation, threw a tin cup of boiling water at him. Falling short, it sprayed over the fire, which sputtered and spat. "Jack Sheridan was a grand dealer, and everyone knew it."

"Girl, if he'd worn a nosebag and been shod once a month himself, he'd have found it hard to recognise another nag," Molloy guffawed irreverently, then waved the bone from the joint at her. "You are different, though, Macha Sheridan. I have watched you and you understand the horses."

"I'll not have you speak of my Da this way. It's all lies!"

"Lies is it? So, what about that grey with splints like leg-irons that he tried to sell in bandages at Castlebar? And the batys mare that used to reverse herself into every lough?" he asked, chuckling. "And then there was that little brute that tossed so many buckeens off its back that Jack Sheridan ran a competition with a prize for whoever could stay on more than five minutes."

A picture of Mick Mulligan being thrown repeatedly over a wall as he tried vainly to win the ten shillings invaded her mind irrepressibly, and she began to lose control.

"And what of the mare that kicked your father's cart to pieces and left him stranded on the roadside in the middle of Joyce Country?"

How could she forget? Macha gave in with a gurgle and completed the tale.

". . . He had to walk ten miles to Maam Cross and buy a donkey off a man to get himself back to us at Oughterard!"

The laughter engulfed them. It shook the girl and rocked the man with crowing and cackling until their eyes ran and their facial muscles cramped. Each time one managed to stop, the sound of the other still hooting was more infectious than yawning. Small night animals fled from the racket, and birds woke up above them with squawks of reproach.

Macha could see and hear her father again. Jack Sheridan trying out ponies with his feet almost scraping the ground; catapulting between the ears of hobbies; careering away on hard-mouthed hunters; jumping carthorses and cursing jibbers. Each recollection redoubled her convulsion. It was as clear as if he were with them beside the fire, and then she remembered his jokes and his stories, and the laughter changed key and became too wild and turned to gasps, and then she was sobbing out her grief, piteously.

The man was there. She hung on to him for the smokiness of his tweed jacket, for its texture against her skin, for the flesh warmth, for the vulcanite hardness of his frame, for the marrow of his humanity. She did not want to stop weeping. After so many weeks of segregation, she wanted to stay there, against him.

His hand was on her head, smoothing, smoothing her hair and then her forehead, and then it was over her face, and she was pressing her mouth against his palm and breathing very deeply. The tears dried, the sobs stopped, a strange calm filled her and she felt light, almost weightless. He took his hand away, and she opened her eyes.

Molloy smiled and went on talking as though it had not happened.

"How would it be if I took the little pony off your hands?" he offered unexpectedly, some days later. "After all, no-one will buy her now with those scarred legs, and she'll not race again."

It sounded a casual offer, but Macha, who had been waiting to discover his interest in her filly, was alerted.

"No," she replied, shortly.

"Don't be hasty. I've developed an affection for her, that's all," he said, with a sincerity that would have fooled a Jesuit. "And I'll give you ten pounds."

It was tempting and Macha thought about it, then decided to call his bluff.

"She's not for giving and she's not for sale, and don't think to cod me, Molloy." She glared her accusation. "I know you would never fret like a wet nurse over any useless screw, so you might as well tell me what you're after."

He looked at her with appreciation, nodded philosophically and asked, "What do you know about that filly? Did your father tell you where she came from?"

Macha's answer was vague. "Da bought the mare, her mother, in foal."

"And where was that?" he persisted.

"Since he traded enough horses to fill Ballinasloe Fair over the past four years, how would I remember?"

"Well, I can tell you where, Macha Sheridan."

That insufferable smugness again, she thought, and scowled.

He continued without noticing, "Jack Sheridan bought that mare from the tenant of a very important and proper gentleman called Mr. Charles J. Blake of Heath House, Maryborough; a steward of the Turf Club, no less."

Macha interrupted, "What's so unusual about that? She was only a common type. Nothing special at all."

"You're right. The farmer used to hunt her, and she even pulled a gig," he agreed. "But she was half-bred, and there was something particular about her at that time, all the same."

"And what was that?"

"She got out a couple of months before she was sold and had a little adventure," he grinned. "The sire of your filly was a stallion called Bel Demonio, which stood at Heath House. Before that, he was the winner of two races in England worth a thousand pounds each. Now, he *was* a bit special!"

"You can't be sure Macha's Girl is his foal."

"Why do you think Jack Sheridan didn't sell her earlier?" he asked, and seeing that she still appeared doubtful, went on, "The tenant farmer sold her quick before questions could be asked and Mr. Blake found out. A local lad who'd been party to the catching of her gave me the tip, except he was a bit late and by the time I got there she'd gone to your father; and that's where I made a little misjudgement."

"A misjudgement!" echoed Macha in sarcastic disbelief.

He ignored this. "I tried to buy her off Jack Sheridan, and either he worked out the reason, or maybe that blagyard lad earned himself another shilling there as well. Anyway, your Da wouldn't part with her; and I've seen the foal enough times since to know that this is the same."

Macha remembered being mildly puzzled that her father had kept the foal after it was weaned, and then the filly had always been given good rations, as good as adult working horses.

"A young creature must build bone, and to do that it needs best feed," he had explained, and she had not thought much more about the matter.

"How would you like to go into partnership?" Molloy reached his purpose at last.

"Share the filly with you?" The girl was confused. "What would be the point, when she's worth nothing now?"

"No, not the filly."

"What then?"

"The foal! Partnership in the filly's foal, when it's born next year!" Molloy was gleeful.

"She's not in foal!" Macha began to think he was slightly deranged.

"No, but she will be," he shouted. "And there's only one horse for her. With him, she'll produce a real goer that'll make us our fortune."

"And which horse would that be?" There was no hiding the scepticism in her voice.

"Gallinule."

"Gallinule!"

Macha gaped at him, incredulously, and then shrieked with laughter.

She was still hiccoughing and wiping her eyes uncontrollably minutes later, when he stood up.

"I've work to do," he said, briefly, and walked off into the darkness.

He might know plenty about horseflesh, but he was obviously also quite mad, and an hour later, she went to bed still breaking into giggles at the thought of strolling along to mate her scraggy three-year-old with the sire of the last Irish Derby winner.

"Mother of Saint Patrick! Are you not up and ready yet?" The hoarse whisper wakened her.

It was not daylight, and she could barely see his outline as he stood in the doorway.

"We should have been on the road half an hour back," he said urgently. "Now, will you collect your pots and cloths and such and let's be off."

He vanished into the dark, where she heard him muttering. The Bow-top gave a jerk, and the clinking of harness announced that the mare from Tulla had been backed between the shafts. Macha stumbled to the steps, rubbing her eyes.

Molloy ran past leading a bunch of unfamiliar horses.

"Come on! Come on!"

Sleepily, she collected tins and utensils from around the dead ashes of the fire. He came past again with the filly and her other three horses and thrust their halter ropes into her hands. Their hobbles had already been removed.

"Hitch them up and follow me!" he ordered.

Then his cart, surrounded by bobbing heads and sharp ears, rumbled by, outlined against the lough, and she found herself flapping the reins and rolling after them.

It could not have been later than three in the morning, and he set a gruelling pace. The sound of hooves on the cobblestones of Killarney hammered a few folk out of bed and to their windows, but all they saw was the high, dark *varda* swaying past. Molloy the Coper's string and cart were already out of sight.

The turning to the racecourse was behind them well before dawn as they journeyed south, parallel to the chasm of Dunloe, and they had crossed Galwey's Bridge and were circling Peakeen Mountain before the first edge of light laced the smooth brows and plump arms of the hills to the west. Ahead, the land sloped for another mile or more to the estuary of a river already brassy with day.

Molloy's cart was some distance in front, with the dozen horses he had kept by Kate Kearney's cottage crowded around its tailboard. Macha wondered whether Kate was one of his women. He looked like the kind of man who would have women all over the place, she thought, with his sly blue eyes and his jaunty walk. She felt unaccountably annoyed, and when he pulled up at the side of the road, she slowed the mare from Tulla, to make him wait the longer before she caught up.

He pointed to the grassy banks below and said, "We'll rest there."

"Where are we going? What's the hurry?" It was the first chance she had had to find out; but he was already urging his horses on and did not hear.

The animals waded into the river and drank, and Molloy, after reassuring himself that the filly's leg was still sound, gathered wood with Macha and quickly set up a fire. After that, to her amazement, he put a large flat griddle and dripping on the heat, broke four eggs into it and added four slices from a smoked ham he produced from the back of his cart. She had never seen a man prepare food before. Cooking was women's work, and the males in the encampment had sat about waiting for meals and always been served first. It was indecent to see a man lower himself so, and she was embarrassed when he held out her share.

"Did you imagine I lived only on neat whiskey?" he teased, not even shamed by her transparent disgust. "Or do you think you're the only one who breaks the rules?"

This was the first time he had referred to her behaviour after her father's death, and she dropped her head and concentrated on eating, admitting to herself with reluctance that the late breakfast tasted very good.

"What about your own people?" It had taken her days to summon up the courage to enquire obliquely why he travelled on his own.

"No family and no people," he answered. "Which is not to say I don't join up with others now and again. But it's best I'm on my own to deal with certain matters."

"Like trying to steal my horse!" she could not resist saying.

He gave one of his quiet smiles and poked the fire with a long stick, so that bubbles of flame bounced up from the logs, and she felt their heat on her uncovered legs and quickly drew down her skirt.

"The Connors and the Wards of the east are good friends of mine, and remember the Maughams if you're ever in need." Suddenly he was looking at her seriously, but she was not sure what he meant.

They were sitting facing the water and enclosed on the other three sides by dense bushes. Molloy had drawn up his cart at a right angle to the trees and had given precise instructions for the parking of the Bow-top to block the path along which they had arrived. No-one could come upon them unnoticed, and they were well concealed.

When they had finished eating, he stood up. "If you don't get a kettle boiled soon, you'll miss the lesson."

"What lesson?"

"You've a lot to learn, Macha Sheridan, now that we're partners" was his only comment, and walking over to the grazing horses, he caught a long-maned bay with a white blaze and two white socks and tied him between the cart and the waggon.

He fetched a large pair of scissors and some clippers, hacked off the horse's lovely black hair and clipped the crest of the neck smooth. By the time he had completed the job and shortened the tail by several inches to a bang, the water was hot. He added some to a reddish-brown powder in two glass jars and mashed in oil and a dash of melted beeswax, holding the jars up periodically until satisfied with the colour of the paste. Then, to one he added black drops from a small bottle.

Whistling, he began to paint it on one of the hindleg socks with a short-bristled brush. Within minutes the pastern and fetlock were almost black and all traces of white had gone.

"Your turn." He pointed to the off hind and handed the jar and brush to Macha, who had been watching fascinated. Now she knew why they had left Aghadoe with such stealth.

"Is this one of the horses that Kate woman was keeping for you?" she asked daringly as she worked.

"Kate . . . ? Oh, you mean Kate Kearney's cottage." He beamed with inexplicable amusement. "Ach, well, it might be and it might not. You know how little ponies come and go! Just like pretty *cailins*."

She would have liked to throw the dye all over him.

"Grade the paint over the fetlock, so that it looks natural," he instructed, and when she had done, cleaned the brush and took up the jar of brown paste, adding, "We'll just turn this blaze into a fine big star."

"Why not get rid of it altogether?"

"Well, the star will draw attention and people will be less likely to think to examine beyond it."

The bay, now with black points, hogged mane, banged tail and a star between his eyes, was a handsome-looking hunter, over sixteen hands high, and Molloy said they would head towards the country of the Muskerry Harriers and Dunhallow Foxhounds, where he would soon find a buyer.

"Will the colour not wash off?" she wanted to know.

"Try and see." He pointed to the river.

Macha untied the rope, curled her tongue between her lips and gave him a sidelong glance, almost a challenge, which he could not translate. The animal took a few steps forward.

Without warning, she gathered the fullness of her skirts into her waistband and sprang. Molloy caught a glimpse of a round, bare bottom before she landed on the broad back and whooped her mount on.

He felt a twist of an ancient terror and shouted out, but they had already cantered to the water's edge, entered without hesitation and started downstream, with spray glittering over them. Her laughter vibrated above the wash. She sat the big horse as though carved there, and he, guided, it seemed, by thought alone, sped safely over the underwater rocks and carried her towards a bend in the river, round which they vanished.

Molloy leant against the Bow-top, shaken by his own reaction, and cursed himself for having brought her with him. For a moment, he almost wondered if he were the victim of sorcery, caught in the trap of a spell cast by a witch.

The syncopated splashing of hooves returned to earshot as the girl and the horse plunged back. The river surged a white frost about them, piercing them with silver needles and slivers of glass which they did not feel. Foam trailed in their wake like a stream of white roses. Macha's hair had come loose and alive in thick, gleaming straps. They seemed to approach in slow motion, aurified by spangles and froth and refracted light, until they rose out of the water and lunged to stand over him, the horse gigantic, with exhilaration in his eyes and red-hot nostrils blowing smoke, and Macha, above and godlike, her clothes moulded to her in alabaster folds, her long hair now hanging forward over one shoulder, covering one side, so that Molloy saw only one eye, one breast, one nipple, one powerful thigh, one foot: the invulnerable oneness.

His heart was in his throat. He could neither move nor breathe. Then the hunter tossed its head and snorted, and he was released.

An uncontrollable desire coursed through him. He seized the girl's arm and dragged her to the ground, thrusting her against the waggon, spreading her legs with his knees and pulling the lank hair until her head was forced back and she was staring at him from a face as white as his own. He saw huge eyes, full, parted lips. He flexed, with teeth bared to devour her.

"Are you angry? You look very angry." Her voice was small and tremulous.

He felt his grip on her body loosen.

"I often ride. I didn't think you'd be angry," she said, standing straight and still as he took a step away.

He was no longer in his own skin. He could see himself moving back from her and hear himself saying, "No . . . no. I'm not angry." He felt violently sick. "I . . . I . . . was a bit worried, that's all."

"The dye didn't come off."

"What . . . ?"

"The dye. Look, his legs are still black." She was pointing to the fake bay.

". . . Of course they are," he muttered, turning away. "It's time we went on."

The hunter fetched sixty pounds, an excellent price, only a few miles further on at a big house. A brown gelding and a grey sold to farms as well, but Molloy did not seem content. He pushed a few of the bank-notes at her and slouched back to his cart, and they drove miserably past the charming Eccles Hotel on the shore at Glengarrif, ignoring the summer-bright water with its garnish of islands and colourful boats as the road wound round the inlets of Bantry Bay.

A wet man and a wet boy walked up the shingle, steam like a cloud of gnats about them under the sun. Rhododendrons and fuchsias brushed blue and scarlet against the Bow-top, and palm trees draped the path with fronded shadows, but failed to delight her.

Since the scene by the river, Molloy had kept distance between them, speaking only if she asked a question and refusing food she had offered during the midday stop.

She stared ahead at his figure, sitting loosely on the cart surrounded by trotting horses, and wished he would look back, and wished he would wave or smile. It was surprising that he was so offended. He had not seemed to care at all about the trouble that followed Jack Sheridan's funeral, and he had often praised her way with horses, yet now he had been incensed by the sight of her mounted on one. She wanted him to pull up until she drew alongside and then join her on the waggon, but of course, he did not.

That evening, they camped on a heath by a broken wooden pier which stumbled into the bay without any obvious purpose. Molloy fed and watered his beasts, then walked off without a word. The girl baked some potatoes in the embers of the fire until the skins were as black and hard as chestnut shells, then ate them from habit.

As the long day ended, the light passed through pale washes of green and primrose and pink. The last crescent of the moon swung like a pendant against the darkening blue, and closing grey clouds were lined with pure gold. Macha waited until the last thin beam went out and the water held no more reflections, but still he did not return.

The hay jabbed and irritated, and there were too many bugs in the bed. She turned restlessly, unable to settle, remembering the smell of his clothes and the warmth of his breath as he had held her at Aghadoe. When he had forced her to the wall of the *varda* in such rage that morning, fear was not all she had felt. She had not cowered. She had waited for something else, something more.

She spread her hands flat on the wood and stretched her whole body against its coolness. Perhaps he was so disgusted by her behaviour that he would end the partnership and tell her to go. She groaned and clenched her fists and pressed her lips to the cold, hard surface. Impossible images flooded her mind, nebulous and sinful, his naked back as he washed in the lough, her arms about his neck, his dark, all-knowing eyes, sinuous flesh, thick black hair; meeting mouths.

Heat glowed in her belly and a light dew sprang from her skin; her right hand moved unconsciously over the jutting edge of her hip bone. With high-pitched yelps, the dogs bundled from beneath the *varda*, making her jump, and she heard his voice chastise them. There was the clatter of a tin can, followed by slurred oaths. He sounded very drunk. Macha knew she should stay out of the way.

Seconds later, she was tiptoeing barefooted towards his bender tent. He had lit a lamp and was sitting on a straw pallet with a nearly empty bottle in his hand when she arrived. He gave her a look she translated as hatred, and for a moment she thought he was going to hit her.

"Get away from here! Go back to your place!" he shouted.

Her mouth filled with saliva.

"Did you not hear me. Go away!"

She knew if she obeyed, he would be gone from her life for ever before morning. She swallowed, stepped inside and knelt on the grass beside him.

"I'm sorry I rode the big hunter. It was *mochardi*, but I never thought you'd mind," she said humbly. "I thought you'd laugh, Molloy."

He looked at her in disbelief and gave a heavy sigh, shaking his head.

"Girl, you ride like a vision. . . . What, in the name of God, is *mochardi* but old wives' tales? . . . You were made to be with the horses. It's a gift the way you handle them. . . . Don't let anyone on this earth ever try to stop you." He spoke with jerky passion.

"But I thought you were in a rage."

He shook his head again and half turned away. He made the accusation in a hard voice.

"You turned down Hugh Mulligan, your father's choice of husband for you."

It was such an unexpected statement that she did not know how to react.

"Why did you reject him?"

"Is he a friend of yours?" she wondered.

"No."

"I did not like him and I did not want him."

"Does a father not know what's best for his daughter?" he demanded. "Is it not a woman's duty to obey?"

She muttered, "Yes" without conviction.

"Well, then?"

"I could not! I could not have Hugh Mulligan. He was like a nasty white jellyfish, a pasty little slug," she protested, with unmistakable feeling.

There was a measureless silence, and then he turned back to her deliberately.

"And what am I like, Macha Sheridan?"

His eyes would not free hers.

"You are . . . You are . . . You are like . . . ," she whispered desperately, and sank against him, closing her eyes tightly, winding her arms around him, finding his mouth with hers so that all the fleeting, incomprehensible images connected and were explained as he responded at last.

She kissed as though parched, drinking relief from him, filling herself to overflowing with ardour, and he, taken by surprise at first, was almost ferocious in return, clamping her to him with a hard arm, heavy-handed on her breast, then gradually becoming more restrained, more tender, until he was able to ease her away.

A deep flush covered her face and throat, and her mouth was a livid and swollen peach. She stared at him through crazy eyes.

"Molloy . . . ?"

"I promised my mother I'd marry a virgin," he said, with a grin.

"Amn't I a virgin anymore?" she asked.

He felt shocked and guilty and enchanted all at the same time and drew her back against him, very gently.

"Of course you're still a virgin, Macha. It takes more than a little kiss to change that, so it'll be all right to wed you—if you'll have me, that is."

She glared into his laughing face and sat up sharply, hitting him a half-playful, half-angry blow.

"You're joshing me again, Molloy!"

He gazed heavenwards in mock despair.

"I suppose a choosy woman like yourself, who rejects sweethearts right and left, expects a man to propose on his knees."

He dumped her on the ground and scrambled to one knee beside her.

"Macha Sheridan," he began, seriously. "Will you marry me?"

She was speechless.

"It's not good for you to travel about unwed with me. Your father and your mother are gone and you have no family. You need to be protected, and I would do that."

"And is that the reason you are proposing?" she asked, with a haughty expression, which he did not miss.

"No! No! My silly filly!" The irrepressible smile spread again. "I'm going to marry you because we were made for each other, because I need help with my horses and don't want the likes of you dealing in opposition; and because I'm growing tired of spending half me life on me knees before you. So it's decided."

He stood up, unsteadily.

"You're a bit drunk, Molloy, and you might think better of this in the morning." She was still not convinced.

"Mother of God, girl! Drunk or sober, I want you, but if you'll not give me a settled answer now, I'll take the offer back. For the last time, will you marry me?"

She gave a squeal of excitement. "Oh, I will! I will! I will!"

"We'll drink to it," he said, producing another bottle of whiskey and a tin mug from a carpet bag on the grass and splashing out a large measure.

It travelled through her body with a comfortable tingle as she leant against him and listened to talk of fairs and sales and deals and wonder steeds which had won races and made fortunes and bred great winners.

In the light of the lamp, his skin was dark and glossy and his eyes glowed, the strong line of his jaw and neck contrasted with the soft silk of his hair. He had a strong, arched nose and pronounced cheekbones and an arrogant way of tilting back his head. Macha saw him through the mist of alcohol.

"I know what you are like. . . . You are like . . . a fine, wild black horse . . ." she murmured, and then, as he pulled her closer, "What would you do if I was not a virgin?"

"I'd marry you anyway, little goddess."

"Then why do we wait?"

"What?" Taken aback, he sat up. "What, Macha?"

She giggled and ducked her head, looking at him mischievously from under her lashes.

"We don't have to wait for the wedding. We could do what married people do now," she said.

"You brazen baggage, and how would you know what married people do?" He glowered in mock disapproval.

"Oh, I know. I know what they do, all right." She lowered her voice, conspiratorially. "Kate Mulligan told me."

"Well, you tell me," he insisted.

"They . . they go to bed . . ." She took a noisy breath and added in a triumphant rush, ". . . They go to bed, together . . . naked!"

Molloy howled with mirth and gave her a mighty bear hug.

"Oh, they do! They do!" he agreed delightedly, ignoring her affronted expression. "And so will we, my darling girl, but not tonight. Tonight, and for every night until the wedding, you will sleep in your proper bed in your *varda*, just as Jack Sheridan would have insisted. For no-one is going to say Molloy took advantage of an orphan girl."

With that, he picked her up and carried her back to the waggon, and by the time he had covered her with the blanket, the whiskey had done its work and she was already asleep.

Chapter FIVE

On the day before Cork races, Molloy had a furtive conversation in a bar with a man whose bow legs and leathery face and age proclaimed him a stable lad.

"The Mister," he introduced him cryptically to Macha, who was to learn that his tipsters were always called the Mister.

On the third race, he won fifty pounds and gave it, all in notes and gold coins, to Macha.

"Spend it on a fancy gown and trinkets for the wedding," he instructed.

"This much would buy the crown jewels of England." The girl, quite accustomed to seeing sums of money change hands for horses, was nevertheless intimidated by the idea of squandering a small fortune on clothes.

"That black pony you bought yesterday is forfeit if you return with one copper left over," he threatened, as the winner was led past by the lad, who looked through them as though through strangers.

"Will you not come with me?"

"And how would I pay for your profligate ways if I went gallivanting about when there's work to do?" He gave her a slap on the behind and headed towards a ring-man.

*   *   *

Macha walked into a grand shop in South Mall and, as an assistant tried to block her way, slowly displayed the money and watched their faces change. A man in striped trousers and a tailcoat pushed the shopgirls out of his way and hurried to her side, rubbing his hands and bobbing his head deferentially.

She bought a length of bright pink satin and cards of coloured ribbon for a skirt, and three white silk petticoats, trimmed with deep flounced lace and insertions, at £1 19s 6d each. The cream chiffon silk blouse, with tucks and different-coloured ecru embroidery, cost over £3. Then, because she had never worn such garments, she bought two pairs of hand-made lawn knickers, trimmed with lace, and was sorely tempted to laugh aloud as the manager backed away in embarrassment, beckoning forward a female assistant as she held them up openly for inspection.

The glint of sovereigns again worked magic at the jeweller's shop, turning rejection into welcome. In no time, trays of necklaces and brooches and rings and bracelets were spread before her. Macha had never seen such treasure. It dazzled and confused as she fingered, hesitating. One necklace of diamonds alone cost £125 (enough to pay a factory worker for five years). But after the initial nervousness, she relaxed and enjoyed herself, watching as they hung gold chains over her wrists and pendants around her neck, as though it had always been so.

Finally, she bought three round gold bangles, a gold shamrock bracelet and matching brooch and, for her other arm, a gold bracelet with two moonstone hearts set in pearls.

The jeweller took £10 15s 6d and looked on as she counted out her remaining money. To her dismay, she still had £21 left. She gazed around the shop and caught sight of a display in a glass cabinet.

"I'll take that one," she pointed, and he unlocked the door, lifted out a solid-gold hunter watch and laid it in a velvet-lined box for Molloy.

She felt sated, as though she had overeaten, and the fun of such luxury unexpectedly faded, leaving her tired and slightly irritable. Pony, or no pony, she would spend no more. A plain silver sovereign case lay at one end of the counter. The jeweller picked it up and handed it to her with a flourish.

"With our compliments, madam," he said, and she slid her remaining coins into it.

* * *

The crowds from Cork Park cantered, red-faced and jolly, downhill to the open, empty bars of the town, impeding Macha's return with her parcels. Molloy was pacing beside the harnessed horses by the time she reached the site.

"You can't pick and choose the time for these things, you know," he scolded. "If we don't move any faster than a hearse against the wind, we'll miss the appointment."

"What appointment?" she asked, throwing the packages into the Bow-top. "We can't be wed yet, when I haven't sewn my skirt."

"Wed? By the saints, Macha, we can wed anytime. It's the filly we've to think of first." He stared at her as though questioning her intelligence. "If she's not at Brownstown by next week, it won't be worth putting her to the horse this year at all."

"Why not?"

"You want to race the foal, don't you?"

She nodded.

"And all racehorses take their age from first January, so the earlier in the year he's born, the better chance he has," he explained. "And this one's already going to be a late arrival."

He set a heartless pace from Cork to Fermoy that same evening, and they covered thirty-eight miles to Clonmel the next day, crossing the railway bridge and drawing up by the racecourse after dark.

All the horses were tired, and the filly was showing signs of stiffness in her forelegs. Macha, cold and wet after driving through rain for hours, was angry.

"I can't see why we're stopping for races if you're in such haste to reach the Curragh," she snapped.

"The services of Gallinule may be had informally, but they won't be had cheap," Molloy replied, and walked off to town, leaving her feeling cross and guilty for having spent so much money in Cork, especially as she would have much preferred to use it on the filly.

He placed successful bets on the first and third races, and she saw him slip silver into a couple of hands with practised deftness. Then he was ready to leave.

"We can't go till I've backed Meadow Lad," she insisted.

"God love us! You've held on to your money all afternoon like a little clerk, and now you want to throw it away on a mule."

"He will win!" Her face set. Since they had met, he had managed somehow to make her feel quite useless, and she was beginning to mutiny.

The runners sauntered in the paddock. Meadow Lad stopped for a moment and turned his head towards them. She met his keen, sure eye and smiled as he snorted and saucily swung his quarters.

"He will win."

"Arrah! With odds at 15–1, you're throwing away good cash—and good time. There's still over eighty miles to go, you know."

She did not mention that she had risked the remaining four sovereigns on her intuition.

The horses were filing onto the track. Meadow Lad gave a high-spirited buck as he was released and then settled into a steady run towards the starting post. In the distance, only purple-and-yellow colours distinguished him. The race dived off. Macha forgot the man at her side and willed the horse.

They came in a pounding, snorting mob and were gone, and Meadow Lad had led all the way. Macha gave Molloy back his £50 and added £15 of her own for Gallinule. Then she gave him the gold hunter watch. He was a man who had never before received a gift and he flushed, embarrassed by the rush of emotion he felt, squeezed her hand hard and turned away. When he faced her again, the gold chain was proudly displayed across his waistcoat with the watch secure in the pocket.

To the east, the last of the black rain cloud was being blown away, horizontally, as though from a factory chimney. Over the centre of Ireland, the sky was dusty blue. Their route, by small, tidy fields, was still lined with white-flowered hawthorn and wild roses, and they were hardly aware of climbing, the gradient was so slight.

Woods of oak and ash and wych elm and silver birch dropped behind a bracken-covered plateau, from which they could see for many miles to the navy blue Blackstairs Mountains.

For the sake of the filly, the pace was not so hard as it had been since Aghadoe, and a donkey and cart passed them easily. There were no houses in sight, only clumps of gorse and the occasional stone wall and a few heifers, mottled roan and white. The air smelt as fresh as water. A lark spun with giddy song into space, and a pregnant brown rat ambled alongside, large-eyed and small-eared, her whiskers twitching with curiosity.

Macha was glad to have left the congestion of towns and racecourses. Her home rocked like a cradle along the way; ahead lay the unopened future, and there was nothing to match the extraordinary blend of adventure and surety such journeying provoked. She leant against the painted wood of the *varda* and daydreamed over the events of the past weeks and what was to come. Her childhood with Jack Sheridan seemed long ago, and her time with Molloy might have been for ever.

He turned around once, and she closed her eyes quickly to pretend she was not thinking of him, but life was secretly exploding within her. She was like a bulb as the earth warms to spring.

Signposts clustered at every crossway, each pointing in a different direction, some to where there was no hint of a path, and all read "To Dublin"; but the travellers continued northeast with certainty.

When they stopped by a stream to eat and drink, Molloy began brushing down two of his horses. Their shaggy winter coats had already been replaced by short, silky hair easily burnished with grooming and health.

"Kilkenny lies ahead," he said. "They pay for decent animals there. Why don't you sell that grey gelding, too?"

Since she had given him her winnings at Clonmel, his attitude had altered. Initially, he had been offended. His money had been a gift, and he would not take hers.

"If we are partners, I must pay my share," she had pointed out.

"Not when we are to marry."

"That makes no difference," she had insisted, and later, sitting close by the fire, had continued, quietly, "Don't leave me out, Molloy. Let me meet who you meet and go where you go. I want to know and be part of it, not just hear the tales after."

He had nodded, and now, instead of telling her to sell the horse, merely advised. She noticed and was pleased.

Dipping a blue bag into the bucket of water, she sponged the grey down. The rinse highlighted the silver and emphasized the white, and after pulling his mane and tail, she eyed him critically. No flat catcher with filed teeth and a feagued tail he. This was a smartly turned-out, genuine hobby of which she could be proud. She wondered which gave more pleasure—skilfully faking a dud, or presenting a classy hack like this—and came to the philosophical conclusion that for satisfaction, the one equalled the other.

Kilkenny proved a good trading town, as Molloy had forecast. The horses sold well, and he bought a half-starved, leggy gelding for a song, because "he looks as though he might have a jump in him."

Three more days and they reached the broad, scrub-covered heath surrounding the Curragh, where races had been held since kings ruled Leinster and before. Cheney had been the first recorded winner here, and Irish Lass, "the Paddereen Mare," had beaten the gentry-backed Black and All Black to become a national heroine. Nimrod had won six sweepstakes from six starts in this place, and although Macha did not know these things, the grass almost smelt of such legends.

A caravan of horses and riders moved silently and in silhouette over a lift in the land, heading for the gallops. Huge banks of cloud and drifts of rain rolled before the light and were sprayed by sudden sun. The racecourse, crowned by its grandstand and skirted by spinneys, bordered the edge of the road to Dublin.

As they drove in with the dawn, the earth shook and the air gasped, leather creaked and metal jangled, there were whispers of silk and cracking whips and coarse, streaming hair, as unseen ghosts rushed past, still battling out the classics of old.

Drawing up, the girl jumped from the footboard to stand on the sacred turf, and the familiarity of it jolted all her senses. It was as though she had returned to the birthplace of a previous self in the age when warhorses trampled and unicorns tilted with golden horns and wondrous white horses with wings like swans glided through the sky, while Macha, the Great Mare, proud-headed, curly-maned, strong-thighed, noisy, fleet and sanguinary, her breath a torrent of shining red fire, overtook flocks of birds.

"I have been here before," she said, as Molloy came to see why she had stopped. "In another time, long ago."

He looked at her pale face and believed it, and found his own credulity perplexing. She was an odd one, with her smoky eyes and that hint of steel still masked by innocence. Since their misunderstanding over the big hunter at the river below Peakeen Mountain, he had put her up on all types and temper of horse, and even the half-trained and unmanageable submitted to her calm direction. He sensed a growing power in her which disturbed as well as attracted him.

"We'll camp about two miles on, in a covert beyond Brownstown House" was all he said.

White-faced sheep with long tails kept the vegetation close-cropped. Training stables and stud farms were strewn round the common, stone-built beside rendered pretty houses, and private within well-maintained hedges and walls. They passed the beech-lined entrance to Brownstown and were soon positioned in the small wood about a mile beyond.

"There are more eyes and ears in the five miles around the Curragh than hairs on a bear," Molloy warned. "Everyone knows we're here already, so we might as well look as open as Nancy, but say nothing."

By eleven o'clock, all the Thoroughbreds in the district had been mucked out, fed, tacked up and worked—or turned out—brushed down, watered and left with full racks of hay; and the head lads were drinking a breakfast pint of porther in the nearest bar.

Molloy took Macha to The Rising Sun, outside which a few goats were tethered and which inside was already packed to standing room only with an astonishing variety of men in bowlers and caps and breeches and gaiters, chesterfields and shabby waistcoats, prosperously fat or small as weasels, with accents from north and south, England, Scotland and Wales, sharing only in common that each pretended to have dropped into The Rising Sun purely by chance and every one was playing the same game, the racing game.

The horse coper paused to look about, then deliberately pushed through to the far side of the room to give his order. While waiting, he turned to a middle-aged man, with a face like a Gladstone bag, seated at a table and asked, "Would there be a Flynn Stephens here?"

"There would not," answered the man.

"I thought so," nodded Molloy. "For he is never usually in his place till six o'clock."

The barman brought their pints and the man stood up, finished his drink and left. Macha opened her mouth, but before she could ask her question received a hard look and thought better of it.

"That was your man," he explained, as they returned to their camp.

"He didn't look as though he knew you."

"Oh, he knew me all right, like he knows his own wages, and when he turns up this evening, keep out of it and don't look interested. He's not to be frightened off."

She gave them whiskey and strained her ears.

"What you're asking is not possible," she heard the visitor protest in a rapid, lisping voice, and Molloy's response was inaudible as they walked behind the waggon, and she tiptoed to open the back window a crack.

"It'll take a deal more than that, man," the stranger was scornfully refusing the money. "If it came out, not only would Captain Greer sack me, but I'd never work again."

"Think about it, Mister! Your usual groom's fee is no more than ten shillings out of a stud fee of two hundred pounds, and I'm offering sixty—no, seventy pounds!" the coper urged. "It would take a marvellous bird indeed to lay you such an egg. In the name of God, man, you could buy out your Captain Harry Greer with it!"

"You've lost your senses," the other replied. "And what about the other lads?"

"How many of them?"

"Ten that matter."

"Well, here's thirty pounds between them."

"I'll tell you what, Coper Molloy," the Mister offered, after a pause in which he had obviously been scanning the fan of notes with a mixture of greed and caution. "I'll tell you what . . . some friends of mine don' want The Bellboy does not win tomorrow. If he does not, Gallinule might have an hour or two in the paddock on a fine morning next week."

"That will be too late; the filly began horsing this day."

"Well, then, I'll see what can be done after tomorrow; but no promises."

Molloy went to his cart and brought back a powder in a twist of paper.

"Tell your friends to add that to The Bellboy's mash and it'll take the edge off him."

"It's not too much?"

"Not a soul will guess. He will still look as fit as a jumping bean." The money was handed over as well.

The travellers stayed in full view on the site all the next day, behaving as tinkers were expected to do. Macha washed out clothes and hung them on bushes and stirred mutton stew over the fire. Molloy whittled at wood and whistled. Their stock, every one properly acquired and none remarkable, grazed by the wood, the filly among them, looking shabby.

Later, in another bar, they heard how The Bellboy, the gambled-on horse in the two-o'clock, had been jeered for trailing ten lengths behind the winner.

"If that was a favourite, you'd not want a harem," one disgruntled punter commented.

They walked back through the dark, checking the starry sky and praying for the fine weather to hold. They did not sleep or rest, but sat by the embers waiting until, in the core of the night, they padded the filly's hooves with rags to cushion the sound and led her by elaborate detour to the far side of Brownstown.

The night was warm, echoing with owls and the wakeful creatures of the dark hunting and being hunted. Molloy worked to loosen the fence, so that it could be taken apart to let the filly in and reassembled in such a way as to appear sound when they left.

At 5A.M., they heard the first activity in the yards as lads prepared feeds of crushed oats and mashes of bran and linseed and the horses hungrily turned and scuffed in their loose boxes.

"Will he come?"

"He'll come," Molloy confirmed. "Or we'll lay the gypsy's curse on him!"

Wheelbarrows clattered over the cobbles and tools scraped on stone as soiled bedding was removed and deep, clean straw was forked in and shaken.

"We could have bought a cracking horse for all that money," she ventured.

"But it wouldn't be the same," he pointed out, chuckling and giving her a squeeze.

The drama of the risk and the proximity of the man combined with days of anticipation to make her mouth taste of salt and her blood race. Her hands were damp and her body jittery with tension, and it was true that even owning a proved winner with a genuine pedigree could never have aroused such a quicksilver reaction as this illegal dare.

Heat permeated the air in advance of the sun, which they watched blaze over the horizon like oncoming fire and then leap, scorching, into a violent blue sky. It was still early when they were forced to move under shade. Trees and freely flowering broom grew up to the northern boundary of the stud, and it was easy to see without being seen.

A bunch of yearlings were loosed into a lower paddock to career about in a boisterous gang, shadowboxing and kicking, chasing and nipping each other and shying at imaginary spooks. Next, the broodmares, round-bellied and stately, stepped out with their foals, dropping their heads to the serious business of grazing, placidly unconcerned by the explorations of their offspring and the demanding butts at their udders after each tiny scare.

The man and the girl chewed absently on soda bread and dripping and felt their patience become brittle. At last, hooves rang in the lane opposite and a man appeared, opened the gate and freed a big chestnut horse with a wide white blaze and three white socks into the nearest field.

"That's Gallinule. That's the sire of the best," whispered Molloy, and added, "Did you know that a horse with three white legs is considered fit for a king?"

For a moment, the great stallion stood with ears pricked and head raised, catching the morning. Then, with a ringing whinny and a plunge of high spirits, he began to canter round the perimeter, moving with serene, loping stride over the sweet grass, the breeze-held ripple of his mane rising and falling and his tail like a plume. In the brilliant light, he shone like living mahogany. He looked fit and hard, virile and strong, and Macha, who had seen all manner of horseflesh at sales and fairs and races, felt her skin creep at the sight.

As suddenly, he stopped, facing them and lifting his head in a series of jerks, his nostrils stretched and fluttering. The filly, which had been standing quietly, took a step and nickered, an eager expression in her eyes. Gallinule trotted forward as she waited at the boundary. She smelled his head and squealed, turning her hindquarters alongside the barrier. The stallion, his ears as sharp as arrowheads, curled up his lips and displayed his teeth. He paced, grunting excitedly and preparing himself for her.

Molloy took out the bottom rails, leaving only the top one between them.

"When he's fully drawn, lead her in," he told Macha.

The filly tossed her head, raised her tail and urinated, and the horse neighed, a primitive, brassy challenge.

"Take the headcollar and stand so that her heels can't catch him, if she decides to kick," Molloy directed, and removed the last bar.

The filly swished her tail and swivelled her ears, and Gallinule took a little run towards her with bass guttural resonance as she backed up, and then he reared to her, gripping her flanks with his powerful forelegs. Macha's Girl stood calmly and received him.

As soon as the stallion dismounted, Macha led her little mare out of the field and into the scrubland as Molloy started repairing the gap in the fence.

"The walk back to the *varda* will stop her straining," he said. "Make her step out, as we want to be well away while they're still hard at work over there in the yards."

Macha was speechless with the thrill of it all, but the little mare was nonchalant and strolled away from the most magnificent stallion in all Ireland without a backward glance.

Everything was packed in readiness, and they moved briskly, heading north. There had been no time for conversation, which was as well, as Macha had become unexpectedly embarrassed and avoided Molloy.

On the encampments with her father, the mating of horses had been strictly organised by men only, the women and girls being ordered to keep away.

Through watching the unleashed power of the stallion, Macha had begun to realise that marriage could not be as simple as she had believed and that what she had seen in some way affected her too. Driving along behind the coper's cart, she wondered why it was the custom in some clans for the bride to scream and weep and struggle against her new husband until he forced her into his bender tent. Her memory resurrected half-overheard murmurings between older wives of agony and blood, and she began to feel frightened.

Behind the Bow-top, the little mare jogged peacefully without any appearance of discomfort, almost as though she had already forgotten the momentous encounter of that morning. Macha looked back at her and felt reassured, although when they stopped at midday, she had little to say to Molloy and found much to do inside her *varda*.

But just before they started off again, he caught her arm and turned her quietly to face him.

"We'll join up with others soon," he said. "For it's time you had women around you; and besides, will there not be the biggest dance at our wedding!"

Macha felt a quiver of alarm. "They'll not want me. I'm *mochardi*. They'll cast me out."

"No-one casts away Molloy the Coper's bride!" He gave her a shake. "And you could never be *mochardi*, goddess. So no more fretting yourself over what is to be a time of joy."

He spoke with emphasis, gazing with kindness into her worried eyes, and she was grateful for his understanding.

"It's to be a long and happy life we'll have together. All will be well," he confirmed.

She glanced anxiously about for listening spirits and put a hand over his mouth before he tempted them further.

Twenty miles on, set at the head of a half-mile-long drive entered through massive wrought-iron gates, stood a grand white eighteenth-century mansion. There were thirty-five windows on its front elevation alone and an impressive portico upheld by a pair of elegant fluted columns. A park spread from this house to the black, gold-tipped iron railings which bordered the road. A flock of sheep grazed on one side of the park, and on the other, half a dozen Thoroughbreds stood lazily swishing flies off each other under an old oak.

Whether he did it to impress her or whether it was to celebrate the success of the visit to Brownstown neither of them knew, but to Macha's fascinated horror, Molloy suddenly swung to the ground, opened one of the huge gates, walked up to the group of horses, put a rope round the neck of one and led it out.

Macha stared at the blank-eyed windows overlooking them, crossed herself and goaded the mare from Tulla into a fast trot, passing the coper as he attached the stolen horse to his string. She could hear him behind, baying with lunatic delight.

Some miles further on, he whistled the signal to pull into the verge.

"You'll never get away with this," she warned, still goggle-eyed at the recklessness.

"The trouble with you is that *varda*," he replied obliquely. "The whole world sees it, so we'll just leave it in here behind these bushes a while and you come and sit alongside myself."

Without bothering to hog the mane, or disguise the one white fetlock, he simply stained out the star on the animal's forehead before they went on.

Beyond the village of Kennegad, they stopped at a yard which was ankle-deep in mud and bordered by rotting wood sheds, their doors secured with twine, the glass and bars from their windows long broken. Cats were draped on the ledges and walls, dogs rushed towards them in a barking pack and horses' heads peered out of every opening.

A short, wizened man who could have been brother to half the lads in Curragh stables rolled towards them, and Molloy indicated his latest acquisition.

"Lord Audley has a gelding as like that one as a look in the glass," the man said immediately.

"Well now, is that not good luck! If his lordship owns it, it must be a smasher, though they say everything has a double," Molloy responded coolly. "Myself, I traded for this one down at Waterford, and I thought of yourself as I did so."

"Same white sock there," pointed out the man, walking round the horse and frowning.

The traveller was conversational. "You'll be going to Tullamore Sales tomorrow, no doubt, Mister."

"I will, Molloy, but not with this nag."

"Your mind would do credit to a Peeler with ambition, but there's no justification for it." The coper sounded regretful. "I'd sell him there myself, if we weren't moving north."

A rider was approaching along the winding road.

"Just put him in there for the time being." The dealer waved towards the nearest shack casually, and the coper moved with unruffled speed.

They stood in the doorway talking for a moment, and as the rider came into view, hands were slapped.

When he laughed, his head fell back and she could see the muscular line of his neck fanning into his shoulders under his open shirt. His mouth turned up unexpectedly at the corners, revealing even white teeth. It was impossible not to laugh with him. Molloy was cock-a-hoop.

The wheels rolled over the grass lane, and the hooves of the pony between the shafts were soundless. Clumps of spurge arched and swayed back into place with green bracts nodding as they brushed past. The afternoon was musky with the scents of summer, honeysuckle and dog roses and hay. Labourers stooked the sheaves in the fields in a lazy, half-hearted way, and bees laboured by, weighted with nectar. It was too hot for birdsong. She nestled into the shelter of his arm, absorbing the spiciness of his body until she felt drugged and closed her eyes.

"Stand and go no further!" a man's voice commanded.

Macha sat up to see two policemen blocking the way with hands upheld. They had reached the covert, and the Bow-top, with its brightly coloured exterior, was garish against the brown tree trunks.

Molloy was still laughing as he was pulled roughly from his seat.

"You're arrested for horse-stealing, tinker," the first officer stated, producing a pair of handcuffs and snapping them onto the traveller's wrists. Macha let out a cry.

"Don't worry, mavourneen," Molloy smiled. "I'll be back before long."

The police ignored her as she ran to the waggon, and twisting in the doorway, she heard the coper protest:

"Every horse here has a sales docket."

"You were seen, man," the second officer said. "That great painted box of yours is hardly invisible."

"It's a dirty lie!" Molloy maintained.

The policeman looked over his shoulder at Macha and shouted, "We'll be back to check all these animals later, and you'll not get far if you think to move on, so don't try it!"

And they led her man away.

The girl hugged herself and paced up and down the restricted space of the *varda*. At first, her mind was full of fear-stricken images of Molloy being sent to some unknown jail, of Molloy in chains, of Molloy being lost to her for ever. She sat and rocked to and fro in agitation. Then, gradually, the ingenuity and instinct for survival which had preserved her people since before the famines began to assert itself.

She examined the situation more rationally. It was true that she and Molloy were the legal owners of the stock tethered on the verge alongside the wood. The dealer would set out for Tullamore under cover of darkness and arrive early at the horse sale, and such a handsome horse would change hands before 9 A.M. and be miles away by noon. She guessed that the police were bluffing when they said the actual theft had been witnessed, and without the horse, there would be only their word against the coper's. It was a pity so much of the money had been spent on bribes for Gallinule. In a crisis there was always use for money, but apart from the few pounds the dealer had just paid for the troublesome Thoroughbred, she was almost penniless.

The officers returned within the hour and meticulously inspected the ponies, peering into their mouths and lifting their feet and rubbing patches of their coats with methylated spirits to see if the colour changed, and examining every grubby scrap of paper she produced as documentation.

"Where is he?" she asked.

"Locked up where he belongs" was the curt answer.

"What's to happen?"

"Well, that could depend on you, tink." The younger man leered at her, slyly. "If you tell us where to find Lord Audley's Thoroughbred and your man pleads guilty, he could get off with a little fine. If not . . ." He mimed the turning of a key in a lock graphically.

"All the *capalls* are here." Macha waved her arm. "And I've never seen the fine gentleman's fine horse. The Blessed Virgin deny me if that's not God's own truth."

"You passed the great house no more than a mile back, so you saw the horses, all right," snapped the policeman.

"Arrah! If it's those horses, then you're right that we saw them in passing," Macha agreed. "We thought what grand bloods they were, but Molloy never went near them. You can see for yourself there's only garrons and batys here."

"You've him hidden somewhere and we'll be back to find him," the older man promised grimly as they left.

She knew they would visit the horse trader, but guessed he was too experienced not to have spirited the animal away within minutes of Molloy's departure.

The resident magistrate, Sir Wynford Beaufort—an Englishman, of course—sat with two Irish colleagues a few days later in Mullingar and listened to the police request to have this suspect remanded in custody while they continued their inquiries, and to Molloy's protests of innocence, then set bail of seventy pounds.

"That's not right! We're just poor travellers!" Macha shouted from the public seats.

She was ordered to silence with the threat of imprisonment and received a broad smile from the prisoner, which left her both elated and sick.

Outside the courthouse, she saw him taken away in a windowless carriage and waited on, leaning against the wall. About an hour later, a brougham drew up and the resident magistrate hurried into it and was driven off.

The girl ran after the second carriage, oblivious of the slippery cobblestones and the pouring rain. The matching pair of horses trotted out of the town, splashing through puddles and sending mud spinning back off the wheels. Macha heaved her wet, heavy skirts above her knees for the freedom to make more speed.

She raced, grabbing breath in gulps, half blind with wind and water-stung eyes, feeling her knees ache and the muscles in her thighs and calves begin to tremble and grow weak with fatigue. Past cottages and then hedgerows and fields, ignoring the stitch in her side, aware only that the carriage was frequently lost from sight around bends ahead and was actually growing smaller as it bowled farther and farther away. And then she rounded a curve in the road and it was gone.

She bent double to catch her breath and ease the pain in her side and the rain deluged over her, its cold drops a relief as they mingled with the sweat on her back. She straightened gingerly and walked on, depressed at having lost her quarry. Trees gathered ahead, and nearing them, she saw, almost obscured, twin stone posts supporting high wrought-iron gates. The overhung drive was freshly churned by hooves and wheels. Her pulse missed a beat.

He had had a pleasant face, looking over the court from behind his mahogany-panelled desk, grey-haired and avuncular. As soon as she had shouted the protest and he had turned mild blue eyes in her direction, she had regretted it. It was then the idea had formed.

A wall backed the laurels which lined the drive, and the heavy carriage doors set into it were open to a meticulously kept yard and stables. Macha slunk past and approached the stone mansion, pushing her hair back and smoothing her clothes and straightening her shawl, not realising that her face was smeared with dirt. On the edge of the lawn she paused, wondering which door to choose. If she went to the back of the house, the servants would send her packing, but the imposing Georgian front entrance was clearly intended for the quality only.

The rain had almost stopped, and as she stood among the shrubs, the resident magistrate suddenly emerged with his family, and another carriage came out of the stable yard.

Macha darted forward, speeding in front of the newly harnessed horses, so that they shied and whinnied and the coachman cursed. She scrambled up the steps and fell to her knees before the astonished party.

"Your honour! Your honour! For the sake of the Blessed Mary and the infant Jesus, let my man free!" she pleaded and, holding up her hand, disclosed the money paid for Lord Audley's stolen horse.

"We haven't such a great sum as the seventy pounds you wanted, your worship! But all I have you're welcome to, if you'll free Molloy, who could never let the littlest lie pass through his mind, let alone commit such a mortal crime as stealing a horse from a noble gentleman!"

"How did this filthy tramp get here?" the resident magistrate roared, drawing back from her and spreading his arms, as though to protect his wife and children from attack.

Macha climbed to her feet and sprang towards him, seizing one of his hands and trying to press the coins into it.

"Take the money, your honour, and set an innocent man loose. We'll be on the road straightaway and no trouble at all to yourself. If you'll just take the money, you'll go your whole life through and not see us again."

" 'Pon my word, I believe the tinker's trying to bribe me." The Englishman, scandalized, pushed her so that she stumbled and fell backwards down the steps, the sovereigns rolling after her.

Two grooms grasped her from behind and pulled her upright, and blood trickled from her cut palm. Another servant collected up the money and handed it to the Englishman, who came heavily towards her, his face dark with anger.

"How dare you attempt to pervert justice by offering money to the Court? If you were not obviously so young, I would have you detained, you disgusting little parasite."

He towered over her, and for a moment, she thought he would strike. Instead, the coins were thrust back into her hand.

"Now, listen to me! Your horse-thieving husband will get the sentence he richly deserves, and if I ever catch sight of you again, you will be locked away for a very long time as well."

Behind him, his daughters giggled noisily, and then Macha was being frogmarched down the drive out of sight of the house to the gates, where without warning, one of the grooms pulled up her skirts and prodded his hand between her legs, making her cry out in pain and shock.

"You'll get better than that if you hang around here, tink," he said.

They released her with a hearty shove and as she fled down the road, stood at the entrance to the great house bawling with laughter and shouting obscenities at her.

In her panic and humiliation, Macha forgot her exhaustion and ran the miles back to Mullingar, slowing only when she had gone beyond it and reached a wayside cottage. There she begged water, and the wife was so alarmed by her appearance of collapse that she made her enter and sit by a peat fire to drink milk and eat bread and cheese.

Macha, appreciative of the kindness and the rest, read her palm and promised money, sons and luck. Rage was rapidly quelling her shame and distress—rage at the resident magistrate and his family, at his grooms and the police; healing, creative rage at everyone. She would get Molloy from jail and leave them all looking daft as sheep for the world to see. She made her way to the horse dealer at Kinnegad, resolution strengthening with every step.

"Ach, it's yourself again," he said. "A mess of aggravation Molloy the Coper left behind here, with the Peelers checking every blade of straw and every nag's hair and every grain of corn in the place."

"If I bring you two good horses, what will you pay?" she asked.

"And where would *you* be getting two good horses, when you can't even pay for your man's release?" The dealer was sceptical. Then, "Ride or drive?"

"Both, to be sure," she replied.

"What colour?"

"Matching bays."

"Thirty pound."

Macha did not even deign to argue the figure, but simply turned on her heel and made for the gate.

"Don't be hasty, now!" the Mister called after her. "It's the bail money you're after, is it not?"

She nodded. There was no point, or time, to try and deny it.

"How much do you have towards it?" he demanded.

"Only what you paid for the Thoroughbred," she answered frankly.

"Well, it so happens I know of a party in Dublin who might be interested in such horses," he said, leaning on the handle of the dung fork he had been wielding when she arrived. "Bring them here as early as you like tomorrow morning, and if they're all you say, I'll make up the difference."

"That's as poor a deal as a pratie pie for a hind leg of beef," Macha was forced to argue.

"And I'll add five pounds to it for the cheek of you, and not a penny more."

They slapped hands.

The rain had stopped when she slid by the laurels she had passed that afternoon. At three o'clock in the morning, no other living thing stirred, but when she reached the stables the horses were awake and munching comfortably at their hay. They turned their heads in their stalls, the wooden weights on the end of their headcollar ropes booming against their mangers like a broadside, their hooves in the straw like crashing timber. They snorted loud as drums.

She waited with prickly skin for footsteps to sound on the floor of the stableboys' loft above, but none came.

Sidling up to the first grey, she stroked with firm movements over his quarters and his ribs, his shoulders and his neck, whispering to him, blowing gently into his nostrils until his tense ears relaxed and he pulled a wisp of hay from the overhead rack. Running a hand down his nearside fore, she picked up the foot and bound it in heavy rags and repeated the procedure until all four hooves were muffled.

The matched gelding in the next stall was as easy to handle, and when she led him out, his steps were as soft as a mop on a polished oak floor.

A figure stood in the doorway, eyes gazing unblinkingly at her. Macha was so startled that she physically twitched and felt her heart race ahead of itself and blood rush to her face.

"What are you doing?"

The clouds cleared, unexpectedly, from obscuring the moon and a girl of her own age was revealed, hungry-looking and ragged.

"Shh!" Macha hissed, and then whispered. "What'll you do if I take these horses past you?"

"I don't know."

She gave silent thanks for delivery. The girl was still standing there, waiting for an offer. She felt in the pouch attached to her skirt and drew out a crown coin, displaying the silver in the moonlight for the other to see.

"It's yours. Five shillings. A whole crown for you, if you say nothing."

The girl's eyes widened. It was obvious she had never had so much money entirely to herself before. Probably, she worked in the kitchens for her keep and a pittance a year. She nodded vigorously and beckoned.

Macha and the two greys were led silently away from the main drive and down an overgrown path to an old gate which apparently had not been used for a very long time. Grass grew high in the centre of the track beyond, and the brambles and wild roses reached out from the hedge with thorny tendrils. If man did not clear it soon, the way would be lost for ever.

"Are you headed south?" the young servant asked.

"I might be," replied Macha warily.

"Well, you'll miss the town if you follow this path, and cut off about two miles."

Macha raised her right hand and curled its fingers into claws; she narrowed her glittering eyes and took two steps forward, so that she was almost touching the other, who flinched and looked frightened.

"You know that I am a gypsy," Macha breathed throatily. "And gypsies cast a terrible curse on those who betray them."

"Mother of God, I'll not breathe a word. It'll be as though this was never a night at all." The girl crossed herself.

Macha mumbled a long nonsense word and weaved from side to side. ". . . and boils will cover every inch of your body and you will grow hairy as an ape with the face of a fish. Man, woman, child and beast will shun you. Food will never fill you and water will never quench, if you let on what you've seen."

"Never! Never! Upon the wounds of Jesus and my own mother's grave, I swear it," vowed the other in terror, and snatching the coin Macha held out, scuttled back to the great house.

Macha grinned to herself. Sometimes there were advantages to being a traveller. She climbed onto the open gate, mounted one of the greys and, leading the other, set off.

Dawn was still no more than a candle glow by the time she reached the Bow-top, but she laid out the dyes and brushes and cloths and decided to start at once. First, the manes and tails were washed and stained black. Remembering Molloy's advice, she left white blazes down their noses and worked with infinite care to achieve coats of light and shade, tinting into the dark rings on the hindquarters as the daylight strengthened, so that they appeared to dapple the rich finish most naturally. From knee and hock to fetlock each leg was coloured to grade from brown to black, and finally, two cream hooves were darkened and polished with linseed oil.

In the clearing in the wood, Macha walked around the two horses as they steamed dry in the sun and admired her own skill. Had Molloy himself been offered them, he would have been hard put to guess the disguise. They looked superb.

She changed into some old trousers and a cap and jacket of his and after checking that the road was clear, boldly rode out and took the matched bays openly to the Mister's yard.

"Is it right into the city they're going?" she asked innocently.

"It is." He gave her a knowing look. "Among a thousand or more carriages."

He handed over the agreed price, adding, "Tell Molloy the Coper not to come this way again before my daughter weds."

"How old is she?" Macha wondered naively.

"I have only sons, girl. Now get along with you!"

She waited until evening before walking into the police station at Mullingar and paying the bail money. Although they questioned her roughly and made all sorts of threats, she would only admit that "a benefactor friend" had lent the money. At last, and with great reluctance, they were forced to free the coper.

They neither looked at nor touched each other until the town was far behind, and then she threw herself on him and passionately returned his kisses. When she told of stealing and selling the resident magistrate's carriage horses, he laughed until his eyes brimmed over and he was rolling on the ground with her in his arms.

"What would I give to see his face!" He looked at her full of glee. "By all the saints in heaven, you'll be a most darling wife for me. If I searched Ireland over, there'd not be another to compare."

"Will they come after you?" she was anxious to know.

"I doubt it," he reassured. "They'll never find Lord Audley's nag now, and without it, there's no evidence against me. And with another pair of fancy horses gone missing while I was locked up, it'll look as though they might have been mistaken all along."

"So they'd have let you go anyway!" She was almost indignant.

"As likely as giving me a knighthood," he grimaced. "No. They believed I'd taken the Thoroughbred, all right, and they'd have pinned blame on me for some other, easier felony to prove, to make sure I remained partaking of their hospitality for a year or two."

"But that is a deadly sin!" she exclaimed, genuinely disgusted at such treachery, and could not understand his amusement.

It was dark when they reached their site, and they left the place at once, pushing the horses hard along the lanes and byways leading north. Macha's Girl, so preciously pregnant, was forced to keep up a fast pace through Athboy and cross country through Bohermeen and on to Donaghpatrick. Molloy, breaking bail, was taking no chances and covering their tracks. All night they travelled, his cart fleeing ahead like a black, many-headed monster pursued by the growling, swaying *varda*. They stopped only once for water, and by morning had covered many miles and changed direction frequently.

During the day they stayed hidden in thick woodland, the vehicles camouflaged with branches, and moved on as quickly the next night.

Macha slept during daylight and once, awoke to see Molloy walking away through the trees. He looked furtive, and something stopped her from calling after him. About an hour later, he returned and she pretended to be newly roused.

"I'd a bit of a thirst a few minutes ago and thought I'd fetch us some milk from the farm down there," he said glibly.

That evening at twilight, although they had plenty of stored water, he insisted she walk the half-mile to the river to scrub out the containers and refill them. Spurred by curiosity, she ran all the way there and, despite the weight, most of the way back, slowing to silence as she neared their camp.

Two strangers were sitting with Molloy. They were quite well dressed in suits and bowler hats and did not look like either travelling or racing people. There was an intensity about the meeting which made her stay concealed until some while after they had left.

"You've been long enough" was the coper's unsuspecting comment. "Were you having a secret bathe?"

"I was not, but the buckets are heavy." She decided not to mention the visitors.

"We'll be there by morning," he said.

"And where would that be?"

"Where kings ruled and fairies laughed and priests wore white and the goddess came to the fair," he answered her with a riddle again.

Sometimes, with his puzzles and mysteries, there was no knowing him, she thought, and bit her lip in irritation.

The Hill was a low pillow on the night, and as they approached, it was as though they stepped into an invisible circle, with the wind left outside. They could hear it whining behind them, but all around the air was still and balmy. They left the Bow-top and the cart and began to climb, compassing the Hill and passing several mounds, which seemed enclosed in ice-cold film. They clambered over a bank, and although they were nearing the crest, the atmosphere closed and sweat began to run from her forehead into her eyes and trickle down her neck and legs.

Ahead, she saw the glint of silver and the flash of a long blade and shadows clashing with each other under the gaze of a ghastly head crowned with horns, and she clutched at Molloy.

"King Laoghaire is here, buried upright in full armour, waiting for his army," his low voice told.

They climbed over two more banks and found themselves enclosed by the circular earthworks which surrounded a bigger hummock on which stood a stone emitting an eerie green light.

Stifled, Macha put her hand to her throat to pull away the choking band about it, but felt only her own skin. The air had become as thick and impermeable as a fleece. Ghosts and spirits jostled and pinched her with spiteful fingers, and she had lost sight of Molloy. Petrified, she turned to escape.

"Wait!" He was beside her. "We must touch the stone."

"No! I cannot!"

Bats flew into her hair and screamed.

"You must!"

He grasped her wrist and pulled her onto the mound. The stone swelled with menace, its surface covered in blood and the light turned black and brilliant. Macha cried out and Molloy forced her against it and she drowned in the open wound.

There was a roar; a thousand voices crashed from the rock and zoomed to the sky, sound waves battering into space. The discord filled her head like a fireball, exploding unbearably against her eardrums. She caught a glimpse of Death with his hollow eyes turned on her. And then she saw beyond him, into a measureless radiance in the centre of which was the Power, massed into a shape which had no shape and an incandescence without colour, but which was all colour.

Then silence, silence, silence, reviving as a long, blessed draught, assuaging as a prayer, a cooling zephyr, the honey scent of heather and wild thyme. Molloy was sitting by her on the grass.

"You are of the ancient people. You go back to the old times, Macha," he said with awe. "*Lia Fail*, the royal stone, knows you and has revealed the secret to you. We'll be wed in *Teach Miodchuarta*, the banquet hall, here at Tara in three days' time."

There was a church on the east flank of Tara, its churchyard invading the Hill. It seemed out of place, and she knew it should not have been there at all, but they camped leeward of it, and she was grateful to creep to a sleep too deep for dreams.

Next day, Molloy woke her by hammering on the door, and she was surprised to find the sun in the centre of its arc and the *varda* surrounded by bender tents, carts and even other Bow-tops (though of different design). For a moment, she was tempted to slam the door shut again and hide. It was the first time since the scandal following her father's funeral that she had been near other travellers.

There was a woman standing beside Molloy, middle-aged and grave, but not obviously hostile. Her hair was thick and grey and swept back into a bun at the nape of her neck; her face was lined and brown. She had the straight eyebrows and full, curving mouth and strong white teeth of a true Romani. She looked weathered and vital.

"Biddy Connor," Molloy introduced her. "She raised me, and now she'll look after you."

The woman nodded to Macha without smiling, and he left them, as though the situation needed no further explanation.

"Wild girls make poor wives. There was a tidy girl kept for a match with Molloy the Coper," Biddy Connor said, without animosity. "But perhaps he needs more than that." There was a pause while they looked at each other. "And maybe you will do."

Macha felt as though she had passed a test.

Everyone present knew her background and reputation, but the fact that she was to be Molloy the Coper's wife seemed enough to overcome any evidence of their reservations. The women and girls of the Connor, Maugham and Ward families accepted her into their circle, working alongside her while making meals, chattering and giving advice and actively preparing for the feast; although she noticed that no-one ever crossed the threshold of her *varda*, which should have been destroyed after Jack Sheridan's death.

Biddy Connor and her daughters helped to cut and sew the pink satin skirt and to stitch the yards of coloured ribbon around its hem. Everybody admired the silk petticoats and the embroidered chiffon blouse, and laughed at the lace-trimmed knickers. Macha wondered which of these girls had originally been chosen for Molloy, but could not guess. They all seemed happy and excited by the prospect of the celebrations to come.

It was good to live in camp again, to waken to the sounds of pots and pans clattering, hungry dogs barking, men shouting and children crying and women singing again; to wipe babies' running noses and avoid being run down by boys galloping horses about and listen to reports of successes or failures in the streets of Navan, to gossip and giggle again; to sit through evenings smoky from half a dozen fires and plaintive with sad tunes played on someone's mouth-organ again.

More families arrived daily, and the encampment soon spread to cover an acre or more. They had journeyed from Armagh and Waterford and Kerry, and even from Connemara. Everybody wanted to be at Molloy the Coper's wedding; everyone except the Mulligans and Dorans and, of course, the Sheridans. No single member of Macha's own family came; but she had too much to do to miss them.

Food was prepared in huge quantities, with money contributed by all for a couple of pigs and a side of beef. Chickens and geese, rabbits and sausages and sackfuls of potatoes materialised, and even the McCanns, who owned only a leaking tarpaulin and the rags they stood in, provided a dozen hedgehogs to bake in clay and several fine hares. The men returned from sorties to obscure copses and combes with carts loaded with barrels of poteen, and those who had been to town brought Guinness and whiskey, enough to make a convent yodel.

Macha did not see Molloy at all, not even the night before the wedding, when she went nervously to bed in the Connor tent with all her jewellery and finery laid out in readiness. Biddy Connor snored comfortably beside her, there as official guardian of her virginity, although there were many who doubted that.

"That juval won't be able to display the sheets."

"If she does, it'll be through taking a pigeon along under her shift and cutting its throat in the night."

She had heard two old women talking, and so had Biddy Connor, who had rounded on them with screeching abuse.

Molloy the Coper would not stoop to marry an unchaste bride, and she was certain sure that despite their addled brains and malicious thoughts, they were not questioning his word that he himself had laid no hand on the girl.

The crones had muttered and scuttled off, and Macha was grateful that for once, she had broken no taboo and done nothing which might have threatened her future life with Molloy.

It was the morning of the day, a dawn tingling with summer, drying the dewy leaves to a shine and reflecting sunlight in the slates of the church roof. The turf, freshly green, lay like a soft mist over Tara, making the Hill appear insubstantial, at once near and yet, at the same time, distant.

The women crowded about Macha as she dressed. They fingered the satin and handed the gold bangles from one to the other with approval. The daughters of Biddy Connor had made a circlet of oxeye daisies for her hair, and their mother gave her a shawl of Aran wool, dyed in elder, blueberry and oak bark to blue, purple and black.

The girl, who had never before received such attention, preened and paraded, twirling so that the skirt flared out. Catching the little glints in the other young girls' eyes, she knew they envied her Molloy, and she felt proud and a little afraid.

The past days had been full of strange rumours in the shape of whispered advice and explanations and the half-understood experiences of the married women, yet still she did not really know what would happen after the wedding, when she was finally alone with him. The flutter in her belly increased. She turned round in a spasm of fear; but the women surrounded her, and it was time.

Scarlet poppies and yellow coltsfoot and teasles and ragwort and cow parsley, all bound with pink-and-white bindweed, bedecked the verges of the path, and the turf over which she walked was strewn with scarlet pimpernel, speedwell and trefoil. They passed the church and began to climb Tara. Molloy and the men were nowhere to be seen. A pair of young jackdaws flew overhead without a sound, and hosts of swallows glided and swooped so high against the blue that their piping cries could not be heard. As on the night she had arrived in this place, there was a huge, warm silence, and it was as though all her attendants had dispersed and she were unaccompanied.

Teach Miodchuarta, the House of Mead Circling, also known as the Banquet Hall, was a long, narrow hollow, enclosed by parallel earthen banks high enough to stop the wind and trap the sun. At the far end, Molloy was waiting, and she saw only him. She walked slowly towards him and, when they met, they joined hands and turned to face the crowd.

"I, Cormac O'Neill Molloy, do take you, Macha Sheridan, for my wife, and I vow to honour and protect you all our days."

In the depths of her cool silver eyes he saw wine-coloured flames.

"I, Macha Sheridan, take you, Cormac O'Neill Molloy, to be my husband and promise to love and obey you all our days."

As she committed herself, he did not smile and she saw in his serious gaze another, stronger man, almost a stranger.

Someone handed them a small, specially baked loaf of bread and two rose thorns. They broke the loaf in two, and Molloy pricked her thumb and she, with a little shudder, pricked his, and the drops of blood fell on the two halves of bread, and each ate the piece which held the blood of the other. This made her part of him and he of her more completely than even their lovemaking would later. She felt potent and tempered, imbued with his maleness. He received a primeval magic, and his perception changed, each strand of her hair, each lash of the fringes of her eyes revealed. To Macha, the mystery of fate was made manifest at last. Through this joining she became complete and, looking at him with wonder, knew all her questions answered.

The travellers cheered. "Jump the budget! Jump the budget!"

Molloy whirled her about. At the entrance to the Banquet Hall lay a box containing the brushes and clippers, the dyes and potions of his trade. With a whoop of joy, they leapt over it for luck and were married.

Hired fiddlers began to play, and with arms about each other, Molloy and Macha led the way back to the encampment. There they filled a single cup with the pure water of the spring and they drank from the cup, which then was smashed into myriads of pieces on the rock, and the feast began.

The fires had been built up and fanned since dawn, and their blue smoke and a mouth-watering smell filled the air. Soup, fragrant with herbs and rich with the plunder of woods and fields, was ladled out of a cauldron; salmon flakes, like pink shells, were lifted delicately from charred skin; slices of roast beef, crusty on the outside and blood-red inside, fell to the sweep of the knife in succulent slabs onto the tin plates, and potatoes were snatched black from the embers and broken open to catch the sizzling fat in their steaming, floury centres. To a background of frantically played music, they ate rabbit legs, pearly pale, and black sausage, fierce and sticky, and ribbons of butter-tender pork, and washed it all down with the gallons of poteen.

The high drama of the day did not reduce Macha's appetite, and she ate as heartily as her man, until her chin and hands were greasy and the silk blouse was spotted with stains.

"Come on, you little porker, it's time you danced your dinner down before you grow as fat as Meg Duffy." Molloy hauled her to her feet and into the grassy circle of the camp.

The fiddlers sawed out reels and jigs without pause, and when everyone else had dropped to the ground from exhaustion, Cornelius Ward sang songs of love in Romani, and then Biddy Connor's daughters and one or two other girls and boys, with shouts and fiery gestures, spun into a dance, wild and exotic, which was never conceived in Ireland. Macha felt gooseflesh rise on her skin and looked at Molloy, to see his face bright as he clapped and stamped to the cross rhythms and bawled encouragement, although most of the other travellers watched placidly enough—but then, they were not the Rom.

A fine streak of beige cloud crossed the sun and tailed away like a fish across the sky. The rays diffused, and the blue paled to the colour of a duck's egg and imperceptibly oozed to gold. There was lowing and the scuffing of a herd of cows ambling home, and the trees darkened against the dusk and the stars came out, and Tara in the half-light, its wraiths stirring, became the more enigmatic, perhaps a temple, perhaps mere earth, perhaps an illusion, a trick of the mind's eye.

The music stopped and the dancers drew aside, leaving the bride and groom alone in the centre of the arena. Then Biddy Connor and other married women ceremoniously unpinned Macha's red hair to cover her breasts and fall down her back to her waist.

"Come!" said Molloy at last, and she followed him gladly.

They did not go to his bender tent, or to her *varda*, but retraced their earlier steps, returning, once more and for the last time, to the occult enclosure of Tara.

A hazy figure walked ahead of them and over the defences of bank and fosse, round to *Rath na Riogh*, a tall man, holding a crimson shield and a sword in a scabbard of gold, his scarlet cloak pinned by an inlaid gold-and-silver brooch; and as the girl gripped Molloy's arm, the figure vanished, and they entered.

"Kings married goddesses here," said the coper, before kissing her unhurriedly and gently, as though for the first time, as though searching, as though savouring.

Together they sat on the grass by the stone, and there he slowly unbuttoned and drew off her silk blouse and the beribboned skirt and the three silk petticoats, one by one, and as she waited, naked and pliant, curiously passive after so many weeks of longing, he discarded his dark wedding suit and white linen shirt and his silver-buckled shoes and lay down beside her, and she found none of this surprising.

His skin was as dark and velvety as a rose under the moon, his hair like the wing of a raven, his eyes like garnets, and as he put out his hand, Macha moved and cleaved to him.

"You are supposed to struggle and cry," he murmured.

"I cannot. I would not," she answered.

The tips of his fingers brushed against her nipple and she felt heat against her thigh and passion consumed her. The fire they lit burned around them in a ring, rising as a tower, illuminating the mystic Hill, awakening the spirits of celestial lovers, reviving aching memories of epochs before Saint Patrick and causing God-fearing people down on the plain to cross themselves and close their eyes.

Macha felt the whirling circles of her life force fuse, contract and concentrate into one pulsing density of power, which gathered energy in pain and ecstasy, sucking the place, the hour, the man and even herself as she had been into its essence, becoming more abstract, more pure, more absolute, until the ultimate implosion which blasted apart her own matter, shattering and scattering its fragments as specks of dust, and for a beat of time, she was without body or soul. She became divine.

Then it was over, and he rested upon her like a milky babe and night cloud extinguished the glowing moon and the warriors crept back to the past. In the bliss of love, Macha and Molloy slept.

Chapter SIX

Macha lost her look of bony immaturity, and the mare was no longer a gawky filly. Throughout the summer and autumn, their angularity became rounded with flesh. Their hair grew glossy and their eyes bright as they travelled the roads to Omagh and Armagh and Dundalk and south to Bray and east to Carlow and then turned north again. By the time they reached the outskirts of Dublin, both were round-bellied and quite matronly.

It had been a good year. Molloy the Coper had bought and sold their horses very profitably, and his frequent interviews in busy bars before race meetings across the country seemed to have paid off well. Occasionally, he had met with other men—not stable lads or jockeys, but outsiders—and Macha had learnt to keep a discreet distance from such encounters and to ask no questions afterwards.

He was a fine husband, caring and lusty and generous. He did not beat her and he made them a good living. He laughed a lot and taught her much, and there was no doubt that he worshipped her, fussing about her health and rest as the unborn child grew, spoiling her with presents—a soft, flock-filled mattress to replace the hay in the *varda*'s plank bed, a sewing machine, silver and tortoiseshell combs for her hair and a handsome, silver-studded bridle for the mare.

Yet there was a part of him she did not know, a concern with matters he refused to discuss. Occasionally he would go away for a day or two and offer no explanation, and more than once, she found his cart loaded with boxes, too securely nailed for her to discover their contents.

Once, she had asked him outright where he went, whom he saw and what he did, and he had replied that every man was entitled to keep his own counsel about his private business.

"Even a married man?" she had demanded.

"Do you not have womanly matters that you keep to yourself?" he had responded.

It sounded so reasonable that she did not know why she continued to feel uneasy, but there was certainly no point in probing further.

Previously, it had been their custom, he alone and she with her father, to continue travelling throughout the cold months of the year, and the decision to stop in an established winter camp was made to conserve Macha's strength and ensure the little mare also lost no condition.

Biddy Connor and her daughters, some of the guests who had been to the wedding and other families who were strangers to the girl were already on the site to the south of the capital when they arrived, but they found a good position, slightly apart from the rest and out of the prevailing wind, and everyone expressed astonishment that Molloy rented a shed nearby for Macha's Girl.

Rain fell week after week and the mud on the encampment deepened into a mire, squelching over bare feet and splashing the trailing skirts of the women to knee height.

The snows came at the end of the New Year hooley, which had lasted for three days and nights, and the temperature dropped so low that icicles hung on the inside of the Bow-top windows each morning. Molloy bought thick woolens for Macha and a blanket for the mare, then fed the girl on steak and the horse on best-quality corn.

Life was not so cushioned for many. The stove in the waggon could be lit, but there was no way to warm a bender tent. With the ground wet and the canvas leaking, men, women and children huddled pitifully together.

They came to the city for the riches there. With no seasonal work, it was simpler to beg a bit of help from the small shops and a halfpenny or two, or some cast-off clothes from the tightly packed houses and tenements; but times were hard for all, and soon the largest travelling families were going hungry. The children developed coughs, and mucus ran continuously from their noses, and open sores blemished their skins.

One morning, when Macha awoke with crystals of ice on her eyelashes and the metal handles on the pots stuck to the women's hands, a baby was found dead and frozen as hard as marble. The police came and berated the parents for their carelessness. A priest assured them the child had gone to hell because it had not been christened, nor the parents married in church. A journalist wrote a paragraph on the tiny tragedy in the *Irish Times*, and some ladies appeared with soup the next day, then became alarmed by the idea of catching some dreadful disease from the tinkers and did not return. Besides, the dirt had quite ruined their coats and shoes.

As January dragged into February, tempers, always volatile among the travellers, became shorter; wives using imagined jealousies to pick on their husbands, husbands replying with blows. There were daily fights among the younger men, and more than one was lacerated so badly that he was taken into hospital.

Macha longed to escape from them all. She rarely saw Molloy, who was often away from morning until late at night, and when she pleaded with him to leave the encampment before spring, he insisted that this was impossible as he still had transactions to complete.

"I don't want my baby born here among the rats and the muck," she complained tearfully. "I want him born in Connemara."

"Now, is that not a strange thing, for don't I have to be in Galway town myself before Easter," he teased. "And it might cast some doubt upon your virtue if you gave birth to our son before then."

When she did not smile, he put his arms about her.

"We'll be on our way at the first breath of spring," he promised.

"I hate the city," she said, glad to have him close.

"Then we'll never return to it. We'll board a ship of gold and cross the sapphire sea to where the sun always shines and there's not a tree that isn't weighed to the ground with nectarines."

What were nectarines? She knew they had to taste more delicious than cherries, or honey, or sugar candy, for he could charm with a phrase and a glance, with that irresistible blend of nonchalance and intensity, at once flippant and yet serious.

It had to be a sin to want a man so much, even her own husband—wanting him more than air, more than food, far more than any freedom. From the time she watched him leave the camp with swift strides until he returned with feline silence in the night, he was her obsession, and it was as though she could not breathe properly in his absence.

Now he was cooing in her hair and caressing the nape of her neck with lightly pressing fingers.

"Molloy . . . Molloy . . . Mmm . . ."

And she forgot all her other needs until the morning of the next day, when he was gone again.

However, he kept his word. When April came at last, they were on their leisurely way once more, and in this final month of her pregnancy, he was by her side all the time.

Crossing stone bridges over streams and brooks and rills and gills and becks and burns and rivers to the sounds of their bubbling and hushing, slurping and rushing, flowing and oozing, waterfalling and sluicing, through rain drumming on the roof and fluttering like moths' wings on the windows, dripping, dropping, spitting, hissing, purl, plash and gurgle, the watery song of Ireland; journeying back to the luminous west.

Past inland loughs and into the mist, feeling the secret way: Westport suddenly materialising from nowhere, clock tower and slim spire, quays and lofty warehouses, jumble of grey streets soon left behind and forgotten at the sight of Croag Patrick, black and glowering and treeless, with lines of water cutting down its dark, deep groin and mighty thighs. Macha had been away for more than twelve months and had not realised how much she had missed the region. To return was like a homecoming.

The reedbeds of Clew Bay spread alongside the track, broken by salty eddies and finally drowned by the hyaline ocean. Countless islets and islands and dazzling white gulls hung on the surface. "The most beautiful scenery in the world," a famous writer of the time had written, but Macha did not need to be told.

"We will stop here," she said, and the Bow-top seemed to guide itself into the very haven under the mountain where Jack Sheridan had drawn up every year since her birth.

The grey town, "Stone Fort of the Oxen," was busy that evening, and the bar was full. The couple did not see the group of young travellers in the far corner as they entered. But the Mulligan brothers saw Macha and turned away. Then those with them nudged and sniggered and pointed, and eventually Hugh Mulligan swaggered up, stopped in front of her and deliberately spat on the floor.

Almost before he realised what was happening, he was pinned against the wall by the throat.

"That is my wife," snarled Molloy. "And you will grovel to her, boy."

As the other struggled, he butted the face with his head, and blood began to dribble from the split lip, which swelled rapidly as they all watched.

Hugh Mulligan mumbled in protest and received a winding jab below the ribs. His companions jeered, jovially.

"That didn't sound like the right words to me," Molloy commented, wrenching the youth's arm hard behind his back and steering him to face her. "Now, what do you say to Molloy the Coper's wife?"

"I'm sorry," muttered her erstwhile fiancé.

"She has a name!" prompted the older man.

"Macha."

"Macha who?"

". . . Macha Molloy."

"And don't you ever forget it, sonny." The coper released him, and the boys trooped out, sheepishly.

The incident took the enjoyment from the outing and left her depressed and tired. She was now so large with child that it was impossible to sit comfortably. Her huge belly pushed up to her breasts, and her back ached. Molloy returned with her to their site, and there, in the fresh night air, she was unexpectedly filled with energy and began turning out the Bow-top.

Despite his objections, he found himself directed to beat the flock-filled mattress, while drawers and cupboards were emptied and cleaned, their contents returned tidily. The floor was swept and washed, and not a cobweb survived in the most obscure corner. All the mugs and plates and pots were thoroughly scoured, and she would have begun washing down the exterior had he not adamantly ordered her to stop.

"Enough of this rubbing and scraping, Macha! You're worse than a currycomb on an ould cow," he berated her. "It's after two in the morning and I want my rest, and you need yours."

He shooed her to bed, climbed in grumbling beside her on the outside edge and was unconscious in minutes. But Macha could not sleep. Able to lie only on her back, she stared up at the stars through the tiny window as her mind checked and rechecked the preparations she had made for the birth.

Molloy had wanted to put up a special tent, as was the custom, but she had rejected the offer, determined to have her child in the Bow-top. Now she wondered if she had been wrong, if breaking another taboo would bring bad luck.

She felt restless and thirsty, and her stomach was upset by the Guinness she had drunk. She shifted her position to ease the cramps, and it was only to avoid disturbing her husband that she did not get up. Pain rumbled through her gut, and her muscles strained; then, to her shame, water burst from her and flooded the bed. Molloy awoke to find her in tears.

"I couldn't help it. I wanted to go outside, but I couldn't get past you." She was distraught. "It was all so quick."

Another spasm gripped her, and she struggled to rise.

"It's all right, mavourneen, lie still," he comforted. "It's the baby coming. I'll fetch the doctor from Westport."

She held fast to him. "No! You're not to leave me! You mustn't go!"

"You'll need help, Macha, and I'll be no time at all."

"Stay, Molloy!" she shouted, but he had gone.

The rain crackled like fire over the waggon and the hound of the wind clawed and howled at the door. Only yards away, she could hear the Atlantic booming in the storm. The contractions came quickly, with but minutes between them when she could lie back, panting and sweating and shaking with fear of the unknown.

The mightiest muscle in the human body, more powerful by far than the biceps of the strongest man in the world, strove to expel the foetus. Macha, ignorant and beyond crying now, felt her body torn apart and prepared to die. Feverishly, she tried to pray, but she could only shout obscenities.

"Holy Mary, Mother of God! Are you in here alone?" The woman's voice sounded far off. "Merciful Jesus preserve us, where's the water? Where's the man? Where's the bloody doctor?"

Macha opened her eyes to see her Aunt Nan peering through the opening to the bed. She grabbed her arm in frenzy.

"I'm going to die, Auntie Nan. Something horrible is happening to me and I'm dying! Fetch me a priest. I want to confess. I don't want to go to hell."

"Ach, Macha, you were always one for the fantasy, just like Jack Sheridan before you," her aunt responded with asperity. "How would you think you've the time to go dying with the babby arriving at any moment? Now let me go, for I've to put a kettle on the stove."

She shook her arm free, gave her niece a little push back on the mattress and bustled noisily about the stove, stoking the embers and clattering the kettle.

The child's head butted ferociously at the opening. Macha let out a bloodcurdling scream. The excruciating pressure exploded and was released, and all at once, Nan was there holding up a damp, red boy baby, no bigger than a handspan, and the infant gave a wailing cry.

Macha held out her arms feebly.

"Patience, girl." She heard water splashed, and then the baby, clean and wrapped in a white wool shawl, was lying on her breast.

They dozed together for a time, and only the continual rolling pain kept Macha from drifting into deeper sleep. When a sharper pang struck unexpectedly, she gave a yelp and sat up.

"Would you credit that!" Nan exclaimed. "If there's not another one in there! By the twelve apostles, it's to be twins!"

But Macha had already guessed and was hard at work once more. It was easier now that she knew what to expect, and without terror, the throes did not seem so cruel. The second child swam into the world like an otter.

"A boy again?" she asked.

"No. You have a *cailin* this time," Nan answered.

The door burst open, and Molloy pushed an unenthusiastic doctor through it. Her aunt rounded on them with a stream of high-pitched abuse—for being too late, for being men and for daring to enter the *varda* at all at such a time. The doctor gave Macha a cursory glance, ignored the twins and left with obvious relief. Molloy was banished to the weather.

Later, Macha, suspended between sleep and wakefulness, just caught her aunt's whisper:

"I'll have to be away now, but you'll be as right as a dab of porther in a mutton stew on a Saturday night. Don't ever let on to Michael Mulligan that I was here, or he'll kill me."

The girl nodded her promise and took the older woman's hand with gratitude.

"You entered the Bow-top for me, although it is *mochardi*," she murmured, marvelling that her aunt would have crossed the cursed threshold.

"Aye, Blessed Mary and all the paragons in heaven forgive me!" Nan crossed herself three times. "An army of Zulus would not have had the courage to do it and, if it hadn't been for Hugh coming back with a tale about your man, I'd not have known you were here. But somebody had to be at your side, even though you've caused enough disgrace to bring bad luck to the ace of hearts and the cattle charms of May besides."

When she had departed, Molloy crept in, dripping wet, and stood with awed eyes beside her, afraid to approach his minute children and too nervous to touch her. It was the first time she had seen him nonplussed, and as she smiled at this, she caught a hint of her own capabilities and that the balance between them had been subtly changed.

The twins were healthy, and both their parents enjoyed them, Molloy even cradling them when he was certain no outsider would catch sight of him, for babies were women's concern. They named them Tom and Molly.

On the road to Galway city, they passed a number of travellers who had been at Jack Sheridan's funeral and who steadfastly ignored them.

"They'll never forget, or forgive you," commented the coper. "And I'll be glad to leave this miserable province and go south again."

However, Macha did not care what others thought. She had her man and her children and her horses and needed no-one else.

The days were lasting and lustrous, leaf buds were fat on the twigs and a green film of early growth flimsily dressed the uplands. The first sunlight of the year was lured to the valleys and changed into fertility.

They passed between layers of mountains, folded one behind the other like theatrical backcloths, colourful and detailed at first with stone walls and dots of sheep, darker the next shadow, and then a lighter, less distinct screen and beyond that another, even paler and so amorphous that it seemed like a hazy reflection of the others, fading ripples into the distance.

One white dawn, by a milky lough in the bosom of Joyce Country, the mare dropped her foal, simply and without fuss. When Molloy and Macha arose, the event was already over and the colt was unsteadily on his feet and suckling.

"Will you look at that! He's the image of Gallinule!" the triumphant coper exclaimed, and Macha saw the same wide white blaze and three white socks as on the great stallion. She squeezed her man and laughed with abandon. Their audacious plot had actually worked!

The foal had huge, guileless brown eyes fringed by girlish black lashes. His head tapered to a soft, small nose with delicately curled, pink-lined nostrils. He had a twitching tuft of a tail, the scrappy beginnings of a mane, curving, alert ears and long, long, slim legs. Legs as straight as saplings. Macha stared at the exquisite creature and wondered if perhaps he was not even more beautiful than her own babies.

"Look at that chest! And that barrel! There'll be a great heart in there. And those shoulders, slopes you could skate down," Molloy was crowing, walking round and round examining the new arrival from every angle, as the mare nickered anxiously.

"Oh, we've a champion here and no mistake!" He lifted Macha off the ground and swung her with a flourish. "We've a winner. There'll be no stopping this one. It's glory and gold we have here."

They called him "Gold," for his coat and his future, and as they drove very gently and with many halts on to Galway, he trotted behind his mother and shied at sheep, scrambled over ditches and bounded after butterflies, slept stretched on the world-famous grass of Ireland and grew almost as they watched.

They pulled up on the waste ground in the Claddagh, where Macha had camped the previous year during the horse sales and races. This time she did not go into the town centre, but walked, with the twins held to her by her tied shawl, past the fishermen's brightly painted, thatched cabins and through the Spanish arch to the docks, where the air smelt of fish and salt and spices.

Coasters and fishing boats were tied up at the quays, and a mail packet was steaming in from the sea. The ferry was taking on stores and a few passengers for the Aran Islands, and two tramp steamers were unloading. An English frigate stood greyly offshore, and in passing contrast, a full-sailed schooner was billowing in from North Africa. Men were heaving cloth-bound bales and lengths of massive rope, winding chains, shouting, singing and puffing smoke as thick as treacle from plugs of tobacco like dried dung. Molloy was in amongst them, somewhere.

That night, he went off with the pony and cart, and this time, perhaps because of her new self-confidence, his wife ignored his instructions to stay in the Bow-top and she followed.

A side lane brought them out on a deserted corner of the docks piled with discarded crates and rusting iron. A decaying hull lay half submerged and blocking the moorings for other craft. There, three men met Molloy, who was soon helping them lift boxes onto the cart.

"Cork is it?"

"Cork it is."

Macha left before he turned and was waiting on the steps of her waggon when he arrived.

"You're to tell me now," she demanded.

"It's best that you know nothing," he parried.

"I must know."

"There are people I help out sometimes. That's all."

"What people?"

"People of the Cause."

"What Cause?"

"*The* Cause. The Cause of Ireland. *My* Cause, Macha."

"Do you mean the Fenians? Molloy! If a thousand saints bless me this instant, I won't believe you've any part of that demented rabble!"

"Not a rabble, and not so mad," he emphasized solemnly. "For one day they will win."

"But what are they to you, a Rom?" Macha was incredulous. She was informed enough to know travelling people were offered no clemency in any society in any land, and in return they gave no allegiance.

"My father died in an English prison—not for horse-stealing. For being a Rom. And my mother died of hunger and cold in the winter of '79, when I was eight years old."

It was the first time he had talked of his family, and she knew he would say no more; nor, out of respect, would she ask.

Macha had heard stories of the famines, of the evictions and emigrations, of the times when the bodies of the starved had rotted on the waysides, being too numerous to bury. Many travelling families, she knew, were descendants of those who had taken to the road when turned out of their homes for being unable to pay their rents after the potato crops had failed. But to her, it all seemed to have happened too long ago to matter. The English, with their soldiers and magistrates and landowners, half of them almost indistinguishable from the Irish, were undeniably in charge, and it seemed impossible that a few men meeting in secret and whispering would ever see them off.

To Macha, Ireland was the endless journey over the peat bogs, through one-street villages, past the remote cabins and the man driving his two cows in for milking. Ireland was the limpid light of Connacht and the clear, pale blue winter water of the turloughs; the Twelve Bens and Macgillycuddy's Reeks; the haunting circles of stones in empty places and the enigma of Tara; the cries of the owl in the night, red grouse, buzzard and wild geese over the windswept, vivid turf. She had little contact with the settled community, and who ruled was unimportant, for whoever rules harasses travelling people.

However, she knew Molloy better now. The times when he stared thoughtfully into the fire, or seemed preoccupied; the serious spirit occasionally detected behind his airy personality; the morality of his passion were all explained. She did not completely understand his commitment, but she admired him and would have helped had he so permitted.

From Galway, they followed the route she had first taken south as far as Cork, where she awoke one morning with an unexplained feeling of liberation and later discovered that the boxes had gone from the coper's cart, although he had not left her side for over twenty-four hours.

He, too, was buoyant and happy and turned their vehicles to follow the coast to a small, hidden bay. The sun had evaporated the rain and dispersed the cloud which had been clogging the sky. They piled onto the snowy strand and were soon running, splashing each other and screaming and drenched to the skin through the shallow waves. The babies were dandled with their tiny feet kicking the spray. The dogs dived in after sticks and stones. The horses stood, looking doubtful, up to their knees in the salt water, and the golden foal squealed and fled from every foam-tipped swirl.

For a month, they lazed by the sheltered sea, protected from the ocean breakers by headlands. Molloy taught her to swim, and each morning they would race straight into the raw, fresh tang wearing improperly few clothes, and when the sun was high at midday, they would swim the horses, riding them bareback through the swell, the now intrepid foal paddling alongside with only his ears and head above the surface. Under the stars, they would plunge in again, completely naked in the darkness.

Then Molloy would catch her ankle, as they cantered back to the shore, and pull her down by their bonfire and cover her with sandy kisses and play and tempt until the elements of her body burned and her sea-cold skin radiated heat. And while they loved, a white flame flickered over the water, and when the running tongue of a wave licked over them, they, too, glowed, phosphorescent ghosts at witching time. Molten, she could feel herself receive him, shape to him and fuse. It was as though, each time they made love, he efformed her and she was reborn.

Nights of eroticism and dreaming were followed by long, lolling days, dozing outdoors until their skin was darkened by the rays of summer, meandering through the dunes searching for puffin burrows and collecting shells, Molloy blowing eerie notes on a reed cupped in his hands and being answered in chorus by gannets veering seaward overhead.

The babies lay in the wooden crib he had made them, rosy and brown and juicy as two Russet apples. The foal grew taller on legs like slender stilts. The mare was sleek and fit again, and even the lurchers put on flesh through the sheer indolence of their life. Her man was merry and relaxed and had lost his stern, distant look. Macha wanted to stay there for ever and even caught herself imagining a thatch-roofed cottage on the edge of the strand where they would all live. It was a shock when he began loading the cart one morning.

"Oh, Molloy, we don't have to be on the road again, not yet," she pleaded. "Could we not stay a few days more?"

"Then you might not get your present," he replied obliquely.

"What present?"

"Why, you know the one. The one I have to go to Dublin to collect."

"I do not know it. You're teasing. Just a day or two longer, with the sun shining like a pawnbroker's ball."

"Which would you have? A day, or a present?" he asked, holding both his hands behind his back as if they contained the choice.

"A day! A day!" She pulled at his right arm.

He unclosed his fist and his hand was empty.

"You have it. You have your day. We'll leave tomorrow," he said, grinning. "And maybe you'll get the present as well."

So, they swam and walked, sunbathed and ate rabbit, rode the horses and played with the children, found coloured stones and sea anemones and, at last, a burrow of newly hatched puffins, waiting with beaks open for their parents to arrive with sand eels for supper. They kissed and made love, and crammed a whole second month into that last day. By the moon, Macha watched him sleep and felt her heart in pain from love.

They did not hurry to Dublin, but zigzagged from Waterford to Wexford to Clonmel to Enniscorthy, back to Kilkenny and on to Carlow and then over to Wicklow, trading horses. There seemed to be no shape or time limit to the route, but wherever they went, there was always someone who was acquaintanced with Molloy. Shadows she now knew to be Fenians came in the night, and other horse copers traded by day.

"When you're dealing, it's always wise to encourage the regulars," he advised her. "And it's never worth letting them down. Sell them good beasts and when times are hard, they will put the bread in your mouth. The tricks are the game, but the trust is the trade."

They drew up on the banks of the River Dodder and the babies were left sleeping as he drove her, finally, into Dublin in the cart, passing the Magdalen Asylum for "unfortunate females, abandoned by their seducers and rejected by their friends, who prefer a life of penitence and virtue to one of guilt, infamy and prostitution."

They arranged to meet in less than an hour at the foot of Sackville Street and he drove on, leaving her to cross the bridge and wander up Ireland's most famous thoroughfare, to gape enviously at the well-dressed folk shopping at Clerys, entering and leaving the Gresham, the Crown and the Granville Hotels, and to buy a bottle of whiskey at Findlaters.

When he picked her up again, the cart was laden under the spread tarpaulin and the pony could do no more than pull the weight at walking pace. They walked, too, at its head, and Molloy handed her a large envelope.

"What's this?" she wondered.

"Did I not promise you a gift?"

She had pictured a dress, or a brooch, or maybe an ornament for the Bow-top and looked at the envelope doubtfully.

"I can't open it here."

"You could slit the end and take a peek," he encouraged.

Inside, she could see documents covered in writing and drawn lines, but was unable to pull them out to read.

"What would I want with such stuff? What's it about?" she demanded.

He was positively smirking. "They are all the papers for Gold—pedigree, registration, every single thing he'll need when his time comes to race."

"But how can you have a pedigree giving him as Gallinule's foal? Everyone from Belfast to London will know it could not be."

"You're right," he agreed. "There is not a thoroughbred nor half-bred running in Ireland, England or even France whose line isn't easily traced, so here's the beauty of it . . ." He paused, looking vastly pleased with himself. "I've arranged for him to be imported—from America. Our little colt is officially the offspring of a Thoroughbred mare called Precious Stone and a stallion called Philosopher, which had a good enough record on the tracks before retiring to stud in Kentucky. Even the import documents are there to prove it."

Macha gazed at him in open admiration. "I'd never have thought of all that. I'd not have known what to do."

"That's why we're such a good team." He winked. "You have the way with the horses and I know the ways of the world, and we won't always be living like this, goddess. We'll have a yard full of quality hobbies and hunters and chasers between Dublin and the Curragh. One day we'll be rich, and you'll be covered in diamonds and I'll be wearing a top hat."

She giggled and took his hand, resting her head on his shoulder as they strolled. They did not see the black, horse-drawn van approaching rapidly from behind until it passed and slewed across their path. The doors of the van swung open and a dozen policemen leapt out.

"Go! Race for your life!" Molloy yelled, giving her a brutal push. "Save yourself, Macha!"

A constable caught her wrist. She twisted and sank her teeth into his bare hand and tasted warm, salt blood before he swore with pain and released his grip.

Instinct and panic gave her speed. Fleeing across the wide street, she looked back over her shoulder only once. Molloy was surrounded; the cover had been pulled off the cart and the wooden boxes exposed. No-one was bothering to pursue her. They were all too intent on the contents. Macha eeled down a dark wynd and into the warren of slums beyond. A long way off, there was a small explosion.

She did not slow down until she reached the riverbank and ran inside the Bow-top, slamming and locking the door behind her. There, sitting shaking on the bench by the stove and still clutching the envelope of documents he had given her, she was unable to envisage the extent of the catastrophe, too afraid to guess at the contents of the boxes, but aware that this time, Molloy was in far more serious trouble than being arrested for horse stealing.

During the previous winter she had come to know Dublin quite well and wondered to which jail they had taken him and whether she should go to each and ask to see him. Then she remembered his voice screeching at her to save herself. He, who had never shown a trace of misgiving before, had struck the note of mortal terror, and she knew she must stay away.

The hot tea she poured automatically began to thaw out her

trembling hands, and she added a shot of whiskey to it and tried to do what he would have wanted, to calm down and concentrate.

There was plenty of money, which could be used to help him through bribery, perhaps. The idea of hiring a lawyer never occurred to her. Attorneys did not deal with tinkers. The unthinkable kept pushing its way into her mind, and every now and again she found herself gulping back tears of apprehension which refused to be controlled.

Feeling helpless and alone, she hunched in a turmoil of impossible ideas, too distracted to light the lamps as evening spread across the city. Then, suddenly, there was someone in the Bow-top with her and, turning, she clearly saw him standing by the door.

"The Connors and the Wards are good friends of mine, and remember the Maughams if you're ever in need." He repeated words of long before, and then, as she stared, he was gone.

The fretting of the babies invaded her reverie, along with the guilty realisation that none of the animals had been fed either. Relieved to be occupied, she concentrated on them, spinning out the tasks to escape her thoughts. But the moment could not be postponed indefinitely when the twins were clean and fed and sleeping again, the lurchers and horses replete and there was nothing more to do except wait, wide-eyed and motionless, until dawn.

The encampment was still heavy with slumber, and even the skeletal dogs found it an effort to rouse themselves to sound the alarm at her arrival. For one moment of dismay, she did not recognise any of the waggons or tents; but then she saw the Connors' distinctive cart under trees on the west side of the clearing.

Jumping from the running board of the Bow-top, she charged into the bender tent, cast herself on the bemused woman and burst into hysterical sobs, loudly blurting out the news.

The slap was as hard as a punch, and stinging, and it stopped Macha's torrent of words in her throat. Biddy Connor's eyes were piercing hers with glittering hatred.

"Hold your noise this instant! Do you want the world to know?"

But the world had already heard, and the sensation was crashing over benders and caravans like a landslide, spreading chaos before it. Already, women were stuffing rags, pots and infants into carts and men were rolling canvasses and rounding up ponies. Dogs yawled and children bawled. The adults cursed and shouted, and horses collided with each other in the haste to leave. As Liam Ward came running towards them, Macha looked about the site in bewilderment.

"What's happening?" she asked Biddy Connor. "Why is everybody going?"

"Because the police will be here in a trice, and probably the army too, you stupid scrub." The older woman glared at her in disgust. "What did you mean by coming here and causing discomposure in us all?"

"Leave it, Mrs. Connor," advised Liam Ward. "Just get her and this thing away." He jerked his thumb at the Bow-top. "I'll go into Dublin and see what I can discover."

"In the name of Mary and Joseph, have a care." Biddy Connor clasped her hands together.

"We'll meet up tonight by Lake Tay," he arranged, and left.

Without addressing another word to Macha, the Connors packed up their possessions and indicated that she should follow. They urged their pony to a canter, and her *varda* whiplashed dangerously as she tried to keep up along the road south to the Wicklow Mountains. They stopped only briefly to water the horses, giving her little time to feed the twins. The foal was white-streaked with sweat and staggering with exhaustion.

"Leave it behind on the road," ordered Biddy Connor ruthlessly.

Macha managed, somehow, to drag it up the steps and into the Bow-top before they careered on again, with the mare neighing frantically and the foal screaming for its mother as they went.

The irregular black outline of the city faded and finally disappeared. The shadowy mountains consolidated, grew immense and surrounded them. They drove under War Hill and Ojouce Mountain and clambered through the Sally Gap before starting a twisting descent on the far side through ravines made by the numerous river sources until, at last, they drew up in a secret valley in the heart of the range.

"You've got to tell me!" Macha confronted Biddy Connor. "What has Molloy done? And why would the police have come to the camp?"

"Christ of Almighty! Are you saying you don't know about Molloy the Coper, and you the one married to him?"

"I know he took messages sometimes for the Fenians," Macha answered.

"Messages is it?" Biddy Connor gave her a glare of disbelief. "That's the first time I've ever heard guns described as messages."

"Guns! Oh, Mother of God, no! There couldn't have been guns in the cart!" Macha felt her world shudder.

"What did you think he was carrying? Woollen socks for soldiers?" The woman, full of contempt, came so close that the girl flinched as though the words were a physical threat.

"You brought this about, Macha Sheridan. You are the cause, with your *mochardi* ways, bringing that unclean waggon among us, bringing bedevilment, tainting him with the curse of the dead. It was Satan's day when he set eyes on you, for you have been a black bride, you shameless harlot."

The Connor girls had gathered behind their mother, faces distorted with loathing, and Macha knew they were going to attack. The oldest reached out and grasped her hair, and the roots crackled as they were wrenched out, excruciatingly. She closed her eyes and rounded her shoulders and waited for the rest.

Nothing happened, and she sensed them withdraw. Looking up warily, she saw that Liam Ward had arrived, his face white and drawn.

"Leave me to talk with Mrs. Molloy. This is her concern," he said.

They moved back, and then she knew. She knew it all. No thick cell walls could entomb Molloy, no iron bars cage her wild, dark man. He would not have been taken.

She must have spoken, although she did not hear a sound, but he was nodding and patting her arm, pointlessly.

". . . and so you see, Mrs. Molloy . . . Macha . . . they never got him to jail. He put the pistol to his own head and shot himself, God forgive him, there in the street before they could stop him."

That distant little explosion as she had been running away through the alleys. It had been her man dying. It had been no more than a balloon bursting, a squib reporting, a chestnut cracking in the fire. It had been her man dying.

His last drop of blood, exchanged for hers on their wedding day, drained from her—just a drop, but it left a reachless pit, an emptiness which would never be filled. There was a high, thin wailing, like a sea creature keening on the sand. She did not know it was herself.

Someone was forcing whiskey into her mouth, and she was choking. The hatred in the women's eyes had been extinguished by sorrow.

Liam was speaking, urgently: "You'll have to get away, girl. They're hunting you."

"Why?" she asked, confused. "What would they want with me?"

"You're his wife. You were with him. They think you were in on it."

She shook her head at them irritably. Her husband would come soon and tell her what to do. If she waited, her husband would come.

Biddy Connor took her by the shoulders and shook her, hard.

"Molloy is dead. Molloy is dead," she stated pitilessly. "And you will die too if you don't get away. They'll hang you, Macha Sheridan, and I would not mind letting them, for it's what you deserve. But Molloy would not have wished that, and Molloy was like my own son. My own darling son, who is now dead."

"You'll need to leave Ireland. There'll be no place to hide here," Liam was saying. "They never give up the search when treason is involved."

She was floundering, quite uncomprehending, as Biddy Connor and the man began to make plans over her head.

"If she goes to Rosslare, she can cross the water to Wales and go on to England. They'll never think to find her there."

"She'll be noticed less if she travels on foot."

"Have you any money, girl?"

Macha nodded, dumbly, at the waggon.

"Well, fetch it and whatever clothes and else you want, for you will not be taking that monstrosity along, with every Peeler in the land on the watch for it."

"It's my *varda*, my father's Bow-top, I cannot leave it," she protested feebly.

"Leave it? We're going to burn it!" Biddy Connor shrieked at her in grief and rage. "We will burn it to cinders, as it should have been destroyed long ago. Molloy might have been alive and here with us now if you hadn't dragged that thing, big as a cabin and unholy with paint, all over the country, showing up his route as surely as if you were informing the police at every station."

She threw herself into the Bow-top. The foal came tumbling down the steps bleating with alarm. The contents came hurtling out after him. Biddy Connor finally emerged, panting, to thrust the twins into her eldest daughter's arms and the tin box of money and jewellery into Macha's hands.

"Get rid of it!" she commanded Liam Ward, pointing at the now empty Bow-top. "Put the flame to it, in the name of God."

Helped by her other daughter, she held Macha back as the man sprinkled the gaudy wheels and walls with paraffin and then lit a piece of oil-soaked string with a taper and they all watched the thin scarlet worm scurry over the ground. It reached the wooden frame, hesitated, and then, with a boom which echoed again and again through the mountains, reared over the Bow-top. And the fine scrolls and decorations split and blackened; the door fell off its melting hinges and lay seething on the ground. Wood splintered and scattered lethal, fire-tipped arrows in all directions and the blaze grew ever hotter. One by one the windows blew out, and with each, she heard again the explosion of his death, and in the incandescence she saw his face blown apart, over and over, and in the red furnace of the interior she saw Hell. The funeral pyre of her father and her husband was burning, and she heard herself howling a long way off.

They left her alone, crouched rocking by the charcoal and the ashes, weeping bitter, bitter tears and listening to the terrible extinction in herself where Molloy had been. The shadow of his face above her, the heat as their bodies met and merged, the way his mind read hers and spoke what she was about to say were gone; gone with the strands on which they had played and the moors over which they had raced and the skies under which they had rested. All her senses would function, but the sound and smell and sight and touch and taste of him were gone. The world Molloy had created for her was obliterated.

When, in the end, someone laid her on a straw pallet and covered her with a rug, it was as though they were protecting a space.

It was strange that she should have slept, but she did, awaking to see Biddy Connor and Liam Ward conversing closely and the girls feeding their babies by the campfire. There was a smouldering black scar on the turf, so obscene that she could not bear to look at it.

As she sat up, Biddy brought over a bundle of clothes. Clothes which had belonged to Molloy.

"We've decided on a scheme to get you safe away," she said. "They'll not be searching for a *chavvy*, so you are to wear these. We'll travel with you as far as Wexford and put you on the road to Rosslare. Take only what you need."

Macha felt frightened. Their plans for her were rushing ahead without giving her time to think.

"I know no-one in England," she protested nervously. "How will I live?"

"Consider that God, or the Devil, smiled on you when he left you well provided for." Biddy Connor flipped open the lid of the tin box and exposed the rolls of bank notes and shining jumble of gold jewellery. "And you've the horses, so you won't starve."

"I don't want to go. I won't know where to go, or what to do. I want to stay here." Macha began to cry.

The woman stood over her with arms folded. Her grey hair hung wispily to her shoulders, and her face was haggard from her own mourning. The hatred which had given it such dreadful verve the day before was no longer evident. Her eyes were cold and lifeless.

She spoke deliberately. "There is nothing for you now in Ireland, girl. And I am not talking about the police and their business. There is nothing for you because with Molloy gone, there is not a traveller will welcome you. You have flouted our ways, and you are to blame for his death. You will get no help and have no friend on the road. So go to England and make another life for yourself far away. You are not wanted here, Macha Sheridan."

It was an annihilating statement, implacable and icy. Macha felt the air chill and recognised the overwhelming truth. Without another word, she took the bundle and went behind the tent to change.

The clothes were warm, as though Molloy had just discarded them. It was like climbing into his skin. She dressed unhurriedly, almost gratefully, savouring the oiled wool of his jersey, pulling it over her head slowly, slowly, breathing deeply, remembering his hand caressing her face. The bottoms of the trousers were frayed and she plucked at the loose threads absently, then fingered the hard tweed lapel of his jacket before putting it on and, strangely, gaining strength. Returning to the fire, she began to push her hair under his cap.

"That will not do at all. How will you keep your head covered day and night?" Biddy Connor drew a pair of long scissors from a bag and as the girl knelt obediently before her, hacked off the long red hair. Ancient punishment. Macha knew it was a woman's revenge.

There was a mist hiding the mountain peaks and falling damply about them. It muffled the bird cries and the running spring and even the grinding of the blades. It induced dull acceptance like a trance in her, protected by Molloy's clothes, held snugly in his aura. She did not care what they did. Her hair fell, its strands coiling into springs on the ground. There was a sense of unreality about the experience: the obscure glen; people unfamiliar to her dominating her present, directing her future; the loss of Molloy, who would never return, although the feel and smell of him was all about her. What did it matter what she looked like, or where she went?

Then they were on their way, the women and babies piled in the cart and the man riding a pony bareback and leading the others in a clattering group behind. For hours no-one spoke. Macha sat with first

Molly and then Tom in her arms, feeding and nursing them, drawing comfort from their smiles and their tiny hands clinging to her fingers and their trusting faces and their small forms resting against her heart. They travelled by little-used lanes, Macha hiding under blankets while passing through Arklow and busy coastal villages.

Late the following afternoon, Liam Ward left them all in a wood outside Wexford while he went into the town to make enquiries. Biddy Connor and her daughters busied themselves cutting hazel rods. Macha wrapped her sleeping babies in their shawls and laid them in a crib.

When the man returned, he came on foot, leading the pony, now laden with a tarpaulin and new panniers.

"There's a cattle boat that'll take the horses leaving Rosslare," he told Macha. "And as you'll need some shelter over the water, I've bought a canvas."

He named the price, and she paid him. The twins had woken again and begun to girn in the background, and he and Biddy Connor exchanged a peculiar look as she turned to attend to them.

"About the babbies," the woman said, grimly. "Liam, here, and myself have been over it together, and they cannot go with you. They must stay here."

"You're mad, Biddy Connor! I'd never leave my children." Macha was more astonished than outraged by the idea. Then her eyes narrowed. "And you needn't think you're getting them, you old witch, if that's your latest plot."

Liam Ward moved between the two.

"Macha, you can be certain the police know all about Molloy and you and your children. They'll be covering every road and every station and every port, looking for a tinker girl with twin babies."

Macha swept the babies into her arms and hugged them, mewling, to her. She did not want to hear him, or to think.

"No! They're my angels, Molloy's and mine. He will not stand for you stealing them," she cried crazily. "I'll be dressed as a man. No-one will guess it's me."

"And what would a lad be doing with two infants? Of course they'll guess." He reached to take them, but she wrenched them away, stumbling and gripping them too tightly, so that their wails became squalls, and she screamed too.

"I'm taking them with me. They're my children. I will not be parted from them. They need me. I am their mother."

A pit was opening up before her.

"What will happen to them when you're arrested?" Ward shouted. "When they lock you away, what will happen to them then? I'll tell you, woman. They will be put into an institution and brought up as orphans. No-one is going to believe you did not know what Molloy the Coper was up to. When you step on the ferryboat and they catch you, they will hang you, and then little Tom and Molly will have no mother at all and no family either."

"Oh, Blessed Mary, Mother of God, have mercy on me and my little ones," Macha prayed, desperately sinking to her knees. "What's to become of us? Save us! Help us!"

"I will take the babbies and look after them as if they were my own, just as I did with Molloy." Biddy, finally softened by the girl's anguish, put her arms around all three. "And, in a while, when the fuss is over, you can come back for them."

"I can't. I cannot do it," Macha keened, rocking backwards and forwards in torment. "I need them."

"Arrah, you do," Biddy agreed, gently. "But it's too late for that. You must think of what is best for them now, and you cannot condemn them, dear innocent souls, to the orphanage."

"No. They cannot go there and I cannot leave them either." She shook her head hopelessly and held to the struggling bodies as though to a branch over the precipice.

"It'll be for no longer than a couple of years . . . a year or so . . . maybe only a few months." Liam Ward reduced the sentence each time she shuddered.

Biddy flapped him away.

"Give them here, Macha." She held out open hands. "They'll be safe and loved dearly until you return. I'll care for them, and every traveller in the land will protect them. Molloy the Coper's children will be treated like princes. What Liam says is right. After a time the Peelers will have better things to do than keep up the hunt, and you will be able to fetch them to England."

"You said the police would never give up. How can I come back?"

The man and the woman exchanged glances again.

"Ach, but aren't there always families crossing the water?" Liam intervened quickly. "Sure, we will send the children over with one of them just as soon as you're settled."

"Do you swear it?" Macha turned to him, fiercely. "Swear by the Virgin!"

"By the Blessed Mary, by my own sons and may the Devil drag me like a horse's head to his fire in hell!" He gave his oath. "Just as soon as you give the word, Tom and Molly, here, will be on their way."

Biddy Connor took the babies from her at last, one by one. Macha whimpered and waited, stunned for a miracle; for Saint Peter to appear in radiance and return them to her breast, for a wand to wave and turn Time back three days, for a thunderbolt to strike her dead. No miracle happened.

The girls had packed the panniers with her possessions and strapped the hazel rods, which would make up the frame of a tent, to the pack pony. The rest of her horses were roped together and ready to move.

Liam Ward outlined the five-mile route to Rosslare and lowered his eyes, superstitiously, as she mounted astride. Macha, unable to see through tears, reached blindly and vainly towards her children as he hit the mare hard on the quarters with a stick and sent her bucking away from them. By the time the girl gained control and looked back, the little group was already shapeless in the distance, and then they turned off the track and were gone.

Macha, at sixteen years old, had lost husband, children, home and country.

Chapter SEVEN

Wales was funereal. The cattle boat docked under a pall of cloud after a crossing during which Macha was repeatedly sick and the bellowing, groaning animals were thrown off their feet, some fatally.

Numb from the dolour of the past days, she wandered through the hills, unaware of the dingy landscape or of anything beyond the shock which strangled her from throat to womb, and the endless, tolling scream where her brain had been.

Bereft of senses, not seeing or hearing, not smelling or touching or tasting, without appetite or aim, sometimes she stopped for no reason, and the ponies drew in water and the dogs scavenged for themselves. She did not know they were there. Rage would well up without warning, making her eyes bulge and swelling the arteries in her neck: rage against Molloy for being dead, against herself for being alive, rage because it was the emotion to blot out all others. More lunatic than sane, once she rushed baying and spreading out her arms to be received into the rapid currents of Afon Gronw and was saved only by a fallen tree, which closed a cage about her as the river swept on. In rage, she frenziedly pummelled a rock face with her fists until they bled and she was breathless and beaten.

Just the thought of Tom and Molly, her babies, their eyes like fathomless fonts of faith, would send her running and stumbling about distractedly with clenched lids and covered ears, as though it were possible physically to escape her plight.

Then, after a time, came the curious awareness, without sensation, of her own actions: of standing still, or lying down under the blanket, of riding or trudging along followed by the horses, moving across a land whose people spoke a tongue she did not understand, through villages and towns the names of which she could not read. She ate nothing and drank only a little and welcomed the rack of hunger and had no wish to assuage it. Soon, she felt light-headed and began to mumble to herself, sometimes believing Molloy was walking beside her again.

One morning, she decided not to get up. She had left the county of Pembroke far behind and had passed over the eastern boundary of Carmarthen. The air was growing dusty and bitter; even in the rain the vegetation was dulled by a coat of dirt. There were solid barriers ahead, polished by the water to look painted—pyramids of iron or jet, outlandish and forbidding. They loomed and receded in Macha's unfocussed gaze, and she thought they were the fearsome fortifications of England. She would go no further, she decided, hunching, foetus-like, with head ducked and clasping her knees; and in truth, she had no strength left.

The cover over her and the earth beneath soaked up the rain and created a cool silk cocoon in which to curl. Yet even this was not enough to extinguish the heat which was consuming her from within. It was as though the pain she had been carrying had turned into a furnace and was burning itself out and destroying her at last. Convulsed in its fever, with limbs shaking uncontrollably and sweat oozing from every pore, she lay passively, glad to die.

Violent shadows and flame and smoke met her eyes when next she opened them. Then a huge black face looked down, and she cried out and cowered. She was in Hell.

The Devil spoke through broken teeth in a booming voice. Demons and sprites crowded behind him. Macha tried to cross herself, but was too weak to raise her arm. Besides, it was too late. She knew she had died and been damned and sent to Hell. Soon they would throw her on the flames to suffer everlasting torment. The Devil held out a mug brimming over with poison for her to drink, and she turned her face to the floor and, when his hairy hand touched her, let out a quavering, high-pitched screech.

There was a scuffling in the shadows and then an atmosphere of space and air, as though Hell had emptied through an open door, and then a woman's lilting voice was talking to her. She felt her head raised and the cup against her mouth. Lukewarm, sweet liquid seeped onto her tongue. It was milk.

Macha dared to look again and this time, saw a beautiful woman sitting beside her. The woman was slim as a quill, with moon-white skin and lips like blood-red fruit, with black hair and black brows and thick black lashes and eyes witch-black. Only her rough red hands persuaded that she was human.

They were in a small, dark kitchen before a cast-iron range with an open fire, and the flames were casting shadows on the ceiling.

"*Peidiwch ag ofni*. You have nothing to fear. You have been very ill. My cousin found you lying by the side of the road and brought you here three days ago. We began to think you would never come round, for you have not moved since. You were wearing man's clothes and seemed like a boy at first."

Unendurable memories of the events in Ireland seethed, and Macha's face twisted with inner agony. The woman took her hand. "Whatever it is, *cariad*, you must put it from your thoughts. To be well again, you must free your mind from the adversities of the past."

"My babies . . . ," whispered Macha brokenly.

"So you have lost *plant*, too, my lamb." The woman held her hand more tightly. "Did they die in childbirth?"

Macha shook her head. "I had to leave them behind in Ireland. They say they will send them to me soon, but I do not believe it. I think I will never see my babies again."

Hot and useless tears trickled down her face, and she wiped them away with angry shame. A traveller never betrayed emotion before a *gaujo*.

"Give thanks to the Almighty that they are alive." The woman's mouth trembled very slightly. "For little Owain was taken from me two years ago, and Mia lived only for one week after she was born last winter."

They clung to each other, made sisters through their sorrow, and Macha found in the distress of the woman the seed of solace needed to grow courage.

She drank the milk and slept and drifted through time, half aware of people around her and of being fed and then everything fading as she lost consciousness again.

When she became sharply attentive at last, there was a man sitting at the table with his back to her, and the woman was placing a plate of steaming food before him. Several boys and girls of varying ages waited around the edge of the kitchen, their eyes following his every mouthful, and when the woman came towards her with a bowl, their watch fixed on that.

After taking a couple of spoonfuls, Macha handed the broth back. "They are hungry." She indicated the children. "Give it to them."

"There's plenty for them, but their father eats first."

The man turned round. She saw again the black face of the Devil and cringed.

The black face grinned and winked. "Have you never seen a collier before, back? Do you think I'm a blackamoor? Give me a cloth, Sian, before the girl collapses with fright."

He took a damp rag from his wife and rubbed vigorously at his cheek, and to Macha's surprise, a white patch appeared.

"Coal dust," he explained.

Sian said, "Perhaps they don't have mines in Ireland, Ifor."

"What do you burn on your fires, then?" he asked.

"Peat from the bog, and sometimes a bit of wood."

"Well, here we burn good Welsh coal, the best coal in the world, dug out from hundreds of feet below the surface of the earth. Feel the great heat it gives."

So that was why the flames were so fierce.

As the children fell upon their bowls of *cawl*, picking out the lumps of bacon before attacking the vegetables, Sian turned the tap on the left side of the range, and boiling water poured into a bucket, which was then tipped into a tin bath on the floor in front of the grate and refilled and emptied until the bath was half full, when cold water was added.

Before Macha's rivetted eyes, the man took off all his clothes, stepped into the water and sat down. She had noticed he was black all over, even his penis, before she collected herself enough to look away. When his wife had scrubbed him, he came out white: a short, broad man, muscles mapped in ranges over his back and arms and chest. Peeping at him again, the girl thought of Molloy and felt her pulse beat a reminder of life. Then she scanned his face. It was impossible to tell his age, only that he was tired; not superficially tired from the exertions of an hour or two, but intrinsically spent from a life sentence to hard labour, tired lungs, tired blood, tired cells, tired pale eyes: so tired, it was as though the marvellously developed muscles were illusions, full not of power, but of air. At any moment they might deflate and there would be nothing of this tired man left.

The family went to bed early, the parents and two youngest children in the upstairs bedroom and three older children in a small back room. Macha was alone on her makeshift mattress among the steaming washing with time to think about her predicament.

There was no sign of the panniers containing her possessions and she wondered whether her money had been stolen while she lay unconscious, or whether she had simply forgotten the tin box somewhere back along the route. The dogs and horses must have strayed. The thought of losing them, especially the mare and Gold, made her miserable. In a way, the colt had symbolised her season with Molloy. All the fun and shenanigan over Gallinule, the thrill and promise of his birth, the hopes for his future. Yet some farmer might, even now, be preparing to ruin him with cart work, not realising his true potential.

Outside, twilight closed in against the window. The kitchen was stifling. Fine black dust had already peppered the clean clothes and the scrubbed table. Macha knew she must leave.

She was afraid. Memories of being hunted, of the docks full of police and officials scrutinising every passenger at Rosslare made her heart thump, as it had on the night she'd escaped from Ireland. It had beat so loudly, like a bodhran that all could hear. While the horses were being loaded, she had waited for the shout of accusation and for the hand to grip her shoulder as she walked up the gangway. . . . There had been soldiers on the ship, and although she had kept her cap well down over her shorn head and tucked herself away in a corner, one had come and lain too near her and whispered something. When she ran away in terror, he and his friends had laughed.

Perhaps they were still searching for her. At the idea of travelling the unknown roads of hostile England without even the companionship and protection of her own beasts, she trembled. Yet she could stay under the miner's roof no longer.

It was still the middle of the night when Ifor and Sian returned to the room and began to move about in weary silence. At first, Macha thought they had come for a drink, but when a taper was lit, she sat up.

"What's wrong?"

"Time for work."

"But it's dark."

"We make our own light." Ifor showed her the gauze-covered lamp hanging from his waist and explained how it was lit in the lamp room at the head of the mine and attached to his helmet. Then, pocketting a brass box containing a twist of tobacco to chew and carrying another box containing bread and caerphilly cheese to eat later, he left.

Sian sat heavily in the Windsor chair by the range with a mug of tea and passed one to Macha.

She took the Welsh woman's hand and stared at the palm.

"Good luck and fortune will be with your next child," she foretold. "He will lead others. He will bring better times to you all."

The other smiled. "I am not in need of your magic, gypsy girl," she said, quietly. "All that matters is to learn to face life without fear."

Macha looked deep into her ebon eyes and saw an ancient strength reach back to a Time as primaeval as her own.

"I'll be on the road tomorrow," she said.

Sian stood up and crossed to the corner cupboard.

"You will want this."

She took out the box of money and jewellery. The girl opened it with the key hung around her neck. The contents were untouched. Taking out a fistful of sovereigns, she held them out.

"No!" The Welsh woman was firm. "We take no money."

"For the food, for all your care," Macha pressed. "I would have died without you."

"I ask only that you use the gift of life well," Sian said. "I have a good man and fine children, while you have no-one and may have far to go. Keep your coin for your own use."

Macha took out the shamrock bracelet and matching brooch. "I wore these at my wedding to darling Molloy, and I want you to have them. It will dishearten me if you refuse."

Sian turned the delicate gold pieces over. The freshly stoked fire and burning oil lamps reflected on them so that they shone against the dark walls. The children had started moving about and giggling. She picked up the wristlet.

"I'll keep this to remind me of you, Macha," she agreed gracefully. "And when you wear the brooch it will always be a bond between us."

"You have taught me how to face tomorrow again through your wisdom." Macha put both hands over the hand holding her keepsake. "The Holy Mother will bless you, Sian Williams, and I shall never forget you."

"Remember that although all things do not always work out for the best, often what you fear most brings the most benefit. Never deny your true beliefs, *cariad*," Sian said, and then called out to a child: "David! When you have eaten, go to Dai Williams and tell him the gypsy will be taking her ponies in the morning."

"You found them? My horses? The saints be praised!" Macha was ecstatic. "I thought they were all lost, or sold."

"Sold? And who would sell them? They're on my cousin Dai's farm, pampered as pets, and two mongrels with them."

"Their keep will be paid for," the girl promised.

Sian grinned. "It will that, for Dai Williams was never one to refuse a farthing; but you'll find them all in good condition, for my husband, Ifor, swears he keeps the best stock in Powys."

As the children ate their breakfast brose of crushed oatcake soaked in beef stock and buttermilk, their mother mixed the scraps from the previous day into swill and carried it to feed the pig at the foot of the garden behind the cottage. When she returned, she filled a copper from the range, dumped in another heap of soiled clothes and set a girl to swirl them about with a wooden dolly, while she cleaned the room, leading the range and polishing the oak dresser with its proud display of pewter and lustre. Macha rubbed up brass candlesticks and the brass bases of the two lamps. Then it was time to scrub the clothes on a washboard, wind them through a mangle and peg them out.

After that, Sian baked: flat barley bread; oatcakes like curling shells and squat drop scones flipped over on the round iron plate over the fire with a wooden slice; fruit turnovers; speckled, batter and round cakes. Macha, whose experience of cooking had been limited to the most elementary boiling or roasting of food over an open fire, watched impressed as batch after batch was mixed from flour and eggs and turned into mouth-watering treats, the Welsh woman hurrying from table to bakestone with flour creeping up her arms and powdering her hair and bleaching her long apron.

The traveller helped peel piles of vegetables brought in from the garden—potatoes, carrots, onions and green beans. The clock in the corner ticked and chimed. The wife went out for a while and returned with a large joint of beef, which was put into a cauldron along with the vegetables, seasoning and herbs and set over the fire.

A crone with a creel over her arm came to the door and sold herrings and pints of cockles and mussels. A very old lady, wearing a peculiar high-crowned black hat with a lace cap underneath and a paisley shawl over her shoulders, arrived: Sian's mother, who sat, mumbling, by the range and eyeing Macha with fierce disfavour. When she decided to leave, with much muttering and head-shaking, one of the children was sent to carry the bag of salt bacon and bread and cake her daughter had packed.

Sian began to put food on the table. The clock struck six. She had been working without rest for over thirteen hours. The door opened and her husband walked in. There was a feast waiting.

"My, my. What's all this, then? Is there a wedding?" he asked, gaping at the spread.

"Macha is leaving us tomorrow, so I thought this would see her on her way in style," explained his wife, untying her apron and smoothing her hair. "You'll have to wash down first tonight."

"That I will," he agreed, showing a big white smile and carefully edging round her, so as not to mark her dress with his blackness.

While he bathed, children were sent to fetch pottery jugs full of small beer, and for once, the whole family sat down together, and all ate and drank mightily.

Later, they drew round the range and leant back in their chairs to ease their stretched stomachs and chattered in their singsong language with explanatory asides to Macha, who took in everything and began to appreciate, at last, living in a house, so protected and enclosed with your own. She drank the strong, dark beer thirstily and watched the children go boisterously to bed and Sian and Ifor grow close and private, and she understood. But there was still nothing to compare with a ring of vans and tents around an open fire and a fiddler playing and the stars above.

Somehow, she had expected to find herself in the country on opening the front door next morning, and so the grimy, bleak terraces of cottages facing each other were disappointing.

Macha kissed her friend farewell, and it would have been easy to cling on and cry. Sian's eyes were also too bright, and they both knew they would never meet again.

As she walked up the hill behind the oldest child, carrying her tin box and a large bundle of food wrapped in a cloth, she turned to look back frequently, and the Welsh woman was still standing in her doorway gazing after them. The street was straight and long, and eventually the only reason they could no longer see each other was that they were already too far apart.

The girl began to wonder when the village would end; but the depressing terraces ribboned on without a break under the overhanging slag heaps, with their sludge-green and rusty growth, and the bare hills behind. A river of dull yellow water slurped along the floor of the valley, with a railway line beside it. When trains steamed through, the smoke belched hotly from their funnels and changed into soot, which rose on the air currents to merge with the smog and settle back on the community.

They passed above gaunt, alien buildings grouped about a mine shaft, and the boy David explained the chimneys and chutes, girders, wheels, cages and the headgear, and that he would be joining his father down the pit in a year or so.

"Wouldn't you like it better on a farm, working out in the open fields?" she asked, and received a glance of contempt.

"Everybody goes down the pit here. My grandfather was a collier, and his father; even my grandmother went down when she was young."

They had been walking for over an hour and climbed on without pause. The lines of hovels were backed by others and, beyond those, more. Dozens, to hundreds, to thousands, all housing the human fodder of the coal mines. There were curtains at the windows, and she knew there was meat on the tables that the poor of Ireland would have brawled to taste. But the mind-paralysing ugliness around her was something at least that the Irish never had to endure.

Another hour passed and she began to believe that there was in fact no end to the road; that it would continue through the mountains and on as far as England and maybe even connect up with the coalfields Ifor had told her were in that land too. Then, without warning, they passed the George IV Inn, crossed a bridge and were on the flat band of country which runs along the foot of the Black Mountains.

Dai Williams' farm lay on the slopes at an angle of sixty degrees. Drystone walls protected his lower fields, but his sheep ran free over the rocky steeps above. He had seen the girl and boy approaching and was waiting at the gate to his yard.

Her lurchers rushed forward with yelps of greeting, and behind him, to her joy, Macha saw her horses. When she called, they nosed forward, blowing recognition through their nostrils. Their eyes and coats shone with health, their hooves had been pared and treated with linseed oil and they had been re-shod. At the back of the bunch, bounding to join his mother, the colt appeared like a young noble.

The farmer was watching her face with satisfaction.

"Looking a bit better than when they arrived, isn't it? And so do you, gypsy girl. Why, I would not have known you."

She began to thank him, but he waved dismissively. "Mother is expecting us in the house."

He led the way, and an old hag with wispy grey hair stood warily close to the fire as they entered. She served tea and a sweet, plummed bread without encouragement, and Macha was embarrassed to eat.

"If you tell me the cost, I will pay for the ponies' keep," she offered.

"And the dogs," put in the woman.

"And the dogs," Macha agreed hastily, opening the tin box.

Dai Williams and his mother craned forward and drew in audible breaths at the sight of the money and jewellery.

"Bread is nothing at all without jam, I am sure," old Mrs. Williams said, suddenly wreathed in smiles and placing a pot of homemade conserve before her guest. "Help yourself! Help yourself!"

"And then you must take a look over the farm before you go," added her son, rubbing his hands, and Macha had barely time to finish the slice before the plate was whipped away and she was being bustled back to the yard.

The waggon shed stored a harvest cart and pony trap, a plough, harrows and other farm implements and, in the most prominent position, a freshly painted spring cart fitted with a canvas cover supported on a wooden frame. Dai Williams stopped purposefully in front of it.

"What do you think of that, then?"

"A grand vehicle," Macha responded, sidestepping towards the stable.

Her ponies shuffled after them full of curiosity. The stalls in the building were empty, except for one, in which was tethered a grey cob with a docked tail.

"Have you ever seen a finer animal?" Dai Williams had somehow moved swiftly in front of her and was there, leading the creature out. "You trade in horses, and I would be willing to give up a Sunday you don't see many like this, but."

The cob looked very useful. He had a deep, strong body, short legs, powerful hocks and a kind eye.

"I've enough horses," said Macha.

"Now, that's just what I wanted to talk to you about," he rejoined, with a winning grin. "You've a pony that would do very nicely for our gig; of course, he's a good bit older than Prince, here, but I thought we might come to an arrangement to suit us both."

He pointed to a neat brown gelding she had brought from Ireland. "What do you say to giving me fifteen pounds and the pony?"

Macha opened her mouth to protest, then closed it. After an unbroken tradition of haggling, it was almost impossible to refrain, but she owed a debt of gratitude to the man and so nodded silently.

They slapped hands on the deal. The pony was whisked into the stall vacated by the cob, and before she could put up her guard, they were standing before the spring cart once again.

"You need a good cart, that's what you need," the farmer was saying urgently. "If you'd had a cart like this, with proper shelter from the weather, you would never have got in such a state of bad health, would you? Young David tells me you're going to England, which is a long distance, and after what you've been through, you'll have to keep warm and dry on the way. It rains a terrible amount in Wales, you know, a terrible amount."

"How much?" Macha was resigned, and besides, she accepted the point of the argument. It would be safer and more comfortable to journey in a covered cart, and this one looked in excellent condition.

"Eighteen pounds—a bargain."

"Eighteen pounds! I could buy brand-new for that!"

"Not with a canvas you could not." Dai Williams looked hurt. "And it is practically new, no more than twelve months old."

She gave in, speechlessly.

He returned to the house like a weightless man, almost skipping over the ground. Inside, he took a grubby piece of paper covered with scribbles off the dresser and murmured laboriously under his breath for a few minutes, his expression screwed up with the effort. Finally the creases smoothed into a face-consuming smirk, as he announced the totals.

"That's fifteen pounds for the cob and eighteen pounds the cart and let's say another two pounds for harness and five pounds for the keep of your ponies and dogs. That would be forty pounds altogether, now."

His old mother's eyes were like treen bowls as Macha counted out the sovereigns and tried to shut her mind to the strain of not beating him down, while vowing never again to buy or sell without haggling properly first.

Dai Williams was right. It did rain in Wales. In fact, it rained without stopping as Macha crossed out of the Rhondda and climbed to Merthyr Tydfil. Rain shrouded the whole route, hiding the stacks of slack and the mountains behind a screen of vapour, stirring the mud on the beds of the mustard-coloured rivers and turning the smoke into a tar to be spewed over the walls and roofs of the little houses. All visibility was reduced to a circumference of a few yards. The rain battered the canvas and weaselled through joins to trickle to the floor of the cart and be absorbed into the clothes and blanket lying there. It did not gurgle and plash and giggle like the rain of Ireland, but flung itself into her face like gravel and flayed the heads and backs of the horses and hissed and spat, attacking like a fighting beast.

She journeyed on to Abergavenny and turned towards England, finally reaching Gloucestershire without having discovered the glory of Snowdon, or gazed over the emotion-rousing vistas from Brecon Beacon; believing that the country she left behind so thankfully was no more than a heavy and dark land of fuliginous stretches of water, towering soot-encrusted buildings and iron-girded bridges. Only Sian Williams' moon-white skin and lips like strawberries and long black hair and brows and lashes and witch-black eyes remained like a pearl amongst her cheerless memories of the place.

No wall or fence marked the border, nor did she notice even a signpost, and yet the frontier had been unmistakably crossed. The difference was as emphatic as a change of world. England was luscious with autumn, her trees hung with gilded fruit, her fields left butter-yellow by the cut corn. Golden motes swirled in the sunbeams, and the leaves were turning to yellow curls.

Macha did not hurry over the rosy slopes of the Cotswolds. She lingered in the harlequin woods and by the fresh streams, content to be seduced. It was a time of recovery. England, with gentle warmth and soft light, calmed and healed and renewed, and the girl, who had previously imagined this to be the centre of all iniquity, followed its tender prompting. She ate well and looked after herself carefully, refusing to think of past or future, but living from day to day, filling the hours with leisurely travel and the grooming and tending of her animals.

Once or twice she took casual work, picking apples and pears for orchard owners. The farms were prosperous, and trading was easy. In Stroud, she sold a couple of workhorses for prices which would have made her blink had she been less of an expert at appearing inscrutable during such transactions. Instinct told her that she was moving into a higher market, and she bought a stylish twelve-year-old hack in their place, then sold him for a fine profit while on her way back to her camp. It was a night for celebration.

She walked to the public house at Slad, where the young men exchanged looks when she boldly ordered a pot of cider. As she raised it to her lips, an old man by the fire slyly beckoned her over, pulled a red-hot poker from the embers and plunged it into the stone tankard.

The cider bubbled and fizzed, foaming over the rim and throwing up stinging fumes. When she took the first sip, it clanged against her tongue like a bell. It was not thick and sweet like Guinness, nor fiery like whiskey, but deceptively thin and smelling of September. She wrinkled her nose, unsure, and they all laughed.

" 'Twill do you no harm, maid. Drink it down."

She held her breath and swallowed, and before she had half-finished, one youth more impudent than the rest placed another pot before her like a challenge. His companions nudged each other and guffawed, but she knew it was feeble stuff compared with porther and so gulped it down.

The faces around her seemed to grow strangely distorted and mobile, noses bulbous and then receding, eyes bulging and cheek-bones swelling. She could see two of everything. It was as though she were drunk, although that was not possible. She was well into her third pint when she began to talk to those around her.

"Ssshhhld tirshhish thsh mirn," she heard herself say and was surprised to find that her mouth had grown too small to accommodate her teeth.

The vacant place on the bench looked inviting, and suddenly she was sitting there. Her eyes closed for only a moment, but when she opened them again, all the lamps had been turned out and the landlord was shaking her and shouting rudely.

It was cold outside. Large stones and shrubs kept blocking the track, and some fool had dug a ditch right across it at one point, so that she fell in and turned her ankle, as well as receiving a soaking. The bender tent seemed much further off than when she had set out earlier that evening, and she began to imagine footsteps in the night behind her, cracking twigs and rustling foliage, and the breath of someone large. There was sniggering and a cough, and her fragile new confidence began to disintegrate. The pain in her ankle prevented her from running, but it rapidly brought a semblance of sobriety, and as the copse appeared like a huge black flower in the starlight, she knew these were no imaginings. Someone was there. Macha felt in the pouch sewn into her skirt.

Hurrying and panting, and then they were standing in her way, looking down and swaggering, the bold one from the pub and two of his friends. They were sweating and excited. Macha grasped the carved horn handle. Their hands reached out, and her arm was seized. She slashed about wildly with her knife and heard their astonished cries of pain as she hobbled into the trees.

The lurchers began snarling, and she cut them loose, to hurtle, howling, after the intruders. A cacophony of baying and cursing exploded over the sleeping valley and retreated as the dogs pursued their quarry back to the village.

Macha resignedly dismantled and packed the tent, gathered her cooking utensils, removed the hobbles from her grazing horses, harnessing the cob to the cart and, lastly, with considerable reluctance, rolling up her straw mattress, which had been laid out in readiness for her tired return. The local lads might have intended no real harm, but that did not matter now. The incident would offend local people and perhaps bring the police. It was time to move on.

The barking sounded a long way off. She gave a number of piercing whistles, hopped into the cart and flapped the reins. The grey stepped into the lane, and seconds later, the dogs returned to their usual place between the wheels.

By the time they came looking in the morning, she was out of the county and still heading south, swearing never to touch another drop of cider as each jolt cleaved her head like an axe blow.

The first travelling families seen since leaving Ireland passed her near Bath, stared with undisguised curiosity, and drove on. That they obviously did not recognise her at all brought an odd feeling of release, and all at once, the fact that this was truly the beginning of another life was given meaning.

Here was an unexplored country where no-one had ever heard of Jack Sheridan, or Coper Molloy, or her past wickedness. Here she could do anything and be anybody she chose. It was no longer necessary even to be a traveller, if she did not wish, and with that ludicrous thought, she drew up behind a hedge on the edge of some common land and, still smiling at the idea, spread the mattress inside the cart and gratefully slept off the unpleasant effects of the previous night, which had obviously left her slightly deranged.

It was only a short walk to the city. In the late afternoon of her arrival, its lights had clustered in the bowl of land below like snowdrops. After sleeping fully twelve hours, Macha decided to replenish her stores, which were almost finished. The sky was a delicate, cloudless blue when she crawled from the warmth of the blanket and stood up.

Bath rose from the misty sea of its gardens and parks like an amber island, its crescents and spires as fragile as honeycomb, its famous stone flaxen in the early sunlight of this morning.

Macha almost ran down the hill. Grand houses behind mature trees lined the wide avenue which led into the Royal Crescent, which even to her untutored eye was immaculate in its discipline of unadorned sash windows, with their slender wooden glazing bars and panelled, dignified doors. She stopped to savour the graceful sweep and the delightful view over Royal Victoria Park and found herself thinking that if ever she had to live in a house, it should be in a house such as one of these.

The terrace led to a circus of equal style and harmony, and soon she was in the centre of the city, so neatly laced in by the river Avon. There were shops such as she had never seen, not even in Dublin, full of exquisite fabrics, and marvellous hats, and shoes so tiny and bejewelled that it was incredible that anyone should allow them to touch the ground, let alone try to walk in them; shops displaying sofas and chairs, covered in flowered material and more luxuriously upholstered than feather beds; shops selling only paintings, or nothing but books, and then, most entrancing of all, a shop filled with toys.

Macha pressed her face against the glass in childish wonder. There were china dolls dressed like fashion plates, and puppets, and tambourines, a doll's house open to reveal three floors divided into perfectly furnished rooms, a rocking horse saddled and bridled in leather, a wooden boat surrounded by pairs of extraordinary wooden animals, some with long necks and some with huge ears and others covered in stripes and spots and then two with humps in the middle of their backs. It was an amazing place. Macha looked longingly at the rocking horse with his lively eye and bounding legs and dappled hindquarters and grinned at herself for being so silly, but she would have loved to have just a little ride on his back.

It was then that she saw the merry-go-round in the bottom corner of the window, seven gaily painted horses with gold-tipped ears and golden manes and tails on a miniature roundabout with a red-and-white-striped roof. It was irresistible. Macha opened the door of the shop and entered.

"Out! Out! Get out of here this instant!"

A fat man with an exaggerated moustache leapt at her with unexpected agility and waved pudgy hands.

"No gypsies. What are you trying to do? Drive my customers away? Coming in here with your dirty face and filthy clothes."

"But I want to buy something," Macha protested as he bundled her back to the door.

"I wouldn't sell you the crown jewels. Now, be off with you and don't come back!"

He gave her a hearty shove, which sent her into the street to land on her back in the gutter. A carriage and pair threw mud all over her as it passed, and the driver did not even notice, but two arrogant ladies did and drew their furs more tightly about them, turning their faces away in disgust.

Shame gave way to rage as Macha stumbled back to the spring cart. She slapped down the welcoming dogs in frustration and fed the horses without spending the usual time fondling and talking to them. Then she erected the bender and flounced inside, without even lighting a fire or preparing food for herself.

For a long time she lay staring up at the arch of hazel rods, imagining all the clever retorts she could have made to the fat man had she thought of them in time, and then how she would arrive at his door on some future date, immensely rich, in her own brougham with footman and liveried coachman, to buy up his shop for a pittance and have him thrown into the gutter as she had been. Then she began to cry over the humiliation that she, Macha Molloy, who had bought gold in the finest shop in Cork, who owned a colt sired by Gallinule, had been refused an infant's toy. Everyone in Ireland had been right. England was hateful.

Much later, unable to sleep, she foraged for a piece of stale bread and a drink of cold water and mollified the dogs by inviting them into the tent to sleep beside her and provide warmth. Because of the unpleasant affair, she had forgotten to buy supplies and would have to return to the town the next day.

The two proud ladies with their furs and scornful expressions haunted her; the way they had minced off as she floundered in the dregs. She remembered their feathered hats and bandboxes. She thought of all the other women she had seen that day in balloon-sleeved jackets and bell-shaped skirts, carrying muffs and with peculiar, fluffy little dogs tripping along at their feet on the end of light leads. No self-respecting girl would want to look so stupid. And yet they were self-respecting, and respected. The toy-shop owner would not have dared evict one of them. Wherever they went, people bowed and opened doors and begged to serve them. Suddenly, she wished desperately that she had a looking glass.

Macha, starting out in this foreign territory, felt confused and began to wonder about views she had always held without question, views about moving from place to place, about her ambition to own and live in another *varda*, about home being wherever she chose to stop on the open road. In fact, without realising it, she was examining her beliefs about freedom.

Also, it would soon be winter, when for months the bender tent would be wet and bitterly cold. And Gold, her treasured foal, her hope for tomorrow, was already showing promise in line and bone. He would need training, and that meant established conditions and a regular daily programme, which could not be postponed because there was nowhere to gallop, or because they were on someone's land, or too near houses, or being harassed by police or local authorities, or any of the other complications which disturbed a traveller's days. By dawn, Macha had reached the most important decision of her life.

There was a spring running out of the hillside, and stripping off all her clothes, she crouched in the stream it fed and washed herself. Having no soap, she used a rag to rub her skin so hard that the icy water's bite seemed mild by comparison, and when she was certain not an inch had been missed, she ducked her whole head in and scrubbed and scratched at it until sure that every flea must have drowned or deserted. She emerged pink and tingling and dried herself with the blanket. From her bundle of possessions, she drew out her tenderly wrapped wedding garments and put them on: the lawn knickers she and the girls at Tara had sniggered over, then a camisole, the three white silk petticoats and the cream chiffon blouse, and lastly, the pink satin skirt with its trim of coloured ribbons. Pinning on her old shawl with the gold shamrock brooch and hoping her friend Sian Williams was praying for her, she descended once more to Bath.

There was a second-hand shop in Cheap Street near the market. She had passed it the previous day and now returned there to buy a plain navy blue coat in Imperial cloth and a blue velvet hat dressed with feathers and a bow. Clad in these and feeling distinctly ill-at-ease, she walked to the nearest haberdashery and purchased the finishing touch, a pair of black doeskin gloves, which cost one shilling and sixpence.

The sound of laughter came through the open door of a market pub. Looking in, she could see the crowd of porters with full jars in their fists, and the desire for a good measure of whiskey to boost her audacity was almost too strong. Only the certainty that no lady could possibly smell of spirits restrained her, and straightening her shoulders, she marched resolutely up the High Street, along Broad Street and into the toy shop.

The fat man came scurrying forward, his puffy hands clasped together and his florid cheeks quivering as he nodded his head and smiled obsequiously.

"Can I help, madam?"

He did not recognise her at all.

"I'll take the merry-go-round," she said with hauteur.

"Certainly. Certainly."

He bustled to the window and turned, holding it out. Then his eyes travelled down her costume, and his smile froze as they fixed upon her hefty leather farm boots.

Macha coolly plucked the toy from him and held out the money. He took it automatically, and within minutes, she was striding through the market, singing aloud in triumph.

"You're happy today, miss," a stallholder called out.

"Going to see her young man, it's a sovereign to a penny," put in his neighbour, a woman selling eggs from a basket.

The girl bought two dozen, and some potatoes, onions and carrots from the man, then picked good lean mutton and two fat pork chops from a butcher's display. Further on, she bought some sherry wine, because she had heard of it, but never tasted it. All the traders were attentive and polite, wrapping the goods, and the butcher even offering to deliver to her house. It was as though the wearing of a simple coat and hat had changed her into a different person.

On the way home, she set one last test and, greatly daring, entered a tea shop. It was full of fashionable women, none of whom gave her more than a cursory glance as a waitress younger than herself showed her to a place and brought her order. Macha relaxed with her elbows on the table, dunking the biscuits in the tea until they were so soft that there was hardly time to catch them in her mouth before they disintegrated.

The affronted glares of the women seated nearest to her were sharper than hat pins. The girl bent her head, pretending to rearrange her parcels, until they lost interest. She could not think what was wrong and smoothed down her coat, checking the buttons, before surreptitiously inspecting her neighbours more closely. They sat very stiffly and did not raise their cups in both hands as she did, but held the handle between two fingers and thumb, taking sips which would not have quenched a bee and eating their cakes and biscuits with mouse-like nibbles, which made the whole process take a very long time. Macha copied and waited for more stares, but they continued talking to each other as though she were behaving perfectly normally.

Her nerves were frayed by the time she returned to the site. Neither horse stealing or dealing had ever left her so shaken. It had been the most extraordinary day. Now, being alone again under the night sky, doing the ordinary tasks of laying the fire and cooking felt like an escape. As the stew bubbled and the potatoes charred in the hot ashes, she twirled the carousel and discovered a little key in the base. Turning it made the horses revolve, and then, to her delight, it began to tinkle a tune with silvery notes. A musical box!

To Macha it was a sign of approval of her decision of the morning, a good omen for the future. Her pluck returned and she knew she would succeed.

It seemed wise to go where the winter climate would be mildest, especially as she did not know what sort of conditions might have to be endured. Perhaps she would not find the right place. After all, the requirements were very specific: a long, wide, flat piece of open country; a large, warm shed; no prying or antagonistic settled people nearby; yet not too far from good roads and possibly a railway. It did not cross her mind that such a location might not exist.

Meanwhile, it was vital to add to the money in the tin box; so as she travelled, she traded cocktails and confidentials, blood weeds and flat-catchers, fresh-legged youngsters and worn-out hobbies, screws, tits and jades.

The days were growing shorter, and she rose very early to have her horses groomed and actually positioned before sales started at Devizes and Warminster and over the plain at Salisbury. In this way, with luck she could sell quickly and have plenty of time to buy up the best bargains, overhear useful gossip about the nags and be back at her chosen pitch by afternoon, while there was still enough light to work the necessary "improvements" on her purchases, by applying a little stain to cover broken knees, or a file and hot iron to teeth (causing ten years to disappear miraculously from an aging mouth), by beaning the lame sound, or simply disguising with colour and clippers a horse which was a well-known rogue locally but with such aid, could yet find a buyer within a few miles.

Along the way, she dealt with rectors and doctors, a manor house and numerous tradesmen, sometimes taking corn and hay as part of the price and once, accepting a side-saddle and lady's used riding habit, complete with shabby top hat, veil and remarkably large boots, in return for a child's bad-tempered pony.

The end of the season came almost without warning. Those requiring hunters had found them; draught horses had already grown accustomed to new drivers and park hacks to new mistresses. At the apex of the equine world, Thoroughbred mares were tranquilly growing next year's priceless progeny, while their owners attempted spiritual bribery for some guarantee that they would not give birth before the 31st December, and willed them all to foal on New Year's Day. At the lowest end of the market, the bolters and rearers, the cat-hammed, cock-throttled, herring-gutted, broken-winded and chink-backs had already grown their scruffy winter coats and lost what little condition they had gained in summer.

The last sale at Ringwood offered nothing worth buying, even to Macha's skilled eye, and she had nothing to sell. Trading was over until spring. She counted up her profit and scrutinized the few genuine animals carefully kept as future investment and was pleased. She had done very well indeed.

The New Forest, with its secret and intimate nooks, its bracken-covered glades and close-cropped clearings, beguiled her with sightings of fallow deer and badgers and a minute mouse with a long, pointed nose which she did not recognise as a shrew, because no such creature existed in Ireland; but, above all with its herds of wild ponies, which nosed without fear around her tent.

Romanies camped there often, leaving behind only ash circles where their fires had burned. Macha had seen them in Ringwood and Lyndhurst, unknown and yet familiar faces. They had looked at her curiously, identifying one of their own, but not approaching out of respect for her obvious wish for privacy. The forest offered security and tolerance.

Gold grazed alongside the mare as the girl considered the possibilities. He was hard and fit from travelling the road. He had good feet and wind and the playful temperament befitting a high-spirited baby. From the day of his birth, she had handled him continuously—first guiding him near the mare, with one arm round his chest and the other round his hindquarters; then fitting on a little headcollar, by which he had soon become accustomed to being led; picking up his hooves, opening his mouth, grooming and petting him. Now it was time he was weaned, and this winter would be the most important of his life, when he would need the best of hay and corn to ensure that his development continued unhindered.

The girl knew the forest would protect him from exposure to wind and snow, yet was reluctant to abandon her aim while conditions were still so easy, and also because she suspected this was to be her last journey.

They would go on for a few more days, she decided, just to see what lay on the other side of the large port to the east. So, hitching the string of ponies behind the cart, she followed the great thrust of the Solent inland, marvelling at the lines of ships chugging and steaming and sailing purposefully to and fro and wondering where they had come from and where they were going, their fog-horns sounding so grand and important, booming across Southampton as she passed and resounding through her sleep.

Then, as they faded and died in the distance, she saw ahead the rolling, voluptuous contours of the Sussex Downs, billowy, green and peaceful, unthreatened by crags or chasms, dangerous cliffs or peaks of grandeur, gentle on the eye, serene and timeless, undulating down to the sea, magical under the sinking sun and the moon rising in the same sky. Macha drove into their fold as though magnetised.

A grove of trees, some of mighty girth, grew in the vale where she spent the night, watched over by the kindly wraiths of Druids who had once worshipped there. For the first time since leaving Rosslare, she felt happy, sensing that the place she searched for was only a handspan away.

The next day, she managed to don the riding habit, after a struggle with its voluminous skirt, and put the side-saddle on a bay gelding, which fortunately behaved like a perfect gentleman as she tried clumsily to maintain balance and sit straight, the way the ladies had done when out hunting in Ireland. Somewhat shakily and much later than planned, she set out along the bridleway which led round Crows Hall Farm and over Haye's Down before climbing smoothly.

It was a breezy, exhilarating morning. Had she been riding astride, she would have galloped over the rotund, smooth slopes, so perfect for exercising and building muscle in a fine young horse. Bracken, red as a fox and crisp as straw, edged the path, and beechwoods, bronzed and crackling with dried leaves, drifted away to the left as the trail widened into a way, which opened out above the weald, rising steadily and studded with many hoofprints.

Macha felt her pulse speed. The gelding, sensing her mood, tossed his head and swung his quarters, sidling over the grass, flintstones sparking against his shoes. The air smelt of herbs and sea and horses. The turf was springy. Macha pressed her right leg over the up-pommel and her left against the leaping-head, leant back slightly and let him go just enough to canter on until their progress was unexpectedly checked by a solid circular rampart, where she reined in, flushed and highly pleased at having kept her seat.

There was an inturned entrance, through which she passed, and she discerned a series of faint rings set in the ground. This fastness seemed familiar, perhaps because of its great age, as though tied to other places she knew.

The Downs bowled before her for mile upon mile, like pale green cloud, their combes marked only by insubstantial maroon shadows, their hangers brooding smokily over villages of cottages clustered as tightly as toadstools. A town with a massive church, new spire shining, lay almost directly below on the level coastal plain, and beyond, the haze of the English Channel floated into the sky, so that the Isle of Wight seemed suspended between them.

A kestrel quivered ahead, like a sign. Her eyes automatically followed its line and saw, set on a ridge directly below, the white-railed elegance of a most beautiful racecourse. The straight, overlooked by a grandstand, stretched for almost a mile before turning into a figure of eight surrounded by trees. She had arrived.

Macha sat on her horse absorbing everything of the shapes and sounds: the wind lisping in the grass and humming in the branches of the spindle tree, berries and gulls bobbing, churches and milk churns chiming, geese and inns cackling, gorse and chimneys flowering, sheep veering like blown snow before a dog and following their master meekly, the racecourse, cool as a lake, challenging as a thrown-down glove, an unknown future locked in its eternal loops. As she sat, the air grew cold, but she did not care.

"Ye've been here a time, missy. Be ye well enough?"

A very old man had ridden up unheard, but she was not startled. She had almost expected him. He had a strong local burr, the words so round and furry in her ears that it was not easy to separate them into sense.

"I could not be better if I had two hearts and had grown twelve inches more," she replied with a smile. "I was just thinking that here is a lovely scene indeed. You could travel for a ship's life across the oceans and never land on such a shore."

He wore a high-crowned hat and thick tweed jacket, and looked too prosperous to be a labourer. She guessed he was a farmer.

"What part do ye come from, then?" he asked, pulling at his beard, his head on one side with curiosity.

"I was born in Ireland, sir, and lived there till my darling father was taken to heaven." She looked suitably tragic. "My dear mother brought me to Wales, and then she too went to the angels."

"And now you're all alone in the world, child?" He shook his head, anticipating the sad confirmation.

"There's just me and my brother. We are twins, sir."

Long before, she had worked out the answers to inevitable questions, and to prevent further enquiry, she now changed the subject to one of her own.

"Could you do me the kindness of giving me the name of the racecourse down there?"

"Why, missy, where else would that be but glorious Goodwood?"

He looked quite taken aback by her ignorance, and Macha gazed at the sweep of emerald again, this time with awe. Newmarket, Ascot, Epsom, Goodwood—Molloy had told her of them all, with regular reports of races held there during their two summers together.

"There's some fair horses come over from Ireland," said the old man, conversationally. "I've won a few wagers on Irish runners."

"The best!" she rejoined, and added, casually, "My brother and I have a few horses ourselves. That's why we're here: searching for somewhere to live and keep them."

"Well, there are houses aplenty in this county of Sussex," he said. "With stables and yards and paddocks and barns enough to keep fifty horses, and I don't suppose ye have as many as that."

"Merciful saints, we have not. And being orphans, we have not the means for such a house and buildings as you describe. No, sir, what we must find is a little cabin with just a wood shed or two and the smallest piece of land for rent."

"And what would ye pay for this plot?" He gave her an oddly veiled look, at once intent and distant, from under the brim of his hat, and she blushed.

It was not difficult to appear helpless, for she had no experience in such a matter and no idea of what constituted a fair price—and farmers were not renowned for their generosity.

"That's not easy, sir. How could I say without seeing it?"

He nodded approval.

"Where is this brother of yours? And what do they call ye both?"

"Our name is Sheridan," she answered, then pointed back to Chichester. "My brother is at our lodgings, near the church."

"The cathedral," he corrected. "And what have ye done with your horses?"

"We left them, all but two, on grazing in the forest." She waved vaguely in the direction of Southampton and hoped he would not ask for precise details.

"Well, missy, come ye with me and see some'at," he said, with a roguish chuckle, adding, before she could hesitate, "There's nothing to fear. My name is Harold Locksash, and I was born no more'n a mile from here near eighty year ago. I'm known to all, and some of that land yonder is mine."

His mount, which seemed almost as aged as he, turned and began walking ponderously downhill, branching off from the path by which she had arrived to lead the way through the woods. There Macha caught up, to ride alongside and listen to him telling of a hunt which had once run to and fro across the country from Charlton to East Dean Woods, through Lady Lewknor's Puttocks and back twice, on almost to Cowdray Park, returning through Goodwood Park and on as far as Slindon, through Houghton Forest, eventually ending at the wall of the Arundel River after a chase of ten hours.

He recalled days with the guns, and cricket matches, point-to-points and cycle races. They rode through West Dean, crossed the railway line and over Heathbarn Down to reach more woodland, passing alarmingly close to the dingle where the covered cart and ponies waited. However, they skirted a hill to the right and entered another, even thicker wood, on whose far side they came quite suddenly upon an empty thatch-roofed cottage, beside which stood a low L-shaped flintstone building comprising a cowshed, store and stable.

"How would this do ye and your brother?" asked Harold Locksash. "There's five acre goes wi' it."

Macha did not notice that the thatch was leaking and the wooden doors and windows were soft with rot, or that the hedges round the two small fields needed laying and there were only gaps where gates should have been. She saw an almost secret place, sheltered from weather and people by the density of Wildham Wood, yet less than three miles from wide-open gallops. She saw four stalls in the stable and grass for her horses' keep. It did not even occur to her to inspect the cottage.

The expression on her face was a mixture of eagerness and apprehension as she asked his price.

"Well, 'tis a fine property, ye know: good stout walls, fertile land."

She held her breath.

"I could not let it go for less than five pound."

Five pounds! Five pounds what? A half-year? A quarter? Surely, he could not mean five pounds a month! Whatever figure he mentioned would have seemed outrageous to someone who had never paid a penny for the right to have a roof over her head.

He gave her another of those enigmatic glances through milky irises, which was when she realised he was almost blind. Mischievously, he was waiting to find out what she would do. Then he relented and said, "Don't ye fret, Miss Sheridan. I like a woman who knows horses, and I would not diddle ye. Five pound a year, to be paid each Michaelmas. Now, what do you say to that?"

"I . . . We'll take it," she agreed firmly, and they shook hands.

Chapter EIGHT

This was the beginning. Old Locksash had neither ordered her off his land nor expected her to accept casual labour on his farm, the only two alternatives normally offered to tinkers. He had given her a position in society, however lowly. She was a tenant and could no longer be harried by authorities or police from this, her chosen home.

The thought quite perturbed Macha as she dismantled the cover from the cart before driving, together with the horses, to the cottage. She was astute enough to realise that local people would be curious about a newcomer and probably expect attitudes and behaviour which were unknown to her. Even by exercising extreme caution at all times, she might yet betray herself, unwittingly.

However, the invention of a mythical brother had been a brainwave. She knew enough about the world to appreciate that a young, single woman could never be permitted to rent a property and live there alone. A *brother* provided protection—apart from which, the restrictions of the side-saddle were intolerable. It might look graceful, but it was a nonsensical way to ride a horse and would not do at all when the time came to break in the colt.

In the guise of her *brother*, she drove to Chichester the next day and enthusiastically, bought one or two cheap pieces of second-hand furniture and some more boy's "left-off" clothes from a stall. On her return, it took nearly an hour to work out how to set up the bed, and then she had no tools to tighten the bolts. Even to her eyes, the kitchen looked bare with only two wooden chairs and a table, and she was glad that her landlord was too polite to enter when he called that afternoon for the first year's payment.

The simple pattern of her life was partly established by a wet and windy December, which filled the track to her cottage with mud and kept folk indoors. The parson from East Marden paid a duty visit and lost interest on learning that she was Roman Catholic, and no doubt this news also deterred a number of busybodies who might otherwise have called. Those whose inquisitiveness could not be restrained were met either by an ungainly Irish boy whose sister was out or by the girl herself, who was remarkably unforthcoming. They felt their excursions had been a waste of effort and did not return.

So Macha was left to her own devices, apart from the occasional appearance of the farmer, who turned out to be a kindly and lonely old widower, liking nothing better than to talk of horses and the sporting days of his youth; and, who, if he sensed anything odd about his tenant, enjoyed the company and interest too much to admit it.

Every day, regardless of the weather, the girl rode out on one of the horses over the Downs, and soon knew the countryside better than many who had been born there but spent inactive days. Other riders, especially the followers of Lord Leconfield's foxhounds, saw her often, more than one young man attempting to attract her attention, but without success. The figure of Molloy remained so powerful in her mind, it was as though he were still alive.

Each fortnight, on market day she went to Chichester to shop. The outing was intended not only to buy food but also as education.

Ladies choosing fabrics, ordering goods, instructing their grooms, meeting friends and exchanging the latest gossip were not aware of being watched, but Macha noted every detail of their clothes and conduct and copied what she could.

The purchase of a coil of false hair over which to brush her own (still far too short after Biddy Connor's vicious wielding of the scissors in Ireland) considerably improved her appearance, as did the plushette pelisse and two worn gowns, which had been modernised by the removal of their bustles and the redesigning of their skirts and sleeves. After the mistake in Bath, she actually had a pair of pliant brown leather shoes specially made. They were fastened by no fewer than twelve little buttons and felt as soft as cream. They were her only extravagance.

At luncheon and tea, she became quite adept at eating without letting a spot of grease mark her bodice, or a crumb fall in her lap, despite the bizarre way of holding knife and fork, the restrictions of limited movement and the need for ramrod deportment.

But the overheard conversations between these well-bred women about matters and people she did not know remained incomprehensible. Who was Hors D'oeuvre? Apparently someone important, invited to dine everywhere. Why did it matter where you sat in a carriage? Was croquet a kind of card game? What sort of house was a yacht? At times she returned to the cottage quite downhearted over her own ignorance.

Gold was her consolation. Immediately Macha moved in, he had been weaned—shut in the stable, whinnying and squealing for his mother as she was led out of earshot to a well-fenced paddock temporarily lent for the purpose by Harold Locksash. He was a big, strong colt and had crashed around the stalls kicking over buckets and rearing at the partitions, smashing some of the worm-eaten wood, although Macha was far more afraid he would injure himself. The farmer advised tethering and hobbling him, but the girl felt this would be a greater risk, and after a few days, to her relief, he had calmed down, and before long, was being turned out with some of the older horses during the day. Much later, when the mare returned, they would behave like strangers.

"He'll need cutting come spring," the old man said, when she was in the yard dressed in cap and corduroy.

Gold playfully butted her in the small of the back as she considered the idea of gelding him.

"He's a Thoroughbred, you know," she pointed out.

"But he's going to be a boisterous brute, too much for a light lad like you to handle. Have him done and he'll be like a lamb."

"I think we'll wait a while to see how he turns out."

"Well, don't let him go screaming and striking about with his forelegs. Keep him in order." Harold Locksash studied him pensively. "He's a fine-looking young horse; reminds me a lot of one of your Irish stallions I saw run at Kempton Park and Sandown Park—a chestnut as big as a bull, with the same-shape blaze and white socks as your colt. Gallinule, that were his name. Ye will have heard of him, maybe."

"Oh, yes." Macha could not keep the grin from her face. "I've heard of him."

" 'Twas a rum thing about that horse, know ye. He ran well as a two-year-old, but he was a roarer and a bleeder—kept breaking blood vessels, and had to retire from racing. Yet he is siring some important horses now."

The green crochet hooks of new ferns and bracken appeared. Toads crouched below the entrance to beehives and snatched the first inhabitants to appear. There were skylark nests hidden on the ground under overhanging grasses, and the elms were dusty pink with blossom. It was past snowdrop time. It was spring.

Macha, who had enjoyed sleeping in a proper bed at night and sitting by the warm range during the February snows, suddenly found the cottage stifling and the hedges around the five acres restrictive. The desire to cross beyond the next hill, or through another wood, or to follow the straight line of the old Roman road on and on, gripped her, so that she could not walk or ride far enough to alleviate it, and in the end there was always the frustration of having to return to the same place every day.

Once, she built a fire outside and sat beside it, seeing the ghosts of others in the shadows and hearing their laughter echoing down the years from her childhood. She sat and remembered Connemara, where the light is as clear and pristine as on the first day of Creation and the white, satin sea is set with islands like spots of blood; she remembered the mountains and the tarns and the wheeling eagles, and wept, but was afraid to lay out her straw mattress and spend the whole night by the burning sticks in case someone saw and realised she was not a respectable girl, but a dirty tinker. She took to pacing obsessively up and down the kitchen, as though caged, and sometimes, thinking she heard an accordion or a fiddle playing in Wildham Wood, she would run out to see if travellers were camping there. They never were.

She was tortured by a mental restlessness which became as physical as a sickness, making her skin crawl and her eyes itch and her mouth dry. The cure would have been to escape through journeys to different regions and to fill her hours with fresh interest; but she was caught in her own scheme, from which there was no way out.

Everything she had to forget returned to torment her, and although the Connors might have been anywhere in Ireland and there was no way of contacting them, she began to long for the impossible. Pictures of her children forced their way back into her mind. She could smell their milky breath again and feel their downy hair and peachy skins and taste the delicate salt of them. Her angels. She wanted to crush them against her, to hold them, to hold Molloy, to hold anyone. The human touch—all at once she was starved for it.

Like women before and after her, Macha sublimated her yearning in work. She mucked out the stable and swept the yard until there was not a loose straw in sight; she scrubbed the kitchen floor and bought white distemper to paint inexpertly over the walls. She blocked gaps in the hedges and drove in two huge posts from which a gate was finally hung, saving the trouble of placing branches across the opening every time she turned out the horses.

Had the cottage and its buildings looked less spruce, there might have been no disaster, but old Harold Locksash had noticed all the work and was impressed. Arriving one morning when she was looking particularly tidy herself and was about to go into town, he issued the invitation.

"My daughter and her husband be coming up from Wiltshire next week, Miss Sheridan, and it would please me mightily if you and your brother would take tea with us on Wednesday afternoon. I know they would be gratified to meet ye both."

Macha looked at him in horror. Half a dozen excuses sprang to her lips; but she knew beyond doubt that there was absolutely no way she could refuse, and if her *brother* did not appear, the family would be justifiably insulted, and possibly suspicious as well.

In a double-edged way, by having the choice removed, her wish had been granted, because the only solution to this appalling problem was to leave the cottage and go back on the road. Lying in the small iron-framed bed that night, she put a hand up and felt her frowning brow and realised this was not what she wanted after all. She had grown to love Sussex and to enjoy the security of the old walls around her, being able to listen to the creaking trees from the snugness of her chair by the fire. She liked being clean and wearing gowns, and most of all, she liked the polite regard which came from being one of the settled people.

It was very early when she caught Macha's Girl and brought her up from a paddock damp with dew. The mare had remained her favourite ride, and despite the injuries received in Ireland, could still have left many a good horse behind. There was a rapport between the two. It was as though the mare knew the girl's emotions and behaved accordingly, prancing and playing up when she was happy, and going on quietly if she was sad.

This was to be their last hack over the Downs, and as they neared The Trundle above Goodwood and saw other horses working there, Macha's Girl pulled and bucked. A pair of Thoroughbreds had just started a trial over the gallops. The mare jerked her head violently, and her rider shortened the reins and urged her on.

They thundered up the incline, quickly closing in behind the two racehorses, whose lads looked back in surprise. The mare's stride lengthened and her ears strained as she passed the second horse with a flourish. The head wind stung Macha's eyes and scored her face, a counterblast against her frame, but she sat completely still, balanced like a ball on a wire. There was no need to compel with hands or legs, for the little horse had her own ambition. Skimming the turf like a swallow, she was narrowing the gap, body stretched, legs reaching. They drew alongside the lead horse, muscles powering tensile sinews, heart as big as a steam engine. A surge of exultation filled Macha. This was the way it had been in the race at Killarney, and she knew the mare remembered too. For one transcendent second, they raced level with the rival Thoroughbred, shoulder to shoulder, nose to nose. There was not a shadow in it.

It was enough. The girl steadied her horse, letting her give ground gradually. The two young sprinters sped ahead and disappeared over the ridge. Macha's Girl slowed to a jog and then a walk. Lather covered her like a fleece.

"You did that for me," said Macha, dismounting.

The mare looked at her owner with a composed and satisfied eye.

Macha laughed. "Be jabus! But you did it for yourself, too."

They moved unhurriedly downhill to cool and rest the mare, whose hooves crushed marjoram and basil and thyme, releasing their aromas into the morning. The mushroom-grey cloud turned pink and then retreated westward before the sun. There were celandines and daisies like confetti in the grass, wheatears and meadow pipits in the sky and a pale lace of buds over the branches.

"Where's the fairness in having to leave here?" the girl muttered aloud to herself. "MACHA OF THE HORSES, how can I train the grandest colt in the land if I'm to be pushed about all the time? When are you going to put a bit of real luck my way?"

And MACHA THE GODDESS heard. A miracle happened.

A shouting figure ran out of the trees, arms waving, ragged and wild as a banshee.

"Stop! Stop! If you take another pace, if a hair on your scabby head so much as falls forward, I'll take the scalp off you and dress a Scotsman's kilt with it."

Macha's eyes widened, and appreciating that it was better not to argue, she stopped.

"I know that horse. I'd know that horse if you surrounded Tattersalls Sales with the cavalry and hid her in the middle. How did you get hold of her? You stole her, that's how. The one that owns her would never have sold her, not if the Prince of Wales and all his courtiers along with the Lord Lieutenant of Ireland and the mayor of Galway City had made the order. You're a thieving little Turk, and I'm going to murther you into a hundred pieces."

His clothes were torn, and the toes showed through one boot where the sole had come apart. Tangles of his hair fell into his red-rimmed eyes, and his cheekbones, pushing through a crust of mud, were white. Gawky and very young, he had obviously been living rough and starving. The girl backed behind her horse for protection. He came up very close and stared at her crazily. She thought he was going to hit her. Macha's Girl snorted and lowered her head in warning. The youth's eyes filled with astonishment.

"Holies! But it's yourself! I'd know ye anywhere. You just had me foxed for a moment." He looked her up and down. "Mother of God! It must be a mortal sin!"

Then Macha recalled; so long ago. The boy on the strand, who had once begged to ride the mare.

"Those clothes you have on are a scandal," he said, heavy with disapproval.

"Just take a look at your own, Declan O'Brien," she retorted, and saw his face light up. "And I can't be standing here all day, letting the mare grow cold. She needs a feed, and so do I. What about yourself?"

"Yes . . . well, no. That is . . . there's no need to go bothering about me."

She was glad he still had spirit, whatever had befallen.

"No bother; I've colcannon and mutton enough for ten," she offered airily, and clicked to the mare.

He started following, and she turned.

"No. Don't walk with me. It might look bad. Come by in an hour, and don't be seen. It's the cottage three miles on, beyond Wildham Wood."

In the stable, the girl worked at top speed, allowing the horse a short drink, picking the mud out of her hooves and winding a rope of straw into a wisp with which to rub and slap her body all over to stimulate the circulation, before she was fed and left covered by a blanket of hessian, under which was a layer of straw for warmth.

Then, after splashing water from the mare's bucket over her own face and discarding clothes as she went, she ran into the cottage, pulled on one of her two gowns and her good shoes, drew her hair over the false coil and jabbed it into place with pins before busying herself about the kitchen as though she had been there all day.

Sometime later, when she opened the door to Declan O'Brien, he entered hesitantly, without taking his eyes off her, confused by the change, but she put a plate of food before him and talked as though everything were perfectly ordinary.

The sight of hot food stripped away all his pretence of indifference. He did not speak as he ate; indeed, he could not have done so, for his mouth had no time to empty before another spoonful was pushed in. Macha poured him English beer and he drank it like a thirsty dog, drew nearer the fire and stretched out his legs with a noisy sigh of pleasure.

For a while, he talked with the urgent hesitance of one who has been without social contact for many months. Long, grinding hours on poor land and too little grown to feed sixteen mouths had driven him, like so many others before, from home and family. He told of crossing the Irish Sea to England with a dream of becoming a jockey, of labouring on farms and being cheated, in his ignorance and innocence, of his pay.

He had slept in ditches and once even stolen a loaf from a kitchen windowsill, where it had been left to cool. At last, he had found work in a yard of 'chasers, only for the trainer to go bankrupt within weeks. Since then, he had wandered from stable to stable looking for employment and growing more desperate.

All at once, he stopped talking and instantly fell into a deep slumber.

Macha did not forget to whisper thanks to her divine patroness as she watched him slump in the chair. She laid out corduroy trousers and a shirt, waistcoat, jacket and hat and was standing before him when he finally awoke.

"There's a pump in the yard. Take off those old things you're wearing and have a good wash."

He jumped up, flustered, and was objecting loudly as she shoved him out.

"Scrub all over, mind, and your hair as well," she instructed, wickedly. "You'll find decent clothes in the doorway when you've finished."

He returned to find her waiting, scissors ready in her hand.

"Sit!" she commanded, and chopped his long wet hair short.

"Now get up and turn round and let's see you."

He looked clean, damp, thin and sheepish.

"You'll do." She rewarded him with another pot of beer. "Now here's the plan."

"If it's a weddin' you're after, it's as likely as a ferret biting a hedgehog, for I'm not wanting a wife, tink," he said, with a very frightened expression on his face.

"Well, glory be to the merciful will of God, if you haven't the cheek of O'Sullivan jigging on the holy sod before the wake." Macha did not know whether to be outraged or tickled. "If I could not do better than you, Declan O'Brien, I'd become a nun, and I'll thank you to remember in future that my name is Miss Sheridan. I might be a traveller, but I'm no tinker."

Crimson with embarrassment, he stared down at his feet and mumbled an apology, but before he finished, Macha's amusement had the better of her and she burst into peals of laughter, which threatened to overwhelm her periodically throughout the rest of the day, every time she thought of his reaction.

While still trying to control herself, she took a bottle of Scotch whisky and two cups from the cupboard and waved him to a seat before handing him a good measure and sitting down with her own. Then she told him of all her adventures in England, only omitting any mention of her reasons for leaving Ireland.

"So you see, it was a gallimaufry of a mess until you appeared."

"Beats Banaghan," agreed the boy. "But what difference do I make?"

"Did you leave your brains over the water? Don't you see, it's not a husband I'm needing, Declan O'Brien. It's a *brother*, and you're the very one."

"The Lord save us! I'm not getting into this!" he protested, starting up again and spilling his drink.

"Will ye stop all that leppin' up and down! Sure it's worse than three witches over a broomstick," she said, refilling the cup with calculated generosity. "Now, what have ye against it?"

"We'd not get away with it. What with you living here all winter, the whole world must know your so-called brother. What about the farmer? No, you can have back your clothes and I'll be on my way."

Macha explained, patiently: "Ould Locksash is about blind, and no-one else round here knows me or my *brother*. Still, you're obviously a man who knows his own mind, and you can keep the clothes."

As he shuffled awkwardly to his feet, avoiding her gaze, she leant forward to poke the fire, deliberately not speaking again until he reached the door, when she suggested, casually, "Before you go bolting off to workhouse comforts, will you not take the littlest peek at my few ponies?"

She led the way out of the cottage and across the yard to the lower paddock and leant on the gate.

"Now, what would you say to *him?*"

Gold was grazing with other horses, his coat burnished copper-red by the brightness of noon. He moved forward gracefully on slim, straight legs with white socks gleaming, then, as he noticed her, suddenly kicked up his heels and cantered off across the field.

Declan O'Brien stood shaking his head in silent admiration.

"He'll need breaking and training." She stole a sly glance at his face. "Then, when he's ready to race, won't he be needing a rider? And who better than my own brother?"

There was a long pause. The colt increased his speed to a gallop, as though aware of being on show. Declan O'Brien gave a groan of defeat.

"I'll do it," he said. "Though we'll be hounded to hell if it comes out."

Macha and Declan O'Brien visited the clothes stall in Chichester and found him a suit in reasonable condition. Afternoon tea at the farmhouse was a success and the fact that the boy did not speak much was not unusual.

"I do declare ye've growed an inch or two since ye came to live here, young Mr. Sheridan," commented Harold Locksash as they were leaving. "Must be our good Sussex air."

They all laughed.

"Right!" said Macha, when they returned home. "Now we can start some real work."

There were sales to attend, horses to buy and sell, money to be made—and most important of all, the colt to handle. With the hindrance of her double life removed, she was bouncing with enthusiasm, rattling off projects and ploys, bombarding him with ideas and dreams until he was bemused.

Declan O'Brien was by nature reserved. His upbringing in poverty on a remote Irish homestead had been severe and religious, leaving him feeling more at ease with animals than with other human beings. He had an eradicable sense of what was proper, and to him, Macha was quite definitely improper. All they had in common was an obsession with horses, and he was torn between terror of living with a fast woman and the desire to race her fast colt one day. Desire won, but he knew he would be damned for it.

However, he was allowed little opportunity to dwell on this, for she filled his time with so much activity that by the end of each day he was too tired to do more than sleep soundly.

The yearling was introduced to the bridle and a bit, fitted with keys, with which he played in his mouth for half an hour twice a day until he grew accustomed to it and was ready to be led. Then the metal bit was changed for one of rubber. He was taught to move forward freely while Macha or the boy walked at his shoulder. The lessons were short, always ending after he had done well and so he began to look forward to them. At a time when most horses were beaten into obedience, this was a peculiar approach, but Macha's instinct knew it was right.

Later in the year, long reins would be attached to the mouthpiece and he would be trained to walk, trot and canter in either a left-handed or right-handed circle, the exercises which would make him supple and balanced.

The other horses required regular exercise over the Downs and, although Declan O'Brien could never see her so without wincing, the girl still put on breeches and rode astride; but when she rode, he was silenced by the simple perfection of style and the way her mounts responded without any visible or audible command. She could whisper a vicious animal docile. It was as though she saw into their minds. But there were also her dealings between market and buyer, fascinating and shocking machinations from which he learnt hitherto unimagined cunning, despite the offence to his moral sensibilities.

Although he did not realise it, Macha had him summed up well. He was like so many of the settled people, and she was experienced enough to know how to cope with them. With subtlety, she decreed the terms of their relationship. He was paid a small wage every week, but she also cooked for him and washed his clothes. In this way, she retained the control of an employer, but they could live as friends, and as they were both alone and sometimes homesick for Ireland, it was an ideal arrangement.

Early in May, they spent a day at the races. Macha took much of her recent profits and they drove the cart to Singleton Station, from where the train took them to Salisbury, via changes at Chichester and Portsmouth.

It was to be a plain meeting, with no big prizes to attract the glamorous—just a straightforward programme of a Selling Plate, a couple of Handicaps and two Stakes; but it was her first visit to an English course, and she was in a state of high impatience to arrive. The racecourse lay some distance from the city, and the walk there took longer than expected. Had they not run the last quarter of a mile, the first race would have been over—and lost with it the chance which changed Macha's life.

As it was, the runners had left the paddock and already cantered down the mile-long straight to the start. Hurrying to the rails, she glanced at the Runners and Riders board and saw only one name. It was a message just for her.

"Hurry up, lady, or you'll be too late!" the bookmaker chivvied.

Without even having seen the horse, she handed him thirty pounds with shaking hands.

"Irish Coper, to win," she whispered, as the shouting crowd announced the off.

She could not look, only hear, the far-off rumble, breaking up into staccato drumbeats, the sobbing breaths and oaths and whistling whips, the final cacophony of sound. She opened her eyes.

"Who won?"

"Some outsider at 100–1," replied Declan O'Brien. "Irish Coper."

She had won. Three thousand pounds!

"Holy God! What will you do?" asked the flabbergasted Declan O'Brien as they sat in the train returning to Sussex.

"Everything!" she replied with certainty.

She had started in Salisbury by going straight to the Haunch of Venison Inn in Minster Street and treating them both to a gargantuan meal, which she had eaten with gusto, but he had hardly touched. Then, loading him down with a baron of beef and two broiling fowls, a jar of preserved pineapple and sweetmeats, bottles of whisky and port, she had hired a hansom cab to take them to the station.

"I'm going to do everything!" she repeated happily. "I'm going to dress in lace and velvet and chiffon. I'm going to be hung with jewels and wear hats with more feathers than a flock of birds and furs round my neck and wrists and the hems of my gowns and over my shoulders and lining my gloves and wrapped into muffs. I'm going to sleep between the finest hand-loomed, embroidered and hemstitched Irish linen sheets. I'm going to pour a whole bottle of French perfume over my head every morning and a bottle of champagne down my throat every night. I'm going to mix with the quality, going racing and dancing and wining and dining. So will you stop looking as though you've lost your best heifer to the debt collector and your sister to a teetotaller and the dog has eaten the last of the bacon. Cock ye up, man! The door of the world has just opened!"

He shook his head mournfully. "You'd be better to buy yourself a little place and put the rest of the fortune away in safety. There's no good can come of all that squandering and frippery."

"And what good will come of hiding all the money in safety? Arrah! That sounds a miserable and pinched kind of life to me. And I'd probably forget where I put it, anyway."

He could be very irritating, she thought inwardly, at the same time giving him a sweet smile. "Come on, now, Declan. We'll have a great time. And you needn't fret that it'll all be frittered. Do you think me so stupid? Most will be used wisely enough, you have my word on it."

His expression relaxed enough to tell her he was mollified, although it was obvious he was never going to develop into a character given to humour.

That evening she would have liked to go to some godless hall full of music and lights and handsome men and half-naked women, and sin. Sitting by the cottage fire seemed far too tame after the excitement of the day, even though the port was a splendid drink which touched the cheeks with heat and the mind with recklessness. After sipping much of a bottle and eating all the bonbons and chattering on about the amazing fantasies which were now within reach, she lolled in her chair and surveyed Declan O'Brien through half-closed eyes. The Scotch on the floor by his chair had diminished considerably, and he was beginning to look befuddled.

"I am thinking that the fact that I am now a woman of wealth and able to bring a handsome dowry might make the divil of a difference to your ideas," she said capriciously.

"What difference? What ideas?" He was bleary.

"Your ideas of a wedding, of course." She crossed the space between them like a cat. "Isn't every man wanting a rich wife?"

"What? What?"

He tried to sit upright, but failed. Macha stroked his hair and knelt beside him and walked her fingers slowly up his arm, talking all the time.

"Here we are, you and me, sitting in the same kitchen and then separated every night like sour milk. Do you not begin to think that is a pity, Declan O'Brien, now that I've won all this gold on the horses?"

"I do not. Will you get away!" His mien was one of sheer terror.

"Well, maybe you're right. Perhaps we should not be married yet awhile. But there'd be no harm in a little kiss or two." She nuzzled his ear and he hurtled himself out of the chair with a yelp.

"You're a wanton Jezebel, that's what you are, Macha Sheridan, but I will not commit sins of the flesh, not for all your gold."

"Sure, it would be no more than a venial sin," she teased, goading his reaction by swanning after him. "You'd never be damned for all eternity or anything like that, not just for a few kisses."

"No!" he almost screamed. "Your sovereigns and lust will not buy me. I don't want a kiss and I won't have a wedding, for I'm not old enough to take a wife." With which he reeled from the room.

Macha plumped to the floor, whooping with laughter. He must have heard the gales of her merriment from the barn to where he had fled, but he did not return, and finally she crawled back to her seat to giggle and finish the port. What fun she would have had with Molloy on such an occasion. It was her last reflection, and when she slumped into unconsciousness, two tears were squeezed from her eyes.

Light of day drove through her head like a polished steel bayonet and he was standing over her, weighed down with solemnity and a small bundle which apparently contained his basic possessions.

"I'll be off, then," he said, mournfully.

She felt weak and rather sick. "Where are you off to?"

"On my way."

"Merciful saints! Declan, don't play games with me. Can't you see I'm dying? What is this about you leaving?"

"After what happened last night, I cannot stay."

What had happened last night? Gingerly, she tried out her memory by peeling away several raw layers. Had anything happened last night? If so, why was he depressed about it, when he ought to be strutting? Surely, she could not have forgotten such an event. No, she decided. She could not.

"You can't cod me, Declan O'Brien. Nothing at all happened last night."

"But don't you see, it might have done! It nearly did. And I cannot go on sharing the same roof with you and risking my immortal soul."

He looked piteous, almost as though he had spent the whole night weeping. Even through her own sorry condition, Macha began to feel twinges of guilt.

"Ach, it was only a game, just the drink talking. Put down your things and let's take a drink of tea."

"No! It was no game to me," he said stubbornly.

Something in his voice made her inspect him more closely, and it vaguely occurred to her that she had never actually looked at him properly before. The unruly sandy hair was damped down into temporary slickness by a liberal application of water. His features were bony, the nose angular and overlarge, the chin and jaw strongly defined. Despite pale eyebrows and lashes, he had a face of character—not handsome, but made intriguing by its remoteness of expression, a face which many women would find attractive before long. Then, to her surprise, Macha saw in his eyes genuine pain, and all at once she understood something he did not know about himself: that he was desperately and impossibly in love with her. For although he was almost the same age, she was an adult, but he was still just a boy.

"Declan, please forgive me. I've been a fool, and I am sorry," she said simply. "It was the thrill of the day, with the races and the winning and all the food and drink. I never meant to offend you, and I'm ashamed of myself."

Shy and deeply distressed, he flushed and shifted position.

"Don't leave," she continued. "For I need you here."

"There are plenty who will be more than willing to work for you, *now*." He spoke the last word with special bitterness.

"Yes," she agreed. "But you've not heard my idea."

"Oh, I heard all your fancies and notions of the high life and grand ways, yesterday."

"Not all of them," she corrected. "For I didn't tell you the one which needs you and no-one else will do."

He waited, sulkily.

"Take no heed of yesterday's blatter and chatter—although, make no mistake, I intend to enjoy myself. But what I want to do most of all is buy the most promising Thoroughbred filly we can find and run her."

"We?"

"You and me. Who else can I depend on to help me choose the best?"

He gave her a hard and doubting glare, then turned on his heel and left the cottage. Through the window, she saw him head towards the path to Wildham Wood. Picking nervously at her nails, she cursed herself for being so cruel and insensitive. She had lost him.

Minutes passed. The door latch clattered, and she looked up. He walked to the fire and took the singing kettle off the trivet.

"I will work with your horses and ride for you, Miss Sheridan," he said formally, as the tea infused. "I will even act as your brother, for the time being; but I will do no more. If you agree to that, I would stay on."

"I do," she confirmed at once. "And I am very grateful to you, Declan."

It was to be years before he used her Christian name again.

After several more cups of tea and a desperate shot of whisky for shock value, Macha recovered from the excesses of the previous day. Buckets clattering and horses' hooves resounding on the cobblestones signalled that Declan was fully occupied outside. She was quite alone and unlikely to be disturbed.

The seed of hope she had not dared consider before now had time to flower. She knew the spirit of Molloy had returned, to ride Irish Coper to win, for only one purpose: to give her the money and security to send for their children, at last.

Trembling slightly, she took six sheets of paper from the cheap pad used to record horse dealings, spread them carefully on the kitchen table and sat staring at them.

She had never written a letter before, and the pencil and blank white squares created a barrier of formality between her ideas and their expression. She did not know how to begin, or where to go from there. Words jumbled in her brain.

After a long time, she wrote:

TO bIddY CONer,

By much later in the morning, she had added:

i aM bY eesT MardEN iN sUsiX aNd i WaNT MOly aNd TOM.

Then she signed the letter MaCHa before copying it out on the other five pieces of paper. This took the rest of the day.

At the post office in the village, they sold her six stamps and six envelopes. She addressed them to SOUTH CaMp dUbliN to

O leerYs diP CONeMara and to The TraVelers CaMps in KerY, KarlOW, KorK and Tara, then handed them over the counter in such a state of agitation that she did not even notice the snigger of the postmistress.

Although she thought it might be weeks, or months, before the letters were delivered and replies sent, Macha could not sleep. Her children glowed like paintings on the blue silk of the night. They were more than a year old now, crawling, perhaps even walking, and she wondered if Molly was pretty and Tom as handsome as his father. She could see some unknown traveller coming down the track to the cottage and herself lifting her darling infants off his cart and whirling around with them held close to her again in blessed joy.

She gazed through the darkness to where their two little beds would be and imagined them sleeping there, rosy and plump, filling the room with mouse-like stirrings and snuffles and their baby smell. She would buy feather pillows and blankets of softest wool and dress them like lordlings. She would feed them with great creamy, sticky cakes and ginger beer. They would have their own ponies, a pair of those tiny black Shetlands she had seen the tots of the quality ride. She would turn herself into the most beautiful and queenly mother on earth, and they would grow up proud and marry a prince and princess, at least. Macha lay awake and still and happy in her dreams that night and for many nights after.

Mr. Toby Dodds was an exclusive court dressmaker in Chichester. Even ladies who spent the season in London often visited his establishment while in the country and were impressed by the range of fabrics in stock and the way their most particular requirements were met within a matter of days. Nothing, it seemed, was too difficult for him to obtain. It was said he had even better contacts in the world of fashion than Mr. J. J. Fenwick of Bond Street. Mr. Dodds was a suitably august figure, tall and silver-haired, sartorially faultless, invariably courteous, without ever being obsequious. However, had the light not been carefully filtered through the frilled and tasselled Madras muslin curtains behind the heavy draperies, the merest hint of a glint behind his calm grey gaze might have betrayed a carefully controlled amusement at the human frailties of some of his most exalted clients.

When Macha walked through the door in that perfectly dreadful puce garment and relic of a coat and a hat which defied description, he knew he had been granted his dearest wish. He was an artist. Now he would create.

She looked up at him and read his thoughts, from his opinion of her appearance to his pleased anticipation of her custom.

"I want the latest clothes," she stated frankly.

He nodded and waited.

"And gloves and hats and shoes."

He smiled.

"And my hair dressed. I want . . ." She could not put it into words.

"You want to be beautiful, madam." His statement confirmed it as the most natural desire in the world.

"Yes!" she replied, with a delighted grin.

"Leave it all to me, madam," instructed Mr. Dodds.

And she knew she had found a friend.

He had her measurements taken and recorded in a leather-bound book. He had fashion drawings and some copies of a magazine called *The Lady* and swatches of material neatly parcelled for her to study at leisure. He was far too tactful to arrange for the hairdresser to visit her at home, but instead, set aside one of his rooms for her appointment that same afternoon. He suggested glycerine cream for her hands and most delicately advised that she should wear housemaid's cleaning gloves as much as possible to give her skin time to soften. He discussed colour and line and suitability. Later, and without being in any way intrusive, he remained near at hand while her hair was cut, suggesting styles which would enhance her most fetching features.

Macha gazed into the looking-glass in wonder. Her shining hair was piled sensationally on her head over an additional hairpiece and with a fringe of the most delicious curls framing her face, which she had never noticed before was this charming oval shape set with wide, silver eyes.

"Oh . . . ," she breathed, turning to Mr. Dodds.

"This is only the beginning, madam."

He even assisted her into her old coat without a disparaging sniff. He was a paragon among men.

She paused to stare in the mirror once more.

"What perfume do you think is the most fragrant, Mr. Dodds?"

"Many ladies like Le Bon Vieux Temps by Guerlain, madam."

"Is it French?"

"Most certainly, madam." He wrote down the name on cream-coloured paper which had his name and address engraved across the top, and handed it to her.

For weeks, all her spare time was taken up with fittings and treatments and lessons, for Mr. Dodds supervised not only her wardrobe, but every aspect of her new persona, and what he could not teach himself, he ensured that she learnt by introducing her to a dancing master, a boot maker and a milliner and to the Honourable Mrs. Henry Wellington, a dowager whose glare could snap the mast on a ship half way to France.

Only the almost imperceptible tightening of her eyelids hinted at Mrs. Wellington's feelings as she viewed her pupil for the first time, but as widowhood in straitened circumstances made such an association necessary, she quashed those feelings with a self-discipline instilled in her from birth.

In a darkly shaded room, overfull of aspidistras, framed photographs, screens, the stuffed heads of dead animals and *objet*-covered tables, Mrs. Wellington instructed Macha to turn around and walk about, while she viewed her from all angles through her lorgnette. Then, without more ado, the Irish girl found herself being ruthlessly drilled in the elements of society etiquette and the Season: when to call; when to leave her card; how to behave in the street, at luncheon, at tea, at supper, at dinner, at a ball, a wedding, a funeral, a christening, on a yacht, at the theatre, at the opera, at Henley Regatta, at Royal Ascot, in Scotland. The rules were endless, and Macha knew she would never remember them all, especially as frequently they seemed so pointless.

She learnt that a lady guest *always* entered a carriage before her hostess and took the farther seat facing the horses; that she should not bow to persons she knew by sight, but to whom she had not been introduced; that she should not add salt or pepper to soup before tasting it; that she must never enter a ballroom arm in arm with a gentleman; that she must keep up a constant flow of conversation with her neighbour during luncheon or dinner, without mentioning the food; and not to use the word "ride" when she meant "drive," or the word "dress" instead of "gown" or "frock." She also learnt to curtsy.

"But what for? Isn't it only maids that curtsy?"

"You may be presented one day."

"What would I be presented with?"

"Not *with,* Miss Sheridan, presented *to*—Her Majesty, the Queen, or to the Prince or Princess of Wales."

"That will never happen," laughed the girl.

"Well, you do attend race meetings and such events and you may even manage to marry well, so it is always better to be prepared." But as she spoke, Mrs. Wellington's tone made it clear that she too doubted the possibility of such an opportunity. "Now we shall try once more. Balance. Sweep the foot out and behind. Head high. Back straight. Slo . . . o . . . owly down. No, Miss Sheridan! You must not wobble!"

It was hard to believe that any gel could so lack finesse. Certainly she could never bring herself to enquire into Miss Sheridan's background.

"It is a great pity you do not speak French," she commented one day.

"Oh, but I speak Irish," Macha offered.

The venerable lady paled and produced a bottle of smelling salts. "Never, never tell anyone that," she intonated. "Irish is the language of peasants."

"You were right!" Macha stormed to Declan when she returned home. "It is all frippery and fal-lals. Do you know they think Irish is the language of bog-trotters? Curse o' God! I'm not taking any more. I will give all the *dresses* away first thing tomorrow morning. I will hand them out in the marketplace, and then I'll go back on the road."

"And what will happen to the colt?" he asked slowly.

Gold! Since becoming so totally preoccupied with manners and modes, she'd not given a thought to him, or to her promise to buy a Thoroughbred filly. Neither had there been any answer about her children from Ireland, although she had sent another letter, promising money. After the first flare of excitement, a sense of realism had chilled her heart with the belief that there would not be a reply at all, and she no longer knew what to do to find them.

"Ach, it's all become a muddle." She was disconsolate. "I seem to throw away time and five-pound notes and get no further than a deaf mute with a fiddle. To tell the truth, I don't know what to do next."

There was a pause as he looked at her, seated outside the cottage on a new wicker chair dressed in a summer gown of white voile, her parasol carelessly discarded on the grass.

"It doesn't seem to me you've wasted either," he said diffidently, and searched for words to explain. "All these frills and ways . . . they are becoming . . . to a lady . . . a lady, like yourself."

"Me? Declan?" She was astonished, and gratified, knowing he would never have made such a comment insincerely.

"Well . . . usually," he added, with a rare touch of banter. "But maybe you should begin to put it all to use."

"This minute!" she agreed, and hurried indoors, emerging shortly with a paper.

"We'll send this off to Tattersalls and have Gold registered."

"Tattersalls only sell horses," Declan informed her. "My old guv'nor's horses were registered with Weatherby's. Mr. Locksash will know all about that."

He took the document and peered at it with a strange intensity and compressed his lips before returning it.

"I could show you, if you'd like," she offered cautiously.

"Show me what?" He was very defensive.

"How to read."

"Who said I couldn't read?" He had reddened.

"And write," she continued, ignoring the interruption. "If you'd like."

"This is his birth certificate." She took the paper and ran her finger along each entry. "Born: 1897. Sex: Male. Colour: Chestnut. Markings: Three white legs and white blaze. Sire: Philosopher. Dam: Precious Stone. And it's signed here—look: G. H. Carter, Sheriff, Bowling Green, Kentucky."

"Where's Kentucky?" Declan had forgotten his embarrassment in his curiosity.

"In America. This is the import paper from Charleston to Dun Laoghaire."

"An American horse, is he? Yet you don't call the mare Precious Stone."

"I renamed her," Macha said, hastily.

Declan gave her a quizzical look—uncomfortably similar to the one directed by Harry Locksash when he perused the document later.

"America, you say?" The farmer sounded equally sceptical. "And him a ringer for Gallinule. Must be a throwback to the same ancestor in the line somewhere."

However, he gave her the necessary information, and the paper, together with a claim for the name "Gold" and the sum of five shillings, was posted, to be returned before long with the confirmation that Gold had been entered in the Racing Calendar, the weekly journal of the Jockey Club.

Macha, to celebrate, shook and opened a bottle of champagne, so that the wine fountained into the air and splashed, sparkling, over the watching colt, who squealed with surprise and galloped off across the field. She then opened a second bottle with more care, which she and Declan O'Brien drank, sitting on the five-bar gate.

"Well, it doesn't matter whether he came from America or was born in Murphy's barn," stated the boy, drunk enough to be indiscreet. "He's a champion of a colt, and he'll leave them all at the start."

He looked Macha straight in the eye, and she knew that he knew the certificate was a fake. Chortling, she gave him a playful push, and he fell off the gate, to land in a freshly deposited heap of dung, where he lay and laughed without a care.

It was already the middle of June. They travelled all the way to Ascot in a smart hired carriage, taking the censorious Mrs. Wellington along as Macha's chaperone with the pledge of a sight of royalty, which was to be duly honoured.

They had started out the previous morning and stayed overnight at a coaching inn. Well before dawn on the third of the four days of the Royal Meeting, the little party drew near the famous course to find equipages of other, even earlier enthusiasts already queueing to enter. Nevertheless, by some very deft driving on the part of the hired coachman and extravagant bribery in the right quarter by Macha, they still managed to secure a perfect position drawn right up to the rails, immediately next to the enclosure reserved for the Four-in-Hand Club and almost directly opposite the grandstand.

A hamper of food had been prepared at the inn, and the coachman produced three chairs and a table covered with a white linen cloth and laid with china and sets of picnic knives, forks and spoons, each in a flat roan case. They breakfasted on a raised pork pie and sliced ham and pickle, and drank tea made from water boiled in a kettle on a spirit stove.

The day grew warm. A fresh haze of leaves quivered on the trees about the course, and the renowned circuit wound like woven green cashmere. Bookmakers established their pitches with brash name signs, lists of runners and chalked prices. Touts in loud jackets and gaudy scarves appeared, moving sideways like crabs. Charms of parasols and brigades of top hats began to wheel around the immaculate lawns opposite, as though taking part in a dance. Breathtaking horses were led by, visions incarnate.

Custom-built private drags and barouches, many with armorial bearings painted on their panels and all drawn by teams of four perfectly matched, high-stepping horses with docked tails, swept into the enclosure alongside, the male occupants sporting the enamelled badge of their exclusive club and shouting greetings to each other.

With a gunshot of a pop, Macha opened the first bottle of champagne to a chorus of encouragement. Turning towards the sound, she saw that the new neighbours were lifting their own glasses to her, with the exception of one young man who continued scrutinizing the horses through binoculars.

Mrs. Wellington hissed and moved with remarkable alacrity to place her substantial bulk between her charge and the admirers, who gave an audible groan.

"Ladies do not uncork wine. Allow Mr. Sheridan to do it if you should require more," she corrected, crossly.

"Oh, but I like the fun of the bang and then all the bubbles being sneezed out."

A mighty cheer rose from the crowd and boomed back and forth as everyone crammed forward and the royal cavalcade, led by the Royal Huntsman and whippers-in, entered the course at a fast trot through the gates at the end of the New Mile. Behind the Master of the Buckhounds in full regalia and mounted outriders in scarlet came several landaus with cane-faced sides, each drawn by four horses with postillions. The first of these carried an imposing, bearded man and his elegant wife, who waved and smiled genially to all.

"Good old Teddy!" someone shouted, and the cry was taken up all round.

"The Prince and Princess of Wales!" quavered Mrs. Wellington, teetering dangerously into an attempted curtsy, while perched on the carriage. Then she sat back, fanning her flushed face with a handkerchief and puffing quite alarmingly after the excitement of the experience.

The royal couple descended in front of the Royal Stand and were soon seen again in the Royal Box. Then the ring began gesticulating and shouting, and money started passing from wallet to hand to satchels and pouches, and the pickpockets moved into action. Horses loped past with their little burdens of silks, race cards were marked, minds were changed, field glasses were trained, the flag dropped, there was a distant strumming and a whirl of colour and the first race was over. Macha, with a most unladylike holla, rushed to collect her winnings.

The young man who had been studying the runners so earnestly from the Four-in-Hand Club enclosure courteously stood back to let her reach the stand of HONEST JEM BECK OF HACKNEY, *PROMPT PAYMENT GIVEN* and watched as the coins and notes were counted into her gloved hand.

"Try Earwig in the next race," he advised.

"Oh, no!" she responded. "Mr. Fairie's Eager will win that."

"You are so sure?" he asked, with a slightly mocking smile.

"Sure certain," she confirmed, and to prove it, put five guineas on the horse, at which moment Declan O'Brien and Mrs. Wellington found her and hustled her away, the former looking stern and the latter lecturing about never addressing *anyone*, especially a *gentleman*, who had not been introduced.

"He spoke to me first," the girl explained.

"Then you should have ignored him," stated Mrs. Wellington. "He is obviously very ill bred."

Eager won the Rous Memorial Stakes by four lengths. The gentleman perched on the next carriage inclined his head in acknowledgement of defeat. Engaging her chaperone in conversation, Macha pretended not to see him.

"Why don't *you* have a little flutter, Mrs. Wellington?"

"Ladies do not bet."

"But the next race is the Gold Cup, with the Prince of Wales' own horse running," Macha enticed. "There can't be anything wrong in supporting the royal runner."

Torn between allegiance to the crown and etiquette, the widow stared crushingly.

"I'll tell you what," suggested Macha, unabashed. "I'll put a sovereign on Persimmon for you with my own wager."

"Your brother, Mr. Sheridan, *must* deal with the bookmaker," protested Mrs. Wellington.

Macha relented and sent Declan with the money while she and the dowager crossed sedately to the tunnel leading to the paddock.

Persimmon was nervous, snatching at his bit and sweating slightly. A bay of quality, he had a lovely Thoroughbred head and perfect shoulders and quarters, and he looked muscled and fit. His jockey, Jack Watts, sat him quietly, well accustomed to his high-strung reactions. As they made their way to the start, there was little indication in the horse's slow paces of his greatness.

Winkfield's Pride jumped off like a runaway. The crowd strained forward, bawling, but the purple, gold and scarlet of the Prince of Wales' colours were trailing behind the other three runners until, at the last turn, Jack Watts brought his horse level and then overtook the main rival. Without being fully extended, Persimmon drew away, to widen the gap, with easy confidence. As he passed Macha's vantage point, he was cantering home, to win by eight lengths. All around, top hats and caps and bowlers were flung into the air with ear-splitting yells by the jubilant crowd. The Prince appeared, beaming, to lead in his winner, and Mrs. Wellington fainted clean away.

Lying in her bed at the inn that night, the room rocking slightly from the effects of the champagne, Macha decided this had been the best day she had spent since coming to England. She had won more than enough money to cover all her expenses since Salisbury; she had seen a Prince and Princess (although it had to be admitted she had expected more ethereal-looking figures to match such titles); and the horses, every one classically bred and classically run, had outshone her most fabulous ideal.

Her rose-pink crêpe-de-Chine gown was hanging from a hook on one of the low beams in the ceiling. Mr. Dodds's seamstresses had worked all night to finish it in time, and she knew it had been responsible for the added *frisson* of the flirtation with the gentleman from the Four-in-Hand Club. He and his friends had passed her carriage with eye-catching panache as they left the course, and all raised their hats. It had been the perfect end to the day.

There were definite advantages to Mrs. Wellington's rising the following morning to discover herself a devotee of racing. Her night too had been filled with echoes of that wonderful day, the mingling with royal personages, the return to society after the death of her dear husband, the brigadier, a decade earlier and, not least, her small winnings from the Gold Cup and the following race. If such a sport was graced by the presence of the heir to the throne and his wife, then who was she to object? She recalled that her late husband's nephew, Sir Frederick Wellington, had had connections with the racing world and resolved to write to him forthwith.

All of which meant that Macha had no further difficulty in persuading the widow to accompany her to Sandown and Kempton Parks, nor to Brighton and Windsor during the next month, when they both benefitted from the girl's winning streak. Each was surprised to discover a growing affection for the other, and although the old lady remained severely formal, at times they were not unlike a pair of conspirators as they studied form and planned their gambles.

However, the greatest benefit from the dowager's new interest was to come. Freddie Wellington had been quite fond of his uncle and had occasionally felt slightly guilty about losing touch with his formidable aunt, so he was happy to salve his conscience by replying to her letter with an invitation to join him in the members' enclosure at Goodwood, and to bring her ward, of course.

"Your ward?" Macha queried. "What does that mean?"

It had been only the tiniest white lie, but Mrs. Wellington became unusually flustered.

"As an orphan, you have no-one to vouch for you," she tried to explain. "And you must be known to someone of respectability before you can meet others."

"But what does it mean?" Macha insisted.

"It means . . ." Mrs. Wellington went turkey-red. "It means . . . you have someone who takes the place of your parents."

Macha looked at the unfashionable purple gown with the bustle, the double chins and ample bosom and nervous hands and the control of a lifetime etched into every facial line, and wondered if the old lady would have offered such an arrangement had she known her protégée was an Irish tinker. Yet it contained advantage to both sides, as the Honourable Mrs. Henry Wellington certainly would not want it known that straitened circumstances since her husband's death had forced her to give lessons in correct deportment.

"Thank you," the girl said, sincerely. "That is a great kindness."

"There is no time to lose." The widow dismissed the subject as quickly as possible. "You must see Mr. Dodds and order your gown at once."

They chose a design in eau-de-Nil silk, trimmed with cascades of cream lace. The minute waist and hip-skimming skirt emphasized Macha's willowy height, and when the train was lifted to clear the ground, deeply flounced petticoats were revealed. The colour complemented her ivory-pale complexion and reflected in the silver of her eyes. The outfit was completed by kid boots, long gloves and a little hat dressed with plumes and tipped saucily forward. Her arrival at Goodwood was sensational, causing monocles to be raised and gentlemen's attention to stray from their ladies and questions to be asked by frosty matrons, protective of their daughters' interests.

Freddie Wellington, on recognising the *grande dame* accompanying this ravishing young woman as his aunt, became conspicuously proprietorial and congratulated himself on the sense of duty which had obliged him to respond to his relation's request so promptly.

Within half an hour, Macha had met more people than would fill a winter campsite. They all knew each other and talked so much that to her annoyance, she missed the first race and the horses were already parading in the paddock for the second as Freddie Wellington began steering her towards yet another group of curious faces. She stopped and faced him.

"All your friends are very pleasant people, Sir Frederick, but could we not speak with them later?" she wondered.

Mrs. Wellington coughed with annoyance.

"What would you prefer to do, Miss Sheridan?" he asked, obviously taken aback.

"I should prefer to watch the runners," she stated, decisively. "Is that not the reason for coming to Goodwood?"

"Many ladies come simply to be seen," he murmured.

"Well, not me," she retorted. "Not when any one of those beautiful Thoroughbreds puts us all to shame."

The gentlemen within earshot snorted with laughter, and their wives and daughters went rather pink and began moving towards the paddock with alacrity.

Freddie Wellington steered her in the same direction and made another attempt to gain her favour.

"You might care to venture a sovereign on one of the races, Miss Sheridan," he said. "So may I advise you on the horses?"

She listened carefully to his opinion of each, before asking, "And have *you* put money on that colt, Sir Frederick?"

"I have indeed," he answered.

"Well, in that case, I'll risk a sovereign on him too." She jingled some coins in her hand. "And would you put five guineas each way on number 12, as well?"

When his horse came in first and her choice third, she bounded about with hoydenish abandonment.

"Arrah! We make a great team!" she commented, as he brought her winnings. Poor Mrs. Wellington appeared close to an apoplexy.

Macha lost on the third race, came placed in the fourth and won the fifth, ending the day well in profit.

"And how does a young lady like yourself come to know so much about racing?" asked a middle-aged man who had been watching her with amusement.

"I read the *Sporting Life* every day, sir," she replied, to gasps from those around.

"Allow me to introduce the Duke of Portland," Freddie Wellington put in, quickly, and told the older man her name.

"Can there be any better satisfaction on this earth than to own Saint Simon?" Macha paid tribute to the Duke's magnificent horse, after they had bowed to each other.

"Only to breed another horse as fine," he replied.

"And will you?"

"That is the secret of Time."

By the end of the afternoon, she had happily agreed to return for the last two days of the meeting and accepted an invitation to a ball at Petworth House from Lady Leconfield (despite the rakish reputation of her son, Charles Windham), but ruefully refused two invitations to supper from two very handsome young men, at Mrs. Wellington's insistence.

On her next day at Goodwood, Macha wore the gown she had worn to Ascot, and on the last day, which was slightly colder, she dressed in a mauve tailored costume, faultlessly cut by Mr. Toby Dodds himself, and absolutely in the mode with its neat fitted jacket worn over a pleated blouse and its gathered skirt with short train and braid trim.

Her delectable appearance, together with her astonishing good luck, increased her circle of admirers, one or two of whom became as attentive to hear the name of the next horse she proposed to back as in the gel herself—a fact which did not escape her notice.

Professional and Gentlemen Riders mixed in the second race of the last day, although the low weights allowed the participation of only the slimmest amateurs. One of these men was up on a brown gelding no more than fifteen hands high, but of such exquisite conformation that Macha found him irresistible.

"A pony on the pony, miss?" Even the bookmaker almost smiled as he took her twenty-five pounds. "To win?"

Freddie Wellington grimaced as she nodded, but he made no comment while accompanying her back to the paddock. The Prince of Wales, surrounded by pretty women and attentive men, was already there, viewing the runners and talking to the Duke of Portland. All at once, His Royal Highness looked straight across at Macha, who felt herself blush, and a very large flowered hat instantly moved between them.

The Gentleman Rider had his back to everyone when he mounted the brown Thoroughbred and moved onto the course with the others. As Macha focussed her field glasses on the start, she saw him balance the horse within the first few strides, gradually draw up to the leaders and then call for a dash within lengths of the winning post. The little gelding responded gamely and just managed to push his nose in front. Macha realised she had been shrieking him home like a fishwife.

"Of course, she is *Irish*, you know," someone said nearby, as though this explained her unbecoming behaviour; but walking among them, openly counting the wad of hundred-pound notes, she would not have given a twopenny piece for their opinion, for at last, she understood that this Society, with all its rules and proprieties, mannerisms and tests, was just another sport, and she was most definitely winning.

The Gentleman Rider's yellow-and-white silks were identifiable first, and then, as he was introduced, she recognised him. The Honourable James Melbaugh, who had just filled her hands with money, was the young man from the Four-in-Hand Club enclosure at Ascot.

"I see your eye for the best horse is still as keen," he said, bowing, without relinquishing her gaze.

"Only a top horseman brings out the best." It was an honest compliment. "And by all the saints, you rode a cracking race."

They drifted politely apart for a suitable interval and then he returned to her side.

"I trust you will be at the ball at Goodwood House tonight, Miss Sheridan."

When she shook her head, regretfully, he added at once, "Then neither shall I. That is, if you will dine with me instead?"

He spoke very softly. Mrs. Wellington was in conversation with another dowager. No-one but Macha heard, and he did have more fun in his blue eyes than she had ever seen and a smile full of enticingly improper promises. Besides, she was thoroughly bored with the straitjacket of decorum.

"I will," she agreed.

Chapter NINE

Macha had the sense to refuse James Melbaugh's offer to send his carriage for her. Even she knew better than to leave herself completely vulnerable.

"My . . . cousin . . . Declan O'Brien can bring me and wait to take me home," she arranged.

Poor Declan, given a whole new role in her family without even being consulted. Immediately, she began to wonder how on earth to persuade him to drive her to and collect her from such an assignation.

In the end, she guessed, rightly, that he would do it only for her own protection, but she had to tolerate his sulking all the way to Chichester.

There were supper rooms not far from the Assembly Rooms, where young blades daringly entertained actresses and the female stars of theatrical productions and visiting music hall, and although she would not have admitted it, Macha was relieved to see other girls of her own age dining. She had supposed the place would be full of harlots, and had then tried to imagine what a harlot looked like, somehow coming to the conclusion that such women were all old.

Heavy crimson paper covered the walls, and velvet curtains of the same colour obscured the windows. Each table had a pair of candles with deep red shades and a bowl of dark, fragrant roses and was sufficiently removed from the others to ensure that no word of an intimate tête-à-tête could be overheard. Macha sat down carefully and tried not to betray her uncertainty at the sight of the three wineglasses and array of silver. This was very different from her light lunches in the tea shop by the cathedral.

There were some small oval green fruits in a dish on the table. She thought they might be a type of grape, and seeing James Melbaugh put one into his mouth, she did the same. To her disgust, it tasted saltier than any seawater, and her face automatically screwed up.

"I see you do not care for olives, Miss Sheridan." He did not restrain his broad smile.

"I've never tried one before," she confessed. "I don't think they grow them in Ireland."

"I don't think they do," he agreed, his grin even wider as he signalled to a waiter, who came forward with a bottle of champagne in a bucket of ice. "This will wash the taste away."

"Is it Laurent-Perrier?" she asked, curiously.

He was surprised and lifted the bottle dripping from the ice with the question, "Do you like Laurent-Perrier?"

"Oh, yes! I always drink it when I've done well at the races," she said, without thinking—the truth being that it was the only name she knew.

"Take that away and bring some Laurent-Perrier '83!" he ordered the waiter, gesturing dismissively at the bucket.

"There's no need to do that," she protested, embarrassed.

"Whatever you want, you shall have, Miss Sheridan," he answered. "Especially as you obviously know your champagne as well as you know your runners."

After the first glass, her feeling of awkwardness vanished. They talked of horses, and he made her giggle with tales of racing personalities and of the spills he had experienced as an amateur rider. He impressed her, too, with reports of his successes. Then, as he began to appreciate the depth of her own knowledge and interest, he became serious and revealed a passion as consuming as her own for facing that long stretch of turf with no end in sight, where only the end matters.

He spoke of striving with back and arms and legs and heels and pride; of the tension, volume and heat in the middle of the rushing, crushing bunch; of the frustration of falling back and seeing the knotted flanks and billowing silks, the whips and coloured caps inexorably pulling away in front; of the relentless rhythm of the run.

An indescribable power was generated, fanatical and almost tangible, when all the minds of men and beasts pursued a goal only one partnership could achieve. He described bolting into that single and unique moment of victory for which every Thoroughbred had been raised since the arrival of the Byerley Turk stallion, the first of the Arab patriarchs, exactly two hundred years before. And Macha felt the breath at his heels and his hunger to win, and win, and win.

They stared at each other and then looked away, unwilling to travel so far yet. The mood changed as he became a light-hearted companion again, passing on some very irreverent gossip about many of the aristocrats she had met during the past few days, and even about the Prince of Wales himself. He made her laugh so much that other, more discreet couples turned in their seats.

Every now and again, she would meet and hold his amused blue glance with a boldness he clearly enjoyed, and the evening passed so quickly that the waiter's announcement that her victoria was waiting came disappointingly soon.

"May I call on you?" James Melbaugh asked.

She looked up at him with an eagerness which faded as she realised how unthinkable it would be for him to come to the half-furnished cottage where she lived alone with Declan O'Brien.

"I think Mrs. Wellington . . . my guardian . . . would not permit it," she said, slowly.

"Leave the gorgon to me, Miss Sheridan," he said, with a confidence which left her too worried to notice Declan O'Brien's silent fury on the way home.

Macha went straight to her room and climbed into bed, sitting upright among the pillows and leaving the candle burning. It was where she always did her important thinking. After a while, she went to the tallboy, took out and opened the tin box, and added the money she had won earlier that day before counting the total. In three months, after deducting all her expenditures, she had made nearly seven thousand pounds. It was time to put it to good use, she thought, lying down at last and picturing James Melbaugh once more, long-limbed and graceful, urging the little brown gelding past the winning post.

"Dear Mrs. Wellington, you have been so good to me," Macha murmured, while sitting in the widow's drawing room the following afternoon, angelically labouring over her embroidery, which she had recently begun as a suitable pastime for a young lady. "My greatest regret in being unable to return here will be the loss of your friendship."

"Unable to return, Miss Sheridan. Why ever not?" The widow sounded startled. "You are always most welcome."

"I could not bear for my presence to distress you, and I am in such a dilemma as cannot be resolved."

"What can it be? You must tell me at once!" Mrs. Wellington insisted.

"It is because we met so many people at Goodwood, and of course, they all believed that I lived here with you, as your ward."

"Naturally, Miss Sheridan. There's no harm in that."

"But some of them expressed a wish to call upon me," Macha wailed. "The quandary of it has kept me awake, and now I realise I have no alternative but to retire from society at once."

"Nonsense! Now, who is it wishes to call?" Mrs. Wellington was avidly curious.

"Oh, Mrs. Cookson and Miss Beresford and your nephew and . . . the Honourable James Melbaugh. It is all quite dreadful!" She looked up with brimming eyes.

"James Melbaugh! But that is wonderful, Miss Sheridan. He is most eligible, the younger son of the Earl of Watersmeet. I cannot think of another gel who would find anything so dreadful in the idea of James Melbaugh's attentions. Is he so really distasteful to you?"

"No! He seems . . . charming . . . although we have spoken only once." Macha sighed, convincingly. "But, if you knew more about my circumstances, you would understand why no-one can call on me and why I feel I must avoid him and others."

"I am sure you have no secret too dark to confide," said Mrs. Wellington, encouragingly. "And I may be able to help and advise."

"You know that I am an orphan," Macha began, trying very hard to look helpless. "And before my father died, certain misfortunes overtook the family so that my mother was left with very little money, and there was even less when she too went to heaven, God rest her soul."

"But surely you are quite comfortably off now?" the widow interjected.

"That is true," she agreed. "But it has come about only recently, and solely because of my good fortune with the horses. The problem is that I live in very humble surroundings, such as I could not endure anyone to see."

Macha gave another abject sigh, hoping she was putting on the performance of her life.

"I understood you had a house and land, Miss Sheridan." The dowager looked puzzled.

"A rented hovel and two fields," Macha confessed. "It is the vision, indeed the intention of my . . . cousin and myself to remove to Newmarket next spring, to buy a house and start a training stables . . . so the cottage is sparsely furnished indeed."

"Your *cousin?*"

"It seemed easier in the beginning just to say that Declan was my brother, but the truth is he is the son of my mother's sister, who died in childbirth. His name is O'Brien, not Sheridan." She held her breath, aware that the tale was becoming more convoluted by the minute and praying that it still sounded convincing.

"But you must have servants? . . . a maid . . . ? You mean that you live entirely alone with your cousin?"

The widow sat with her mouth open for some moments. Macha stared down at her needle and waited. If her plan did not work, she knew she could never see James Melbaugh again. She heard a bone-china teacup clink onto its saucer.

"Well, Miss Sheridan, you are quite right. Such a situation cannot continue." The voice sounded severe. "And there is only one solution."

Macha wondered if she was about to be dismissed.

"You must live here!"

This was far more than had been anticipated. The idea of spending all day every day complying with such rigid standards of behaviour and stifling formality was too disagreeable. The girl thought fast.

"Mrs. Wellington, you are the kindest of ladies, and the Holy Mother will bless you. Indeed, to be able to live here would be joy unimaginable; but I vowed to my mother on her deathbed to care for Declan, and what would become of him if I came to you? Then, there are my horses—Gold, which I've told you so much about, and the others, and the filly we're about to buy. I could not dispose of them and give up all our plans. No, I am afraid I must cease going out until such time as we obtain a property, for it would be my ruin if my present position were to become known."

"And can you afford such a property now?"

"I think I can."

There was a very long silence and then Mrs. Wellington said, slowly, "If I were prepared to consider allowing acceptable friends to call upon you here, I should have to insist that you employ a mature woman as a housekeeper to live under your roof at once and that you start searching for a suitable house as soon as possible."

Macha glowed. The ruse had worked! She was so grateful that she dropped her sewing on the floor and ran across the room to kiss the old widow.

"Young ladies should behave with restraint at all times," Mrs. Wellington chided, but with a straightening of her shoulders and an unaccustomed little smile.

Macha felt only the slightest twinge of conscience when she assured her mentor the next day that her landlord had recommended a local widow, who was prepared to move in and act as housekeeper and guardian of her morals. The old lady would never visit the cottage, and what was not known caused no vexation.

On the following Sunday, Freddie Wellington, accompanied by his friend James Melbaugh, waited upon his aunt and her delightful ward. They discussed the forthcoming ball at Petworth House, and each reserved dances with Macha in advance. They bemoaned how quickly the flat-racing season passed and talked of Macha's plans to buy a Thoroughbred filly, a project on which both gentlemen were almost too eager to advise. It was agreed that all should attend the next Tattersalls auction in London.

Macha scrupulously divided her attention between them, while aware that James Melbaugh too was doing his best to make it appear as though he were there only as Freddie's companion during a duty visit. She could not resist passing close enough for her skirt to sweep over his shoes, and he postponed their departure at least twice with entertaining anecdotes.

"I didn't know all the world and many others were going to have a say in this new horse!" Declan O'Brien argued, reproachfully, on hearing of the proposed excursion to London. "I thought the filly was for us."

"For me," Macha corrected, with asperity. "I shall be buying the filly with my money. I will train her and you will ride her—that is, you will ride her if you stop all this huff, because I'll not pretend, Declan O'Brien, that an old donkey with constipation and the wind would be better company than you have been since I had supper with Mr. Melbaugh, and I am putting up with no more."

"I don't want to see you destroy your good name, that's all," he muttered, kicking at the ground.

"It's not my good name you're minding, but me going out with a fine gentleman. Don't think I don't know, and it's to stop, or you will have to go." The time had come to establish herself firmly and she gave him no quarter. "I know what I'm doing and I know where I'm going, and you can either stay on working with my horses and maybe one day riding a winner for me, or you can leave. What you can't do is tell me how to run my life, even if I'm wrong."

Her own harsh voice surprised her, and he was looking as though he had never seen her properly before. She thought he was about to stride away and felt a prick of remorse. He was standing very straight and had gone very pale.

"Right," he said. "The mangers need filling."

"Declan," she said, as he reached the door. "We are friends."

"I know," he confirmed, curtly.

He had recovered his normal dour demeanour by the time they met Mrs. Wellington on the train. To Macha's rapture, James Melbaugh's carriage and four met them at the station in London. She surveyed the Cleveland Bays and the impeccable green equipage and was determined to ride outside.

Mrs. Wellington and her nephew demurred immediately, but Macha's mind would not be changed, and eventually, one of the two liveried grooms helped her up to the box seat, with a sly squinny at his master.

"And you'll let me drive for a bit?" she pleaded.

"Certainly not!" the widow and Sir Freddie chorused from below; but James Melbaugh, who had not spoken throughout the argument, winked.

It was a perfect turnout: the paintwork built up from twenty coats of primer, paint and varnish was not sullied by so much as a fingerprint; the harness leather was as soft as gloves, its silver gleaming. People craned their necks to see them, and Macha had difficulty restraining herself from inclining her head and waving a regal hand.

They passed the Albert Hall, and James Melbaugh turned into the Kensington Gardens end of Rotten Row, where London society rode or drove each day. He handed the reins to Macha.

"Hold the reins in your left hand only, never in both hands," he instructed. Then he called the caution to the passengers: "Sit fast."

He touched the wheelers with the whip, and the horses moved off along the Drive in superbly trained unison. She guessed it must have taken upwards of two thousand pounds to purchase such a team.

"Take the whip in the right hand, so, and readjust the reins to keep the horses straight, so." The pace increased to a trot.

Memories of the rough ponies and broken-down nags which had

drawn the waggon and cart across Ireland flitted through Macha's mind as she concentrated hard on keeping her touch light and not making any accidental signals which might cause the team to jib or bore to one side. The contained power held within her one small hand, the instantaneity of their reactions, the way they synchronized their strides with military precision, leaders with wheelers, never jarring, never out of step, turned the ordinary act of driving into a new and sensational experience. It was surprisingly tiring on the hands, and she did not know that her face was pink and tense with the effort, the tip of her tongue curled over her top lip and her fringe slightly damp on her forehead, or that James Melbaugh was gazing at her with a light in his eye and those passing in carriages or on horseback were outraged. While it was acceptable for a lady to drive a gig, to be allowed charge of a four-in-hand was not just irresponsible, but downright dangerous, and several of his acquaintances resolved to have a serious word with Melbaugh after luncheon at the club.

On reaching Park Lane, he took over and with remarkable skill wheeled about and returned along the Drive to navigate the traffic congestion of horse-drawn omnibuses, hansoms, waggonettes, coaches, broughams, phaetons and barouches through Albert Gate to reach the vast premises of Tattersalls. There, by coincidental misfortunes of bankruptcy and death, several dispersal sales of bloodstock were taking place over the next two days, the auction having already been in operation since early morning.

"Do you think we have missed any good buys?" Macha asked anxiously. "I've studied *Ruff's Guide* and the catalogue and marked those I fancy. Most seem to be coming up this afternoon or tomorrow."

He gave her his own well-thumbed catalogue and they began to compare notes, pleased and impressed with each other on discovering many identical entries.

"What about Lindos Venus?" she asked.

"I looked over the horses on Sunday night, and that filly won't fetch a penny under four thousand guineas," he answered with a smile.

"Oh. Well, why do you not think Kerry Lady a possible?"

"I saw her run a couple of times, and frankly, although she had a win and a place, she was in poor company and did not look impressive."

Freddie Wellington looked over their shoulders with the comment "I see neither of you thinks much of Tulip Mary."

They had almost forgotten him.

"She hasn't done at all well this season as a two-year-old," his friend pointed out.

"No, but she started late because of coughing in the stables, and then a foreleg filled. Besides, I've never been convinced that the results of racing such immature animals are much to go on. At a trial last week she was very promising and she is full sister to Captain Paul, and he was not really at his best until he was a three-year-old."

The name was ringed; then Mrs. Wellington was made comfortable in one of the chairs provided in the gallery, and Macha, to her consternation, was left with her while the men made their way below to the vast, glass-covered yard to stand by the fountain under the eyes of the famous stone Fox.

The auctioneer's voice echoed through the building, punctuated by the shrill whinnying of the horses.

"Eleven hundred. Eleven hundred. Twelve hundred. Against you, sir. At twelve hundred guineas, this filly's certainly a snip. One three. One four. You're losing her, you know that, at fourteen hundred guineas. Last time, any more anywhere? At fourteen hundred."

This was not at all what Macha had expected. With her experience at innumerable horse fairs and sales, she had thought it would be a matter of haggling directly with the individual owners and had been confident of striking a good bargain. Now, here she was, completely excluded from the proceedings, glaring down on a mob of top hats and bowlers and caps, and not an owner in sight on whom to practice her wiles.

The last filly was led out and another Thoroughbred led in, bucking slightly with surprise at the crowd and strange surroundings. The often incomprehensible tones of the auctioneer rattled off again.

"Three-year-old colt, Ling's Turn. Placed in his first season. By Beckett's Request, with lots of winners in the pedigree. Give me three thousand for him . . . two . . . one . . . what you will. . . . Eight hundred guineas, thank you, sir. . . . Nine. . . . One thousand guineas . . . one one . . . one two . . . one three . . . Come on, now! One thousand three hundred. Keep your eye on me. One four, one five . . ."

Macha could see no-one bidding and looked down to see Declan O'Brien looking panic-stricken by the whole business.

"The buyers make secret signs arranged beforehand." Sir Freddie had returned to her side and guessed the problem. "Watch how Bill

Beresford rubs his fingers together and that Johnny over there keeps stroking his beard. Many of them are regular here and the auctioneer knows what to look for."

"At three thousand five hundred guineas, I sell him here, the good-looking Ling's Turn, at three thousand five hundred. Quickly, if you want him! At three thousand five hundred . . . are you bidding, sir? At three thousand five hundred. Gentleman by the Fox. Three thousand five hundred guineas and cheap. I'm going to sell him if I can get no more. Three thousand five hundred guineas." There was a long pause. Everyone stopped talking, and the sound of the hammer rapped through the silence.

It was an immense amount of money and yet the auctioneer had called it cheap, for a horse that looked like a dog. Until that moment, Macha had believed herself to be wealthy. After all, until the past few months, whom had she met in the whole of her life with seven thousand pounds? As another gleaming, dancing animal was led in, it finally occurred to her that she was probably the most impoverished person standing there and that the purchase of a racehorse might not even be possible, for she was certainly not going to waste money on a non-starter.

As the names marked in her catalogue came and went, she shook her head at James Melbaugh's enquiring glances and remained very quiet, listening and watching everything without comment. By the end of the afternoon, the party was quite downhearted. Bloodstock had been paraded before them by the dozen, prices of seven and a half thousand and eight thousand guineas had been reached and she could not have afforded one single decent horse.

It was as well Freddie Wellington had taken a box for them all at the Gaiety to see *The Circus Girl* that evening, or Macha might well have given up and returned to Sussex. However, she had never been to a theatre before, and from the minute the curtain rose until the curtain calls at the end, she was mesmerised, magically drawn into the Artists' Ball in Paris and the circus scene in which a real white horse actually appeared on the stage. Even the intervals did not break her involvement, and during the ride back to the Savoy Hotel she sang Connie Ediss' song "The Way to Treat a Lady" without restraint until Mrs. Wellington stressed that its theme of a woman being left in a public house by her husband, who had not paid for her port and lemonade, made it most unsuitable music; so she sang Ellaline Terriss' song instead.

Just a little bit of string,
Such a tiny bit of string,
Tied as tightly as a string could be
So that if I tried to play
I could never slip away,
For they'd put me on a string you see.

It had been just the right outing to restore her spirits, and her approach to the sale was considerably more optimistic the following morning. Even after Melbaugh had been outbid three times on her behalf, she remained keen, although it was growing late and most of the best names had gone.

"I don't have to buy here," she said, philosophically. "We can always try the auctions at Reading, or Epsom, or Hampton Court, Selling Plates or even private stables."

The last crowd-drawing colt sold for six thousand eight hundred guineas, and people began leaving. Sir Freddie's recommendation was brought in to very little attention. She was an extremely pretty filly with a pert, shapely head; long, sloping shoulders; and hard marks of muscle in her well-developed hindquarters and that slinky stride which indicates good action. Macha felt a familiar tremor sharpen her wits as the auctioneer began his cajolery.

"Tulip Mary, a two-year-old filly by Gameberry. Raced this season and ready to go on. Full sister to Captain Paul. Am I bid four thousand? three? two? Start her off, gentlemen. One thousand five hundred guineas, one five, one six, one seven . . ."

Macha, strained as a bearing rein, waited and watched. James Melbaugh was talking to an acquaintance and seemed oblivious to the auction. The filly walked elegantly up and down. "Two thousand in the pulpit. She's very small money at two thousand guineas, but I'm here to sell her. Two thousand guineas . . ."

Macha leant over the edge of the gallery with her arm out. The auctioneer stared and repeated. "Two thousand guineas, gentlemen. Your turn by the Fox, sir."

Macha flapped her hand wildly, but again could not hold his eye.

"Two thousand guineas. Last time."

"Two thousand, one hundred," Macha bellowed in a voice trained to carry across the loughs of Connemara.

The man looked up quizzically at Sir Frederick Wellington, who nodded his affirmation, and then at her.

"Are you bidding, madam?" he asked in astonishment.

"You know perfectly well I am. My bid is two thousand, one hundred guineas," Macha retorted without dropping a decibel.

The auctioneer looked behind to his superior. The man shrugged his shoulders and nodded.

"Two one," the auctioneer announced angrily, and then, with relief, "Two two."

"Two thousand five hundred guineas," the girl called out, ignoring a restraining hand on her arm.

"Two thousand five hundred guineas," the man echoed. "You're losing her, sir. She's worth more than this. Two thousand five hundred guineas. Any more anywhere?"

He exhorted and bullied, spinning out her bid in a desperate but unsuccessful attempt to find a male buyer. "Two thousand five hundred. Two thousand five hundred guineas. I'm going to sell her if I can get no more. Selling at two . . . thousand . . . five . . . hundred . . . guineas. Will you have two six? Last time, *gentlemen*. Two thousand five hundred guineas." There was an agonisingly long pause before the gavel knocked so faintly that it would have failed to open the door of a house of ill repute; but Macha's shriek of joy was audible outside the building, and the whole yard cheered.

"Oh, I can't thank you enough, Freddie . . . Sir Frederick." She remembered the proprieties too late to stop herself grasping his hands.

"My dear Miss Sheridan, it was absolutely nothing," he disclaimed, with unmistakable adoration.

"Let's hope the filly lives up to all this faith," James Melbaugh put in sourly as they all met up and hurried towards the stables to organise transport.

Tulip Mary was waiting in charge of a groom. Declan O'Brien went straight to her as though mesmerised.

"What do you think, Declan?" Macha asked.

"You've done all right, Miss Sheridan," he answered, actually beaming with approval.

Society lost much of its appeal after the purchase of Tulip Mary. One of the outbuildings had been turned into a large loose box deeply bedded with straw, and some very expensive tack had been bought beforehand, and Macha suddenly realised how much she had missed the daily stable routine and those carefree rides over the Downs.

The filly's arrival caused an unexpected transformation of Declan O'Brien's personality, too, for he fell in love with her instantly, and she with him. They spent hours each day together, as he worked her, groomed and strapped her, fed her, mucked her out, fussed around the yard near her and spoiled her with snacks of carrots and apples. He took to whistling and did not even raise a protest when Macha began appearing again in trousers and an old jacket to ride out.

"You look like a sack of potatoes on a side-saddle, anyway," was his only rude comment. He was certainly considerably easier to live with.

They spent much time discussing the various merits of the American Tod Sloan's astonishing forward seat versus the orthodox style of riding well down in the saddle with long leathers. To Macha it seemed obvious that the horse would carry weight over his shoulders and forehand more easily than in the centre of his back, but Declan was not convinced, until learning that the American "monkey up a stick" had already ridden twenty-one winners from forty-eight mounts in the few months since his arrival in Britain that year. With great reluctance, the Irish boy shortened his stirrups.

"Now, who's the sack of potatoes?" laughed Macha on his first attempt; but he improved rapidly, and when it became obvious that the method suited Tulip Mary, he denied ever having thought otherwise in the first place.

Gold's education continued in careful steps. After each session on long reins, she would lean over him, gradually adding more of her body weight, until she could sit on him and Declan would lead her a short distance, but not enough to strain the colt. It would be another few months before he was ridden regularly at the slower paces of walking and trotting, up and down hills, rarely cantering, and he would not be galloped at all until he was well muscled and developed.

He was a spirited and tough young horse, and progress was not without battles, which she had to win by determination and guile, rather than strength. At times, when he was being particularly stubborn and she was on the point of losing her temper, it was as though Molloy spoke to her as he had done so often while alive:

"Every vicious horse has been treated viciously by someone, and an animal which has always known kindness is always kind in return."

Then she would swallow her fury and return to the patient insistence which brought the best results.

It was fortunate that Macha was so occupied, as this left less time to brood over the facts that there had still been no reply to her letters to Biddy Connor asking for her children, and neither had there been any word from James Melbaugh since the visit to Tattersalls. Although she was "at home" to callers one afternoon a week at Mrs. Wellington's house, he did not appear, seemingly having taken umbrage at the way she had bought Tulip Mary and at the attention she had unwittingly paid to his friend.

Sir Freddie Wellington became a regular visitor and displayed a solid knowledge of horses and racing which provided them both with a topic for endless conversation. He was not a dashing companion, but she became very fond of him, sensing a rather bashful man masked by superficial eccentricity. It occasionally surprised her that Mrs. Wellington did not try to discourage her nephew's interest in someone of dubious background, but then, the dowager too was not as she appeared at first, having revealed in her ventures with racecourse bookmakers a remarkably daring nature beneath the severe exterior.

There was no avoiding some of the obligatory return visits to sit in stuffy, overfurnished drawing rooms making small talk for fifteen or twenty minutes before taking leave and moving on to another stultifying call, but Macha persuaded her chaperone to cram as many of these as possible into a single afternoon, in order to leave her free to return to the holding and in the hope they would not have to be repeated often.

The day of the Petworth House ball drew nearer, and the necessary fittings at Mr. Dodds's establishment resulted in an exquisite lemon-yellow chiffon gown adorned with clusters of ribbon, the bodice, sleeves and the tiers of its skirt edged with lace, and with a satin train decorated with hand-painted flowers. On Mrs. Wellington's advice, she paid over twenty pounds for a necklace of pearl daisies with diamond centres and had her hair dressed with pearls intertwined.

The days were already short. It was dusk as they crossed the Downs and dark by the time the carriage drew up at the entrance to the long, grey house with its windows all ablaze and they made their way to the Marble Hall. Macha was speechless at the sight of opulence she could not have imagined: the huge rooms with their wall carvings of fruit, leaves and flowers, birds and mythical beasts and cherubs, shields and angels; the chandelier of ormolu and porcelain reflected in the looking-glass over the fireplace. She quite forgot having promised the first dance to Freddie as she strayed away from the party, beguiled by the marble and the gold leaf, the paintings, murals and sumptuous furniture.

She had already seen the jewels and clothes and carriages, the shops, the service, the confident superiority of the gentlemen and the impregnable position of the ladies, their horses feted and pampered like heroes, their dogs faithful and fit and privileged above human servants. She had seen their parks, the exteriors of their country seats and their town houses; but until this moment, she had not appreciated the real meaning of the word "rich." Did they eat off gold plates and sleep only in specially warmed eiderdown? Now, she knew that they did.

"My nephew has been looking for you everywhere. It is not just thoughtlessness on your part, Miss Sheridan, but unforgivable discourtesy. May I remind you that but for his connection on his mother's side with Lord Leconfield, you and I should not be here at all."

It was the presence which had induced the vapours in generations of young officers' wives. Mrs. Wellington cut Macha's ashamed reply by marching back to the ballroom like an advancing regiment, with her ward bringing up the rear as the solitary camp follower.

"Freddie . . . ," Macha began, abjectly, as he revolved her expertly round the floor.

"Tell me more about this colt of yours," he put in, quickly.

"But I want to apologise . . ."

"Your cousin, O'Brien, tells me he's a real dandy." He was determined not to let her humiliate herself.

"They say he's just like Gallinule," she said, and gave his hand a grateful squeeze. "We want to take Tulip Mary and him to train at Newmarket, and I'm about to start hunting for a house there."

"My aunt should have told me your plan, for you may not have to search at all," he said eagerly. "I might know just the place."

"Where? What is it like? Oh, tell me about it!" Macha turned her head to look up at him.

As she did so, James Melbaugh swept by them with a radiant girl and Macha, watching as they swirled away, did not hear a word of the answer.

The next waltz on her programme had been reserved by Melbaugh when he had first called upon her and they had talked of the ball. It was an arrangement he could not fail to honour and would give her the chance to put matters right between them, she thought. She found herself anticipating how he would hold her with such fervour that she did not notice her partner break off in mid-sentence with a bewildered look as he returned her to her seat.

Melbaugh bowed, stiffly, and maintained enough distance between them to contain another equally estranged couple. They could have raised their arms and simply allowed others to dance through them. Macha's plans of a sidelong glance and a flirtatious giggle were iced.

"Is this not a wonderful ball?" she said, tentatively.

"Tolerable."

A Rom traveller in the same situation would have raged at her for all to hear and she would have screamed back, or maybe even laughed in such a way as to invite him to join in, but she had no idea how to respond to this cold gentleman who knew her so well, but was treating her like a stranger.

She tried again. "Have you been racing recently?"

"Of course."

"We have not for several weeks."

"Really." He stared over her head with an expression of extreme boredom, which suddenly changed into a brilliant smile as his previous partner danced by.

Macha narrowed her eyes, apparently missed a step accidentally, stamped heavily on his foot and had the satisfaction of seeing him wince.

"My new filly is doing very well indeed. I expect you've heard as much from Sir Frederick. We're all sure she's going to be in the money next year."

He was still trying to appear uninterested when she dangled the bait.

". . . Of course, it's a fine rider she'll be needing then."

"If she's as good as you say, I should be delighted to ride her."

He was hooked.

Macha gazed up at him with wide eyes, seemingly full of regret.

"How kind of you to offer, Mr. Melbaugh," she said silkily. "But I should not dream of imposing on someone with so many other engagements and so little time to spare. No, I am afraid my cousin, Declan, will just have to be the one to take her first past the winning post."

It was a victory which brought her little satisfaction during the rest of the ball, although England's most aristocratic young men were so keen to be introduced and to partner her that she did not sit out a single dance. But then, neither did The Honourable James Melbaugh, who glided and twirled and waltzed and spun past her, each time with a different beauty in his arms and another nodding, smiling Mama on the sidelines and enough diamonds between the two to buy the royal horse Persimmon outright and still have sufficient left over to purchase a castle.

Macha laughed and tossed her head, flicked her fan open and shut, and trapped unwary gallants with a devastating mixture of silver eyes, soft Irish voice and naively outrageous witticisms.

Countless nights spent dancing at travellers' feasts and weddings had given her natural grace. This music was more staid, and the quality moved as unrhythmically as wooden dolls jerked by strings, but the polka contained strains of the wild flamencos and Irish jigs she knew best, and she tripped it with verve.

Altogether, she was quite proud of her performance and even succeeded in enjoying herself in a savage kind of way for much of the evening.

Yet she was glad when the time came to leave and wandered into the fresh air with relief. Just ahead of her, James Melbaugh, in scarlet-lined black cloak and silk top hat, sprang athletically into the driving seat of his carriage, played the thong of his whip and skimmed off down the drive. She would not think of him again, she vowed. Then thought of little else.

The train crossed the autumn landscape, through the yellowing woods of Surrey with their flashing copper beeches and over the commons of harshly rust bracken; past fields full of cattle fat from summer and still diligently storing food against the cold and hungry months to come; over the Thames and into the foggy, shrieking, packed, hooting, echoing, glass-vaulted chaos of the London Station.

Macha and Declan O'Brien and Mrs. Wellington and Sir Freddie traversed the city with difficulty and boarded another train. They were on their way to the heath where King Charles the First built a stand from which to watch the running of a Gold Cup and King Charles the Second rode winners on his favourite horse; to the gallops of the Limekilns, Long Hill, the Bury and the Warren Hills; to the hub of English racing.

As they travelled east, the skies broadened and deepened and widened until the land was reduced to a frieze. Then wisps of fine grey cloud were drawn across, like strokes of Oriental script, and the window panes were tinted by the last rays of the sun setting behind Cambridge. Macha, oblivious to the others, was lost in thought as they steamed past an encampment of travellers on the outskirts of the little town, then large houses surrounded by paddocks enclosed with white post-and-rail fencing and into the curry of hay and crushed cats, molasses and straw, manure and leather, which all make up the inimitable smell of horses that is Newmarket.

Rooms were reserved for them at the Rutland Arms Hotel, and at first light next morning, Macha's eyes and mind opened to instant alertness, as though she had not slept. Without disturbing the others, she dressed and went out into the whistle-gay, bucket-clanking, hoof-clattering, wide-awake streets, through which the first strings of racehorses were wending towards the Heath.

She passed the newly completed Clock Tower; turned right and then left up a narrow alley which led to the foot of the stiff slope of Long Hill. Sea-gulls wheeled and wailed overhead, and wind was noisily hoarse in the fringe of trees. Mist softened the contours and colours of the turf and gave a rhapsodic quality to the sight of hundreds of Thoroughbreds converging on the gallops: bays and browns, chestnuts, greys and blacks, walking or trotting gently one after another, clouds of breath about their heads, lads crouched on their backs coughing in the cold morning, flint-eyed trainers hacking alongside on solid cobs unimpressed by the magnificence of their companions.

Here were no coloured silks or numbers, no way to differentiate between the stars and the also-rans except by genuine expertise; here, without cheers or éclat, the sprinters and the stayers, the aged and the maidens, the blowers and the legs simply worked together.

As Macha watched, a small stable of horses began to play up, prancing and bucking, sidling and whirling about, running backwards, rearing and shying, and as suddenly settled down again, as though to a signal. A spread-out group galloped over the brow and became a sedate line passing diagonally through another, part of a mystic ritual, an act of worship to an ancient god.

"I thought I'd find you here," said Declan O'Brien's voice by her side. "Was there ever anything like this?"

"Never." She drew in her breath with a sob.

The bells for Matins rang out from All Saints and still the horses came, each tired bunch leaving to be replaced by new arrivals fresh and raring to go, unconcerned by the men lurking in the trees seeking secrets through field glasses and the strangers riding with apparent innocence near every trial and casually strolling onlookers chancing across the turf.

The lads rode past loftily, talking to each other not about their sublime mounts, nor of speed, triumphs or prizes, but about the night before and the kitchen maid at Cheveley and Mary, the head lad's daughter, and the barmaid at the Red Lion.

"You'll be out there with them soon," Macha promised, reading his thoughts.

With arctic cries, a thick cloud of greylag geese flying south from Iceland for winter descended from the sky to graze as the very last horse and rider diminished in the distance to vanish over the skyline.

There was the usual fuss from Mrs. Wellington when they returned; but Macha did not care, and Sir Freddie came to her defence.

"Do not be too hard, aunt. When I take you to the gallops tomorrow, I'll wager you will not be persuaded to leave before luncheon either."

That afternoon he drove them out of the town, up Cambridge Hill, past famous Egerton, where Richard Marsh trained horses for the Prince of Wales, finally turning into a short carriage sweep leading to a pretty red brick house.

"Is it for sale?" asked Macha.

"To rent," he replied, and when she looked doubtful, continued: "I realise you may consider it to be too small, but such an arrangement would give you time to know the area and look for a larger property to buy, if you so wished."

Macha could not help smiling as she scanned the rows of windows and compared the building with her *varda* and the Sussex cottage. To her this appeared palatial.

The door opened into a large oak-panelled hall with a staircase curving to a galleried first-floor landing. An agent for the owner, who had been awaiting their arrival, led the way from drawing room to breakfast room, dining room, smoking room, billiard room, master bedroom, family bedrooms, spare rooms for guests and nurseries, then off the hall to the service quarters, servants' hall, kitchen, pantries, cook's room, maids' rooms, up and down countless flights of stairs, until the girl completely lost her bearings and was totally confused. She could not imagine how she would fill such a place or control all the servants required for its upkeep, and was thinking up excuses to extricate herself as they followed the back drive to the yard, where her whole opinion changed.

Most of the stables were brand-new, a south-facing block of the latest in loose boxes, their top doors opening so that each horse could look out and see his neighbours and the activity outside. At an angle was an old building of stalls for draught horses. Unlike so many of the dark, dank and dirty stables she had seen, these had been opened up with windows to be airy and dry, refloored to be easily mucked out and drained. There were a large tack room, a harness room and an open-fronted coach house and a barn stuffed to the roof with top-quality hay. On the west block was a stallion box, exactly right for Gold. The problems of coping with a large house vanished. The yard felt right, which was all that mattered.

The rental for Ebberly was agreed, and it was arranged that Declan would return to Sussex for the horses as soon as possible and they would all stay on at the Rutland for the next few weeks while the house was made ready.

All the way back to Newmarket, Freddie kept exclaiming that everything was "top-hole." Mrs. Wellington, who was to come and live there as Macha's companion, had insisted on taking sole charge of the household organisation and conducted a monologue on curtains and furniture and staff. Declan O'Brien discussed training and future races with unaccustomed animation, and Macha verbally filled every box and stall with new horses of impeccably classic credentials; and none listened to a word the others were saying.

The dowager retired to rest, after agreeing her nephew could show her ward around the town, *on foot*, and provided they returned within the hour. The two strolled up the lane behind the inn, past the house where Nell Gwynn had lived and coming to Palace House, where the Prince of Wales usually stayed while visiting Newmarket. It was built of ordinary, light-coloured brick.

"Why, it's not so different from my house!" she exclaimed in disappointment. "It's not a real marble-and-gold palace at all!"

"Macha! Macha! My dear Macha!" Sir Freddie unexpectedly seized her hands and gazed down at her with a peculiar expression on his face, so that she thought he was about to burst into tears. "Macha. I know I'm rather a chump—that is, in some ways, not a particularly clever fellow—but I would treat you like a goddess . . ."

Macha was taken aback to realise he was making a proposal, although it was unclear whether it was a marriage proposal or a less respectable proposition. She waited patiently as he floundered.

"The truth is I've never met a gel like you, such a sport, y'know, and so . . . with such conformation . . . pretty, d'you see."

"Sir Frederick . . ." she began.

"Freddie. Please, please call me Freddie."

"Freddie . . . what on earth are you trying to say?"

"Well, I'm asking you to marry me, of course, old girl," he blurted out. "I mean, we could have a topping time together . . . plenty of horses . . . racing and so on . . ."

"Oh Freddie . . . ," she began, genuinely moved.

"You don't have to answer now. I expect you need to think it over," he interrupted.

"Freddie . . . I am truly honoured that you should want me for your wife," she said gently. "But I cannot accept your proposal."

"No . . . no. I did not think you would." He let her hands go and his face fell into mournful folds. "Prefer Melbaugh, I expect. Good-looking chap and all that."

Macha did not answer.

"I have something for you, you know." He began to look worried again as he spoke. "You won't refuse it, will you? I mean, you won't let this marriage nonsense of mine prevent you from accepting a gift?"

"I don't know what to say," she replied honestly, wondering what to do if he produced a ring. "What is the gift?"

"A surprise . . . nothing to cause you any disquiet . . . Arranged its delivery at Ebberly House tomorrow. . . ." Once again he had instinctively understood her reaction.

"I love surprises. Give me a hint?" She took his arm with an improper familiarity which removed the awkwardness between them at once. "Just the littlest clue?"

He shook his head firmly. "Wait and see."

By the time they returned to the hotel, Mrs. Wellington was waiting with an ill-concealed impatience which made Macha wonder whether she had really gone to rest, or just contrived to leave them alone together. During tea, the widow looked at her with raised eyebrows and once actually appeared to mouth a question. Eventually, she sent her nephew off on some unnecessary errand and turned on the girl a face which would brook no prevarication.

"Well?"

"Mmmm?" Macha pushed too much cake into her mouth.

"Did Freddie propose?"

"Why should you think such a thing?" she fenced.

"Because naturally he asked my permission first," retorted Mrs. Wellington. "Now, when is the wedding to be?"

Macha dabbed her mouth with a napkin before responding with singular lack of tact, "There's to be no wedding, because I've turned him down."

"You've refused to marry Sir Frederick Wellington? Surely you cannot have been so foolish, Miss Sheridan!" The dowager equally forgot all courtesy. "Do you know he has an income of £25,000 a year, and is not only a baronet in his own right, but also the sole heir to his uncle, the Marquess of Angleton, from whom he stands to inherit a fortune and the Huish Cher estate? Marriage with him would give you position and wealth, and you would not even be required to bring a dowry. He is also my nephew. Such an opportunity will never come your way again, you can be absolutely certain of that."

"Please don't be offended, Mrs. Wellington," Macha pleaded. "Sir Frederick is everything you say and much more. He's gentle and kind, and there's nothing he doesn't know about racing, and he will make a saint of a husband to someone much better than me. I know he's a great catch for a girl without background; but I also know we would not make each other happy. Besides, do you not feel that at only sixteen years old, I am too young for marriage?"

"He would have waited a year or so for you, I am quite sure," her chaperone pointed out, angrily lancing a cake so that cream squelched unpleasantly from it.

They sat on in uncomfortable silence, Macha toying with her tea and Mrs. Wellington eating in such a way as to give herself severe indigestion. Eventually, it was the older woman who spoke first.

"Well, you have made your decision, and I admit to being disappointed, but the matter will rest there."

With which she twitched her hat straight, stood up with dignified grandeur and marched from the room.

"Do not concern yourself, Miss Sheridan. The dear old trout will soon be back on form again." Freddie had returned in time to catch the end of the scene. "She never did like being thwarted. My Uncle Harry, who fought in the Crimea '54 and '55, used to say he would not have needed the brigade had my aunt been there. One glimpse of her advancing would have sent the entire Russian army into retreat. The old bean was so terrified of her that he used to hide behind the wall of the kitchen garden before daring to light up his pipe. But she's a good sort, really."

His assessment was accurate. The next day, Mrs. Wellington, followed at a suitable distance by a cowering draper and several random servants who appeared to have been seconded from the hotel, was driven to Ebberly House to embark on a ferocious programme of cleaning, measuring and ordering, in which appeared to lie the cure for her chagrin over the failure of her marital plans for ward and nephew.

Macha and Sir Freddie and Declan O'Brien tiptoed thankfully

away to the gates to the yard, where she was told to close her eyes while the two men led her over the cobblestones. She tried to guess the surprise—definitely something to do with horses: a silver-mounted whip perhaps, or maybe a saddle, or possibly even her chosen racing colours made up into jockey's silks.

"No peeking!" commanded Declan, sternly, as she screwed up her eyes and attempted to cheat.

A door creaked somewhere ahead and there was a lot of scuffling.

"Right! You can look now!"

She opened her eyes. She was facing a loose box, and a bright bay horse with a white blaze was looking straight at her. Declan O'Brien, grinning idiotically, led him out.

"May I present Macmonist," beamed Freddie. "I'd like your opinion of him."

Macha walked slowly round the gelding and then signalled for him to be led across the yard. She felt rather silly at having anticipated a present, when Sir Freddie had only brought over his latest purchase for her to view. The horse was outstanding. If he had been drawing a milk float and neglected under a shaggy, ungroomed winter coat encrusted with dirt, his quality could not have been disguised. It was there in the loose, free action, the big, honest eyes, the poise and supreme confidence.

"By Saint Simon out of Highland Lass." Sir Freddie confirmed his class.

"He's a pearl." She turned, full of pleasure at the sight of the dazzling animal. "You've picked the best in this one."

"He's yours, Macha. I brought him here for you."

A wave of heat broke over her and she felt her stomach fill with moths. The Thoroughbred walked calmly round and round as she stared in an agony of covetousness.

At last, she turned her back deliberately, and managed to say through numb lips, "It would not be proper for me to accept, Sir Frederick."

"Since when did you care about what's proper, Macha Sheridan?" Declan O'Brien shouted in disbelief.

"Yesterday, you gave me your word that you would not reject my gift. Is it not improper to break your oath?" Sir Freddie moved to block her way. "Or perhaps you do not care for the horse?"

"Don't care for him? Wouldn't the haloes of a congregation of saints and a host of angels look tarnished beside him?" She was on the point of tears over the predicament.

"I know how much you admire Saint Simon, and so I thought he would suit you," explained Freddie.

"Oh, he does! You know he does! And if our conversation yesterday had ended differently, nothing would keep me from him," she admitted in a low voice only her suitor could hear. "But how can I take advantage of the fact that you intended him for your fiancée?"

"Now, you're wrong there, old girl." Freddie was hearty. "That gelding was to be sold last, and I kept him back for you before the thought of getting spliced entered my noddle."

"Oh, Freddie, that can't be true," she said with longing.

" 'Pon my honour," he replied, and she did not dare look to see if he was blushing. "Now, will you have him? Or am I going to have to send him to Tattersalls?"

What did it matter what people thought? Declan O'Brien was right. She did not give a fig for them, and having already been crazy enough to refuse Sir Freddie, she was not going to repeat the madness by turning down his horse.

"It's the most wonderful present I've ever had, or ever will have," she vowed ecstatically, and gave him a public and smacking kiss on the lips.

Chapter TEN

It was a working winter. Society deserted Newmarket for the social imperative of London, leaving behind a community totally engrossed by the raising and training of racehorses. Every day was programmed to the timetable of feeding, cleaning out, grooming, riding work, polishing tack, mixing mash, measuring corn, checking legs and feet and eyes and coat and appetite. In sickness and in health, however dark and bitter the morning, the human servants of these most cossetted of animals still had to crack the ice on the water buckets and face the blasted heath at an hour when all sensible people were deeply asleep in their feather beds.

The blades of the east wind sliced unhindered across the flatlands, cutting open lips until they bled and chapping skin and skinning eyes raw. The wind stabbed into naked bodies as though the protective layers of clothes were tatters. Blood became thick and slow in the veins and arteries, and bones were as brittle as crystal. It was common knowledge that winter falls meant broken ribs. Trainers and horses grew bad-tempered, and the lads shivered and cursed, their hands stiff on the reins, and regretted not having apprenticed themselves to shopkeepers, or gone to work on the railway.

Yet few ever left this life of labour and luck, muck and money. They lived in overcrowded mess rooms over the haylofts and their charges, on wages that would have shocked most other manual workers even in this underpaid age, dreaming of riding winners. If they grew too tall, or too old to be jockeys without having achieved this ambition, still they stayed on, hopelessly addicted to the atmosphere, to the gossip in the yards and taprooms and tracks, to being in the know; above all, to the exquisite aristocrats in their care; and the dream of personal triumph was transferred to that special horse in each individual's charge, the one he knew was a champion.

Declan's thirteen-year-old cousin arrived from County Clare to be employed in the stables of Ebberly House. An experienced older man might have taken too much control of the yard, and Macha was jealous of her position, already vulnerable because she was female. However, a young boy fresh off the Dublin ferry posed no threat. He could easily be kept in order, and no-one was likely to pay much attention to his incomprehensible chatter.

A locked room above the stalls was set aside so that she could change secretly and ride out before the domestic servants were up. Everyone knew that she went to watch her horses training each day; if anyone suspected odd goings on, certainly no-one ever whispered it to Mrs. Wellington, who remained in contented ignorance.

In their loose boxes, the horses moved forward to look curiously over their doors into the twilight of the yard. Five o'clock, the time for evening stables. Gold was waiting, his eyes like black marble and his white blaze luminescent. He blew gently as his owner hung her lantern on a hook in the wall and fed him chopped carrots and stroked the silk of his neck. The nobility of the stallion was always marvellous to her, the fiery hair of mane and tail, the camellia texture of his skin, the curved shells of his ears, the strength displayed in muscle and bone. Darkness emphasized the feel and smell of him. She ran the hand down each of his legs to search for heat, but all was well. He arched his neck and nudged her as she put her arm over his crest and scratched between his ears and confided a mixture of the news and nonsense of the day. It was their Evensong. He could have crushed her by merely shifting weight, or seized her in his yellow teeth and flung her away like a toy, or felled her with one striking hoof; instead, he purred.

Above all things she loved him, as though, like Macha the goddess, she had given birth to him herself. He was her last link with Molloy and her children, her tie to Ireland, and her dream was the same as that of every lad in Newmarket: to ride her horse first past the post.

But even Macha, with her natural disregard for rules and convention, realised this was a hopeless aspiration, and she compensated for the frustration by overseeing every aspect of Gold's life, from his rations to his shoeing to any necessary veterinary attention to the meticulous planning of his future career. He was already entered in the Brocklesby Stakes and the Darley Maiden Stakes at the beginning of the next flat season. By now, he was almost as big as his renowned sire and showing no sign of having inherited the weak blood vessels which had helped to end the racing of Gallinule.

The furtive horse watchers who loitered around the gallops were well aware of him. Macha, as she cantered by, sensed their tracking binoculars. No matter how early she started out, or on what obscure part of the heath she rode, they were always there.

It must have been the wettest day of a wet, chilly spring, as she left the woods at the top of Long Hill, when another horse and rider suddenly came up from behind and bolted past, causing Gold to rear in surprise and deluging them both with mud. Without a thought, Macha dug her heels into the stallion's side in anger, and the horse leapt gigantically to the challenge, swallowing the incline in massive strides and closing on the other like a vengeful missile. Too late, she realised she had been tricked, probably by the touts in the trees, into revealing his true speed. Gold had the bit between his teeth and his rival outclassed and was not to be stopped until he was lengths ahead. As they flared past, the girl heard a shout, which faded into a mere bird note behind, and she felt herself burn up with exhilaration.

Let them all see! she thought, recklessly. Let them see what my horse can do! And she urged him on, as though it were the Killarney Races over again.

The unknown competitor was only halfway down the hill by the time Gold drew up at the foot. Macha waited with head flung back and a suitably coarse observation ready on her tongue. She noticed the man had adopted the Tod Sloan seat, although it had done him no good in this case. Then, as they drew nearer, she saw, to her horror, that the rider was James Melbaugh.

Wheeling Gold about, she started to canter away, but Melbaugh crossed the turf at an angle and cut off her retreat. He stopped his horse directly in her path and stared. She ducked her head.

"My God! I would not have believed it!" she heard him say, but still did not look up. "Hiding your face will do you no good, Miss Sheridan, for I know perfectly well who you are."

So she lifted her head and glared back.

"Macha Sheridan! Macha Sheridan!" He was grinning quite idiotically.

"Well, it's meself right enough, James Melbaugh. And you can make of it what you will." She launched into attack. "Now get that weed of a nag out of the way and let me pass."

His laughter was wild, and then he asked unexpectedly, "Have you thought of me, Macha?"

"I have not," she lied, stoutly.

"Well, I have thought of you . . . constantly," he admitted, to her amazement. ". . . and now here you are in cap and breeches, looking . . . ravishing."

It was obvious he was teasing. She threw him a look of contempt.

"Poke fun all you like, Mr. Melbaugh, and tell all the world!" she retorted. "But be sure and tell them at the same time how me and Gold thrashed you and your brute, for all your breeding."

"You did indeed, Miss Sheridan," he agreed. "You have a very remarkable horse, and you are a very fine rider."

"I will be on my way," she said with dignity, shortening her reins and starting to move off.

"Wait!"

She turned, suspiciously.

"Marry me!"

"What?"

"Marry me, Macha Sheridan! I must have you!" There were little lines of desire at the corners of his mouth. "Marry me tomorrow!"

"Merciful saints and little cherubs. You court me for a couple of weeks, then ignore me for long enough to grow an oak from seed and build a ship from it, then you cut up me horse like a road hog, lose the race and expect to marry me!" she stormed. "Well, Mr. Melbaugh, I'd as soon hitch myself to a Turk."

"No, you wouldn't." He drew alongside with a heartbreaking smile.

She looked into his compelling blue eyes. They glinted like cut sapphire, and behind the humour, other hard, exciting facets could just be detected. She felt a surge of pure greed.

"No, I would not," she echoed, weakly.

"Marry me!" he insisted.

Oh, she wanted him, too.

"I will," she consented, unhesitatingly.

That was the moment Declan O'Brien chose to arrive, ride Tulip Mary between them and round on the girl.

"What happened? Where did you get to? Don't you know you had me fretting enough to lose my teeth, haring away downhill as though you'd no reins." Then, before she could answer, a look of panic froze his features as he realised James Melbaugh had been holding her hand. "Lord God of Almighty, he knows! You've told him! You're ruined!"

"Don't worry, dear boy, just congratulate me—and yourself," Melbaugh drawled. "We're about to become cousins, for Miss Sheridan looks so irresistibly delicious in her novel outfit this morning that I had no option but to propose marriage at once, and she has accepted."

Macha felt dizzy and was far too excited to notice the colour drain from Declan O'Brien's face as he mumbled something about wishing her happiness and turned the filly to ride blindly ahead.

"I shall call on your guardian and we'll settle the matter at eleven," said James Melbaugh cheerily, as though arranging a picnic outing, instead of the most momentous occasion in their lives.

Macha flung off her cloak and unbuttoned the dress beneath and stepped into the bath of hot water which was always ready for her return from the gallops. She poured in most of a bottle of bath salts and created such a lather of Fleur d'Amour soap that it floated on the surface like ice cream. Once dry, she sprayed herself with lavender water and smoothed milk of cucumber over her cheeks and rubbed grenadine into her lips, while a young maid tried to salvage the wreckage of her wet hair. Half a dozen frocks were brought out, tried on and discarded before she decided on the azure cashmere with the collar of tucked lawn, a demure and pretty gown which she hoped would obliterate the image of herself in breeches and boots from James Melbaugh's mind.

At breakfast, she dropped her toast and spilled her tea and behaved so nervously that Mrs. Wellington was convinced she had a fever and began to talk of calling a doctor.

"I am perfectly well," Macha assured her breathlessly. "I am merely elated that Gold ran so superbly this morning, better than ever before."

She paused, before adding, in what she hoped was a casual tone, ". . . We met James Melbaugh, exercising a horse."

"Indeed!" Mrs. Wellington's fruity contralto exclamation made it clear that she was not fooled.

"Yes. In fact, he did mention his resolve to call."

"Really! After all this time! And did he happen to mention on which day he would call?"

"Well, he suggested . . . today, actually."

"What a pity we shall be out," said the dowager, rising from the table.

"Oh, no! Oh, please, Mrs. Wellington, we cannot be out!" Macha jumped up in agitation. "It is most important that we be at home."

The widow waved an interested servant from the room before commenting with some severity, "My dear Macha, James Melbaugh has not made the slightest effort to see you for months, and as I recall, behaved with minimal courtesy towards you at Lady Leconfield's ball. It would be most unwise if he were given the impression that you are eager for his company."

"But he wishes to see you. . . . He has something to ask you." Macha was close to tears.

The old lady was imperturbable. "I am sure whatever he wishes to ask can wait."

"It can't! It can't!" The girl lost her head. "He wants to marry me, and I've said Yes."

Mrs. Wellington carefully poured herself another cup of tea. Then she sat down again and sipped it slowly with slightly trembling hands.

"When did all this take place?" she asked at last.

"This morning, as soon as we met again. He said he'd never stopped thinking of me." There was no point in lying.

"Well, his method of becoming engaged seems very bad form, if not actually peculiar. Were you a daughter of mine, I should forbid it; but a gel in your situation must find a husband, and he is certainly an excellent match." Mrs. Wellington shook her head in some confusion. "Really, you hardly know each other; but then, young people nowadays are so impatient."

"You will give us your blessing?" begged Macha.

"Are you quite sure this is what you want, child?" The old lady still looked very uncertain.

"Yes. Oh, yes!" Macha had no doubts.

"Then we shall wait for the young man to arrive and hear his intentions" was as far as Mrs. Wellington would commit herself.

However, two hours later, she was drinking a toast to their future in sherry.

There could be no wedding, Macha firmly told her new fiancé, until after Gold's first race in April, for she had to devote all her attention to training.

"I never thought to find myself in competition with a horse for a lady's affections," he complained with a wry smile.

"But what a horse!" she responded, and he had to agree.

* * *

Declan O'Brien and his cousin, Ulick, were wiping the morning's dirt off the saddles when Macha went into the yard a few days later.

"I won't be able to ride out tomorrow," she said. "I'm off to London to buy my trousseau. So you can put Ulick up on Tulip Mary, and you go out twice on Gold and Macmonist."

"Ulick's not working Tulip Mary," Declan retorted sullenly.

"Then he can ride Macmonist and you can lead Tulip Mary with Gold."

"Gold won't stand for that," he pointed out correctly.

"Well, work something out," she snapped impatiently. "For it's certain I'm to London."

He caught up with her again as she crossed the lawn.

"I want a word with you, Miss Sheridan."

He looked tight-lipped, and she hoped he was not going to protest about her engagement.

"I've had an offer from Cheveley Park," he informed her.

"What sort of offer?" She was completely taken aback.

"A good offer, Miss Sheridan, with maybe the chance to ride some topping horses for them."

"Better than my horses?" she queried with a piercing glare.

He refused to meet her eyes. "There's more money, too."

"Well, if it's more money you're after, why not say so?"

Money had never been mentioned between them, yet he had always seemed satisfied.

"There are three Thoroughbreds, a number of hacks and carriage horses and a lot of extra work here now," he pointed out with justification.

"You're right, Declan. I should have thought of it myself," she nodded, calculating quickly. "Would half a crown more a week do?"

"It wouldn't do at all, Miss Sheridan." He was adamant. "I will need at least another five shillings to stay on."

She was so stupefied that she simply nodded. The idea of Declan's leaving had never occurred to her, and she found it deeply disturbing. Although they were not cousins, the family charade they had played out for so long had almost persuaded her that he was her close relation who would always be there, riding her horses and running her yard.

"Is there anything else on your mind?" she wondered, with an unreasonable sense of betrayal.

"No. I am perfectly satisfied now, Miss Sheridan," he replied, with a formality which kept him out of reach.

Had the wedding plans not occupied her time, Macha would have been bewildered and downcast, but she was being hurried to the station, and the journey was so dominated by talk of fabrics and designs that there was no time to dwell upon the incident or to appreciate its significance, which was that Declan O'Brien had made an important decision about his future. He intended to become a rich man.

Mrs. Wellington took her to Liberty's, in Regent Street, where they bought yards of ivory satin and flounces of Brussels point lace to be forwarded direct to Mr. Toby Dodds in Chichester and made up in a style Macha chose from a magazine. The bridal veil was of Brussels appliqué lace, so delicate that the manager of the department would not allow any of the assistants to touch it, but insisted on packing it himself in layers and layers of tissue paper. They ordered lingerie and tea gowns and linen and, finally, visited the shoemaker, who was to make the satin shoes with lace bows.

After this, the old lady was so exhausted that to Macha's dismay, it seemed they might not be able to return to Newmarket, but have to stay in the capital overnight at the Savoy. The city, with its overcrowded streets and overheated shops and overpowering smells from the gutters and colliding French perfumes, always made her feel slightly jittery. It was like being crawled over by a plague of caterpillars, and despite the fun of spending so much money on so many gorgeous clothes, all she really wanted was to return to the breezy heath of Newmarket as quickly as possible.

They took a hansom to Fortnum and Mason, where a sharp whiff of smelling salts followed by a leisurely tea brought about their recovery.

"Are you certain you would not prefer *white* satin, Macha dear?" the dowager pressed for the umpteenth time. "The ivory shade is lovely, but a bride should be dressed in the white of purity."

Macha thought of Molloy. If he were able to see from beyond the grave, she knew he would not blame her for marrying again; but a virgin-white gown would seem like a denial of their marriage and their children. She could see the faces of her lost babies behind all her thoughts and actions, so close and yet beyond reach. Her letters to

Ireland asking for them had brought no response. Now, by marrying James Melbaugh, she knew she was ending all chance of ever being able to have them with her. She flinched a little at the pain of their memory, and she shook her head.

"The cream is my favourite; and besides, it is already on its way to Mr. Dodds."

As they sat in the train, going home again, she remembered the day in Cork, so long ago, when she had ventured into that smart shop and bought the bright pink satin and coloured ribbon and silk petticoats and the hand-made lawn knickers for her first wedding. She fingered the shamrock brooch she always wore for him and for Sian Williams. If they could see her now.

Without warning, the High Street and surrounding roads became busy with carriages and fashionable couples as spring brought an influx of owners to see how their horses had progressed during the winter. The atmosphere heightened as the start of the flat season drew close. At Ebberly, training intensified, as it did in every other yard, and another lad and an old groom were hired.

It was decided that James Melbaugh would keep his London house on after the marriage, and they would also continue to rent the Newmarket property for a while; he did not feel it was large enough, but they needed a base in the area. He called daily and spent much time in the stables with Macha, and Freddie Wellington returned from town, generously to wish her joy and to become a regular visitor once more. The experience of the two men was invaluable, and all three racehorses improved as a result.

Declan O'Brien worked Gold most mornings, for although her fiancé was highly amused by Macha's riding astride, there was now too much to do, and with too many people around, for her to risk riding out as before. Therefore, each morning, she mounted one of the hacks side-saddle to accompany James Melbaugh on Macmonist and then had to watch, with a mixture of pride and irritation, as the Thoroughbreds left her behind, to arrive back sometime later, their riders flushed and satisfied.

A trial was run for Gold against Macmonist in which he distinguished himself by cantering past the older, more developed stablemate. The opening meeting was only weeks away.

"That stallion needs a really experienced man up," commented

Melbaugh after the trial. "It would be far better if I rode him for you at Lincoln."

"But I've promised Declan," Macha protested. "It's what he's worked for."

"He can have a ride on one of my string sometime; but it would be a great mistake to put a chalk on your horse and spoil his chances, so I will ride him." The man gave her a soothing little pat on the head, as though the affair were decided.

"No, James!" Macha irritably shook his hand away. "It is good of you to offer, but Declan is racing Gold in the Brocklesby Stakes."

"My dear, this is not the way I expect my pretty girl to behave." He wagged a finger at her, half mocking and half serious. "You must realise that I know best."

Macha tilted up her chin and fixed him with quelling arrogance. "James Melbaugh, I am not your wife yet, and when . . . if . . . I become so, it will be my duty to accept your decisions in all marital matters. However, while your advice will always be as welcome as new bread, my horses are my business and are to remain so. I shall decide when and where they run and who runs them."

"What? Without any help at all?" A broad grin made the fleeting shadow which had darkened his glance seem like an illusion.

Macha felt rather silly for having been so aggressive. "No, no, of course not, but you do understand about Declan, don't you?"

Her fiancé shrugged his shoulders. "I wish him every success," he said, with only the slightest edge in his voice.

Gold with emerald-green hoops were the colours she registered, paying the annual fee and opening the necessary account with Messrs. Weatherby, where eyebrows were raised at the effrontery of a woman revealing her own name as an owner. The Duchess of Montrose had certainly owned and raced horses, but she had had the decency to do so under the male pseudonym of "Mr. Manton," and it was common knowledge that "Mr. Jersey's" horses belonged to actress Lillie Langtry, onetime mistress of the Prince of Wales. But the owner of Gold, Tulip Mary and Macmonist insisted on being publicly entered as Miss Macha Sheridan, and was therefore damned as no lady.

Macha also actually travelled in the train van with her colt on the day of his first race, leaving the bemused party of Mrs. Wellington, Sir Frederick Wellington and the Honourable James Melbaugh, to make the journey in a first-class passenger compartment. All the way, she had to restrain herself from lecturing Declan O'Brien, who sat grim-faced and preoccupied on a pile of straw in the corner.

He had been *wasting* through a combination of near-starvation and purgatives since Christmas and managed to weigh in at six stone seven pounds. The faces all around him were unfamiliar, but he ignored them, concentrating all his thoughts on the horse.

"Sit still and no whip. I don't want him put off the game on his first outing." Macha gave him her last instructions for the race as he mounted in the paddock. Gold had walked round quite quietly, showing a natural interest in the other two-year-olds and the crowd, but no sign of nerves. It was a mild day, and with the sun warm on his back, he cantered down to the start with skittish enjoyment.

Macha's knuckles showed white as she raised her field glasses. With so many inexperienced youngsters, there was a lot of playing around before they came under starter's orders, and she could not breathe as she saw Gold back away from the line. The flag was up. He gave a little bounce forward and they were off. She picked up her colours among the leaders, and then Gold was alongside Lord Rosefield's horse. They were neck and neck. She did not hear the full-throated voices or the thundering hooves. It was as though the race were a silent photograph. Declan was riding home with hands and legs, perfectly, like a part of the chestnut's own body.

She remembered how the men had sneered in Galway at the ugly little filly who had borne this magnificent colt and how they had scorned her; the army sergeant in Gort and the farm boys in the Cotswolds and the man in the toy shop in Bath. Now she had left them all far behind. The spirit of Molloy was laughing in triumph with her at them all as Gold thrust forward and stormed past Helm's Vintage, picked up a length, then two and sprinted home to win the Brocklesby Stakes by three lengths.

Macha did not remember the tears streaming down her cheeks, or leading her horse through cheering onlookers, or Declan O'Brien's ecstatic face. The explosion of the cork recalled her attention. She was almost startled not to see Molloy's face looking down at her.

"Laurent-Perrier," James Melbaugh murmured significantly in her ear.

Before he had time to fill a glass, she took the bottle from him and shook it hard until a spume of champagne fountained into the sunlight, spraying everyone around until she tipped back her head and poured the last of its irresistible bubbles straight into her mouth.

More races were run; the colours blazed; the horses arrowed; the ladies floated round stand and paddock like water-lilies in their fresh spring colours; the sun opened petals, parasols, and faces and bathed the scene in an enchanted shimmer. James Melbaugh's eyes were brighter than blue meteors; his handsome lean face emphasized white, even teeth as he smiled possessively over his bride-to-be and introduced her to dozens of strangers, who congratulated him on winning Macha and Macha on winning the race. Acquaintances from the previous year bowed and smiled, not a few of the young women with very strained politeness. The girl herself seemed to move several inches above the ground through the rest of the day.

"What do you think of the first week in June?" asked James, as she leant on his arm in a haze of euphoria.

"Derby week," she replied, promptly.

"Oh, of course. That's out. We'd never persuade anyone to come. What about the end of May?"

"The week before Derby week," she giggled, squiffed more from excitement than from champagne.

"I'm talking about our wedding day, goose," he said, tapping her small nose. "Shall we marry on the 30th May?"

"That would be lovely," she responded eagerly. "Then I can go to the Derby as the Honourable Mrs. James Melbaugh." It sounded hilarious.

"And what about the honeymoon? I thought you might like to go to France for a month."

"During the flat-racing season?" She came out of her reverie at once. "Oh, James, do we have to? How will my horses get to their meetings?"

"Why can't your cousin take them?"

"Without me?" She was aghast. "They can't run without me. I must see every race. If we go to France, think what we'll miss here!"

He rubbed his chin and shook his head, chuckling. "You're the only girl in Britain who would turn down Paris," he said ruefully. "All right, we'll postpone the honeymoon; but you'd better produce plenty wins to compensate."

There were journeys to Gloucestershire and Hampshire to meet her fiancé's family: uncles who were captivated and aunts who were not.

Poldonith Castle, the family seat, was a thirteenth-century stone pile on the borders of Wales, clearly built for defence, with battlements and towers, a drawbridge and a moat. Its small, guarded windows made it dark and cold within, and its vastness reduced Macha to near silence for several hours during her first visit; but James's mother was dead, and his father, the Earl of Watersmeet, was a kindly man, whose absentmindedness put her at her ease.

He seemed more concerned with the stock of partridge in his coverts and the development of the pineapples, nectarines, melons, grapes and figs in the estate glass houses than in the future of his youngest son. After all, his heir, Charles, had done the right thing by marrying that American with her multimillion-dollar fortune, and this little Irish gel of James's certainly knew horses, so they were probably well enough suited. There were three small sisters still in the schoolroom, and overwhelmed by endless formalities of behaviour and conversation, Macha sometimes wished she could join them. They were to be her bridesmaids.

She was constantly catching trains. There were innumerable trips to London for more shoes and gloves, *twelve* nightdresses (although she had never worn one before), handmade French chemises, camisoles, combinations, petticoats, corsets, vests, white silk hose, garters, lace handkerchiefs, mantles, coats, gowns for dressing, breakfast, tea and balls . . . and cycling knickers!

"But I can't ride a bicycle!"

"Everyone has cycling knickers nowadays, madam."

Toby Dodds came twice from Chichester, and she travelled there once for fittings. She seemed to be for ever taking off her clothes.

There were discussions with caterers, the marquee to be erected, flowers to be arranged, unknown hymns to be chosen for a choir, unfamiliar procedures to be memorised, invitations to be sent to scores of people of whom she had never heard. James Melbaugh was a little reckless, as was the way with youngest sons, but although he was captivated by what he saw as her rebelliousness and eccentricity, instinct told Macha that if he discovered the truth of her background, his interest would end at once.

It was to be a very traditional ceremony, and to meet the convention that the bride's family paid, she had invented a story of inherited money; but the wedding breakfast alone was to cost ten shillings a head. Then James decided, for romantic reasons, that they would all drink nothing but Laurent-Perrier. She was relieved when he said he would settle this last item himself, and even more relieved when he rode Macmonist first past the post at Brighton and Declan O'Brien brought in Tulip Mary second at Newmarket. She had gambled heavily on her own horses, and the risk paid off, which was fortunate, for the cost of the wedding was becoming prohibitive.

At night, she would flop naked into the friendly cloud of her feather mattress and let her man drift through her mind with his long, muscular legs and wide, straight shoulders and slender hands and apple of a *derrière*. It was as well she was so exhausted by the preparations and the business of overseeing her yard, or she would have been unable to resist indulging in delicious sin. Whatever the price, he would be worth it, she thought, and his wickedly inviting stare was the last image in her head as she went to sleep.

The wedding dress arrived at Poldonith Castle with the imperturbable Mr. Dodds. With seed pearls from five hundred oysters, mists of lace and satin, as heavy and cool as water, slipped over her head. The hairdresser gathered her thick hair round a wire frame, created a fabulous confection of curls and arranged the exquisite veil. Macha gaped at the ravishing transfiguration in the cheval-glass.

"Did I not tell you to leave it all to me, Miss Sheridan?" The court dressmaker, highly satisfied with the results of his work, reminded her of his original promise to make her beautiful.

Mrs. Wellington, resplendent in mauve, dabbed her eyes and sniffed loudly.

The family coach, with crest and motto and heraldic bearings emblazoned on its panels, gave a jerk and then bumped off down the mile-long drive, through the high, gold-tipped wrought-iron gates and along the lanes. Macha was on her way to church and passing the open common.

There, drawn up on the turf, was the most ornate and elaborately decorated caravan she had ever seen.

"Stop! Stop!" she called to the liveried coachman, and the horses halted, snorting. The two vehicles stood side by side.

Macha stared and stared at the magnificent Bow-top. It had a scalloped frame and intricate scrolls of gold. Carved, brilliantly painted leaves and flowers and birds embellished its front panels, and on the door was a horse painted with gold leaf. Its tall wheels were crimson and yellow. She could not take her eyes off it.

A hand touched her arm, and she turned, full of an unbearable nostalgia.

Declan O'Brien, who had so generously offered to give her away, read her feelings and shook his head.

"The past is gone. We must drive on. You don't want to be late," he said gently, and gave the instruction.

Villagers gathered with respectful curiosity; among them, although she did not know it, were the three young men who had once pursued her from the local inn, one still carrying the scar from their encounter. The church was crowded. The cream of the aristocracy and sporting society was waiting. The three little bridesmaids in shell-pink organdie sewn with silk rosebuds, with floral fillets on their heads and posies in their hands, grouped solemnly before her. Declan O'Brien, very young and grave in morning coat and pinstripe trousers, highly polished shoes and spats, gave her his arm. The organ sounded. Her bridegroom, so dashing and pedigreed, was standing before the altar. It was all totally alien. She had never felt so excluded. The country, the people, the setting, the ceremony, the atmosphere, even the religion had nothing to do with her. Wildly, she started to turn, to run from the place, to fly home to the *varda*, to return to the freedom of the road and never look back. Declan gripped her arm very tightly against his side with his elbow and took the first step forward.

"I, Macha, take thee, James George Sebastian, to my wedded husband. . . ," she heard herself repeating.

The expression on James's face was one of pure delight, his eyes dark and glittering, and not even the solemnity of the vows could subdue his grin. He winked and squeezed her hand, the creases at the corners of his mouth deepening. All at once, she was not thinking sad thoughts any more, or even serious ones. She was wondering what it was going to be like.

The consommé was as cold and salty as jellied seawater, and the sole in aspic had the texture of porridge. They were followed by some very old chickens and tough braised ham. A bit of poaching and a good campfire would have produced better, she decided, trying to banish the figure of ten shillings a head from her mind. But all the unknown wedding guests ate heartily, talking industriously in their extraordinarily carrying voices at the same time, so that the marquee seemed bloated with wind and on the point of ballooning away across country. She hiccupped.

"That's quite enough champagne," whispered her new husband. "There is to be no sleeping tonight."

That made her giggle. A Rom would never have said anything so *risqué*. Marriage to James was going to be fun.

His hand closed over hers on the sword to make the first cut in the four-tiered cake. She made her wish. It should have been to live happily with him ever after—but instead, she wished that one day Gold would win the Triple Crown.

There were toasts and speeches, and a girl in a daringly low-cut and clinging gown caught her bouquet and glared at her with transparent hostility. Macha had no idea who she was and would have asked James had the horses not jolted forward and thrown her into his arms.

The carriage took them to catch the train which chuffed to Bath and then far beyond to Taunton, where they changed onto another which wound very slowly round the coast until it arrived at a tiny station where an ancient carriage with an even older coachman waited. It was dusk by then, and as she leant drowsily against James the way only a new wife was permitted to do, they were driven through a village twinkling with lamps and up a winding drive which climbed round and round an unusually steep hill, past what seemed to be a tower, to end at an open oak door, at which a butler was waiting.

"Where are we?" she asked.

"As Paris did not meet with my lady's approval, some friends have lent us their castle." James helped her to the ground with a playfully exaggerated gesture of courtesy. "They are abroad, and we shall stay for as long as you wish . . . well, for at least a week, until the Derby."

Another castle! She was silent as the housekeeper led them through the great hall and up the heavily carved staircase and to her puzzlement, showed her into one room and James to another.

As she stood alone and wondering what to do next, a maid knocked and entered, drew the curtains, turned back the bed and stoked up the fire. Macha sat on a stool and inspected herself in the looking-glass, fiddling with her hair in an effort to hide her unease. The door closed behind the girl and another opened equally softly. James Melbaugh stood in its frame and stripped his bride with his eyes. He had not touched her, but Macha felt her colour and temperature rise and shut her eyes and waited for him to take her at last.

When nothing happened, she opened them again. He had turned away from her into the dressing room.

"We must change for dinner quickly, as it is fairly late," he said.

"I'm not hungry. We've been eating all day," she protested.

"It has already been prepared," he answered. "And in any case, it would be rather vulgar not to appear at all."

Couldn't they be "vulgar," even on their wedding night? she asked herself, grimacing at the ceiling, as the door opened again and another maid appeared to unpack her boxes and help her dress.

The food came, rotated round the table and was taken away. They sat one at each end, with five yards between them, and talked politely of the day, as if they had attended someone else's wedding instead of their own. The room was full of other people who they pretended were not there. It was not the first time she had found the whole existence of servants a preposterous invasion of privacy. Brandy was not a drink for women, but she ignored her spouse's tiny frown and insisted on drinking two warm and generous measures after the port, just as she guessed he had finally decided they might rise with propriety.

They walked stiffly up the stairs, and he left her outside her bedroom. She began to take down her hair slowly and was wondering if it was possible that they would not make love at all when he finally came through the adjoining door again.

"You are a coquette, a naughty coquette." He caught her round the waist.

"What's a coquette?" she asked, not struggling too hard to escape.

"A woman who drives men out of their senses with her wiles," he growled, still gripping her with one arm while taking the pins from her hair with his free hand.

"Are you really driven from your senses, darling James?" She laughed, tilting her head against his as the hand fondled her throat and slid slowly down beneath her bodice to her breasts.

It was a very experienced hand. She caught her breath and felt the gown drop from her shoulders to the floor and then, without any effort on her part, they were lying on the bed.

Molloy had been a very straightforward lover. James Melbaugh was much more adventurous; he used every part of her, and the most extraordinary areas of her body became responsive—earlobes, eyelids, toes.

"Brown nipples," he observed, with surprise.

"Arrah! I'm no English rose," she replied.

He bent and took one in his mouth the way a Rom would have considered *mochardi*, and she felt the thrill circle through her from the point.

In turn, his fairness was unexpected, his sunny skin and smooth broad chest, the little line of pale gold hairs running down from navel to crotch. She had always thought of men as being dark and hairy and knotted with muscles, which could be quite ugly. He was fine-toned and strong, a thoroughbred.

His inventiveness turned sex into the game she began to realise it ought to be. The intensity she had always associated with making love was replaced by light-hearted gratification which freed her from the embarrassment of earnestness. He stopped her thoughts with sensation. Her skin glowed. His bone was hard on her bone. It had been so long. She could not wait, she could not wait; she felt herself explode like the bubbles from the bottle. No wonder people loved champagne.

James Melbaugh found himself with a bride who was lithe and willing and something else . . .

"You're no virgin either," he commented as they lay back, but he did not seem displeased.

She bent her head and nuzzled his belly, then looked up at him, panting and happy.

"Again," she demanded. "Do it again."

"With pleasure," he assured her.

And he did it again . . . and again . . . and several times more. True to his word, there was no sleep that night.

Making love with James Melbaugh was like a drug, and after an acrobatic week in Somerset, they returned to Newmarket, where every time they bounced off their horses, they bounced straight into bed. She began riding again and it seemed to arouse him to see her astride Gold, and he encouraged her onto the gallops far too often; the greater the risk of discovery, the greater his passion, it appeared. They played sexual games, in which he displayed limitless imagination, and explored an extraordinary range of convoluted positions, most of which worked, one or two of which did not, with ludicrous results. Lying breathless and slightly bruised, she often thought with glee that she had married a boisterously virile bucko; then she would creep upon him again with stealthy fingers and little bites, and he would coil her red hair around his hand and turn her about, and another night would be lost. Yet to her amusement, they always had to be back in their separate rooms before the servants arrived with their trays in the morning.

In every other way they lived life at a frantic pace too, training the horses, hurrying back and forth and up and down England to race meetings, going to garden parties and one country house party after another and playing a lot of cards. Not only Epsom, Royal Ascot and Goodwood were socially obligatory: there was also Henley, where all the men wore straw boaters and she had to sit in a boat watching other people in boats all day; there was the Eton and Harrow cricket match at Lords, where she sat in an open carriage watching men dressed in white playing an incomprehensible game in the distance all day, and there was Cowes, where she stood on shore in the wind watching even more distant yachts reportedly racing for several days.

In fact, it was an idyllic summer, danced through one glittering ballroom after another to the music of all the most popular orchestras: a voluptuously hedonic time, each day begun lifting silver lids off silver dishes of kedgeree, eggs, bacon, mushrooms and kidneys, which she ate with gusto, and ending with a different feast for which she had as much appetite.

She became quite an acceptable partner at bridge, a skill which was *de rigueur*, and she learnt to play croquet ruthlessly. It was bizarre the way this game could rouse the phlegmatic English to such venomous choler. Old wounds were reopened, revenge for past slights was taken, scores were settled and friends were turned into lifelong enemies when a shot knocked a ball out of play. Macha brought a steady hand, an unerring aim and a Celtic sense of mischief to the lawns and entertained herself greatly watching the consequences.

Her horses ran well, Gold winning a further three races with Declan in charge during her absences. Her husband's successes further enhanced his reputation as a Gentleman Rider, and the money poured in—one thousand guineas here, five thousand guineas there, purses and prizes and a gigantic win of £10,000 at Sandown Park, where she had always been lucky. Then it was August and James announced that they were going to Scotland.

"There's the Newmarket summer meeting," she reminded him.

"Of course, but we obviously won't be going up before the glorious twelfth," he replied, leaving her wondering what was so important about the twelfth.

"Whatever happens, this is one invitation we are certainly not turning down," he continued, misinterpreting her look. "The Mackintosh owns some of the best grouse moors there are. You will love it, my darling. All your friends will be there, and as we chaps will be at the butts all day, you'll be able to gossip to your heart's content."

It sounded ominous. Wherever they went, she found herself in the same circle of single girls to whom everything, and especially every man, was "simply deevy," and married women who talked only of love affairs, or planned matches for their unmarried daughters or sisters—but, above all, they talked about where they had been and who else had been there.

They were a tightly bound group, each family known to all the others, often for generations back; not held together by wealth, for some were not rich, or intellect, for some were exceedingly stupid, but by connections of background and marriage and a secret network of unspoken familiarities and customs which no outsider could ever unravel. In this, they were just like Romanies, Macha thought, and in their perpetual trundling from one house to another, and their seasonal migrations to Ascot, Cowes and Scotland, Baden-Baden and Monte Carlo, they were no different from travellers moving from site to site.

They arrived at a gaunt stone pile in Inverness-shire. Even to Macha, hardy from years on the road, it was bitterly cold. Fires, she was informed, were never lit in the bedrooms before mid-September at the earliest. She changed, shivering, in the one she had been assigned, next to James's room, and trusted he would lose no time coming to join her after they retired, or she would be frozen stiffer than the stone effigy of the first Countess of Watersmeet in Poldonith Church. As she descended to the sepulchral hall, Caroline Legh-Temple arrived with a skip and a wave.

"Isn't this just too divine!" she trilled.

"Simply deevy," agreed Macha.

"A fortnight? Does that mean we have to stay here for *two whole weeks*, Archie?" An outraged American voice sounded above her. "With no fires, and all that rain pouring down outside?"

Macha turned to see a couple crossing the gallery. The man's voice was too low to be heard, but the girl's reply was quite clear.

"Yes, I know I said I'd love to visit a Scotch estate, but I did not say I wanted to die of cold in one."

Her husband was obviously English and equally obviously embarrassed, but his American wife was too appalled by her uncomfortable surroundings to care.

"So why can't you arrange a telegram from Daddy or something . . . anything so we can get back to London."

She caught Macha's eye as they rounded the corner. "Do you have a fire in your bedroom?" she demanded.

The Irish girl grinned and shook her head.

"There you are, Archie. I told you it was no oversight," the other said triumphantly. "And do you know that the men are going to be out all day, every day? Can you imagine what we are supposed to do with ourselves? If we don't perish of the polar temperature, we shall become moribund with boredom."

Thankfully, seeing that she had attached herself to a female guest, her husband melted away.

"Daisy Fitzclarence." The American ignored etiquette by introducing herself and holding out her hand. "I was a Vanderbilt before I married Archie."

Macha, who had the distinct impression that the other wished she had remained a Vanderbilt, took the hand and gave her own name.

"Oh, you're not English either!" Daisy Fitzclarence was delighted. "Have you ever met such a lot of stuffed shirts?"

She was as tall as Macha and excessively pretty, with chestnut hair and a creamy complexion, large, clever hazel eyes and a ripe, pink mouth for which men would have betrayed their brothers. Macha wondered if she painted it, but later realised that she did not.

Unlike Macha's sister-in-law, who had crossed the Atlantic and blended into her husband's background expertly enough to have become invisible, this girl was resolutely American, and the title and society into which her Mama had persuaded her to marry were apparently fast losing their glamour.

She and Macha liked each other at once and became allies for the rest of their enforced stay, first of all exchanging tales of some of the more outlandish customs they had encountered among these odd people, then talking of their own lands and admitting to their homesickness. By the second day, they had decided that nothing would persuade them to sit about for another minute in such conditions.

"We could go into Inverness and shop," Macha suggested.

"Shop! Have you seen Inverness? We were forced to stop over there for three hours waiting for a train. My dear, skirts with bustles have only just arrived up here."

Then Macha had her brainwave. "I know! We'll do what they do!"

"What's that?"

"Shoot, of course. Why didn't I think of it before."

"Oh my, *ladies* can't shoot, Macha."

"I can. So can lots of ladies in Ireland. I've seen them."

"Well, I don't know how." Her friend was doubtful.

"Sure, and will I not teach you myself?"

"They'll never allow it."

"They will so."

"You're right. We'll make 'em."

Lord Bentland, Daisy's husband, quailed at the idea, but James Melbaugh thought it had the makings of a capital caper, although he drew the line at lending her his new Purdeys with the ejectors.

"How good a shot are you?" he asked. "The truth, now!"

"Oh, I'm good enough to bring down a few of those little birds," she replied airily. "And you can keep your precious Purdeys. Any old shotgun will do for me."

It was a challenge he could not decline.

"I'll ask Gordon Mackintosh if you can pot a rabbit or two in the glen."

"And what about the grouse?"

"My dear Macha. What outlandish ideas you Irish have. You cannot just turn up at the butts. There are some very fine shots here this week. It would ruin the day's sport."

"By my safe soul! Ruin the sport, would I?" She was affronted. "Well, I'll show you, James Melbaugh."

So far north, it stayed light in summer for much longer than in England, so there was plenty of time after the day's shooting was over and they had dined to go with James to the glen. Quite a party accompanied them, the event being a diversion for the bored wives and an entertainment for the men, who went along expecting to be highly amused. Gordon Mackintosh lent her an old Cogswell & Harrison which he had used as a boy, and his disapproving Highland keeper was instructed to keep an eye on her.

The glen was sheltered, peaceful and partly wooded. She missed the first rabbit; then all the reflexes which had bagged her countless suppers in Ireland took over, and in rapid succession she shot a hare, half a dozen rabbits, then a pigeon and a brace of woodcock put up by the keeper's dog. There was a little burst of spontaneous applause.

"You have an eagle eye, Mrs. Melbaugh," complimented the Mackintosh.

"I'm out of practice, or I would have had that first rabbit," she confessed. "Now may I join the shoot?"

"Oh, grouse are a very different matter." He smiled, deprecatingly. "Much, much faster."

"Percy de Vere won't be shooting tomorrow, with that wrist of his," James reminded him. "I'll wager a monkey my wife bags at least . . . well . . . twelve brace."

Macha beamed at him for such a public display of faith.

"A hundred guineas she shoots no more than six brace," called out the whiskey-gravel voice of Millbank's son.

"Two hundred she does not hit one bird."

"And another pony she hits a beater."

Macha glared at the Carew brothers, who saw themselves as the jokers of the group.

The Mackintosh, too polite a host to ignore anything which

obviously entertained his guests, although it did not seem to him to be very good form, reluctantly agreed that Mrs. Melbaugh might join the shoot for the one day only; but he retaliated gently by suggesting that Melbaugh share the Number 6 butt with his wife. Monty Millbank looked dismayed, realising this would give her much less time to achieve the target he had set, and James was rueful as, having brought about the situation by making the first bet, he now had to give up some of his own shooting in her behalf.

"You've deserted me!" her friend Daisy wailed, on hearing the news. "How am I going to survive now?"

"They won't be after letting me join them more than once, that's certain," Macha pointed out. "So there'll be the rest of the week to give you a few lessons. James thinks he will never be asked back, but he's so tickled that at the moment, he doesn't care. Oh, he's a darling man!"

The heather smelt sweetly sharp after the rain. The blustering wind which had blown the rain on westwards met them head on as they dismounted from the stocky garron ponies and climbed to the butts, which were placed in a line just behind the ridge ahead.

There were elements of this place which took Macha back to Connemara. The mountains were different in shape and height and even colour, but with the same grandeur they illustrated the endlessness of time and the smallness of mankind. Their wildness was invigorating. She realised she had missed such rugged and awesome beauty while living in the cushioned green of the south of England. Here, the myriad trivial rules which so constricted her life there were reduced to absurdity. She felt mentally released and free, and hitching at her skirts, she strode out keenly.

The butts were made of stone and peat, about seven feet square on the inside, with seats of heather sods in each corner, where the guns could sit hidden from the oncoming birds. Macha, dressed warmly in a tweed costume with velvet collar, perched on her shooting stick beside James until alerted by the halloas of the drivers.

The first grouse came over in groups of about twenty-five, quite low to the ground. The Mackintosh had been right; these birds were very small and very fast, and they flew like snipe, with a wrench and a twist. Macha was glad James had decided to shoot first, as she would probably have made a fool of herself.

She watched how he fired both barrels; handed the empty gun to the loader and took the newly loaded gun from him without once looking away from the target; swung onto them and fired again. Bundles of fluttering feathers thudded out of the sky. The thirty red-and-white flags of the beaters appeared, spread across the ridge, with the birds before them in hundreds, flying higher now and straight. Gunfire and the smell of cordite, and the first drive was over.

The dogs, eager and confident, ran forward on command to retrieve. James Melbaugh was a reliable shot, who could be depended upon to make a decent contribution to the day's pick-up, but although the individual scores were not counted, everyone knew that Daisy's husband, Lord Bentland, was far and away the best shot and whose record was a bag of over five hundred grouse in a day.

They walked the two hundred yards to the next butts, on higher ground, for the return drive. Macha felt a tremor of anticipation, a rising excitement combined with a steeling of her concentration.

"Keep your eyes constantly running over all the ground from right to left until they come," instructed James. "And if your bird is flying low, remember to keep your left arm up and to shoot well over him."

This was quite different from poaching a wood pigeon or a wild duck for supper. The competition, not only against the men, but against the birds themselves, put her on her mettle.

The drivers sounded far off, but suddenly, the first flight was there. She aimed and swung and fired, and fired again, seeing too many birds at once and fumbling during the changeover of guns.

"Never look round; just put out your hand and let the man do the rest. Keep your eyes on the birds," James instructed her urgently.

The air was vibrating and shattering against the bombardment. She focussed on a speck, swung again, one bird in her eye, one bird in the sight. She squeezed the trigger. The red grouse dropped to the ground.

"Good shot, madam." One of the loaders was impressed.

"Well done, my darling girl," said her husband. "Twenty-three more of those and I'm up £2,000."

By the end of the day, his win was assured. She had knocked down fifty-one birds. On the ride back the gentlemen were full of cordial camaraderie.

As they reached the great house, they saw a brougham drawn up at the front entrance and a woman being helped to step from it. She turned, and Macha recognised the girl who had caught her bouquet at her wedding.

"Who is that?" she asked James.

"Victoria Paxton, of course. She was at our wedding. You cannot have forgotten, surely." He sounded testy, as though she had made a *gaffe*.

The ladies congratulated her on her day's sport with faultless politeness, beneath which Macha clearly discerned disapproval; but she was quite accustomed to that, so it did not explain her ennui.

In some way, the triumph of the day had ended in her feeling jaded and tired. While dressing for dinner, she kept visualising the grouse fluttering and tumbling out of the skies in their dozens. What had been the point of it all? To see such a multitude of birds shot left her depressed.

It was the way of country and travelling folk to kill for food, or in order to make a small sale to another for food, and she had been accustomed to shooting a rabbit here, a hare, maybe a pigeon or two, but never more than enough for her need. There had been satisfactions in it, too, of having the ability to hit the quarry cleanly and of providing the next meal for herself.

Shooting with these society people was quite different. Theirs was an obsession, which seemed to stem directly from gilded lives in which no smallest wish remained ungranted, from the planting of the truffle inside the foie gras inside the boned quail to the perfect dressing of a curl. They could satisfy the merest whim, slake any desire. They could go anywhere on earth, do whatever they wanted. Only one element was forbidden. They could not be seen to labour. They could not build, or thatch, or plough, or saw, or weave, or cook, groom or shoe their horses, carve or turn wood. They could not strive. They could not work. But they could indulge in a skill; the skill to kill.

Seated between old Count Speransky and the slightly deaf Lord Ernest Marshall, she found it difficult to concentrate on either and was aware of a slight, but persistent pain behind her eyes. Afterwards, at bridge, she played forgetfully, and therefore badly, to the annoyance of her partner, Tony Arran.

"I have a little headache," she confessed to him apologetically.

"Quite common after a day with the guns, my dear Mrs. Melbaugh," he replied with courteous understanding.

James, who had overheard, came to her side at once.

"Why don't you retire early," he said.

"Will you not mind?"

"Of course not, sweet girl; and I shall not disturb you later."

He could be very kind and considerate, she reflected as the maid unbuttoned her gown. How lucky she had been to find such a husband.

Still the birds plummetted from the sky as she lay unable to sleep in the dark. They filled her aching head with struggling wings and quivering breasts and scattered red feathers and limp, lifeless heads. The hours went by. There was the muffled sound of others passing her door on the way to their rooms and then, later, the creaking of a floorboard as a gentleman crept towards the bed of his mistress—most probably Sir Henry Talbot going to Lady Anthony Arran, or Lord Anthony Arran tiptoeing to Baroness Radley's arms. She wondered if James was still awake and guessed not. It would be comforting to curl up against his warm, sleeping back all night. The inexplicable uneasiness she was experiencing would disappear. Reaching for her satin wrap, she crossed the room quietly, opened their adjoining door, tiptoed towards his bed and slid under the eiderdown.

It was as cold as a glacier. The linen sheets were starched and unyielding. She felt about with her hand and then sat up. The bed was empty.

Chapter ELEVEN

Lighting the candle on the table beside her, Macha stared around the room. James's shoes lay discarded on the floor from where the valet had forgotten to remove them, and his monogrammed slippers were not to be seen. The bed had not been slept in.

Perhaps he had forgotten his pipe and returned downstairs, or been unable to settle without her and gone to fetch a book from the library, or even for a short walk, she thought, fear shredding such logic even as it presented itself.

Her throat constricted and her hands tightened. A footfall sounded softly outside the room. Happiness! Her guess was right. He had been far away. She sprang to the door and stared into the unlit corridor.

"James! Are you there?" she whispered. "Is that you, James?"

A shadow, insubstantial as a puff of cigar smoke, hovered ahead and then was gone.

"James?"

There was no answer.

Macha ran into the darkness, her mind gabbling and crackling with half-formed and horrible ideas, her hand hissing along the bannister which guarded the landing, past the Bentlands' rooms and Percy de Vere's door, accidentally turning right into the cul-de-sac of four rooms set aside for the Carew brothers and their wives, stumbling blindly back past the snores of deaf Lord Ernest Marshall and along another passage lined with solid-oak panelled doors, each with a big brass handle like a polished eye keeping watch for the unknown occupants. She stopped, straining to catch the smallest susurration, the faintest sigh, and then was convinced. Uncaring of the consequences, she flung open the third door and stood shaking and ready to attack.

"Who is there?" asked an angry Scottish contralto. It was the mother of the Mackintosh.

Macha gave a loud sob and fled. Back in James's room, she climbed into the empty bed sweating coldly. She knew and could not bear to know.

Repeatedly, the slim hand reached up and caught the wedding bouquet, with a movement both determined and defiant, and followed by that look of deep dislike. The hair was sleek and blond, the eyes cool and pale, the swan-like neck created, it seemed, to wear emeralds by Cartier and priceless family pearls. With what poise and grace she had descended from the carriage in her immaculate costume by Worth. How effortless and amusing had been her conversation at dinner. Aristocratic, confident and beautiful. Victoria Paxton! The feminine counterpoise to James Melbaugh. Oh, Macha knew where her husband was.

An irresistible lethargy overcame her. She lay motionless, in a trance of misery, her eyes wide open and unblinking, her breath so shallow it would not have misted a doctor's glass. Numb and dumb, she was not conscious of violent emotion—no rage, no agony—and yet her heart throbbed like a wound as the hours passed and the voluptuous moon became a fragment of tissue fluttering ahead of the stealthy dawn. The furniture in the room emerged gradually from the dusk, old wood and heavy draperies closing in to suffocate, the window mullions thickening and solidifying into stone prison bars against the light. She waited in limbo as the first bird fluted its sad, recurrent note and the rain tattooed on the stone walls and the scullery maid flinched as her sleep-warm bare feet touched the harsh stone floor.

The bow of morning began to tune the house, and Macha, still immobile, became tense with effort to catch the easing of that distant door and the whisper of his return. Then the handle turned, and the room gave a small gasp. She lay and stared at him.

"I awoke early and . . . ," he began, and saw it was useless.

"I . . . she . . . ," he floundered again. "Don't look like that! It is unimportant . . . the way of the world. . . . I've known her since we were children. . . . By gad, woman! Everyone does it . . . it means nothing."

Macha, naked, rose from the bed and crossed the floor. At the entrance to the dressing room, she turned.

"You are a whore," she spat, and he quailed before the scorn in her eyes.

A maid arrived in response to her summons and was instructed to pack her boxes and have them transported to Inverness Station immediately. Macha was dressed in travelling clothes by the time her husband found the courage to come to her room. He gazed at the packing operation and dismissed the servant with a gesture.

"What is all this?" There was an expression of appalled disbelief on his face. "What are you doing?"

"It is quite obvious that I am leaving," retorted Macha, tucking the last strand of hair under her hat.

"That is quite impossible. It would be unthinkable to create such a scandal."

"Me create a scandal? I think not, James Melbaugh. It was yourself who created the scandal by fornicating all the night long with that Paxton slut."

"Don't be absurd, Macha," he drawled. "There is not one married man in our set—and probably not one in the whole of England—who does not have a mistress or two. It is something every wife accepts."

"Not this wife." Macha rang the bell again.

"You cannot seriously mean to leave here over this business. We shall be a laughing stock. I absolutely forbid you to go."

"Apparently you do not understand, James." Macha sat down on the stool in front of the pier-table and faced him calmly. "When I return to Newmarket, all your belongings will be sent to your London address. I am not simply leaving this place. I am leaving you."

James Melbaugh went pale.

"You don't know what you're saying. Look, I'm sorry about last night. I did not mean to hurt you. I did not think you would find out. Why don't you rest in your room today? We'll tell Gordon Mackintosh that you are unwell. It will give you time to recover yourself."

"I am leaving you, James," Macha repeated patiently.

"You'll be ruined, rejected by Society—don't you understand?" He gripped her arm and gave it a little shake. "No woman leaves her husband. You will become an outcast. You cannot survive."

"Oh, I survived well enough before I met you and I shall doubtless survive again. As for being an outcast, it is certain I'll find a way to pass the time of day with a few folk before reaching my dotage, for it may surprise you to know that you and your little group of friends do not make up the whole world."

"Well, expect no help from me! I'll see you damned for this!" he snarled, and slammed from the room.

A carriage was brought to the front of the house and Macha's boxes loaded into it. A footman informed her that all was ready. Most of the shooting party were discussing plans for the day's sport, unaware of her impending departure.

When Macha reached the breakfast room, Victoria Paxton had just spooned a lightly coddled egg onto a plate. Macha took the plate, gently laid it on the sideboard, and slapped the blonde hard across the face.

"That is for stealing my husband!" she announced for all to hear.

She clenched her fist and swung her arm. The punch landed with heavy accuracy on that well-bred nose and the mouth silly with surprise.

"And that is so that you won't forget!"

Blood flowed satisfactorily down the girl's chin. Macha turned on her heel before the speechless breakfasters and walked out.

The train steamed south, leaving the purple mountains behind, passing the black coal pits of Fife and crossing the new wonder of the world's longest bridge spanning the River Forth on the way to Edinburgh, where porters hurried forward to transport Macha's boxes to the London train.

Macha submissively ate the food placed before her in the dining car. To other travellers she appeared, deceptively, as a composed and charming girl, expensively dressed and with that slightly vacant air of one protected from birth and untouched by experience. Indeed, her mind was empty, and her blank eyes directed towards the speeding view saw nothing. She merely felt tired and mildly surprised by her own lack of reaction.

It was later, as she lay sleepless and the train whistled mournfully through the midnight of Carlisle, that her heart cracked. A jumble of memories and impressions and emotions suddenly crowded the compartment: his beautiful body, lithe and muscled; the smile which made her pulse race; the fun of him; that private look kept only for her; his loving—all lost; her love, her faith, her hopes, their secrets—all betrayed. She was betrayed and James was lost.

The bitter tears coursed, and with them came the wishful doubts, that perhaps in fact nothing had happened—he might have been too drunk to make love. Perhaps he really believed there was no harm in it, for it was true that such behaviour was commonplace in their circle—ladies took lovers and gentlemen took mistresses; maybe she should have pretended not to know, or perhaps she should have condoned his infidelity: his hand on that lily-white breast, his mouth on that mouth, his tongue stroking her tongue, his arms holding her close, pulling her close . . .

Jealousy, green and spiked and all-consuming, rage as mordant as acid clawed at Macha. She pitched from the cot and vomited into the china basin, retching and hawking until her muscles ached and her eyes burned, and she sank back, at last, reeking and exhausted. Much later, she recovered sufficiently to turn up the dimmed lamp. Her skin felt damp and sticky, and when she looked down, she saw that her silk nightdress was ripped and her skin scored with weals, self-inflicted in her torment.

Eventually, she reached Ebberly and the refuge of her boudoir, which she locked, and the womb of her own bed, into which she crawled to curl like a foetus, deaf to the knocking of the servants and the anxious enquiries of Declan O'Brien and Mrs. Wellington. Trays of food were left outside and taken away untouched. A doctor was summoned to offer the comfort of laudanum and urge her to eat. He left the house shrugging and spreading his hands. Twenty-four hours later, her husband returned, to shout and plead against the door, and be ignored.

Macha remained trapped in that final night in the Highlands, picking over each minute, goading herself with her own imagination until the whole episode was so clear it was as though James Melbaugh had actually pleasured Victoria Paxton in her presence.

"If you do not open this door, I shall order it to be broken down," he bullied on the third day.

Macha lifted the shotgun from the floor by the bed and blasted in the direction of his voice. A blessed silence followed.

It was dark when Mrs. Wellington tapped. "There is someone to see you, my dear. A friend who has come a very long way," she said nervously. "Do talk to her."

Then a warm, young voice. "Honey, please let me in. It's worse than Siberia out here. The draughts in your English houses would freeze a penguin."

Macha opened the door to Daisy Fitzclarence. And then she talked and cried, and her friend held her hand and listened and poured out glasses of brandy from the bottle smuggled in beneath her cape, until the words became slurred and the pain became blunted.

"I love him, you see," she mumbled. "You won't leave yet, will you?"

"If there's a fire in my bedchamber, just try to get rid of me," replied Daisy, and drew the quilt over the now incapably drunk Irish girl.

In the morning, she returned with a tray, insisting that Macha eat every mouthful of the kedgeree and one slice of toast with butter and marmalade.

"There," the American said, removing the remnants of the meal. "You are in a much better state to think sensibly and make proper decisions now, and I have a letter for you."

"*My dearest, darling girl,*" he had written.

> Forgive me, I beg you. It was all a monstrous mistake, brought about, I am sure, by too much port.
>
> Had I been in control of my senses, I should not have hurt you for a king's ransom, and I am now demented with regret. Upon my most solemn oath, such behaviour will never, ever occur again. Permit me to see you and talk with you, my angel, and I know I shall be able to make you forget the whole affair. I am waiting only for your word.
>
> Your abject, but adoring husband,
> James Melbaugh.

Macha read it twice and then stared out of the window.

"What will you do?" wondered Daisy.

"Leave him."

"If you do that, what sort of life do you think you'll have?" asked her friend. "It will not be the same as before."

"Why not?" demanded Macha. "I still have my horses and enough money."

"Society will cut you. You were single and eligible before. Now you are a married woman, and if you leave your husband, you will be ostracized. No invitations, no weekends, no balls and only me and

Mrs. Wellington and Sir Freddie for friends. You will be ruined."

"That's what James said," Macha recalled. "And yet I have done nothing wrong. He is the one who has been unfaithful."

"Men can do what they like." Daisy was resigned. "Look, Macha, you love him and he loves you. Oh, I know he does. He is absolutely distraught over the matter. And it is not as though he had a long affair with this girl. It happened just the once. Why not forgive him, forget it and start again?"

"When I think about it, I feel sick . . . diseased . . ." She shuddered and looked about to break down again.

"Then don't think about it," Daisy advised briskly. "Put it right out of your mind. Get out of that bed and out of this room and back to your horses. Nothing will be resolved while you sit here brooding."

"Yes," agreed Macha. "But I know I will never be able to forget, and I don't think I can forgive either."

"Well, take time to decide. James has gone to London until he hears from you, so there is no hurry." Daisy gave her a hug. "You know I really want to see you two together again; but may I give you a tip?"

"You've given me so many good ones already, another must be welcome," Macha replied with a weak smile.

"If you feel, in the end, that you cannot take James back, then do not stay in England. Go to the United States. Life is not so restricted there. Anyone with guts and determination can be a success in America—and there are some very fine horses, too!"

Flowers began arriving in bunches and baskets and boxes and eventually a whole carriageful; chocolates and bon-bons followed, then hats with plumes and veils and blooms and fruits and ribbons and seed pearls, then a diamond bracelet; and finally he telephoned.

"Are you at home tomorrow?"

She thought for a long moment, about America.

"Darling? I have something special for you and I want to see you, to talk to you."

"I will be at home," she said reluctantly.

Unusually, he arrived on foot, walking up the drive and hesitating at the front door, as though about to grasp the iron bell pull, then changing his mind, and entering with some diffidence. Macha, sitting in the drawing room, listened as he made renewed apologies and promises and forecasts for their wonderful future together.

"We'll buy some more horses. I hear Gold has done particularly well in the past two weeks. We'll employ more lads and expand. I'll take you on that honeymoon to Paris. We'll forget what happened. Everything will be as it was before . . . better, in fact."

But she knew it would not. Yet she hated seeing him so downcast. Her golden, proud and laughing man, looking lined and humbled. She stood up and went to him, putting her arms round his neck and her head on his chest, and felt his own arms tighten about her.

"Thank God, Macha," he mumbled.

They were both crying and then, catching sight of each other, gave tremulous smiles and then began to giggle.

"Don't move an inch! Stay exactly where you are, and no peeping out of the window!" he commanded. "I shall be gone for ten minutes."

She waited, trying not to remember Scotland and hoping she had made the right decision.

There was a cacophony of noise outside and Declan O'Brien burst into the room.

"Will ye come and take a look at this! The saints have mercy! It'll rattle the plants from their roots and the teeth from the head of every crone for fifty miles!" he shouted excitedly, grabbing her hand and rushing her from the room and across the hall.

There, at the foot of the broad flight of stone steps leading to the entrance, was a gleaming scarlet Mors motor-car. James Melbaugh stood beside it, beaming.

"It's for you, my darling wife," he announced, in a voice loud enough to be heard by all the servants and Ulick and the old groom and Mrs. Wellington, who had hurried to discover the cause of the commotion and were now gazing at the machine with open-mouthed admiration.

Macha gave a halloo of delight and hurled herself down the steps and into the seat, to run her hands over the buttoned leather upholstery and the steering tiller and bounce about. It was like a phaeton without the horses.

"James, you are surely not going to allow her to drive that dangerous contraption," exclaimed Mrs. Wellington, her awe changed to consternation.

"Of course she is/I am!" exclaimed James and Macha in unison, and he climbed in beside his wife and began the first lesson.

"There's how to start the engine and that's the brake lever and those are the three speeds you can choose." The motor erupted into life. "It has the power of eight horses, you know."

Macha released the brake and the vehicle shot forward, scattering onlookers. It careered down the drive, the gates looming closer at a fearful pace until just in time, she pulled the handle over and bucketted over the lawn, screaming with the thrill, James roaring with laughter beside her, round and round, narrowly missing trees and devastating flower beds and finally, taking aim and scraping between the gates and away down the open road.

By the time they returned, after plunging through a hedge, sending a herd of bawling young bullocks thundering off down a lane pursued by a furious farmer and his dogs, and causing chaos among the hansom cabs and carriages waiting down the entire length of Newmarket High Street, she had an approximate idea of how to drive and managed to stop safely within inches of the brick wall surrounding the yard.

"Nineteen miles an hour! There'd be less fright in hurling over a cliff-top and being swallowed by a whale. Oh, isn't this the greatest fever since the day I was born!" she gasped, crimson with the mixture of terror and exhilaration. "Did you see how we stopped Lady Manners' carriage, and how that fat man leapt straight into a pothole full of water? Blessed Mary and Jesus, when that hedge came lepping at us, were not heaven's millions lined up in expectation of our arrival! I was waiting for the horseless carriage to rise up and clear it like Manifesto at Becher's, and instead it went straight through and I lost my hat."

"I almost lost my scalp," James pointed out, rubbing the scratches on his forehead.

"Oh, it's a swank of a present. An emperor would envy it." She kissed him, gleefully and then deeply, and all the familiar desires returned, and they almost ran upstairs to bed.

To her surprise, James Melbaugh was right. The following months were as good as they had ever been before Scotland and their life together was the same . . . well, almost the same. Macha noticed other women more; their figures, their hair, how they smiled and whom they flirted with, aware of them as rivals for the first time; and she had to banish certain memories and pictures ruthlessly from her mind, and sometimes she burst into tears without reason. Nevertheless, they had wonderful days, their winning streak continuing to the end of the flat-racing season, entertaining their friends and being entertained, dancing all night at "Harty Tarty," the Duke of Devonshire's ball at Chatsworth.

He kept his word and took her to Paris, to dine at Maxim's and stay at the Ritz in dazzling luxury. She bought a gown at Worth and congratulated herself on looking far more fetching in it than Victoria Paxton, who had no bosom to speak of and whose complexion was really rather washed-out. As they strolled down the Champs-Elysées with other lovers, she told James how remarkably clever she thought these foreigners were, because every one of them spoke such perfect French; then could not understand why he kept chuckling over her comment.

It was late November when they returned to England to Poldonith Castle for a few days out with the Beaufort—a hunt which Macha felt would have done justice to Ireland, an opinion which her husband repeated to numerous friends, all of whom laughed as though she had said something witty.

They removed to the London house in Mayfair in time for Christmas. A great fir tree had already been transported there from the estate and set up in the hall, and tinsel and candles and little wooden figures and the most fragile glass baubles were brought from some backstairs cupboard for her to hang on the branches. Holly, thick with berries, and evergreens were tied around picture frames and chimneypieces with scarlet ribbon and wound between the banisters up both sides of the staircase.

Old Watersmeet had given up Christmas as being far too much bother years before, and so the actual day was spent at the family house in Park Lane with James's eldest brother, Charles, his American wife and their children, joined by the three young sisters and the assortment of relations whose only other appearance was at funerals.

To Macha, who had known nothing of the traditional English family Christmas before, it was all wondrous, from the hanging of the children's stockings to the pulling of the crackers with their spark and bang and scattering of bon-bons. Her parcel from the tree contained a musical clown in a box, which reminded her of the merry-go-round she had bought in Bath, and she was as pleased with it as with the solid-gold horse brooch from James and the crocodile dressing case with silver-mounted brushes, jars and bottles from Charles and Hannah and the box of floral cachous from two spinster aunts, although her favourite present was the Ascot racing game, self-winding, with eight large horses fitted in a mahogany case, from Declan.

After the feast of goose and plum pudding and candied fruits, they all played charades. Macha and a venerable great uncle and young Maud and cousin Bertie chose the word "pilgrimage"—the Irish girl acting the patient being given a *pill* by "Doctor" Bertie, the protector of Maud against Bertie's *grim* villain and daughter to James's uncle in his great age. She had no idea of the meaning of some of the later words, but she acted the roles in their syllables with unselfconscious expertise, and no-one managed to guess the right answers.

Both before and after Christmas Day there were dinners and games of bridge, parties and balls, and at the New Year, James and Macha gave their own very modern "dinare and dansare." As well as the usual young members of their set, James invited a number of the fancy, including the notorious prize-fighter Charlie Mitchell, who he insisted was an old friend. Everyone agreed the event was a "rip."

The following evening, James and a number of male guests from the night before went to Crockford's, the gaming club, to play hazard, leaving Macha alone for the first time since the crisis in her marriage.

She dismissed the servants and went to her room early, enjoying the novelty of undressing by herself and folding her clothes into a small, tidy pile, the way living in the *varda* had once made absolutely necessary. It had never been possible to feel genuinely comfortable with another woman fussing around her body, easing the silk hose over her bare legs and lacing her stays and pinning and unpinning her hair. She slid into the already warmed bed and snuggled down luxuriously to flip through some magazines.

The fire flickered in a homely way, and the swan-necked gas lights around the wall gave a softness to the room, leaving the corners in grape-dark shadow and causing the crystal and silver on her dressing table and the round occasional table to glint like candles. It was such a relief to escape from the ringing voices, the vacuous conversation, the endless games of cards and the artificiality of London society. The periodicals slipped carelessly from her hands, and she lay back to enjoy the peace of solitude.

These days she spent all her time changing her clothes from morning gowns to tea gowns to ball gowns, and waiting for the carriage to arrive or depart from pointless calls to leave cards or sit with incredibly tedious women for the obligatory fifteen minutes before being driven to the next house. Weeks had passed since she had been out in the open air other than in the occasional formal appearance in Rotten Row driving her gig down and back in order to nod to her acquaintances. She never rode at all, and any involvement with the training of her horses had ended with the journey to France, since when James had propelled them from one engagement to the next without pause. Declan O'Brien ran the yard at Ebberly now.

She found herself growing conscious of her own dissatisfaction at the thought of the years ahead containing nothing but dress fittings, chit-chat and pointless pastimes, an existence which was already turning her into a flabby, brainless ninny.

Although it could not be explained, it seemed important to rise at dawn, instead of nearly midday, to be cut by the cold east wind on the gallops, to catch her breath at the speed and power of the Thoroughbred in her control. She wanted to work again, to feel the sweat run down between her shoulder blades and breasts and legs, to wipe damp hair from her forehead, to ache with effort. She longed for serious discussions and planning with men who smelt of horses and harness, instead of being flowery with words and scented soaps. She was losing touch with her true aims and with the up-to-date knowledge which might make them possible to achieve; even losing touch with herself.

Staying at James's side helped to ensure that he did not stray, of course, but she was practical enough to accept that he could not be guarded from temptation twenty-four hours a day. Even at this moment, he might not be at the tables at all, but off with his cronies to some brothel. In this rare mood of introspection, she questioned whether it was worth sacrificing so much just to try to keep a man, even a man she adored. For too long, she had been following her own nose instead of deciding her priorities, and now a choice had to be made.

"Did you enjoy Crockfords? And did you win?" she asked James over breakfast.

"Yes to both questions," he replied. "I finished £500 to the good, so you may buy yourself an outrageous new hat."

"A pair of Bedford cord breeches and some new boots would be more outrageous, don't you think?" She smiled.

He cast a quick look in the direction of the footman bringing in another dish, then grinned back and wagged a finger at her in roguish silence.

"Actually, Alfred . . . and Tom . . . thought we all had such a good time last night that we should do it more often—once a week or so. . . ." He sounded casual, but the phrasing signalled his uncertainty of how the scheme would be received. "We used to spend every winter about town together . . . young bloods, y'know. Of course, it's different now . . . married men, you understand . . . but a few hours' gaming . . . on Thursdays . . ."

"It sounds a good idea." Macha took a deep breath. "James, I want to go to Ebberly House."

"Certainly, my angel." His delight at her immediate acquiescence was transparent. "Want to take a quick look at Gold, eh? Will you be back by the weekend?"

"I want to stay there till spring, James."

His expression changed. "What? Leave here? Why? Because Alfred, Tom and I thought we'd have a few evenings playing hazard?"

"Oh not at all, not at all! It's nothing to do with that. Sure, it's a fine thing to pass more time with your friends," she said hastily. "But to tell the honest truth, I'm needing the country life, and poor Mrs. Wellington is on her own up there, and someone should oversee the training, if we want the horses to do well next season."

"Well, I'm not at all sure about this, Macha." He adopted a husbandly stance. "Your place is here with me."

"Ach, and isn't it less than ten weeks till the start of the flat!" she pointed out. "And are there not countless ladies with young children who are never seen in London with their husbands—and them the more grateful for it."

"We're not likely to have a single young child if you're going to spend all your time in another house," he grumbled.

"Mother of God! If you don't make a midden out of a speck of dust," she teased, rising to walk to his end of the table, put her arms round his neck and blow gently in his ear. "Now, what was that you were saying?"

"We've just had breakfast!"

"So we have," she agreed. "Isn't the morning the best part of the day?"

"Mmmm. I shall miss this . . . you," he murmured, a while later, rolling onto his side and drawing her contentedly against him.

"Me too," she agreed, ungrammatically.

The effect of Ebberly and Newmarket Heath brought colour back into Macha's face and put a spring in her step. Within days she felt healthier, although it took a little longer to reach the pitch of physical fitness previously maintained so effortlessly.

"Don't think you're riding work until you've stopped all that huffing and groaning," Declan told her cruelly. "I'm not having a decent animal wrecked just because you've been sitting about eating like next year's bacon for six months."

Oh, the pleasure of hearing a man speak his mind without

compunction! From uncoordinated and bony boyhood, Declan O'Brien had become hard and capable, tending to humourlessness just as much as before, but with an affinity almost matching her own with the horses and still light enough to race. Riding both for the yard and for one or two other owners, he had had plenty of winners during the last season. His wages had been revised again and were now generously aligned to his responsibilities, and although only eighteen, already he had gained substance and respect.

He told Macha the latest stable gossip, and together they went over the prospects of her runners and the best races for each to enter, discussing distances, conditions and possible rivals. She read back through three months of *The Sporting Life* and caught up on form.

"That colt I rode in the Middle Park Stakes is for sale," he said. "He had a poor season as a two-year-old, but I had the idea he might find his way to the front as a three-year-old, and he's going cheap."

"Buy him, then," agreed Macha, with complete confidence in his judgement.

"And there's talk of Archibald Hanley being short of the readies and about to sell off most of his string."

"Well, keep your ear to the ground on that," she advised. "There's one or two of them I wouldn't like to see get away from us."

It was like old times. She stretched with satisfaction before opening a feed bin and measuring out an illicit treat for Gold. The big horse stared down his nose as she approached and then turned his head away, unmistakably offended.

"I know I've been away, but you've been looked after better than Mary O'Houlihan's Sunday stays," she said persuasively, and then shook the scoop.

He tossed his head and ignored it.

She filled her hand with corn and held it out flat. "Come on!"

He blew noisily, and the corn flew off her palm and scattered on the cobblestones.

"Now, stop being a toad," she scolded, taking another handful and offering it once more. "This is your last chance."

With enormous condescension he arched his neck and accepted, his lips so delicate on her skin that they tickled.

"I'll lunge you in the paddock tomorrow, seeing I'm not allowed to ride out," she promised.

Declan went past, looking well scrubbed and very smart in a good-quality tweed jacket and new trousers. He had grown a moustache and walked with the fluency of an athlete. As he waved casually, Macha thought of asking where he was going and whether she could join him, but something held her back.

Much later, wrapped in her fur, she went for a last walk around the property, for the pure enjoyment of feeling the frosty grass crunch under her boots and looking up at the blue-ringed moon and canopy of stars. On reaching the path to the servants' entrance, she heard a sound and hesitated. The gas lamps in the kitchen cast a soft circle of light through the windows onto the figures of a girl and a man. They were kissing enthusiastically under the cedar of Lebanon. Macha started to smile as they drew apart to walk with their arms around each other towards the back door. Then her face froze as she recognized Declan O'Brien with one of the maids. A wave of fury swept over her. How dare they? How dare he? She would sack them both. She stepped forward and the couple stopped, startled.

"Good night, Mrs. Melbaugh," Declan said calmly, and the maid bobbed a curtsy.

"Good night," Macha heard herself reply, as the rage was replaced by the embarrassing shock of realising that she was jealous.

How ridiculous, she told herself as she returned hastily to the house. Of course, lots of girls must chase after Declan O'Brien. He was very attractive, but she could not possibly be jealous. She loved James Melbaugh. She was a married woman. It was just that she had never imagined Declan being interested in anyone—other than herself. With a little shrug, she climbed into bed, put her feeling of sulky depression down to the shellfish served at dinner and resolved to speak to cook about it the following morning.

The routine of the yard dominated everything again. It was as though she had never broken from it. Indeed, she seemed to be even more involved than ever, taking no time off for the kind of social interruptions permitted before. The employment of extra staff meant that her riding astride on the heath became the most open secret in Newmarket. At any other time of year, when the place was full of the rich and powerful, this would have been impossible, but now it merely resulted in some curious looks from the lads from other stables. To the winter professionals, being an expert in the saddle was all that mattered.

She hardly thought of her husband, James Melbaugh, and, had she not missed his physical presence on those rare nights when she was not tired enough to fall asleep immediately, she might have forgotten him altogether. He telephoned quite often, but their worlds were so different that there seemed to be little to say. She was too absorbed in her work to recognise that his single night with Victoria Paxton had effectively destroyed the prospect of abiding matrimonial love developing between them. Only lust was left and that, too, burned less fiercely.

When he burst into her room before dawn, she thought at first he was an intruder and reached for the shotgun she kept by the bed, just as her father had taught.

"Macha, darling! It's me . . . James."

He fell across her body and began sobbing. He smelt of stale tobacco and alcohol.

"Mercy on us! Are you hurt? Are you ill? What has happened?" She was breathless from his weight.

He sobbed louder, like an angry child, and she struggled to sit up, growing vaguely frightened.

"James, tell me, for the love of God, what's up?"

She leant towards the bedside table.

"No light. Don't light the lamp," he begged.

She put her arms round him and held him tightly. "Come, now. It can't be that bad. How did you get here at this time of night?"

"I drove four-in-hand." His voice was muffled in the eiderdown.

"All the way? The Devil's father! The horses must be in a fine state. Does Declan know?" She released him angrily.

"I'm ruined!" he said.

"Those horses are ruined, more like." Her sympathy had been doused. What was he thinking of? Driving them such a distance, galloping all the way, no doubt. "Why didn't you use my little motor-car?"

"It's gone," he mumbled.

"Gone? What do you mean, gone?"

Shouting, he grabbed her in the darkness and shook her until her neck cricked.

"I'm ruined! Don't you understand, you silly bitch? I'm ruined! I've lost everything—money, house, everything."

"No, I don't understand, James," she said, slowly, when he finally let her go. "How have you lost everything? What do you mean?"

"I mean I've lost everything at the tables. I'm ruined," he groaned.

"You've gambled away *all* your money . . . and your house?"

"And your bloody horseless carriage!" he added with bitterness.

Her mind ran over the news quickly, checking its seriousness and probable effect on their future.

After a silence broken only by his gulping and sniffing, she said, "Well, James Melbaugh, you've been a damned fool. It's as well I've some money and we've rented this house."

"Oh, God!" he moaned. "How can you be so stupid? What's yours is mine in law, and I've lost everything—every penny we had. We'll have to move from here, dismiss the staff, sell the horses. There is nothing left."

"Sell the horses?" she screamed. "Sell the horses? You're not selling my horses. You got yourself into this and you are not having my horses to get you out of it. I will shoot you dead, James Melbaugh, before I let you take one of my horses."

But despite her howling protests and threats, the horses had to go.

The carriage horses, the Welsh cob, the three-year-old colt she had just bought, two yearlings purchased in the previous year's sales—even Freddie Wellington's gift to her, Macmonist—were all sold. Only Macha's suicidal fury saved Gold and the mare, his mother. It was fraudulently arranged that Declan O'Brien bought them and Tulip Mary for a token figure.

All the servants were sacked, and the lads. Declan's cousin, Ulick, was found a place in another yard. Mrs. Wellington went tearfully back to Chichester, and most of the furniture was auctioned, along with Macha's furs and jewellery. She hid only the gold shamrock brooch, the gold bracelet with two moonstone hearts set in pearls and the gold bangles she had worn at her wedding to Molloy.

James stayed drunk throughout the weeks during which the entire dismal process took place, and showed signs of awareness only when they finally climbed down from the hired carriage which had met them at Singleton Station and carried them to the old Sussex cottage.

"Where the devil are we?" he asked blearily.

"Home," she said.

"Home? This hovel?" He stared at it aggressively. "You can't expect me to stay here. I wouldn't let a cat piss in this hovel! I'm a Melbaugh. My father is the Earl of Watersmeet."

"Then you can be an earl's son under the hedgerows, and you'll soon find out which is the more comfortable."

She left him swaying with his mouth slack and went to supervise the unloading of the cart which had arrived with the few essentials they had managed to keep back from the dispersal sale.

The cottage had stood empty since her departure to Newmarket, and Farmer Locksash had been so touchingly happy to see her again that he had not even increased the original rental. Now it was furnished with two beds and a scrubbed table and a few chairs—almost exactly as when she had first moved in there.

Her husband slumped into the chair nearest to the range in the kitchen and remained there from morning till night, his only demand being a continuous supply of bottles procured from the inn at West Dean.

There was no time to do anything about this situation, as Macha and Declan were far too busy settling in the two Thoroughbreds and the Macha's Girl and continuing training on the Downs with as little change as possible in their daily timetable. Both realised that the only chance of salvaging anything from the situation lay in the success of Gold and Tulip Mary in the coming season. The two horses had to be in peak condition, and they had to win.

Since word of James Melbaugh's ruin had spread, not one of the friends with whom he had been on such intimate terms since childhood had called or sent any message offering help, support or even sympathy. A stiff accusatory letter had arrived from the Viscount Midburst, his brother, and his father had paid his debts far too often before to be prepared to do so again. They had left Suffolk without a single well-wisher to say goodbye.

"Not even the lowest tinker would have behaved like that to one of his own in trouble," Macha commented to Declan.

"Nor the poorest cabin dweller," he agreed.

So they were both surprised when a coach complete with a pair of footmen on the rear platform lurched down the track. The doors were opened and Sir Frederick Wellington stepped out, followed by his aunt.

"Oh, Freddie! You delightful man!" Macha flung her arms round him and then, with tears of joy, swept Mrs. Wellington into the embrace as well. She was overcome by their appearance. "I thought I'd never see either of you again."

"How could you have imagined such a thing of your friends?" He sounded hurt. "Had I not been in the South of France, I should have called as soon as James got into this hole, but I only heard of it upon my return yesterday. Now, where is he?"

Macha grimaced and pointed to the open door of the cottage. As they went in, Mrs. Wellington gave a gasp, but her nephew was far too considerate to betray his shock at the state in which they were living. James, having consumed two bottles of port since staggering downstairs at noon still drunk from the day before, was unconscious again and snoring too loudly to permit conversation. Declan led the way to the next room, where there were two upholstered chairs, one wooden chair and a rug. Tactfully, he went to stand by the window, so that the other three could sit down.

"Will you ever forgive me that I had to sell Macmonist?" Macha was too embarrassed to look at Freddie.

"You must not worry about such trifles," he reassured her instantly. "Had I been here, I should have bought the horse and kept him for you."

"We still have Gold and Tulip Mary," she said quickly, not wanting him to feel sorry for her. "They are in such splendid condition you could hammer out iron on their muscle, and they're running like gunshot. They'll win back our fortunes for us this year, for sure."

Mrs. Wellington dabbed at her mouth and looked upset, and Freddie patted Macha's hand, muttered gruffly that she had "tremendous pluck" and lit his pipe without asking the ladies' permission, which showed how distraught he was over her predicament.

After a few puffs, he asked, "Who's to ride for you?"

"Declan and James, of course," she replied.

"How long has Melbaugh been in that condition?" he asked bluntly.

Macha shrugged, and Declan put in, bitterly, "Since Christmas, I shouldn't wonder."

"Well, if something isn't done about it, he'll be in no condition to ride." Freddie voiced their fear. "So I propose that I take him back with me, give him a good shaking and keep him off the wallop until he's fit to return and work."

I should have married Freddie, Macha thought, and catching Mrs. Wellington's eye, knew she was thinking the same.

The two friends stayed for tea, served in fragile, but cracked, porcelain cups from an ugly brown teapot, and then James was heaved into the coach. Mrs. Wellington was helped in after and sat fastidiously in the farthest corner from him.

Freddie turned to Macha and pushed a small roll of bank notes into her hand. As she started to protest, he whispered, "Take it, please, if only to keep the horses fed. Don't be proud with me. Give yourself a chance."

"Thank you, my friend," she said simply. "I shall repay it one day."

"It is a gift."

"No," she corrected gently. "A loan."

After the Wellington coach had driven off, the girl and Declan O'Brien counted the money. It came to £100. Then they sat on the cottage windowsill in the spring sunshine and discussed how to put it to the best use.

"No windfall could have been better timed," commented Declan. "I'm down to my last few pounds, and we're almost out of corn."

"If it hadn't been for your savings, we'd all have starved," acknowledged Macha. "So I want you to know that Tulip Mary is your horse, and when we're back on our feet with our own yard again, you and me will be partners, 50/50."

"Maybe" was all he said, but she knew he was pleased.

Because of the complications of the sales and removal, the horses had already missed a number of races for which they had been entered before the calamity. It was agreed that transporting Tulip Mary that week to Epsom for the Spring Meeting was the first expense to be met. Enough fodder would be bought in to guarantee the maintenance of the Thoroughbreds for the rest of the year, and Macha would take £25 to the next local horse auctions to invest in a couple of bargain working animals for private and profitable resale.

"There won't be much left over for emergencies," pointed out Declan, ever cautious.

"This is the emergency," she answered.

Everything seemed so much easier to organise without the presence of James Melbaugh, whose drunken insults and obscenities had sapped the heart of their fight for recovery. Now they were able to work together with the familiarity of two who knew each other's ways and could almost read each other's thoughts.

Although Gold ran a bit green and went down by half a length at Hurst Park, Tulip Mary won at Epsom. The odds had been low, but Macha, who had not disclosed her intention of gambling some of the little money left over, felt free to disclose the return of £30 on her stake. Declan looked disapproving.

"Half is yours," she said, handing over the coins and quietly amused at the slight relaxation of his expression.

The following day, her husband returned, stepping like a dandy from the hired carriage and staring at her and about him with obvious revulsion. He was his former elegant self, clean, shaven and immaculately dressed. Macha, dirty-faced and dishevelled from mucking out, caught his look. The sight of her in breeches certainly did not seem to be having the same effect on him as of old.

"It would appear you've seen your tailor," she observed acidly.

"Freddie Wellington settled the outstanding account, so I ordered another couple of suits," he drawled.

"So you're in debt again!" She was furious.

"Good God! Do you expect me to go about like some slum-dweller? A visit to your dressmaker would do you no harm. You are a perfect disgrace," he snarled back. Then he stalked towards the loose boxes, from which Declan appeared.

"I shall be riding Tulip Mary on Thursday at Alexandra Park," Melbaugh told him. "And again on Monday at Chester."

"But she's entered for the City and Suburban Stakes on Wednesday, and next Saturday we're taking her to Lincoln," he objected.

"Good show! The more the merrier. I hear she's running well."

"Four races in a week's too much for her," Declan pointed out.

"Rubbish, man! The brute's far too cossetted as it is." The caution was disregarded. "Now, what about that old lazybones of yours?" James Melbaugh turned to address his wife.

"If you mean Gold, he needs another fortnight's work because he looks unfinished," she answered.

"My God! You're not running a nags' rest home here. May I remind you that we are in bloody big financial trouble," he snapped. "That horse is in the three-o'clock at Lingfield a week on Tuesday. It's no competition, so he'd better win."

Macha and Declan were dismayed, but James Melbaugh was already boarding the carriage again.

"I shall meet you at the course on Thursday. If you have to contact me before then, I shall be at my club."

With that, the driver cracked his whip and the vehicle lurched noisily away over the potholes.

"The filly will be wrecked." The Irishman was distraught.

"We'll pull her out of the City and Suburban," Macha decided. "And take a good look at her on Friday to see if she's fit for the Saturday meeting. Otherwise, we'll keep her back from that too."

Declan gave her a look of gratitude.

"You know," she continued, wistfully. "It was always my dream that Gold should win the Irish Derby, and now he'll never even have the chance to enter."

"There's always the English Derby," he pointed out.

"Too soon."

"The Eclipse, then."

"I had that in mind, if we can stop James running him into the ground first."

Tulip Mary came second in her race at Alexandra Park, and would have come first had Melbaugh not pushed her out in front from the start instead of riding the waiting race Macha advised. When he dismounted, he slashed the filly across the face with his whip, and only awareness of the watching onlookers prevented him from hitting his wife, when she intervened, as well.

"Get that dog out of my sight," he snarled. "She's got as much stamina as a sick drab."

Macha knew he had lost more money on the race and smelt the brandy on his breath.

"She's a grand little filly, and you know it!" she raged. "She was doing handsprings before the start, and if you hadn't been at the bottle and then thrashed her to ribbons, she'd have cantered it."

"Well, if she doesn't canter it on Monday, the knacker can have her."

Macha glared at him in revulsion. The features she had once thought so handsome were now seen to be weak, and the mouth she had found so arrogantly attractive was petulant. She wondered how she could have been so infatuated with him that his slightest touch made her shiver with passion. The golden aristocrat she had married was in fact merely a vicious and stupid young man. She began to walk away.

"Where are you going?" he demanded.

"Home."

"To the hovel?" he sneered. "Yes, that would be 'home' to you. You were probably raised along with another ten or fifteen snivelling brats in a pig-sty just like that."

"Not quite like that, James," she said, with a strange little smile.

At evening stables that day, she felt heat in Tulip Mary's offside foreleg, which was treated with compresses. There would be no racing at the weekend, and it was unlikely that the filly would be fit for Melbaugh on the Monday.

"We're supposed to meet him at Chester," Macha told Declan. "But if she's not right, we simply won't turn up."

However, as though he had read their minds, James Melbaugh appeared unexpectedly at the cottage very early on the morning in question and insisted on taking the filly to the station to be transported by rail to the course. Both Macha's protests and Declan's wish to accompany the horse were denied.

When the horse was not returned by dusk, they imagined he had arranged for her to be stabled overnight; but when she did not arrive the next day, they rode into Chichester to telephone James at his club, only to be told he was unavailable.

The rest of the week passed without news. Declan, never an optimist, believed the worst.

"She fell and broke that leg. She's been put down . . . shot," he kept saying.

Macha could offer him no comfort. With a sinking feeling in her stomach, she knew that if the horse had not been injured, then it had certainly been sold. Again and again, she cursed herself for having been stupid enough to marry such a man as James Melbaugh.

An irate hansom-cab driver decanted her husband on the track some days later and demanded the fare from London. James was helplessly drunk, and a search through his pockets revealed that he was also penniless. Macha grudgingly paid out of her limited resources.

Then she filled a wooden bucket from the water butt and emptied it over him. Kneeling in the mud, she seized his collar as he spluttered and blinked unfocussed eyes, and shook him until his head lolled alarmingly.

"Where's Tulip Mary? Where's the filly?" she shouted.

"Sold." He was barely coherent.

"Who's bought her? Where is she?"

"Don't know. She won the Seller and was auctioned off." His slurred words tailed away and he lost consciousness again.

Declan came running up from the paddock, his face anxiously questioning.

"He entered her in a Selling Plate and she won," Macha explained bluntly, and looked away as his expression crumpled.

The body on the stones jerked and groaned, and she twisted round in time to see the Irishman land a second heavy-booted kick in Melbaugh's ribs.

"No! Leave him!" She jumped between the two and grabbed Declan's arms. "If you hurt him, there'll be more trouble. He's not worth it."

"I loved that filly," mumbled her friend, and stumbled away.

* * *

"I'll tell you what, my little shamrock. If Gold wins on Tuesday—and he will win—I shall find out who bought your precious filly and buy her back again. 'Pon my honour. Now fetch me some more port and leave me in peace."

James was slumped back in the chair by the kitchen stove once more.

"You'll not be fit to ride in a cart by then, let alone in a race," she said bitterly.

"Wait and see. Wait and see."

On Sunday he stopped drinking at midday. On Monday he scrubbed himself in cold water drawn from the well and made the rest of the day a misery with his evil temper. On Tuesday, Declan woke at dawn to find he had already fed and watered Gold and was impatient to be on the way. He appeared vigorously athletic, and the horse was bright-eyed and eager. As a pair, Macha thought, they looked unbeatable, and she decided to risk the rest of her money on the race.

Far from being no contest, as Melbaugh had suggested, the three-o'clock at Lingfield included some very powerful opposition. The Duke of Westminster's Good Luck was the favourite in a very strong field.

Gold was sweating as Declan led him round the paddock, and Macha wondered if the journey had upset him, although he was quite accustomed to travelling. He reared as James Melbaugh mounted, and she could see him fighting for his head all the way down to the start. Then when the flag dropped, he rampaged ahead of the field as though pursued by the hounds of hell, and not even the Duke of Westminster's classic colt came near his heels.

As he tore first past the winning post, Macha's field glasses were trained only on his bulging eyes and froth-covered coat, and, when he went on careering round the course, she ran onto the turf in agitation. In the distance, her husband was trying to stop him, leaning back with all his weight on the reins and sawing at his mouth. Suddenly, Gold veered without warning and as his rider lost balance, crashed into the rails, fell to his knees, struggled up and began galloping flat out straight for her.

"Gold! Steady, Gold!" she called, but he did not slow down. Then she saw, as he hurtled closer with ears flattened and teeth barred, that he did not recognise her and his eyes were blind and mad.

"Gold! No!"

She felt his breath like a torch. People were screaming somewhere. He rose in the air before her. The whole length of his belly was streaked with foam and blood.

"He is going to kill me," she thought.

Then she was lying on the ground and the horse was shuddering and groaning beside her and Declan O'Brien was crossing himself and staring down at them both.

"Holy Mary, Mother of Jesus, that was a blessed miracle." He helped her up, and she saw that he was shaking. "The colt was in the air, his great hooves flailing down upon you. There could be no saving of you—and in that very split second, it's the sacred truth that he was lifted back. His head went up and his mouth opened and his neck bent round and he was carried up from you by the hand of God. It was a divine miracle."

"Look at him! The devil's father! What's happened to him?" Macha was concerned only with her darling horse stretched twitching on the grass, his tongue hanging from his mouth and his shins bleeding profusely.

"He's been doped," Declan said.

A shadow fell over them as James Melbaugh walked up, covered in mud.

"You gave my horse dope?" She shrieked the question at him.

"He won, didn't he? And we've all made a packet, haven't we?" was his contemptuous reply.

Macha stood up, straight and stony as carved vengeance. "I curse you, James Melbaugh, and I call on my father and my father's fathers to curse you from the grave. Your bones will crack into smithereens. Your tongue will be swallowed into your throat. Your body will stiffen as though encased in ice so that not even your little finger can move, or your eyelids blink, or your voice speak, but you will hear and never be heard, thirst and never be quenched, see and go unnoticed. You will become the living dead." Then she spoke the words which must never be repeated.

James Melbaugh gaped and then gave a nervous laugh. "A gyppo. . . . You're a gyppo. . . . I should have guessed. . . ." He looked round hurriedly, afraid some of the crowd might have overheard, but they were too far back. A group of officials were running towards them. He drew close to his wife.

"You may have fooled me into giving you my name, you filthy gyppo strumpet, but that's all you're going to have from now on," he hissed in her ear. "I never want to set eyes on you again. And if word of your noble antecedents ever reaches my family or friends, I shall have you finished off for good." He stabbed a sharp finger against her ribs like a dagger.

"All your plans are dust, all your tomorrows are pain, James Melbaugh." The silver of her eyes fixed upon him and seemed to pierce his angry gaze with slivers of glass and needles fine as silks and deadlier than venom. He felt dizzy and put up a hand as though to ward her off. "All your future is past, James Melbaugh."

He stumbled back, shielding his face.

"Are you all right, sir?" A course official reached his side.

"Nothing a large brandy won't put right, old boy" was his answer as he was helped away.

The journey back home was a nightmare. Gold, with his gashed legs bandaged, had to be tightly hobbled, blinkered and restrained by a twitch on his upper lip to prevent him from kicking the horse compartment on the train to pieces. A special van drawn by two shires was hired to carry him from Chichester station to the cottage, where it took the driver, his mate, Declan O'Brien, old Locksash's son and Macha over an hour to manoeuvre him into his converted loose box. There, he was rugged up and fed a warm bran mash in total darkness, while Macha whispered and breathed into his nostrils and ran her hands over and over his face as Molloy would have done until he was calm enough to have the hood removed and hobbles loosened. She stayed with him all that night.

The top door of the box was opened next morning. Gold stood with head down and dulled eyes and hollow flanks. As the light poured in he crashed backwards, neighing in terror, so that they were forced to shut the door and dress his legs in near twilight. She used the same ointment the horse coper had used to mend the old mare's leg, but without real hope.

The cuts healed quickly, but the tendons remained inflamed in one leg and it was five weeks before the injury went cold.

"We'll have to fire it," Declan O'Brien said aloud what they were both thinking.

"Perhaps blistering would do." The thought of inflicting such pain on the colt made her blanch.

"You know very well it will not. If it is not done, he will live on in misery, or go to the knacker's yard."

Three strong farm lads were brought from the village to construct a primitive brick kiln in which a fire was lit and built to furnace heat.

Gold was prepared, the hair from the injured area cut away and the other legs tied in a complex net of rope which, when pulled, cast him brutally to the ground, where the three boys struggled to hold him down, one sitting on his head.

The firing irons, with their smooth edges the thickness of a worn shilling, were heated to a dull red.

"Will you leave it to me?" he asked.

"No," she replied, with set face. "I must do it."

He poured chloroform onto a thick rag and held it round the horse's nostrils. After some minutes, Gold's ears flopped limply and his head nodded and his eyelids began to droop.

Macha rejected pity from her mind and replaced it with the merciless willpower of love. Clenching her teeth and fixing her eyes on the swollen leg, she pressed the red-hot iron into the flesh.

The horse woke, screaming and jerking. The skin scorched under the metal. Declan drew a second iron from the fire and ran to her with it. She thrust it against the flexor tendon, desperately trying to ignore the screaming animal and the sizzling wound and the nauseous smell of burning meat. She worked quickly, each time with a fresh, hot iron, until there were nine parallel straw-coloured lines across the back of Gold's foreleg and the job was done.

Then, taking the last iron, she rammed it into the palm of her left hand. For a moment, she felt nothing, and then the pain exploded through every nerve, carmine in her sight, shrilling and livid in her head. It was as though her brain had been blown apart.

"Why did you do it? Why?" Declan was bending over her, his voice like an echo behind the agony which returned with her consciousness.

"It is my penance," she whispered.

"You are as crazy as a heathen!" he shouted, anguished.

"Paste the ointment on Gold's leg," she moaned. "And then give it here."

He dressed the horse's lesions first and then, with a touch like a wren's wing, dressed her hand.

For the next few weeks, the colt was nursed and rested, first in his loose box and later allowed into the paddock to let the sun on his back and to graze the sweet summer grass. Like Macha's hand, his leg healed, leaving scars behind, but regaining strength. Eventually, he was able to canter again over the Sussex Downs with the old mare, his mother, for company, until at last he was physically fit and hard once more.

But he was not the same as before. He shied at birds and slender branches and rustling leaves. Any unexpected move near the stable made him squeal and roll his eyes in fear. Sometimes he would stop in the middle of the field for no reason and stare trembling at some nameless horror. His courage was gone. Macha, gazing into his frightened eyes and remembering the mischievous, bold look of before, knew her virile and splendid horse was broken.

"He'll never race again," she said to Declan.

"Ach, come on now, you can't be so certain of that." He tried to sound reassuring.

"I know. I am sure."

They worked on in silence, for there was nothing more to say.

A trainer at Pulborough took on Declan O'Brien at his yard, which was near enough for the Irishman to return to the cottage to help out on days off and some evenings. Macha returned to the buying and selling of working horses and ponies, just as she had done in the beginning. Between them, they made enough money to survive and even to put some aside for the coming winter.

Macha, mentally drained from the bombardment—giddy heights and depths, the triumphs and devastation—of the past three years, lived simply. After completing the daily chores made necessary by her stock, she would go walking through the serene woods of Sussex, and find their filtered green light soothing and be quietly amused by the serious preoccupation of her lurchers with nosing out clues to the lives hidden all around them.

She did not permit herself to think much, but drew in the pure air and enjoyed summer on her face and arms and the rampant honeysuckle and petals fluttering to the earth from the dog roses, leaving hips as small and new as jade beads. She picked wild strawberries and relished their prickly-sweet explosions on her tongue, like balls of sherbet. Her feet dangled in cool pools, and her eyes were satisfied by the curving womanly body of the Downs as it lay against the satin ocean below. Touch and hearing and sight and smell and taste, her senses were fulfilled as she allowed herself to be healed.

In autumn, Declan was riding one of his new employer's horses at Goodwood, and she decided to go and watch. It was the first meeting she had attended that year, and now there was no question of gliding graciously round the members' enclosure in a gorgeous gown. She bought cheap entry at the turnstiles and there mingled happily with the countryfolk out for the day and the trippers, touts, tipsters and bookmakers down from London, happy to be part of the company and noise after her seclusion. Her pulse beat a little faster; a familiar tingle shivered over the fine down of her skin; her heart contracted as the horses cantered past. It was like returning to a lover, familiar, glad and anticipatory.

The multicoloured ball of the race bowled past—and suddenly, on that balmy autumn day in the rub and heat of the crowd, Macha Sheridan became colder than snow, and those around drew back from her, shivering inexplicably, and as her lungs emptied and her hands clenched and her eyes stared without seeing and a despotic tension gripped her to rigidity, the other MACHA was there.

MACHA sanguinary and dripping with war. MACHA, the Great Mare Goddess, vengeful with her breath of knives. MACHA with the fangs of the snakes in her hair bared, with the death moon shining in her horns, with tusks unsheathed on her hands and feet and her hounds baying about her. MACHA was within her.

Macha Sheridan, perfectly still, saw her husband with X-ray vision raise the flask to his lips, watched his imperceptibly uneven stride from the weighing room. His chestnut horse was parading with the others. He mounted at the second attempt. The two passed before her, golden and exquisite in a spangled aura, the spirit of autumn, a symphony of muscle and motion, almost floating down to the start.

Macha Sheridan waited without turning her head for the beating thunder and the rasping breaths, waited for the shouts of the jockeys, the brawling, striving scrum of runners, the jostling inches from the crowd and raised her silver eyes. He was pushing his horse between two others, driving one into the side and causing the other to swerve, lashing out at them with his whip. Desperate to avoid the rails, the rider on the inside yanked his mount back, catching the chestnut across the nose with his stick. Racing for the finish at thirty miles an hour, the three horses collided and lost balance; the chestnut stumbled; James Melbaugh fell into the melee of hooves behind. For vital seconds, his body was rolled and jerked and knocked about the turf. Then it was left behind like a cast-off coat. Macha went home.

They sent for her, of course, the Earl of Watersmeet and Lord Midhurst, and she put on a plain coat and hat and journeyed to Poldonith Castle by train, walking from the railway station to the great gates and up the long drive down which she had travelled dressed in satin and pearls in the crest-emblazoned coach to her wedding less than eighteen months ago. The footman who opened the door did not recognise her and after looking her up and down, advised her to go to the servants' entrance. She gave a wry smile at the expression on his face when she announced herself.

The Earl was his usual vague and courteous self, and Charles Melbaugh, the Viscount Midhurst, stiffly polite. She was shown upstairs to a chamber overlooking the park, and as the door closed behind her, she found herself gazing at the immobile figure of her husband lying in the great curtained tester.

She walked to stand over him. Splints encased his arms; his eyes did not blink or waver from their fixed stare. The icy cold which met her touch froze as deep as the marrow in his bones. He was the living dead.

"Yes, it is the Romany woman," she said, knowing that he heard. "The filthy gyppo strumpet you married."

Taking the glass of water from the table by the bed, she put it to his lips. A few drops oozed between them, and the rest dribbled down his face into the pillow, like tears. His mind gabbled against hers in terror.

The image of Gold screaming and thrashing and bleeding in his darkened box filled her head, and her look became stone.

"You have a long way to go yet, my friend," she said. "A road without end."

Turning, she left the room.

They expected her to stay and care for him, and Lord Midhurst's facade of civility cracked into anger when she announced her intention of leaving.

"You are his wife! It is your duty to remain by his side at such a time!" he bullied.

"There is nothing I can do for him. He will receive every attention here," she replied, her face expressionless. "My duty is to myself."

"It is imperative that you stay and can give him the comfort of your presence."

"I think not. My presence ceased to be of comfort to James some time ago, as I am sure you are aware."

"It would be most improper for you to live elsewhere. What will people say?" put in her shocked sister-in-law, Hannah.

"I do not give a fig what they say," Macha retorted.

"Your place is with my son, my dear." Even the Earl was driven to intervene in his gentle manner. "This must be your home now."

"It is not my wish to be unkind, sir, but when your son deserted me and left me penniless, this family did not offer me a home," she reminded him with calm stubbornness. "I have made my own home now and, as the train departs in under an hour, I am afraid I must take leave of you and return there. If there is any change in James's condition, I trust you will inform me."

But she knew there would be no change, and she felt no pity.

Chapter TWELVE

Winter, crisp with frost and hard, bright days, feathered the Downs white. Brittle twigs snapped off the trees, and the turf crunched under the horses' hooves. Animals and humans were invigorated by the tang of the mornings. They skipped and bounded about, snorting and swinging their limbs, chasing foxes and scampering after rabbits, guzzling hot mashes and broths.

An underfed, ill-treated brown gelding bought for a song earlier in the year had filled out under Macha's care into a jaunty giant with a jump like a stag's and bounced home ahead of the field in his first steeplechase, with old Locksash's son up. He repeated the process enough times over the next weeks for his mistress to invest some of her winnings in a cheap five-year-old retired flat-racing mare, which looked a prospective 'chaser and was boarded out at the farm, because there was no more space in the cottage outbuildings.

She was a drab and sulky-looking beast, and Declan O'Brien was not at all impressed with the purchase.

"She's cow-hocked, and that's as mean an eye as you'd see on a Kerry bull. Nothing but trouble there," he commented. "Waste of good money."

"You didn't see her break free at the sale and take a five-barred gate as though it was a skipping rope," Macha gave her reason.

However, Declan was right. There was no doubt that the mare could run and leap, but only when the mood took her, which was rarely indeed.

Macha cajoled and whispered, bribed and bullied, threatened and, once, even lost her temper. The mare just humped her back and flattened her ears and showed the whites of her nasty little eyes and dug her big feet into the ground and refused to budge. Other horses made her more intractable, and eventually, her owner gave up the struggle, turned her out in a paddock with a shed, tossed her feed over daily and left her until the spring, with the intention of getting rid of her at the first opportunity.

It was Macha's first failure with a horse, and she felt affronted. The defeat irked her as she sat by the stove. Molloy would have known what to do; but none of the tricks and secrets he had confided worked in this case. Sometimes she could feel his presence again, vibrant and wise, both father and lover, a true husband, so close it seemed that if she leant back her head it would rest against him, if she climbed the stairs he would be waiting. But the bed was always empty.

The twins were three years old now. She could see them as though they were in the room: Tom, the boy, black-haired and vital like his father; Molly, silver-eyed like her. She would put out her arms; but her arms were always empty.

James Melbaugh came to her too, raging and cursing at first and then, as the weeks passed, weeping with self-pity and, later still, pleading for forgiveness and, at last, begging to die. Her nights were full of ghosts and guilt. She pushed them all from her and endured until dawn.

Despite the undoubted thrill of competition, the striving horses with their flying manes and tails sailing over the fences and ditches and spattering through the mud across rough stretches of the countryside, steeplechasing was not her sport. There were too many broken necks and backs and legs, too many falls with jockeys carried off on litters and big, proud animals shot. The risk to her own filled her with a sense of dread which the jovial, relaxed company on the course and the necessary fiery swallows of brandy from the flask did not alleviate.

Yet the start of the flat did not hold the same excitement as before, when she'd had entries of her own with the prospect of success—and money. The earliest meetings took place while the east wind was still chill and the trees bare. She attended because Declan was riding and found the sight of the gleaming, streamlined Thoroughbreds galling.

Somehow, there had to be a way back into ownership. She had to see her colours, gold with green hoops, streamered by speed along the rails and passing the post in a blur of glory. She had to lead her own sweating, triumphant winner through the crowd again.

Thoughts of the future preoccupied her, and with them, the realisation that her position was far worse than when she had first arrived in Sussex. Then she had been beautiful, single and mysterious. Now she was a married woman, her history known to all. The door to her ambitions was through Society, but she was Society's reject now. The paralysed figure of James Melbaugh lay across her way. She was as if manacled to him, and he to her. If she released him, she would be free; and yet she could not do it. But for as long as Gold stood whimpering in his loose box and trembling at the sight of the gallops, she could not forgive.

The snowdrops appeared like scatterings of pearls and vanished just as quickly. Primroses and crocuses, fat buds and bursting chrysalides followed. The grass began to grow again, sweet and juicy as steak to creatures shut inside and fed on dusty hay since November.

Gold was taken to the lower pasture for the first time. She comforted him as he backed, shaking, from the open space. Bucking and shying, he reluctantly permitted her to lead him gently round the perimeter; and then, at the far side, he stopped and screamed. Sweat broke out on his shoulders and flanks; his nostrils flared and ears strained.

"Gently, gently, darlin'," she murmured, putting out a hand.

He plunged away from it and stood glaring over her with head flung back and every muscle quivering.

Declan was away. There was no-one she could call to come to her aid. If the stallion used his strength against her, if he attacked, she would be helpless.

"Steady, Gold. Steady, my baby."

To her amazement, the horse gave a deep, grunting whicker, the unmistakable sound of love. The nose of the sulky brown mare appeared over the hedge. Gold broke free from Macha's grasp, galloped to the first break in the bushes and charged through.

The Irish girl raced after him. The mare was not in season. She had viciously kicked and bitten every companion released near her, and Gold was in no condition for battle. Macha scrambled through the thorns, ignoring her torn skin and ripped jacket.

The two horses were standing, their nostrils almost touching, and, as she watched, Gold slowly nuzzled his way up the side of the mare's face and along her scraggy neck until he was tenderly nibbling her withers. The ugly mare looked astounded; Macha could almost see her thinking. And then, very hesitantly, she arched her neck and paid him the same compliment. For a long time, they nuzzled and nibbled and blew softly at each other, and then a gleam, which could have been described only as flirtatious, came into the mare's eyes. She squealed, kicked up her heels and wheeled to canter off across the field, hindquarters swinging saucily. The stallion sped after her, neighing with pleasure. For over an hour they galloped and shadow-boxed and chased each other. Once, Gold pranced over to Macha, tossing his head and almost grinning, before returning to the game. At last they came to a halt and bent their heads and grazed, nose to nose.

From that day, they were inseparable, sleeping in the same loose box, sharing the same corn, exercising side by side over the Downs, where the stallion forgot all fear at last and the mare raced and jumped against him as though her life depended on it.

A fortnight later, Macha put on her coat and hat and boarded the train to Gloucestershire. This time, the footman did recognise her, although his disapproval remained as severe. James Melbaugh was still lying in exactly the same position as when she had left him, his eyes fixed ahead, his arms, with the splints removed, lying transparently on top of the eiderdown. She drew up a chair and sat beside him. The glass of water on the table, just as before. She put it to his mouth, so carefully that none spilled this time.

"I cannot cure you, James," she said sadly. "That is not in my power."

Tears filled his eyes and ran down his face. She dried them with her handkerchief.

"I know. I know." She could hear him pleading for release, although he was speechless. "There's been enough suffering. Don't fret no more, dear James."

She stroked his head and then leant over and put her arms about him. How cold he felt! She closed her eyes and joined her thoughts to his.

"Yes, I forgive you. I forgive you with all my heart."

She pressed her warmth to him and kissed his glacial lips.

"It is over now. Be at peace."

The lock turned. His hand grew warm in hers. Colour, more delicate than a water tint, spread over his skin. His eyes looked into hers, quietly. He was freed.

"Be at peace," she repeated, and left.

James Melbaugh died that night. The family sent word to the

cottage, and Macha attended his funeral veiled in black. As the coffin was lowered, she remembered the laughing man of her hopes, her golden man, her spoilt child-man, and she wept.

"What waste," she thought. "What waste."

Sir Freddie and Mrs. Wellington came to admire Gold's remarkable recovery. They had both visited frequently since James Melbaugh's bankruptcy and subsequent death, and expressed persistent distress at the conditions in which Macha was living. The old lady had even tried to press some of her limited resources on the girl and, when this had been refused, offered to share her home in Chichester.

The girl had remained adamantly where she was.

"Lady Fortune will smile on me before long, you'll see," she assured her friends.

All outings and entertainments were denied her following the death of her husband, but the time passed quickly. There was little money, it was true, but Declan obtained quite a few rides and winners and she felt more at peace in the ramshackle cottage than she had ever felt in high society.

Then, almost without warning, autumn and winter were gone and it was spring and, to Macha's ecstatic delight, the ugly mare was found to be in foal. Gold, well aware of his achievement, was irrepressible. Much of his old conceit returned as he preened and strutted and herded his love about. Although his injuries and the damage to his courage had been such that he would never be able to face crowds and race again, he became a tearaway on the gallops, streaking away and back before her benign gaze and causing chaos round the cottage with his high spirits. The coming foal became the star of the future.

On the day Macha's first year of officially ordained mourning finally ended, Sir Freddie's carriage rattled down the track.

"Marry me!" he demanded, with far more resolution than in his first proposal.

"Arrah, Freddie! Was ever a man so desperate to reach the altar?" she teased.

"Marry me and you'll be adored and secure for the rest of your life. I'll give you everything you could wish for: jewels, gowns, palaces—anything," he vowed in one breath.

"Horses?" she quizzed.

"Triple Crown winners, every one."

"But there's one thing you cannot give me," she told him, kindly.

"What is that? Name it! You could do whatever you liked, go wherever you wish. You would have status, a title, respect, what you will. What's left?"

"You can't give me your happiness, Freddie."

"I'd be as happy as the day is long with you as my wife." He was totally convinced.

"Darling man, no-one could have a more loyal friend, and I love you dearly. . . ."

His face brightened. "There you are, then. . . ."

"I'll always love you," she promised. "But not with the love a wife should feel for her husband. And without that, I cannot make you happy."

He took her face between his hands and looked down earnestly.

"I'd be happy with anything you could give, so long as you were with me, and I shall ask you again and again and again, old girl."

She hugged him.

"In the meantime," he went on, "what say we go to the races? It's high time you 'came out' into Society again, and there's a meeting at Salisbury."

She laughed and then remembered the rules of her mourning. It was true that after one year she was permitted to go out again, but she was expected to wear black for two or three years.

"Oh, I've only rags of weeds to wear," she wailed.

" 'Tis every lady's complaint," Freddie mocked. "But I think my aunt and Mr. Dobbs may have a surprise in store."

The gown was velvet, trimmed with velvet ribbon and with lace at the cuffs. Small panels emphasized Macha's tiny waist and the curve of her hips. It may have been black in colour, but it was surprisingly daring in style, and her reflection showed the transformation from unkempt working woman to a figure which would make heads turn. She stroked the rich material and realised, for the first time, how much she had missed all the feminine frills and fancies which had dressed and surrounded her before.

"A little gift," Mrs. Wellington smiled. "To mark the beginning of a new life."

Macha's throat was so tight that she could not reply. She pulled the old lady to her and burst into tears.

"How old are you, child?" asked Mrs. Wellington, flustered.

She gulped and considered. "I must be twenty-one now."

"Only twenty-one." Mrs. Wellington shook her head and sighed. "A widow so young."

Making an obvious effort to regain her composure, she said, briskly, "Well, although black is no colour for a gel of twenty-one, I must admit you look most fetching in this frock. What think you, Mr. Dobbs?"

"I think madam is fortunate to have such large silver eyes and an ivory complexion, so perfect against *noir*. But just look at those hands, madam!" Mr. Dobbs scolded. "I thought I told madam to use glycerine cream *every night*."

Macha looked contrite. She had forgotten all such nonsense.

"Cover them up at once with these!" he ordered, waving a pair of flimsy gloves. "I cannot have one of my creations seen with hands like those. It would ruin my reputation."

He hurried behind a curtain at the back of his salon and reappeared with a large jar. Its label proclaimed that it was full of the ointment used to dress sores on cows' udders.

"Desperate situations require desperate measures, madam," he explained severely. "So be so good as to keep your hands creamed with this at all times, *and* wear housemaid's gloves."

With which he bowed them out.

Macha and Sir Freddie and Mrs. Wellington took the train from Chichester to Salisbury, Macha jigging about on her seat and chattering nonstop, full of the memory of her first visit to this racecourse with Declan and of the money she had won then. It was going to be her lucky day. When they arrived at the station, it was all she could do to restrain herself from jumping out before Sir Freddie had time to help her down.

At the far end of the train, some Thoroughbreds were being led from the van. As they watched, the last one reared and slipped off the ramp. His lad fell and let go of the reins, and the horse bolted through the screaming passengers and made for the iron railings with their lethally pointed tips.

Without hesitation, Macha sped across the platform into his path, grabbed the flying reins and was dragged several yards before the terrified animal stopped.

"Easy there, boy, easy. What sort of behaviour is this for a gentleman like yourself?" She had picked herself up and was already holding his head and quietening the horse as Sir Freddie rushed up.

"Macha, my dear, my dearest! Are you all right? Macha?"

"Is she hurt? My God! She might have been killed!" Another

worried-looking man appeared close behind. "My dear lady, that was a crazy thing to do!"

"I'm right as hounds speaking on a nip of a morning," she said, grinning; and then, "Oh, the Devil's father, if I haven't ruined my brand-new frock! What ever will Mrs. Wellington say—and Mr. Dobbs?"

But Mrs. Wellington had swooned and was lying on the ground, with several ladies waving bottles of sal volatile under her nose.

Freddie was patting Macha's head abstractedly and talking sheer rubbish in panic. The stranger was lifting her arms and moving her fingers up and down one by one.

"Ouch!" Macha flinched. "What on earth are you doing?"

"Wiggle your toes!" he commanded. "We must be sure no bones are broken."

"Of course nothing's broken," she retorted. "And if this horse belongs to you, you'd be better off looking to him."

"Allow me to introduce the Earl of Ashreigney," Freddie remembered propriety at last. The stranger kept her hand in his as a red-faced groom ran up, took hold of the racehorse and began to lead it away.

"Stop! Don't move that creature another inch!" Macha swung round without acknowledging the introduction, and pushed the startled lad aside. Then she ran her hands down each of the Thoroughbred's legs and carefully felt his quarters and shoulders and checked the head and belly.

She rounded on the groom. "What sort of man are you? Trying to shift a horse without seeing him right first?"

Turning back to the stranger, she added with severity, "There doesn't seem to be any damage done, but there's to be no racing for him today."

"I shouldn't dream of it," he agreed solemnly.

"And be sure the veterinary examines him."

"Of course." He smiled slightly.

Macha raised her eyebrows with dignity, unaware that her face was smudged with dirt and that she had lost her hat.

"Are you sure you are all right?" Sir Freddie was asking anxiously.

"A bruise or two. Nothing that a very large brandy could not put right," she replied.

"Then permit me at least to offer that and to take you and your party to an hotel where you may recover and repair your . . . disarray." The stranger, who had drawn back to talk to his groom and watch his horse led off, rejoined them.

He was a tall, grave man with the patrician features and aquiline nose of so many aristocrats. His clothes were faultlessly tailored, and he had an air of accustomed authority. He was quite old, she thought—at least twenty-eight—and his face in repose was guarded to the point of austerity with grey, haughty eyes. She gazed into them steadily and realised, with surprise, that it was not arrogance at all. The expression in his eyes was reserved, almost diffident. Richard Withington, the Earl of Ashreigney, was, in fact, a very shy man.

"That won't be necessary, Ashreigney." Sir Freddie was rejecting the offer on her behalf.

Macha gave the stranger a radiant smile. "Thank you, Lord Ashreigney. I should be grateful for both the brandy and the chance to tidy up this mess." She beamed. "We should be delighted to join you."

As she said his name, she remembered.

"Holies! You're the owner of the Beckworth Stud. Garnet Fox belongs to you. You bred Blackthorne and Aldern Boy and Beau Musician." The names of a string of classic runners registered in her mind.

He inclined his head with another smile, and by the time they reached his waiting carriage and lifted the still gasping Mrs. Wellington onto its leather seat, they were already far into that informed discussion which can keep two horse lovers talking for a lifetime.

They were shown into a private suite, and while the gentlemen remained in the sitting room and Mrs. Wellington lay resting on the bed, a chambermaid clumsily parted Macha from her torn garments, which were whisked away to be cleaned and repaired and replaced by a simple dark blue voile day dress which Lord Ashreigney had somehow arranged to have sent in and which fitted perfectly.

In less than an hour, Macha emerged to find a table set for tea before a merrily burning fire.

"A fire in Summer!" she exclaimed.

"We thought you might feel chilled from shock," explained Lord Ashreigney. "And that the rooms might be damp. I realise you are in mourning, Mrs. Melbaugh, and regret it was not possible to find anything suitable for you to wear in black."

"I don't regret it," she smiled cheekily. "It is lovely to have the excuse to discard widow's weeds, and very clever of you to find such a deevy frock, sir." She fingered the flimsy skirt. "But I shall have it cleaned and returned to the shop as soon as my own is ready."

"Please accept it, Mrs. Melbaugh. I would not wish to cause you any further embarrassment, but the circumstances are exceptional and it is such a trifle," he pressed. "Pharaoh is a favourite horse of mine, and he could have been seriously injured—as you could yourself."

"Ach, curses! The races have started. We've missed the first two already with all this palaver, and there was me with the winners in the bag for certain," Macha suddenly exclaimed with disappointment. "If we hurry, we'll catch the rest, though."

"I think you should stay here and eat some of these little iced cakes," the Earl said firmly. "You have had a very frightening experience and need time to recover, and there are many more days to go racing."

"Ashreigney's right, old girl," Freddie, who had been silent for an unusually long time, intervened rather bossily. "In any case, we can't leave my aunt stranded here, so sit down and take your tea."

She obeyed with a flounce and then discovered that she was indeed rather shaken and tired, and the cakes were very good.

By the time Mrs. Wellington's quavering voice called from the bedroom, Richard Withington, the Earl of Ashreigney, was laughing without restraint at Macha's stories of horses and races.

The old lady joined them looking very frail.

"I should like to go home," she said faintly.

"May I beg you to accept my sincerest apologies for the distress you have been caused today." Lord Ashreigney bent over her hand. "And allow me to suggest that you are in no condition for the privations of a train journey."

"Well, perhaps a night spent here . . . ," Mrs. Wellington murmured, still as pale as parchment.

"Beckworth House is but a short distance," he said. "Please permit me to have you conveyed there, where you and Mrs. Melbaugh may receive the care and comfort which I am sure is absolutely necessary and which an hotel cannot provide."

"We could not possibly put you to such trouble," she protested weakly.

"It would be the greatest honour, madam, and would enable me, in far too humble a way, to try to make amends for everything you have suffered."

"Oh, we must go. I would give anything to see the stud," Macha burst out. "You will show me round, Lord Ashreigney? I want to see everything."

"Oh, Macha, Macha." Mrs. Wellington was unable to do more than shake her head over the Irish girl's lack of modesty.

"Be jabus! Isn't a 'respectable widow' entitled to speak her mind more than a maiden, Freddie?" demanded Macha.

Sir Freddie looked boot-faced, and Mrs. Wellington closed her eyes in despair.

"First thing in the morning, I shall show you every corner of my stables," promised the Earl.

As they slowly covered the three miles in his carriage, Macha queried why he and his horses had been on the train, when he lived so close by.

"I had been in London, and those horses are in training near Chichester," he answered. "Only the brood mares, foals and yearlings are kept at Beckworth. And, of course the stallions, including Garnet Fox."

The horse he named was the finest stallion in the country, a legend, winner of the Triple Crown in his time and now sire to winners of almost every important race.

"I still haven't had a Derby winner from him," he commented ruefully.

"But you will, and soon." Macha was certain. "I have a mare in foal to my Gold you know."

He remembered Gold, and as she described her vision of the foal to come in every detail from fetlocks to the curve of his ears, Richard Withington listened with as much attention as if she were talking of the royal winner, Diamond Jubilee.

Beckworth House was not as forbidding as Poldonith Castle, lacking the gatehouse, with its bastions and towers, leading to the protected central courtyard. It was built of warm old brick which glowed in the sun, and from its Tudor roots had grown wings and turrets without the application of any disciplined symmetry, and although it contained over one hundred rooms, it had the warm and friendly atmosphere of a much smaller dwelling.

The lodge-keeper had touched his cap and his wife bobbed a curtsy as the carriage swept through the gates, past a wide lake with a temple set on a knoll in the distance and through an avenue of limes, to arrive at the south entrance.

As they drew up, Sir Freddie suddenly muttered something about having business to attend and asked to be returned to the railway station. He took his leave with a puzzling expression on his face. He was probably annoyed at having missed the day's racing, Macha guessed, and then was so entranced by the sight of the house that she thought no more of it.

The original timber roof still arched over the great hall, at whose far end was a carved and painted wooden screen with minstrel gallery. Macha and Mrs. Wellington were led up the wide staircase, across a large saloon with pictures of half-naked women on the ceiling and through the long gallery hung with portraits of Ashreigney ancestors and lined with chairs and chests and tables. The old lady was flagging by the time they were shown into two adjoining bedchambers.

Macha's room was decorated with Chinese hand-painted wallpaper and lacquer furniture the like of which she had never seen before. Delicate gold trees and birds decorated the doors and drawers of a cabinet and tallboy. There were ornate gilded mirrors on the walls, a wide floral carpet almost covered the whole of the polished oak floor and solid-silver candlesticks, a heavy silver inkstand and silver fountain pens and pencils stood on the small mahogany writing table. The only disappointment was the ragged state of the bed hangings on the tester, which were embroidered with crests and scrolls and in her view, should have been thrown out and replaced at once. Had she known they were more than two hundred years old, she would have been even less impressed.

They dined formally that evening, as she had expected, the carving being accomplished by the butler at the serving table and the food being handed from the left on silver salvers by footmen. Yet Macha did not feel uncomfortable as so often before in such circumstances. The room was not large enough to be intimidating, and the pictures of the stud's most illustrious horses and other sporting scenes which surrounded her gave plenty to talk about.

Lord Ashreigney answered all her questions and added many of his own anecdotes. The footmen, accustomed to his taciturnity, carried surprised reports back to the kitchen. It was the first time since the death of his young wife and baby in childbirth years before that they had seen their master so animated, and this led to considerable speculation in the servants' hall, of which the two subjects under discussion were completely unaware.

It had been such an eventful day after her long stay alone at the cottage that Macha hardly remembered reaching her bedchamber, let alone falling fast asleep.

"Aaeeh, Madam!"

The maid let out a screech as the Irish girl struggled from bed the following morning and revealed a body covered in bruises where she had been dragged along the ground by the runaway horse the previous day. She could hardly move from stiffness and had a headache.

Mrs. Wellington was summoned and immediately bustled her back under the eiderdown.

"I knew we should have called a doctor yesterday," she said. "And I shall do so at once."

"I don't like doctors and I don't need one and I will not see one," Macha responded with decision, believing, like many travellers, that the attentions of a medical practitioner hastened the arrival of a coffin. "Tell Cook to make up dressings of pennyroyal and vinegar and a decoction of powdered angelica root, Carduus water and treacle and I'll be right as ninepence before you know it."

"Only if you give me your word that you will stay in bed and not move," Mrs. Wellington agreed reluctantly.

The herbal mixtures arrived, together with a breakfast tray of weak tea, arrowroot and a lightly boiled egg.

Macha's face fell. She was very hungry.

"I'm not an invalid," she protested to Mrs. Wellington.

"I ordered the nourishment most suited to your debilitated state," answered the other.

"Then I will simply die of starvation. Not the littlest shrew could survive on this." Macha was most ungrateful.

Mrs. Wellington snorted. "Don't talk such nonsense, child. Eat it up, or I shall not give you these magazines to read."

Macha took a sip of the arrowroot and screwed up her face.

"It's horribilissimo!" she exclaimed, pushing it away. But the old lady pushed it back and stood over her until she had finished it.

Outside, the morning was filled with sunshine and birdsong. Macha flipped through the magazines, all of which contained only articles on fashion and rather silly stories. She wished someone had had the sense to send up a copy of *The Sporting Life*.

A message came from the Earl urging her to rest and not to concern herself with anything until she had recovered. Another maid removed the tray and, after waiting until all the footsteps had died away along the corridor outside, Macha tiptoed across the room to open the window.

Her room overlooked an immaculate topiary garden, the yews clipped into spheres and pyramids, cubes and weights, and two shaped like fan-tailed doves, all set on knife-edged lawns divided by a gravel path and surrounded by a high hedge, like a game on a green board ready for play. An archway through the hedge led to a pleasure garden in which fountains played in twin pools surrounded by beds of tulips and wallflowers. Wisteria formed an arbour round a stone seat, and a pergola of trained laburnums led to a walk of spreading old lilac trees, from which scent as strong as eau de cologne wafted back to the house. A small crescent-shaped wood to the east sheltered the gardens, and the Wiltshire Downs rolled away south, more gentle in their swell than the hills of Sussex. To the west she could see the acres of Lord Ashreigney's paddocks.

The fresh air banished her headache, and she began to wonder where her clothes were. Carefully locking the adjoining door to Mrs. Wellington's room, she padded across the room to try the door on the other side. It opened into an exquisite oval dressing room, the grey silk-covered walls of which were crowded with watercolours painted by the same gifted hand. Ivory brushes inlaid with silver, enamelled and porcelain pots and jars and perfume bottles of crystal adorned the modern dressing table with its triple mirror, and there were two upholstered boudoir chairs, a graceful little walnut table and a cheval glass.

Hearing the sound of someone approaching, she scampered back across the bedroom and under the covers just in time. Mrs. Wellington entered the room bearing an unpleasant-looking drink.

"I am coming down to luncheon," Macha announced with determination. "And I should like my clothes, please."

As Mrs. Wellington demurred, she held up a hand.

"I am perfectly well and I cannot stand being cooped up here any longer. I am bored to tears. It is quite insufferable."

The old lady sensibly saw there was no more point in arguing, and minutes later, a maid showed Macha back into the oval dressing room and opened one of the built-in cupboards cleverly concealed in the walls.

It was full of a woman's gorgeous clothes, morning frocks and "teagies" skilfully embroidered and embellished with priceless lace, evening gowns of gold-and-silver-worked velvets, and silk and brocades and taffetas sewn with pearls and precious stones. Mrs. Wellington had whispered of Lord Ashreigney's dead young wife, and Macha knew these had belonged to her.

"His Lordship wondered if you would care to choose one of these for today," the middle-aged servant told her.

"But I could wear the blue frock I arrived in," said Macha.

"I'm afraid that is being pressed, madam."

Because it was her favourite colour, she picked out a light green walking gown, while the maid produced a chemise and petticoats and silk stockings from the drawers and then helped her into them with an expertise which came from long practise.

"Were you Lady Ashreigney's maid?" Macha asked.

"Lady Charlotte's lady's maid, yes," the woman corrected snootily, in a strong West Country accent. Servants always knew whose background was questionable. "Her were the Duke of Pennine's daughter, you know. 'Twere a terrible tragedy when her died. Her were that beautiful, with a waist no bigger than my own wrist yere."

She hauled on the corset laces with a sniff which indicated that Macha's figure left much to be desired by comparison.

"And her were that sweet-natured, allus singin' like a nightingale, and playing the piano and painting pictures. All them pictures were done by her," she went on. "Oh, her were an angel. His Lordship's never got over her passing, and I don't reckon he never will."

She chattered on as she dressed Macha's hair, until by the time she had finished, the Irish girl felt gauche and gross as she stood before the cheval glass.

The woman produced a delightful matching green hat from a round box and a pair of gloves.

"Madam may wish to take the air this afternoon," she explained. "Seeing as the weather's so fine."

"I certainly will." She could not wait to tour the stud.

The maid looked her up and down, searching for faults with a professional eye. At last she nodded.

"Madam looks quite nice," she concluded, and Macha was immensely relieved at even this limited approval.

The Earl was talking to Mrs. Wellington in the hall as she descended the stairs. When he turned and saw her, he stopped in mid-sentence, and a muscle twitched slightly in his cheek. An awkward second passed before he stepped forward to greet her and enquire after her health.

During luncheon he was much quieter than at dinner the previous night, and she began to wonder whether he was finding their continued presence irksome. However, at the end of the meal he invited them with marked willingness to view the stud.

When Mrs. Wellington expressed a preference to retire to rest, he escorted Macha to the main entrance, where a pony cart with fringed canopy was waiting.

"It would be inadvisable for you to overstrain yourself today," he explained. "So I thought it better to drive you round."

"That's very thoughtful of you, sir, but I'm as fit as a bug, you know." She grinned, and his face softened at last.

They drove to the paddocks. There the lovely brood mares, full-bellied as ships, bobbed gently over the rippling grass, grazing. Elegantly turned legs, long, sloping shoulders and fine heads told of their impeccable breeding, but the highly strung skittishness of youth was long behind them. Now they created an atmosphere of tranquility, with their unhurried movements, their calm eyes and lazily swishing tails. Their foals lay stretched out in the warmth of the sun after the games of the morning.

Macha felt her eyes grow moist at the sight. All at once she understood that this was the halcyon balance to the conflict on the turf. Most people were interested only in the thrills and spills, the winning or losing, the poverty and riches of the racing game. But it was the breeding of the Thoroughbred and the running of the race which, together, formed the unique perfection of the sport. Divorce one from the other and a cheap sensationalism would be left on one side and straight commerce on the other. It was the combination of blood and courage, the line and the contest which made the flawless whole.

After absorbing the scene in silence for a while, she turned to Richard Withington with a sigh of contentment.

"Ah, there's nothing like it, is there?"

"No," he replied. And their minds were in harmony.

The lane curved as they drove on, bringing the pony cart round behind the stable blocks to the gate of another field by the main yard. As they approached, a gang of about twenty young horses cantered up, full of interest.

A lot of nonsense and nipping went on amongst the group, the bold nosing up, lifting their top lips and showing their teeth, the shy sniffing and backing off. Every ear was pricked. Richard Withington produced some sugar lumps from his pocket and handed them to her with a furtive look over his shoulder.

"Stacey, the stud groom, doesn't approve, you know."

By comparison with the gawky foals, the yearlings had the beginnings of grace. They had grown taller and their bodies had filled out, but they were still untidy, leggy babies, innocently inquisitive. Older horses had a knowing curiosity, but to the young ones everything was still new.

Macha fed them the sugar, giggling at the timid ones trying to decide whether to push forward and those at the front making sure they did not get the chance.

"Don't bite me, you," she reproved, raising her elbow at the most daring.

The whole bunch jerked back in astonishment, wheeled about, bumping into each other, cantered off, squealing, and returned seconds later.

Macha laughed helplessly. "Oh, I could take every one of them home with me."

Richard Withington gave her an unfathomable look and then a slow smile. Leaving the pony and trap, they walked towards the buildings and he explained how the horses were moved through the various yards. Early in the year, the brood mares were brought up from the bottom yard to foaling boxes, where a groom lived in, as their time neared; then, after three months, they were taken with their foals to another yard. Later, the yearlings and foals were removed to the yard which had originally held the in-foal mares: most to be sold in the autumn; the best to be retained for training and running in Ashreigney's colours.

They came to a grass enclosure containing a number of upright square stones.

"It looks like a cemetery, only smaller," Macha observed.

"It is." He looked pleased at her perception. "A cemetery for horses. My great grandfather started this stud, you know."

He led her from stone to stone, and she saw each was carved with a famous name and the dates of birth and death, and he told her the histories, races won, legendary offspring sired, descendants still at Beckworth, carrying on the strain.

"Hermitage: Now, there was a holy terror. Used to come out of his box kicking and bucking; there wasn't a lad wanted to go near him. Then a goat somehow found its way into his paddock one day, and by Jove, if the horse didn't turn into a lamb from then on, so long as the goat stayed with him. It was the most extraordinary thing. The old chap had been lonely, I suppose."

His expression had become tender at the memory.

Lonely, just like you, she thought, and, taking his arm, she recounted the story of Gold and the ugly mare. "Horses aren't so different from us," she concluded.

"That is quite right," he said, as though she had revealed a truth.

At last, they reached the stallions' yard. It was much smaller than she had expected, with the three horses standing at Beckworth in neighbouring beech loose boxes.

The stud groom, a short, fast-talking man, brought out the first with a clatter of hooves.

"We don't really know much about him yet. He had a good racing career before I bought him, but it's his progeny which matter now, and the first of his get are only yearlings," commented her companion. "Everything depends on his performance, and he has a lot to do."

In his involvement with the subject, he had forgotten that such matters were considered to be unmentionable in front of ladies. Macha asked the right questions, and he answered, unselfconsciously, as one horseman to another.

"We'll know his fate after a few years. A good horse could cover fifty mares in a season and will go on working as a stallion until he's eighteen or nineteen years old."

The next horse was led out, sixteen hands high and heavily powerful; almost too muscular, she thought.

"We could do with a better type of mare for him. Most of my own are covered by Garnet Fox, of course, but this chap has a beautiful pedigree. An Irish horse, a stayer, and too many people want horses which come up quickly."

Finally, as they stood back from the door, Garnet Fox was brought out of his box, 16.1 hands high, a superlative bay.

". . . full brother to Flying Fox. He won the Triple Crown and the Gold Cup," Lord Ashreigney was murmuring, staring at the horse with adoration. "He's a great horse."

Macha scarcely heard him. She caught her breath at the sight of the stallion. Here was eminence, the culmination of the centuries of breeding, the countless hours men had spent poring over documents and records and studying form. This horse was a prince. No. This was the king.

She took off her glove and stretched out a hand. The groom clicked his tongue in warning, and Lord Ashreigney made as though to restrain her, but Garnet Fox breathed delicately against her palm and, as she moved to him, inclined his head until their faces almost met and she was rubbing his ears.

"Well, my lord, I've never seen him do that!" The man was staggered. "He's a tricky customer, madam. I thought he was going to have your fingers there."

"Oh, no," she said, ecstatically as the stallion playfully pushed her hat off and nosed in her hair. "They always tell you when they're going to misbehave, and he's far too good-mannered for that."

"Don't you believe it," the groom retorted with feeling.

Mrs. Wellington watched the Earl of Ashreigney and Macha return across the lawn from a window and was seated, waiting, on a sofa in the drawing room when they entered.

"It is time for tea," she said. "You have been away for almost three hours."

"My dear Mrs. Wellington, how remiss of me. I had no idea we had been so long. I do hope you are not vexed."

Richard Withington was immediately full of apologies, and Macha prayed he did not notice the sly and knowing look on the old lady's face. She hastily tugged at the bell-pull to distract him with the appearance of the butler.

On the way back to Sussex, there was no stopping Mrs. Wellington's wittering plans for Macha's future.

"I could see how taken he is with you, my dear, and of course, he's one of the most eligible men in the country, and then, you have so much in common, he being a widower and you a widow, and there's your interest in horses, too. Oh, it would be the most perfect match."

"We may never see him again, yet here you are with us wedded already," Macha protested mildly. "And the truth is that I am not at all inclined to remarry."

"What a thing to say!" Mrs. Wellington was horrified. "You must marry again, child. How ever will you survive otherwise?"

"I hardly know Lord Ashreigney; and besides, he is far too old."

"Old! Don't be ridiculous! The man is in his prime. Sometimes I despair of today's young people." Mrs. Wellington leant forward in her seat to give emphasis to her words. "It should be your priority to find another husband, Macha dear. Frankly, I cannot imagine why you do not marry my nephew, Freddie, who is the most charming and considerate of men. However, although I am forced to accept your decision there, I intend to do everything within my power to find you a suitable husband."

"I cannot marry a man I do not love," Macha pointed out.

"Love! Fiddlesticks! What has love to do with it?" The old lady dismissed such sentimentalism with a contemptuous wave. "Do you think I loved Harry at first? Of course not. In fact, I thought him quite feeble, but I was wrong. He proved to be as brave as a lion and was mentioned in despatches in the Crimea. And no more great-hearted a husband walked this earth. I grew very attached to him, very attached indeed."

Her mouth trembled a little and she dabbed at it with her handkerchief.

"Marriage is the protection every woman needs. In marriage, the man provides security and the woman gives him heirs. It has absolutely nothing to do with love," she lectured. "And I do declare, Macha, that if you are so foolish as to reject a proposal from Richard Withington, Earl of Ashreigney, heir to the Marquess of Bridgemere, I shall wash my hands of you."

Seeing that the old lady was quite upset, Macha did not argue further. In fact, she was not at all averse to seeing Richard Withington again. The hours spent in his company had been the most enjoyable she had passed for a long time. Admittedly, in some ways he was rather staid and would probably disapprove of many of the wild friends she had known with James Melbaugh. She could not imagine him dancing the polka all night, or accepting invitations to some of the more notorious house parties; but those friends had proved fickle, and she herself had found many of the weekends interminable. Certainly, her heart did not race as it had once done over Molloy—but it did race at the thought of those magnificent horses.

When his invitation to attend an opera in London arrived the following week, both the Irish girl and the old lady were delighted.

"Oh that's a kind of music hall, isn't it?" said Macha.

"Absolutely not! Oh, dear, you have so much to learn." Mrs. Wellington looked dismayed and launched forth into a dissertation on how to behave at Covent Garden.

Mr. Dodds, on learning of the forthcoming evening and the illustrious name of her escort, decided Macha must wear white.

"Simplicity. That is the secret," he pronounced, producing a sketch.

"I thought widows weren't supposed to wear white," commented Macha.

"Strictly speaking, madam is quite correct," he agreed. "But Madam is so very young that only a few old fuddy-duddies could object. The Earl of Ashreigney should see madam looking at her most, dare I say it, *virginal* and luminous. But madam really must do something about her cheeks. They are far too highly coloured. It is not at all becoming. I do beg madam to spend less time in the fresh air."

He was matchmaking too, she thought. It was a conspiracy. But the gown, when it was finished, was heavenly; white wild silk, cut very low at the neck to reveal the curve of her breasts and with sleeves puffed to the elbow and then tight to the wrists. Macha looked down at its pure flow and fingered the star-shaped flowers of beads and gold thread scattered over its skirt quite often during the opera.

"What the devil is she saying?" she whispered to Mrs. Wellington, as the soprano shrilled after the overture. "I can't understand a word."

"The work is in Italian," she was informed. "This is a young maiden telling of her love."

As the diva looked like a sofa and her love, when he appeared, had several chins and a huge paunch, and not only the first aria, but the entire performance turned out to be in the incomprehensible foreign tongue, Macha quickly lost interest, even though some of the tunes were catchy. She stood up with relief at the first interval, expecting to collect her cloak, and was crestfallen to learn there were another two acts to come.

"Stop fiddling, child!" hissed Mrs. Wellington, an hour later.

"Are you enjoying it?" Lord Ashreigney whispered from the other side.

Clasping her hands firmly together in her lap, she managed to reply that the opera was "deevy."

Supper afterwards was much more fun. Romano's in the Strand was packed with theatregoers, fabulous women in sables and jewels, and handsome, top-hatted men with silk-lined cloaks and silver-topped canes. The smells of French perfume and rich food mingled, waiters scurried about, the sounds of chatter and laughter filled the air. A stream of people greeted Lord Ashreigney and were presented to the ladies, many names which meant nothing to the Irish girl, but which produced a frenzy of quivering from Mrs. Wellington's fan: Lord and Lady Castlerosse and Mr. W. B. Yeats, Sir Henry Irving and, finally, Lord Salisbury, the Prime Minister. Macha had certainly heard of him, and her cheeks grew even pinker. Richard Withington thought she looked delicious.

The Earl followed up the evening with more invitations: to the Private View at the Royal Academy of Arts, to the ballet and, of course, as his partner to the colossal ball given at Goodwood House at the end of the week's racing by the Duke of Richmond. Once again, the Mamas who had seen him as a prize for their daughters were scowling in Macha's direction; some even attempted to have her ostracised for appearing in colours other than black less than two years after being widowed.

However, the power of the Withington name was sufficient for acquaintances who had ignored her since James Melbaugh's downfall to eagerly acknowledge her existence once more. In a remarkable display of the subtleties of English Society, Lord Ashreigney included in their circle only those of irreproachable character and excluded the rest without even raising a discourteous eyebrow.

It was while taking tea in Gunter's one afternoon with Mrs. Wellington that Macha heard a familiar voice calling across the crowded tables and twisted to see Daisy Fitzclarence, waving dangerously while dodging towards them between the potted palms and salver-sized hats.

"Where have you been hiding yourself, Macha?" she demanded, after the briefest of greetings. "After your misfortunes, I tried everything to contact you, but you simply disappeared; and when I heard that James had died, I tried again. Archie was very unhelpful, I might say."

"How is Archie?" Macha asked, to avoid going into the details of her position.

"Still huntin', shootin' and fishin'—and not much else," replied her friend, raising her eyes to the ceiling.

Mrs. Wellington lifted her lorgnette in an arch gesture which was quite lost on the American girl, who went on, unabashed:

"Anyway, honey, a whole flock of little birds tell me you've a deevy new beau," she said, in ringing tones which made it impossible for the ladies sitting nearby not to eavesdrop, much to their relief.

"Then they've been singing the wrong song, as usual." Macha tried to suppress her with a certain coldness, but Daisy was irrepressible and so engaging that she could not remain annoyed.

"No man takes a gal right through the Season without intending to make her his bride. Has he proposed? Archie knows him, of course, and says his father's so old he could kick the bucket any time and your beau will inherit the marquessate. Being a marchioness has just got to be an improvement on being a widow—would you not agree, Mrs. Wellington?"

"Those are my sentiments, Lady Fitzclarence," agreed the old lady, who suddenly perceived an ally in the outspoken American and warmed to her accordingly.

Macha made a *moue* at them both; but there was no denying her own pleasure at being out and about in company and lavish surroundings once more. To return to this lifestyle on a more permanent basis was certainly going to demand planning and action, and could not be achieved by a young woman on her own, especially a young widow.

She had no jewellery, and rebuilding her wardrobe was a constant problem. She won some money at the races and sold a few working horses at a profit. She suspected that Mrs. Wellington was dipping into her own savings to augment Mr. Dobbs's charges, which seemed to have gone down rather than up. But still, the bill for materials mounted until she was driven to mention her fears to the court dressmaker.

"Madam's star is in the house of the ascendant," he replied, calmly. "And madam is not to be concerned with minor matters."

Nevertheless, she did worry and was forced to plead previous engagements to several of Lord Ashreigney's suggested outings, in order to avoid being seen in the same costumes too many times.

However, she could not refuse too often, for fear of appearing discouraging, and fortunately, the Season ended just as she was running out of solutions. Freddie Wellington, of whom she had seen little recently, left to winter in France, as was his custom, and Society departed en masse for Scotland, or to winter pursuits which did not interest the Earl.

When he insisted that she and Mrs. Wellington come to Beckworth House for Christmas, Macha's lingerie was not fit for the servants' eyes, and that necessitated more expense. Her financial situation so preoccupied her that she was far quieter than usual throughout their stay.

On Christmas morning, he gave her a necklace of cabochon-cut star sapphires set in gold. As she held it up, they sparkled the cornflower-blue colour unique to the very finest stones.

"Oh . . . oh . . ." gasped the old lady.

"Sapphires symbolize constancy, hope and heaven," Richard Withington murmured as he fastened it round Macha's neck.

She, to her shame, could only wonder how long it would be before she had to pawn it, or even sell it.

That afternoon, he took her down to the stables. The loose boxes were full of majestically pregnant mares, their coats patinated with condition, each with a fortune in her belly, contentedly waiting out their time in the warm, deep straw. She fed them cut carrots and stroked their velvet noses and would have given her necklace for any one of them.

"The Christmasses of the past are special. They are like roses, each with its own scent and colour and shape," he said, unexpectedly. "Sometimes one imagines they can never be repeated, and of course, they cannot. But as each flower is different, it is also of equal beauty to the others, and so there will be other flowers, Macha."

She looked up, puzzled.

He went on, "I know you have not been long bereaved, but I hate to see you sad. . . ."

"Oh, no, it is not that . . ." she began, realising he had misread her abstraction, and then stopped. How could she tell him that she had no longer cared for James Melbaugh in the end.

"It is five years since my wife died, and I do understand how hard it is to bear such loss. At first, one is sure one cannot recover, but time does heal. Not a day passes when I do not think of my wife, but now I no longer remember with pain. Please believe me when I say that the memories become sweet and welcome."

Molloy surged through Macha's mind. Her heart squeezed, and she closed her eyes.

"I know. Oh, I do know, my dear." He took her hand in both of his. "The past cannot, should not be forgotten, but we have to learn to make life anew. He would not wish you to mourn for ever. He would want you to be happy, fulfilled, just as Charlotte would want for me."

That night, Macha lay awake and thought about Richard Withington. She did not love him; or perhaps it was that she was not "in love" with him. Yet that afternoon, for the first time she had wanted him to take her in his arms and hold her very close. She had wanted to hide in him.

He was a splendid catch. Even Queen Victoria herself, had she still been alive, would have thought him a fitting husband for any of her grand-daughters. But he was a good man who deserved an honestly caring woman, someone to give him the cherishing and purpose he craved. Macha could not have brought herself to dupe him into marriage, and she was very unsure of her feelings.

They spent Boxing Day in the library, where he showed her the stud books, tomes bound in morocco. The ancestry of every one of his horses could be traced back to one of the three founding arab stallions—the Byerley Turk, the Darley Arabian and the Godolphin Arabian—from which every Thoroughbred was descended. He explained about bloodlines and inbreeding and outbreeding, revealing an huge new area of knowledge which perhaps Molloy himself had not dreamed existed.

"The most remarkable occurrence took place this year," he told her, taking down a volume reverently. "Some long-lost papers by a monk called Mendel were found and have been published. He discovered the principles of heredity—the inheritance of nature and characteristics from parents and ancestors—and I am convinced they must affect the thinking of every breeder of bloodstock. It is a discovery of monumental importance."

Macha eagerly assimilated everything, astonishing Richard Withington with her retentive memory and rapid grasp of the subject, as well as with her own sagacity. They regarded each other with increasing respect.

"My wife, Charlotte, was a fine horsewoman, but not greatly inspired by such details," he admitted as he began to replace the records in the bookcases.

Macha found herself quite pleased to hear that the paragon had had a failing.

"I suppose I've never been interested in anything much except horses," she confessed. "And I thought I knew a lot about them, until today. Now I see I'm as ignorant as a mooncalf."

"If that is ignorance, old Mat Dawson must be sitting up in his grave," he responded, admiringly. "For I have never met a more informed lady."

It was necessary to return to Sussex the following day as Gold's foal was almost due. The mare had grown matronly and actually pretty and the stallion stood over her possessively in their shared box.

"They should be parted before she reaches her time," Declan said worriedly.

"You can try it, then," replied Macha. "Because I'm not going to. He'll eat you alive."

So the two horses stayed together and a few nights later, the mare lay down in the straw and gave birth to a colt as Gold stood over her in a lather of excitement and the girl and the Irishman watched, holding their breaths.

"Thank God, he takes after his father," commented Declan, viewing the damp new arrival, as it began to climb shakily to its feet. It flaunted the familiar wide blaze and three white socks and light brown hair which would darken into the bright chestnut passed down directly from the great Gallinule.

It was New Year's Day, the official birthday of every racehorse, the day every owner prays strong foals will be born to give them the months of extra growth over their future rivals.

"Gaelic Gold," Macha named him with delight.

"Let's hope so," said Declan cryptically.

After three weeks in Sussex, she returned to Beckworth in January, in time for the arrival of the first foals there. Now there was no question of her not accompanying the Earl to the stables, no matter how far into the night he was called.

Each time the minute hooves emerged and the elfin nose appeared tucked between the fragile legs and the diminutive body slid out, still wrapped in its silver skin, they were openly moved by the miracle of birth.

"When is your birthday?" he wanted to know, as they strolled back to the house in the earliest hours, after the arrival of a peerless dark bay filly.

"May Eve," she replied, and wished she could have told him of her father, but said instead, "I shall be twenty-two."

"You are only twenty-one." He gave her that same half-sad look Mrs. Wellington had given at the information. Then he went on, "May seems far too long to wait. I think you should have your gift now. Macha, would you accept that new filly as an early birthday present?"

"Oh, Richard, how wonderful, wonderful!" She skipped beside him and then put her hands up to his face and kissed him. "I can't thank you enough, but thank you."

He gave a little groan and pulled her head against him and held her tightly for several seconds. Then he released her as suddenly and walked ahead so fast that she had to run to keep up.

It was the first time they had kissed, and she was taken aback at how shaken she felt. Catching sight of his remote expression, she wondered if she had upset him. He was lonely and perhaps he thought of her only as a friend. Perhaps he would never recover from the death of his Lady Charlotte enough to want another wife. Macha, afraid of being hurt, decided to distance herself from him.

"But when is he going to propose?" Mrs. Wellington demanded impatiently. "Never mind gifts of jewellery and horses, welcome though they are. It is time you were betrothed."

"It is not the kind of friendship that leads to marriage," Macha replied.

"Of course it is. What other kind of friendship is there between a man and a woman?" The old lady would have none of this theory. "And if it is not such a friendship, then it is unsuitable and high time you saw less of him."

They left for Sussex that afternoon, and although flowers arrived at the cottage, and several affectionate but guarded notes over the next two weeks, Macha politely refused his suggestion to return, and, later, to attend the opening meeting of the flat in early spring.

This was not easy to do, for she missed him much more than she would have imagined. Although she was sure she did not love him, it was strange how he seemed to be always on her mind as she mucked out her horses and rode work, and especially, during the solitary evenings as she ate on her own and then sat on her own, reading the *Pink 'Un*, or sewing in the kitchen.

The hours and days in his company had passed so quickly, bonded by a shared vocation, and now time seemed heavy. Without him she felt melancholy.

Another invitation arrived, and she was tempted to accept.

"No," instructed Mrs. Wellington.

The following morning was unseasonably mild and Macha decided to treat herself to a day off. Most of the working horses in stock were tough enough to be turned out by this time of year, and, after feeding Gold and his mare, she packed a nosebag of corn and a saddle-bag with bread and cheese, apples and a flask of cider, tacked up the stallion and rode off through Charlton Forest and along the top of Graffham Down to picnic at Woolavington.

It was a blowy, noisy day, the clouds sweeping across the sky from the southwest, the grass streamlined into a fast-flowing current, the breeze rowdy, trees sizzling like frying pans. Gold whinnied and kicked up his heels as they cantered back through Eartham Wood. His red mane whipped into her face as she gave him his head on the gallops above Goodwood. Macha, bursting with energy, revelled in the health and vitality of her body, its supple joints and muscles tempered to athletic fitness, and turned for home, at last, tingling with the exhilaration of spring.

They went back through more woods behind the cottage, and so she was actually riding into the yard before she saw the strange horse tethered at the end of the track. Thinking Freddie Wellington must have returned from France, she urged the stallion into a trot and then, to her horror, saw Richard Withington step out from the old farm buildings.

They stared at each other in silence, Macha dressed in old breeches sitting astride the big chestnut and the Earl of Ashreigney standing by the dung heap. It was impossible to know who was the more appalled.

Macha recovered first. Dismounting with a flourish, she walked straight up to him and shook his hand.

"Aren't you the one for springing more surprises than a plater winning the St. Leger!" She grinned, her face flushed and eyes brilliant from the ride. "But sure, there couldn't be a better day this side of heaven to come visiting."

"My God, Macha! What are you doing here, and . . ." He stared at her clothes, but a lifetime's training in good manners prevented him from going further.

"I live here," she said, simply.

"But where is your house?" He looked about, uncomprehending.

"I've no house. Only this cabin; but go in and sit yourself down while I put Gold away and then we'll drink some tea." Her own life's experience made her instantly philosophical. There was no point in trying to conceal anything, and if the truth of her circumstances repelled him, then it was as well to find out now and save herself any further soul-searching.

He gazed distractedly at the stallion; collected himself sufficiently to comment, "Fine horse"; then turned to do as she suggested, walking like a man in a daze.

She joined him quickly, and, chattering all the while about her picnic and ride, filled the brown teapot from the kettle always kept hot on the hob above the stove and poured tea into two cracked porcelain cups. Handing him one, she sat down in the chair opposite, stopped talking, looked at him calmly and waited.

He was still stupefied.

"What? . . . I . . . I . . . I don't understand . . . ," he began, and then stopped.

She said nothing.

". . . You live *here?* . . ."

She nodded.

"You live here," he repeated, as though trying to grasp one fact at a time.

They sat for a long time, while he regarded her and then the room and then looked back at her.

"My dear . . . my dear . . ." At last, his face crumpled. "I had no idea . . . no conception. This is quite, quite dreadful."

"I like it well enough," she responded with dignity.

". . . that you are so destitute. . . ." He did not seem to have heard. "That that swine Melbaugh left you penniless . . . that Watersmeet and Midhurst are permitting you to live in such conditions . . . I cannot believe it."

Near to tears, he swallowed and rubbed his brow with his hand.

"It is my choice," she told him hurriedly. "And in all truth, I did not care for my late husband . . . in the end."

"My God! I'm not surprised. The man was a cad, an unspeakable rotter." The Earl of Ashreigney forgot himself completely in his outrage.

"Arrah, now! He wasn't all bad." Macha felt forced onto the defensive. "He was just a weak boy, spoilt."

Richard Withington stood up with an abruptness which startled her.

"Macha . . . Macha, my dear . . . I beg you to forgive me," he said.

Believing he was about to excuse himself and leave, she became deliberately impassive.

"No . . . please do not look like . . . I know I had no right to . . . make advances to you as I did at Beckworth. . . . It was inexcusable, and I would not have distressed you for the world."

For a moment, she wondered what he was talking about.

"I vow it will never happen again and do plead with you to allow me to make amends," he went on.

Then she understood. He thought she had been affronted by his embrace.

"But . . . ," she began.

"I cannot allow you to live like this," he interrupted her. "It is unbearable. Please allow me to help you . . ."

"Richard . . ."

"Upon my oath and honour, I shall never impose upon you in any way. I could make you an annuity. You need never see me again; if you would only accept it, accept my help . . ."

"Oh, Richard, darling man, you're quite wrong." She managed to push her words into the flow of his wretchedness. "I wasn't in the least displeased when we kissed. Quite the contrary. I thought it was you who thought me forward, a bold hussy."

"You believed that? Why, Macha, you are the most chaste and perfect of women." He was shaking his head in bewilderment. "Don't you know . . . do you not know that I love you? I've loved you since I first saw you racing after that horse with your bonnet flying off and your lovely hair tumbling loose and your dear face all covered with mud. I thought you were the most beautiful woman I'd ever seen, so impossibly brave . . . so loyal, even to that wastrel James Melbaugh. It is as though I've loved you since the day I was born. Don't you know that?"

Macha put out her arms and he lifted her out of the chair into his and their kiss was long and searching and imparted a history of secret knowledge each to the other.

Then he sat her back in the chair, stepped back and, to her astonishment, actually went down on one knee.

"Macha, my immaculate Macha, will you marry me?" he asked, and kissed her hand.

"It's a fairy tale!" she gasped. "And there's you the prince."

"And you are the princess—and in every fairy story, the prince and princess marry. So will you be my wife, Macha?"

"And live happily ever after." She sighed with joy.

"Unquestionably." He was absolutely certain.

Chapter THIRTEEN

Richard Withington's riches, status and love cocooned Macha. Magically, they swept her back to the pinnacle of Society and into a state of exclusive impregnability once again. She no longer had to worry about money, or food, or clothes. There was no more pushing and shouting her way in the horse auctions, no more shivering through unheated winters and, above all, no more living a double life in constant fear that her true position would be revealed.

As the Earl of Ashreigney's fiancee, every door was open to her and, as though to make up for the privations she had suffered, he heaped jewels and luxury upon her. Elegantly dressed once more, she was photographed for *The Queen* magazine. At Richard's insistence, they were to be married as soon as possible and, meanwhile, Macha removed immediately to Mrs. Wellington's house in Chichester.

It was the wedding of the year, the ceremony performed in St. Mary's, Westminster. Had the arrangements not been made too quickly to allow the royal family to break previous official engagements, King Edward VII and Queen Alexandra would certainly have attended. Others, not fortunate enough to receive invitations, were so mortified that they felt obliged to invent pressing reasons for being out of London that day.

Macha wore a gown of finely tucked peach chiffon frothing with

Chantilly lace and garlands of tiny silk roses, and an elaborate matching hat dressed with ostrich feather. With limitless funds put at his disposal, Mr. Dodds and his seamstresses excelled themselves.

After the wedding breakfast held in the ballroom at her husband's Grosvenor Square house, she was driven away in the family coach to the cheers of the five hundred guests, to the train at Victoria Station, which carried her to honeymoon in the South of France.

There, sitting under her parasol to protect her skin from the sun, she smiled at Fate and relaxed at last, reaching out every now and again to touch her new husband as though to convince herself that he was real.

They met the crowned heads and aristocracy of Europe, and were invited to their banquets and fancy dress balls. She went swimming, as she had done in the loughs of Ireland, and could hardly be persuaded to return to dry land, so much did she love the sea. He took her to the casino in Nice, where her beauty and uninhibited delight and seemingly infallible luck at *trente-et-quarante* made her a great favourite. In his eyes she could do no wrong.

Dismissing their carriage, they would stroll back through the balmy night to their hotel suite to lie with the windows open, gazing into a sky brilliant with stars, and then they would make love. Lacking the fire of Molloy and the frivolity of James Melbaugh, nevertheless Richard Withington was a sensitive and accomplished lover, who gave more than the simple pleasure of her previous experience. He revealed his true self and his feelings with trusting and unguarded innocence in a way no man had done before. He filled her with a sense of belonging, of lifelong shelter, of finally having reached the one place on earth for which she had always searched. He made her feel more loved than ever before.

They returned to England after a month. The walls of Beckworth House were rosy with welcome. Mrs. Wellington, who had been prevailed upon to come and live with them as Macha's companion, was waiting in a drawing room filled with flowers. Declan and his cousin, Ulick, were working for her again. Her horses were in the fields, Gold with his ugly mare and their foal in one paddock and Macha's Girl with the brood mares. Macha knew she had come home.

In the few weeks with Richard, she had lost the restlessness which had previously created an atmosphere of nervous tension around her. Her movements had become calm and her expression more tranquil, her body bloomed and her face had filled out and lost its hunger.

"I think the dear girl has a secret already," Mrs. Wellington so far forgot herself with excitement as to confide in Declan.

Declan thought so, too. He had learnt a lot about mares in foal since leaving Ireland.

After the death of Queen Victoria the previous year, Edward VII had refused to be crowned while the country was at war with the Boers, but in May 1902, while Richard and Macha were in France, the armistice was signed. Soon after their return, the summons to the Earl and Countess of Ashreigney to attend the coronation on 26th June of that same year was borne to them on a silver tray while they sat at breakfast.

". . . These are to Will and Command you (all excuses set apart) to make your personal attendance on Us . . ."

Macha let out a squeal as Richard read it out and, from then on, immersed herself in the rushed fittings for her gown. Richard would wear the ermine trimmed scarlet robe of an Earl handed down from his father, who had attended the coronation of Queen Victoria before inheriting the marquessate.

Then, two days before the great event, disaster struck. The King had to undergo an emergency operation for appendicitis and the coronation was postponed.

When the new date of August 9th was announced, Macha chattered in excitement to Richard.

"What if the King had died, I might never have got to a coronation and now I can hardly contain myself. Of course, I shall have to have the gown let out now I've expanded a little. Do you think I should wear the sapphires, or would diamonds be better?"

Her husband looked at her strangely.

"My darling, I realise how much this means to you," he began slowly. "But it is unthinkable that you should attend now."

"What? Not go to the coronation!" She was flabbergasted. "Why ever not? Of course, I am going. I would not miss it for a Derby winner . . . well, perhaps I would for that, but not for anything else. Why should I not go?"

"As you yourself have just pointed out, your condition can no longer be concealed, Macha. It would be most improper," he told her.

"Oh, Richard, don't be so stuffy. Every married woman in the land has babies. Most of them have one a year. It's no secret," she scoffed. "And, besides, it hardly shows at all."

But he remained serious. "You know perfectly well that the King is an absolute stickler for etiquette and you cannot possibly appear *enceinte* in Westminster Abbey. He would be outraged. I am afraid it is quite out of the question, Macha."

Macha exploded into tears of fury, rushed from the room and locked herself in her boudoir. An Irish tinker girl attending the coronation of the King of England could go no higher. It was as though the ultimate victory were being snatched from her. She refused to be consoled by Richard's anxious promises through the closed door of gifts and journeys and the giving of a ball in Grosvenor Square to compensate and, even less, by Mrs. Wellington's sensible support of his decision.

At lunchtime, Declan O'Brien was sent for and banged on the door.

"You stop that caterwauling now and let me in," he demanded.

She turned the key and then her back, snivelling as he marched in.

"Your trouble, Macha, is you've always had your own way. No-one's ever stopped you from doing a single little thing you wanted. God's honest truth, you're like a young flipe fed on nothing but Conny Wabble." He was callously unpitying.

"But it's the *coronation*," she wailed. "I can't miss the coronation."

"And how do you imagine you can parade that belly all round the Abbey without causing a scandal?" he demanded.

"There's nothing wrong with my belly," she whined, pettishly. "It's no size at all."

"Well, if you confront the King with it when they're about to put the crown on his head, he'll probably give one of his great roars and have you thrown in a dungeon and the whole world will know it was Macha Sheridan that wrecked the damned coronation," he said. "That belly of yours could topple the throne."

She gave a watery smile.

"Will ye be reasonable now, woman?" he went on. "You're driving your husband demented. There's the poor man offering you gems and trips and all manner of fal-de-lals and you behaving like a spoilt ninny. He'd be better giving you a slap, I'm thinking."

"I want to go to the coronation," she repeated, mulishly.

"Well, you can't, so there's an end to it," he said, with equal firmness. "Now, get off your backside and down to the yard, for there's a very late foal on the way and I can't waste any more time with you."

She pouted sulkily.

"This one's by Garnet Fox out of Regency Queen." He grew crafty. "And if you give Richard a big kiss, he'll most likely let you have it."

With that, he turned on his heel and left the room. Macha sat frowning for a few moments and then caught sight of her petulant face in the looking glass and felt abashed. Declan was quite right. The wealth and position which had come with marriage to Richard must have gone to her head. She was being ridiculous. Out in the mares' yard a foal from one of the finest classic lines in the world was about to be born and here she was fretting over a bit of pomp and ceremony. Had Molloy been alive, he would not have believed it. She picked up her coat and hurried out.

The mare was stretching her back and neck and yawning with discomfort. The strain of another contraction made her lean back and curl her tail over her flanks. Before long, she was half lying and half sitting and the opaque silk of the membrane protecting the foal began to appear. Another rest, another push and the hooves and pasterns of the forelegs became clearly visible through this bubble.

Regency Queen stood up and nosed absent-mindedly at her haynet, tossed her head and stamped a hind leg before lying down again.

It was a scene Macha had watched countless times before and yet she felt the same exquisite anticipation. Here was creation working its miracle before her, as soon it would again with the birth of her own child. This was the split moment before a new heart gained its independence and the first breath of another life was drawn.

The mare heaved and the forelegs pushed at last through the placenta as the outline of a head appeared, streamlined between them and followed by the shoulders. Then, the rest of the foal's body slid onto the straw still wrapped in the gleaming membrane, which had pulled back to reveal a little blond head with a white star. Mother and foal lay flat out for a while and, finally, Regency Queen pulled her legs under her and sat up, pricking her ears and bending her neck to turn with that uniquely eager, anxious love to see her newborn colt for the first time. Macha remembered that mesmerising second when she, too, had gazed upon her lost twins and she thought with a slight flutter of panic of the baby to come.

Just as Declan O'Brien had forecast, Richard gave Macha the foal.

"We'll call him King's Coronation," she decided, her frustration completely forgotten in the comical sight of the dear creature tottering to his feet for the first time.

"I shall tell His Majesty and he will be pleased." Richard Withington was touchingly gladdened by the revival of her spirits. "There will be other great occasions, darling, and the King is a generous man. When he hears of the reason for your disappointment, I think he will arrange something very special for you.

"What?" she asked. "What will he do?"

But Richard merely put a finger to his lips and looked mysterious.

Macha's days took shape. The senior staff were retainers, having worked for Lord Ashreigney all his adult life. They needed little guidance and, apart from choosing a menu from the selection presented each morning and holding slightly more detailed discussions with the butler, housekeeper and cook when she and her husband entertained, Macha was thankfully able to leave the running of the household to them. That she was a sensible and considerate mistress who made their master happy, ensured their goodwill, despite the older members of the household being wary of her dubious background. Even Doris, her lady's maid, thawed into motherly fussiness after Macha arranged for her old father to be moved into a cottage on the estate.

Although there was still the chore of paying calls and leaving cards, one card bearing her own name and two bearing that of her husband now, and they were to still able to attend some of the events of the Season, it was a relief to find that Richard did not care for the interminable round of house parties and bridge playing which she had found so stultifying with James Melbaugh.

So Macha was able to spend nearly all her time with the horses, or with Richard in the library, poring over their leather-bound records. The arrival of each visiting mare led to the tracing of new pedigrees until the elaborate labyrinth of blood lines began to form a clear pattern in her mind. She learnt that a great winner did not necessarily throw great winners and that horses which had had average racing careers could prove mighty sires and dams. She began to study genetics.

Declan O'Brien had feared she might become bored with such an ordered existence. He knew she had spent her life travelling and living by her wits. Even her marriage to James Melbaugh had been an unsettled affair, with the two of them constantly crossing and recrossing the country to racecourses and friends. However, Macha, although as high-spirited as ever, stayed contentedly settled.

By now, everyone knew of her condition and she found herself pampered and cossetted by a husband, both joyful and terrified by her pregnancy.

When she insisted on continuing to ride during the first months, he put her up on a mare too ancient to do more than walk sedately round the estate and then accompanied her in a state of constant agitation which quite ruined the outings.

"You'll have me on a leading rein next," she teased.

"You should be resting, lying on a couch, not gadding about all over the countryside," he replied, with alarm in his eyes.

"Gadding about! Come now. You know the doctor said the light exercise would do me good."

But she knew the memory of Lady Charlotte's death in childbirth was driving him to distraction and, eventually, she stopped the rides for his sake, rather than her own.

The family doctor had helped her husband into the world and had regarded her shrewdly during her first examination. Too late, Macha had remembered the tiny stretch marks which would tell him that she had previously carried a child. She had stared back at the elderly man with a mixture of defiance and pleading and he gave an almost imperceptible nod as he patted her on the head. When her time came just before Christmas, he sent the midwife from the room and they brought forth the child alone. He was to remain her physician and a good friend for many years and never reveal her secret.

Unlike the parturition of her twins, this was an easy birth. A boy was born and Macha and Richard were overjoyed. Macha clutched the baby to her with all the fierceness of a woman who has lost earlier children. No-one would ever part her from him, she vowed, silently, as she gazed down at the little sleeping head covered with fine blond down and melted with love.

In the weeks which followed, she spent every minute of her time with him, leaving Richard's old nanny, who had been brought out of retirement, with nothing to do, much to her chagrin. Macha and her husband, each with their individual experiences of past sorrow, were and remained doting parents. This child was to have everything love could give and money could buy.

They planned a splendid christening to be held in the chapel at Beckworth and the family christening robe of exquisite Honiton lace was brought by special coach from Rapsleigh Palace, the seat of her father-in-law, the Marquess of Bridgemere. It was spread out like a mist on a damask-covered table and an expert lacemaker was hired to come to the house to clean it and make any necessary repairs.

Immersed in preparations for the ceremony and attention to her son, Macha had long ceased to think of the coronation, which had taken place months before. When the envelope bearing the royal seal arrived, she was taken by surprise.

Richard opened it in the library in a leisurely fashion designed to rag her, turning away as she tried to crane her neck over his shoulder.

"Ah," he said, without a glimmer of a smile, "just as I thought."

"What does it say?" Macha was giving little jumps in her effort to see.

"Hmm." He pretended to read it again and shook his head.

"What? What? Is it bad news? What has happened?"

"His Majesty has agreed . . ." He put the letter carefully back into its envelope.

"Yes? . . . Oh, Richard, you are being purposely perverse to torment me," she stormed.

"Would I do that?" His eyes twinkled.

"Yes you would. Now tell me what the King says, immediately," she commanded.

"His Majesty, King Edward VII has agreed . . . to be godfather to our son," he announced.

Macha whooped and flung her arms around him, covering his face with kisses.

"Oh, that's far, far better than the coronation. Everyone went to the silly old coronation, but how many of them will have a son whose godfather is the King of England? You arranged this, darling Richard. I know you did. You're more of a saint than Gabriel, so you are."

"It is a very great honour," he agreed, in his conservative way, but with a smile that was only happiness at her pleasure.

Preparations for the event doubled. Every one of the hundred rooms of Beckworth House was spring cleaned, although King Edward would see only the chapel, hall and salon, which were completely redecorated and refurbished. Mrs. Wellington, between swoons, ordered herself a gown in plum-coloured *merveilleux* trimmed with black lace for the occasion and Macha chose cream cashmere over which she wore a Russian sable stole and matching hat and muff.

His Majesty arrived in a swirl of equerries. Thanks to Mrs. Wellington's rehearsals, Macha made a perfect curtsy and received gallant approval from the King's renowned roving eye. Knowing he was a man intolerant of boredom, she made every effort to keep him amused with jokes and tales throughout the visit and his rumbustious laughter was proof that she succeeded.

The child was named Edward Richard Percival. Standing by the font in the chapel, the rotund figure of the King watched as the godmother, the Duchess of Westminster, took Macha's son in her arms and passed him to the chaplain.

Memories of two other babies crowded in. There had been no pomp and circumstance for them, no king's hand stretched out to them. Their baptisms had been in the streams of Ireland and now they were hidden by the mists of Macha's homeland, growing up without her. She would no longer be able to recognise them, if she saw them. Her eyes filled and, at that moment, her new baby grinned up at the monarch, who grinned back. The Irish girl blinked and smiled with pride. To her, the royal vows made then were for all her children.

The chestnut colt by Gold and Midnight Blue, the bay filly given to her by Richard not long after they met, would be ready to start training before very long. Both yearlings looked promising and Richard began to talk of where they should be sent after the initial stages of their handling were completed. His own trainer near Chichester and some of the leading names of the Turf were suggested; John Porter at Kingsclere, the best of them all; Richard Marsh, the King's trainer at Newmarket, or Sam Darling, who trained for their friend "Harty Tarty," the Duke of Devonshire. Macha listened without enthusiasm.

At last, she said, "Why can't they stay here? I want to train them. I've always trained my own horses with Declan and, in any case, I'm worried about him. He's not a stud farm man, he's a jockey, and if we can't offer him some rides soon, he'll leave us."

"We haven't the facilities here," he demurred.

"What facilities did I have at the cottage? It only takes a couple of loose boxes and a bit of grass. The gallops on the Downs are splendid."

"We've no spare stabling," he pointed out.

"So build another little block. There's plenty of room behind the foaling boxes and we could keep back some of your own young stock, or buy some in, as well."

"Hold on, Macha." He looked alarmed. "Now you're talking about taking on a string here."

"Not at all, not at all." She wrinkled her nose at him and smiled engagingly. "What difference would one or two more horses make?"

He shook his head at her. "What am I to do with you?"

"I like the brood mares well enough, but I miss the racing side, Richard," she told him. "Seeing my horses being ridden out and their trials and all the talk about which races they should enter. I miss holding my breath for them."

"Well, we'll give it a try, my dear," he relented. "You know I can't refuse you anything."

She sat back, satisfied, and then, seeing he was in such an accommodating mood, decided to broach another problem.

"Will you let Gold stand this season?" she asked.

He gave her a penetrating look. "Do you think I should?"

"Well, you've seen his papers, his pedigree." She felt uncomfortable.

"Indeed," he replied and, after a pause, asked again, "What do you think?"

Since first coming to Beckworth, she had spent countless hours reading and memorizing the blood lines. She had watched the care with which he selected which mare to mate with which stallion, insisting on only the highest standards and the finest breeding. She had come to understand the value of the purity of the thoroughbred, the sacrifices which had been made, the fortunes spent, the centuries of painstaking attention which had gone into its creation and preservation. Macha knew what she had to answer.

There was a long silence between them before she muttered, "Maybe better not."

"His sire was Gallinule, was it not?" Richard Withington was benignly certain.

"No . . . I . . . I don't know . . . Yes . . . yes, Gallinule," she admitted.

He waited.

"Father dealt in horses in Ireland," she said, by way of explanation.

"Ah." He did not ask for more details.

"You think I should have Gaelic Gold gelded, too," she accused, in a voice angry with guilt. "Well, I cannot. I cannot do it."

"Macha, you must decide what is right," he pointed out.

The outrageous vision she had shared with Molloy was being annihilated by the very mildness of his response. Already, she had accepted that the stallion could live on with his bad-tempered mare only if their future foals, quick as lightning and streamlined as dolphins, were raised and sold as half-bred. There could be no pure bloodstock from this line.

"I know what is right," she admitted. "I know Gold and the colt must not stand as thoroughbreds, but I cannot geld the colt. I cannot do it."

On Gaelic Gold and on him alone depended the achievement of victory ideated and schemed for by herself and Molloy in that secret pairing of Macha's Girl and Ireland's finest stallion. The colt would have more power and stamina if left entire.

Richard Withington's gaze remained steady.

"You don't understand!" she stormed, as though he were arguing against her. "It was the dream, the dream to breed a horse to win the greatest race in the world. I've wished and waited years, thinking it was to be Gold—until James Melbaugh destroyed him. Now Gaelic Gold is my only chance. He has the right conformation and temperament. Gelding will ruin him."

"My dear, do you imagine we cannot breed your winner from Garnet Fox here?" he queried.

"That's not the same at all. No." She was adamant. "The horses at Beckworth are yours. Gold and Gaelic Gold are mine and my . . . my . . . father's . . . all I have left to remember him by. Oh, I know how you feel about them and you have my word, I swear by all the saints in heaven, Richard, that no foal of theirs will ever be passed off as purebred. But the colt must have his chance."

The underlying disapproval began to surface at last in her husband's expression. The breeding of racehorses was his life's work and his passion. All her senses warned of danger, and she gambled.

"The colt must run against the best, Richard, to honour my . . . father's memory."

"I see," he said. "Very well."

Macha knew she had displeased him for the first time.

However, work on the new stable block was begun and Declan O'Brien given charge of the young horses. He also commuted to the yard of Richard Withington's trainer to race from there and did so well that he became much in demand by other owners. Macha, true to the word she had given when he had used his own money to feed both herself and her horses, gave him a half share in any thoroughbreds she bought herself; although those given to her by her husband were obviously exempt from this arrangement. She also made shameless use of Declan's inside information to win herself some considerable sums of money.

* * *

Although Richard occasionally counselled caution over the amounts she was prepared to gamble, her independence amused him and he was intensely proud of her comeliness and intelligence.

He had discovered she was a gifted hostess, combining flair with the care for details and the perceptive selection of complementary guests which are the principal ingredients of successful entertaining. The choice of wines was always left to his expertise but, appreciating its importance, she became knowledgeable about food and when, a few years later, Escoffier's masterpiece, *A Guide to Modern Cookery*, was published, it became the bible in her kitchen.

Many of the social restrictions which had guarded the closed circle of their class during the reign of the old Queen were already eased by the time her son came to the throne. The Edwardian era had begun and Macha was able to combine aristocrats, politicians and racing personalities with a rare sprinkling of theatricals and operatic stars and create evenings more sparkling than her husband had experienced previously.

She smoked cigarettes openly through a diamond-set holder and had even been known, on occasion, to discourage the ladies from retiring to the drawing room to leave the men talking over their port and cigars after dinner at Beckworth.

"If people are sitting having a good crack, why let some daft old custom spoil it?" she would say. "And, anyway, I like port and the smell of a good cigar."

Lord Ashreigney's parents, the Marquess and Marchioness of Bridgemere, were quite elderly and had brought up their only son with some severity. Naturally reserved, he had never rebelled and had continued to live by their formal rules. Macha, with her wicked sense of the ridiculous and clever flouting of convention, brought fun and even a little daring into his life.

During these early years together, he gradually learnt to release his own dry humour and to relax in the unusual company she favoured. Their tastes broadened to adapt to each other. She learnt to appreciate his classical concerts and operas and he found that the theatre was not as lowbrow as he had imagined. He even consented to visit the Tivoli music hall and watched Dan Leno and Little Titch with an expression of stupefaction on his face, which made her laugh more than the acts.

They dined frequently at Windsor with the King, of whom she was a great pet, managing to deflect his flirtatious approaches without giving offence either to him or to the Honourable Mrs. George Keppel, his mistress, who was often present. Queen Alexandra usually dined separately with her own guests. Macha was able to divert the King without ever crossing that fatal line between permissible bon mots and the familiarity which would produce that dreaded bellow of outrage feared by all around him. Edward VII had a prodigious appetite and little time for those who picked at their food. That Macha could put away a twelve course dinner with gusto earned only his approbation.

"You have a lovely little wife, Ashreigney," he would say with an envious sigh. "See you look after her."

"I shall, sir," Richard would reply, gazing at her.

He had given her a diamond and sapphire tiara, to conform with the King's insistence that tiaras must be worn by ladies at dinner. Macha wore hers with a panache which was almost rakish and looked adorable.

"I am relieved he did not meet you when he was younger," he said to her once.

"Why? What do you think would have happened?" she asked, knowing perfectly well.

"Who can tell?" he replied, mournfully.

"I can tell, Richard Withington, Earl of Ashreigney," she responded, with asperity. "His Majesty would have just had to whistle."

The year passed like a long, slow, perfect dream.

At half past eight each morning, young Edward was always dressed in time to accompany his mother to the yards. By then, all the horses had been fed and were ready to turn out into the paddocks. Even the stallions were let loose in a separate field for three or four hours, depending on the weather, just as Gallinule had been. Then, all the stables were mucked out and the veterinary surgeon called to see any injured or sick stock, and those which had overreached and cut a fetlock were bedded down in peat to avoid straw scratching open the wounds.

There was always plenty of activity and the baby, sitting first in his perambulator and, later, toddling, watched it all. While he was still a tot, Macha would lift him up in front of her on Gold's dam and ride off around the estate. If they broke into a trot, he gurgled with delight and bounced up and down. Edward was going to be a natural equestrian.

When one of their horses was running, Macha took him to the races and blithely ignored the glares from fellow racegoers, which bothered her not at all. Besides, the infant recognised which was their horse and cheered it on to win with all the fervour of a seasoned layer with a monkey on the nose.

Gaelic Gold won six races as a two-year-old and Midnight Blue had a brilliant season crowned by winning the Cheveley Park Stakes at Newmarket in October.

The following year, the filly fulfilled her breeding by romping off with the classic One Thousand Guineas run over Rowley Mile at Newmarket. The colt, after ending the following winter half coated, had to be scratched from the Two Thousand Guineas, but then showed something of his true running with a four length win at Salisbury.

As Derby Day grew nearer, Macha closed her ears to Declan O'Brien's warnings and her eyes to the evidence before them that the horse was still not in top form. This was the race she had set her heart on his winning; the triumph which, in some way she could not have explained, would be the justification of the bartered and compromised life she had led since leaving Ireland.

From her place of privilege in the members' enclosure, she looked across the racecourse to the Bow-tops and carts, Brush and Showman waggons spread like a coloured rag rug over Epsom Downs. She could see the *chavvies* chasing and fighting each other round the painted wheels and the little *raklies* selling their artificial flowers and rush baskets, brushes and lace and pegs to racegoers. Their mothers and grandmothers would be telling fortunes and the men exchanging news, perhaps even news of travellers she knew.

Macha remembered the letters she had sent, before and during her marriage to James Melbaugh, to vague addresses in Ireland—the South Camp, Dublin; O'Leary's Dip, Connemara; to Kerry and Cork and Carlow, to Tara itself. None had been answered. Possibly none had ever arrived. Now, there were travellers on the other side of the racecourse who would know where her children and Biddy Connor were. Yet, how could she leave her noble husband and the presence of the King to go to them? They might as well have been in Africa, they were so unattainable.

She gave last advice to Declan O'Brien, already up, and stroked the colt's neck, trying not to notice that he was already sweating. The horse was not only running for her. Although they did not realise it, he was running for all the travellers on the Downs.

No more than a second's hesitation at the start left Gaelic Gold at the back of the field, but he gained ground rapidly, passing more than half his rivals in the first mile, then running his heart out to push up among the leaders. Macha stared until her eyes burned, but the challenge was too great. Their friend Lord Rosebery's colt, the favourite Cicero, sped forward to win the 1905 Derby by three quarters of a length.

This had been the last chance for Gallinule's secret bloodline to take the blue riband of racing. Macha's disappointment was so intense that her fingernails cut through the silk of her gloves as she clenched her fists to avoid breaking down. All she wanted was to be alone, but there was no escaping the crowd and the rest of the day passed in a confusion of small talk and necessary politeness.

"He really is running extraordinarily well, but is not quite at his peak. Another week or so should do it," Richard commented, seeing her still looking so downcast over breakfast the following day. "I don't think you should give up quite yet. What say, we take a bit of a chance and enter him for the Grand Prix?"

The Grand Prix de Paris was the championship and most valuable race in Europe. Macha's hand shook, spilling a little of her coffee at the idea. Then she groaned.

"We're far too late for that. He'd have had to have been entered last year, while still a two-year-old. Arrah! What a shame. Why didn't we think of it?"

"Well, as a matter of fact . . ." Richard sat back, looking smug.

"You did it! You entered him! You've known all along he was going to run in France and not said a word!"

Macha and her family and Mrs. Wellington drove through the entrance gates to Longchamps Racecourse and were soon strolling towards the tree-shaded paddock, Macha wondering what kind of superhorses were about to run against her chestnut colt.

Gaelic Gold had developed into a beautifully made horse, seventeen hands high, with plenty of lung space and faultless shoulders, and enough courage to take on a posse of giants, which was just as well, as the finest competition in the world was now parading with him in the centre of Paris, with the Eiffel Tower in the distance. Swallows swooped above their heads. The pungency of manure was oddly homely amid the glamour of thoroughbreds, both equine and human. It almost overpowered the smell of money, but not quite.

The French ring thought little enough of her horse to give outsider odds of 25–1. Macha placed her bet, one thousand pounds to win, then returned to the paddock, just as Declan O'Brien was mounting. Putting both hands on the horse's white blaze, she breathed out sharply two or three times and whispered close to his nostrils. Gaelic Gold tossed his head, took a couple of steps backwards before wheeling onto the course.

He had to make a good start. This was no race for a horse to come up from behind. Macha trained her field glasses on the bunch as it streaked away and thought she could see Declan's cap quite well up before distance blended horses and jockeys into a speeding cloud. As they passed the old windmill at the end of the straight, there was only confusion and she put a despairing hand up to shade her eyes.

Then, like a red spear, Gaelic Gold pierced the jostle of runners through and scorched to the front. The trees of the Bois de Boulogne misted, the rest became mere abstract brushstrokes and only the green and gold of her colours and the aurated horse dazzled as brilliantly as jewels. As he swept over the emerald turf, Macha saw again her little brown mare racing along the strand with the boy Declan on her back, and then the great Gallinule cantering over the meadow towards her, and the newly born Gold staggering to his feet and taking his first step, and then she felt the presence of Molloy himself standing beside her again.

"Did I not promise you the greatest horse in the world?" he murmured.

"Ah, darling Molloy. You did."

No need to urge, no need to whip. Declan O'Brien sat still and immaculately balanced, as Gaelic Gold, triumphant over the thunder of the field and the howl of the French crowd, flared past the post like a star and winged the dream they had shared, her whole life's purpose, to fulfillment.

The colt descended from that illicit long ago mating of Ireland's finest stallion with a tinker's mongrel mare had become the champion of all Europe. In a daze, Macha led him to the winner's enclosure, her mind whirling with memories of that first race at Killarney and the precious wedding night at Tara, of her babies in their wooden crib, of the pistol shot and the flaming Bow-top, of Macha, the great mare goddess, and the string of horses clattering along the endless road. She buried her head in the neck of her hot, damp winner and smelt the scent she had known since birth, the warm and friendly smell of the horse. Molloy's heart lay against hers and she was crying.

Declan dismounted and she was in his arms and then in Richard's arms and they were being mobbed. Strangers shook her hand and words she did not understand gabbled from their smiling faces. She felt her shoulder slapped and her gown tugged. A shining trophy was pushed into her hands. Macha spoke without knowing what she said. This was the moment of her destiny, electrifying beyond even her most secret fantasies. Even her one ride in that single race, and Gold winning his very first race could not compare. It was hours before she came down to earth again.

That night they drank champagne at the Cafe des Ambassadeurs with the King, who had watched the race and was staying in Paris incognito as usual, as the Duke of Lancaster, although everyone knew exactly who he was and he would have been most upset had they not. He gave Macha a solid gold bracelet with the design of a horse's head with emerald eyes to mark the occasion.

Richard knew all the leading names in the French racing world, including every member of the French Jockey Club, and a constant stream of mutual acquaintances came to the table to bow to King Edward, greet the Earl of Ashreigney and congratulate his wife on her colt's success.

Stylish French women clustered around the monarch, who smiled expansively and puffed on his big cigar. They were like swans and left Macha wide-eyed and feeling like a country bumpkin. Dressed by Worth and Paquin, Drecole and Rouff, they not only wore their clothes with a chic unrivalled in London, but they made no secret of their admiration for the handsome English Milord, her husband, flirting with him openly despite her presence.

The next day, Macha took herself to Worth and Cartier and squandered every franc of the fortune she had won on the cream of the latest collection and a parure of flawless emeralds, inspired by the King's gift. She had no intention of allowing what had happened with James Melbaugh to happen with Richard Withington, although, had she had more self-confidence, she would have realised that her husband had eyes for no-one but her. Were she dressed in rags, he would not have strayed. For Macha, with her long, silver eyes, her witchery and wit, her wanton loving and tender maternalism, held him captive.

Richard smiled indulgently on all her activities, except one. He could not abide her riding astride and, although she pointed out to him that sitting straight on a horse while both legs were forced to one side had to be the most illogical way of riding, however graceful it might appear, he remained adamant. Eventually, in deference to his wishes and because she saw how much it upset him, she relented.

Almost before little Edward could walk, Richard and Macha had bought him a shetland pony and, when he was not much more than two years old, he was fearlessly galloping around on its back. Each spring, they took him to the South of France and he spent the summer days playing and riding around the estate.

For his third birthday, they took him to the Boxing Day meet of the Wilton, although he was still far too young to take part in the actual hunt. It was an earthy autumn day, ginger sharp with an early frost and smelling of damp bracken and leaf mould. The horses stamped and mouthed their bits, and hounds drawing the first covert found quickly and, suddenly, went away. The followers streamed behind, their faces reddened by the wind, their hearts beating in time to the thud of hooves, over the Downs.

Macha, as usual, was well up in front. Mounted on a gun-metal grey and wearing her new, dark-blue habit, she was like a song, her husband thought to himself, rhythmically fused to the cadences of the hunter's motion, lyrical, her translucent skin reflecting the sun and her silver eyes as bright as lights.

Side by side, they cleared the low hedges and chased through the woods, splashed through the streams running along the valleys and climbed back to the brown of the Downs and the sight of Salisbury Cathedral spire once more. In the midst of their friends and with the music of hounds like a Pied Piper ahead, they spilled out down a bank to the hedge below to take off simultaneously.

Too late, he saw the fallen horse and huntsman on the other side and shouted warning. The grey, in midair, saw at the same moment and twisted to avoid landing on them. A branch hooked in the girth, wrenching the saddle round under his belly and, hampered by the pommels and the apron of her habit, Macha was not thrown wide, but fell under him onto the tree stump which had caused the first accident.

It was a very bad fall and the delay in her receiving medical treatment caused by their distance from home made matters worse. She had lost a lot of blood by the time the doctor came from her room to the library wearing a serious expression.

Complete bedrest for at least two to three months, he directed. "She has severe internal injuries and any movement at all could cause haemorrhaging. Now, I know your wife is a wilful young woman, but if you do not want to lose her, you must insist that she follows my advice to the letter. Have a nurse in that room day and night."

"Will she live?" Richard asked, white-faced with fear.

The doctor spread his hands and shrugged his shoulder. "God willing. But she is very ill indeed."

He issued some more instructions and prepared to leave.

"Oh and by the way, my lord," he added, as he reached the door. "There'll be no more children."

Macha thought she was back in Wales. She could see the open fire in the darkness of the kitchen and she called and called for Sian. But Sian did not come. Sometimes, a woman she did not know made her turn over and the flames of the fire sprang from the grate and turned her body into a torch and her body screamed and howled while she stared down at it in horror from somewhere far above. Then, it seemed, she would blink and find herself back inside the prison of its pain calling and calling for Sian.

But Sian never came and, when she cried for her Da and her Aunt Nan, for her babies, Tom and Molly, only strangers came and shook their heads at her and went away, leaving her to drag her agony along the empty roads of Ireland, searching and weeping for the faces of the past.

Richard Withington sat by her bed day and night, until he began to grow ill himself from lack of food and sleep.

"Who are these people she begs to see?" he asked Mrs. Wellington, in desperation. "Who is Sian? Tell me and I shall find her and bring her to Macha."

When the old lady could not answer, he brought in Declan.

"Who are they? You are her cousin, you must know. Who is Sian? Who are Nan and Tom and Molly, and the man she calls Molloy? We must get them here, or I think she will die."

The man was broken and, avoiding his eyes, Declan wondered whether to confess that he was no blood relation to Macha.

At last, he said, "Truth to tell, we lived at the other end of Ireland and I only met her once before coming to England. I've never heard tell of the folk you mention."

"But this Nan, Aunt Nan. You must know her," Richard insisted. "You are of the same family."

"That must be someone on her mother's side, or perhaps she was just a friend of theirs that Macha called Auntie, as is the way of Irish children," Declan muttered, not knowing what to do. "The name isn't one of ours."

"Well, we must do something. You must write to your father at once for the information and I shall write to the authorities in Ireland. If I have to contact every Sheridan in the country, I shall do so."

Fortunately, the Irish administration replied that the task was beyond them and Declan lied that his father had replied unable to help and, just as the household began to fear for Richard Withington's sanity, Macha opened her eyes and looked at him with recognition.

"Oh, my dearest, dearest one, if you only knew how much I have missed you, how happy I am to have you back," he sobbed openly.

"Well, you've a fine way of showing it," she whispered and put up a feeble hand to dry his tears.

From then, she recovered remarkably quickly and, to everyone's surprise, was most docile in her obedience to the doctor's orders.

"It is lucky she was so fit before the accident," he told Richard. "And that she is as strong as your Garnet Fox, and a fighter to boot, but ensure nothing is permitted to disturb, or distress her. I did fear she might never walk again and we have a long way to go yet."

Richard kept the news that they could have no more children to himself and fussed around her daily, entertaining her with news of the horses and gossip of friends and the messages of concern from the King and Queen and, when she slept, he watched over her so that the presence of the nurse was hardly necessary.

Winter passed, and Macha was allowed to bask in an invalid chair in the first warm sun of spring on the sheltered terrace.

"I tried to find them for you," he said, one day. "I did everything possible, but could trace none of them."

"Who?" she asked.

"The people you cried out for when you were ill," he replied. "You wanted Sian, but I had no idea who or where she was."

Macha closed her eyes for a moment. Her thoughts went back to the miner's cottage and to the slim, moon-pale woman with black eyes whom she had loved so much. She wondered if Sian still wore the gold shamrock bracelet and remembered her.

"She was a friend. A very good friend," she said.

"Tell me where she lives and I shall bring her to you," he said eagerly.

How lovely it would be to see her again. Macha would shower her with presents, share all her fortune with her, lift her and her family out of poverty for ever. But Sian would not accept the gifts, or take the money.

"All that matters is to face life without fear," she would repeat, and turn back to Wales.

"It was long ago, too long ago," Macha said.

"Then what of your Aunt Nan?" he pressed.

"It is unimportant, Richard." She tried to stop him.

"But Tom and Molly . . . ?" he insisted. "You wanted them—and someone called Molloy. Who are they, my dear? They are important to you and you shall see them."

The little flush created by the sun drained away. She wondered what she had babbled in her delirium and stared at him, wildly, to see if she had revealed all her secrets; but his eyes were full only of a loving anxiety to please.

"Dead," she said tonelessly. "All dead."

Her pallor so alarmed him that the nurse was called, and Macha was hurriedly wheeled back to her boudoir and lifted into bed. Then, to her relief, Richard was banished from the room.

That night, as the nurse dozed in the chair by the fire, Macha lamented, bitterly and silently, her husband and her lost children and her friend, and Ireland.

She could walk again and then she could run, playing with her son round the topiaried yews and over the grass. She felt as free and vigorous as an eagle, and one day in May she summoned Declan.

"Saddle up," she ordered. "I'm going for a ride."

"What does His Lordship say to that?" he asked.

"And what would he be saying?" She tossed her head imperiously. Richard had become a little authoritarian recently, no doubt out of concern for her recovery, but now she was fit and raring to return to active life. "It's me that's saying. Now, bring the old mare round."

"Not without your husband's approval," he retorted stubbornly. "Mother of God, he'd have me away from here and on the boat home if anything happened to you."

Richard, as she had known he would be, was more than doubtful of the plan, but finally agreed on condition that he and Declan both accompany her.

"Arrah! You're a pair of old women," she scoffed, but shortly after, three horses were brought to the main entrance to save her from walking to the yard.

The two men were surprised that she was not waiting, full of impatience. They looked up as she appeared at the head of the stairs dressed in a jacket and divided skirt.

"Ah, I'm glad you thought better of it, my dear," said Richard with relief. "I feel you are not yet ready for such strenuous activity."

"I am perfectly ready, thank you," she responded, running down to the open door. "However, you can have that side-saddle taken off the old mare, because I shall be riding astride."

"No. I absolutely forbid it." He was emphatic. "Ladies do not ride in such a way, and after your injuries, it is unthinkable."

She faced him, her expression set.

"Richard, my injuries were caused by riding side-saddle. If I had not been caught up in the damned pommels and habit, I'd have fallen free. Nothing will persuade me ever to mount into a side-saddle again, even though I know that means no more hunting. But as I have absolutely no intention of giving up the horses as well, you'll just have to put up with me riding as God surely intended a horse should be ridden: with one leg on each side of its back—astride."

"It will be bad for your health. Women are not designed to ride so. People will be appalled," he protested. "His Majesty will never approve."

"Mary and Jesus! I'm not riding with the King. I'm riding here, privately, on our own land. And I don't give a fig for what people say. You should know that," she argued. "As for the design of me, in twenty years of working, hacking, hunting and lepping on every size and description of jade, I've found no fault with it, until I tried to twist meself into a corkscrew to ride lopsided. Richard, me darlin', lots of little girls ride in divided skirts nowadays, so where's the difference?"

He waved an irritated hand at her intransigence, but the mare was returned to the yard and resaddled. However, when eventually she rode off with Declan, he did not accompany them.

Hacking gently through the woods, Macha reflected on him with a sigh. He really was classically English and typical of his class, so obsessed with propriety and good form. After over four years of marriage and especially since her accident, this side of him had become more apparent, as though after an interlude in which her unconventionality had been captivating, he was now reverting to type, a kindly man of tradition and patriotism, who wanted nothing more than a punctilious, tranquil life and whose only real passion was the breeding of racehorses. She would have to set about livening him up again, she thought, or they would both be old before their time.

The following week, they were included in the King's party in the Royal Stand at Ascot. They drove to the course, like His Majesty, in a Mercedes motor-car, which Richard had recently purchased at her instigation. It was Macha's first outing to the races since her accident, and the monarch commanded shade and that cushions be arranged so that she might watch everything through the open window from the best and most restful vantage point.

Despite being of a peppery disposition and a very poor loser at any kind of game from cards to croquet, Edward VII was a man well known for his generosity and kindness. He loved giving presents, seeking appointments for his friends and, occasionally, even arranging for the payment of their debts.

"What you need is to take the waters, my dear Lady Ashreigney, and we know just the place." He bent over the reclining Macha and patted her hand. "Bad Ischl. Bracing mountain air and mineral baths. Put you right in no time. You and your wife will join us there in August, Richard."

They travelled in the King's special train across Europe, and Macha was impressed by the deeply comfortable furniture, luxurious carpets and curtains and the fully equipped bathroom assigned to her. France became Germany and Germany flowed into Austria. Within thirty-six hours of leaving home, they were steaming past the big farm-houses, wooden balconies brilliant with geraniums, and along the shore of Fuschlsee under mountains smoking in a heat mist.

His Majesty was in excellent form. He loved travelling and crossed the English Channel several times a year, approaching each journey with child-like anticipation. He alighted at the Bad Ischl railway station wearing an Austrian hat and stepped into a motor-car which swept him to the Hotel Kaiserin Elisabeth, where all the royal party were to stay.

A tired Macha went straight to bed and awoke the next morning to find herself in an enchanting little town surrounded by lakes and overhung by fir-coated steeps which rose to snowy peaks. The air reminded her of Ireland, it was so pure and sweet, and after a day or two of treatments and walks alongside the River Traun, she felt healthy enough to swim the length of the Rhine.

Kaiser Franz Joseph was in residence at his mustard-coloured "villa" set above the river in a private park which climbed the lower slopes of the mountains. The presence of the two monarchs, together with Bad Ischl's popularity with both the aristocracy and many world-famous artists, left not a spare bed in the town.

Each night there were concerts of music by Strauss and Brahms, both of whom had spent several years there, and favourite of all were Franz Lehar's operettas. The composer still lived in Bad Ischl, and Macha went to no less than three performances of *The Merry Widow*.

The theatre played to capacity audiences, its success owing much to the wiles of its manager, who used to have a red carpet rolled out at its entrance if insufficient tickets had been sold. Patrons, believing the Kaiser or King Edward VII was about to arrive, hurried to buy the surplus seats.

Despite the reputation of the Austrian ruling class for rigid etiquette, the atmosphere in the little mountain town was informal and almost classless, with local farmers and workers talking unselfconsciously to their noble visitors.

Although a formal dinner was given for Edward VII in the Kaiser's villa, the British royal party also dined with him one evening in the delightful small Marble Palace on a hill above the official residence. As it was a warm evening, the doors and windows were opened, and the scent from the roses climbing the iron balustrade was overpowering. A band played waltzes outside, and as darkness fell, lamps were lit one by one along the length of the drive.

Opposite the hotel was the Café Zauner, a confection of mirrors, chandeliers, marble, the most beautiful women—and the lightest, most original, mouth-watering and intricately decorated cakes in Europe. From the moment Macha gazed through the window at the icing butterflies and flowers and birds, the bite-sized pink marzipan pigs and hearts, the glossy chocolate rolls, the tartlets and pastries filled with kirsch cherries, she was addicted. She could hardly wait to finish breakfast each morning in order to hurry across the street for cups of hot chocolate and the first delicious tidbit of the day.

It was while sitting over a hefty slice of sponge roulade, stuffed with cream and topped with almonds, that she was suddenly engulfed in shrill greetings, sable and scent.

"Honey! What ever are you doing here? My, but don't you look just deevy in that gown. Worth, isn't it? And just take a look at those emeralds! Do you like this?"

A ring with a diamond the size of a meringue was flashed in front of her nose as its owner went on without pause.

"Wilbur gave it to me on our engagement. You have simply got to meet him. He is absolutely the sweetest man. He's a senator, you know, and his family's in coal. They own half of the Appalachians."

"Daisy!" Macha gasped, as soon as she could disentangle herself from the embraces of her exuberant friend. "Daisy Fitzclarence! I thought you'd left Europe for good. I wanted to write to you, but no-one seemed to know your address."

"*Pretended* not to know it, more like, after the scandal," Daisy said grimly. "Macha, I was never so glad of anything as I was to leave those English stuffed shirts behind and get back to the States."

"Mm." Macha could sympathise. "What are you doing here? Oh, it's good to see you again."

"Wilbur and I are on our honeymoon," the American woman explained. "I'm Daisy Schultz now."

Macha regarded her friend in disbelief. Daisy's desertion of Lord Bentland had been the talk of the season a few years before. That the woman had been brazen enough to snatch back her freedom—and her fortune—had caused incredulity and outrage in Society.

"But . . . but . . . you're divorced!" she blurted out, unable to stop herself.

"Not any more," Daisy replied, with satisfaction.

"No-one marries a divorced woman!"

"They do in America."

Macha finally remembered some manners. "Well, I can't tell you how happy I am for you, Daisy," she said, with genuine pleasure.

She indicated the seat beside her, and the two sat exchanging their own news and gossip of mutual acquaintances until, finally, Daisy revealed the truth behind her drastic action of divorcing her titled English husband and returning to New York.

"I could have stood all the rules and regulations, and endlessly hanging around in the rain watching yachts, or guns, or horses, or even cricket. I could just about tolerate paying those tedious social calls and staying in freezing English country houses. But it was worse than any of that," she confided, and lowered her voice. "Archie didn't like women."

"No Englishmen like women, Daisy. They don't know what to make of us," Macha laughed. "And frankly, looking at Englishwomen, I'm often not surprised."

"I don't mean that, Macha." Her friend shook her head. "I mean, he didn't *like* women. He liked *men*."

Macha tried to look knowing, but remained puzzled as her friend continued without a pause.

"When we discovered I couldn't have children, he was no longer interested in me."

"He'd have been disappointed, I expect," Macha said. "They all want heirs for their family names and lands, you know."

"Lordsakes, Macha! You're not listening!" Daisy hissed. "He had never been interested in me, nor in any other woman. He *loved* men—or, rather, boys."

"You mean . . ." Macha could hardly believe that she was being told something so unspeakable. There had been that monstrous scandal a few years before. She was not sure what it really meant, but she knew it was something so dreadful as to be unmentionable. "You mean . . . like Oscar Wilde?"

"Exactly." Daisy leant back in her chair and drew her fur around her in a gesture of righteous indignation. "I found him with a stable boy. So I just up and left him and went back home to my Daddy, and my Daddy wanted to come over to Britain and thrash Archie Fitzclarence to within an inch of his life, but my Momma said we were to put it all behind us. And then I met Wilbur."

Wilbur himself appeared, a broadly smiling man with outstretched hand and the most perfectly white and even teeth Macha had ever seen. She was enveloped in the kind of immediate familiarity she had not experienced since living in Ireland.

"We don't stand on ceremony with our friends, so no more Mr. Schultz, d'you hear, now. Just call me Wilbur. And I can't wait to meet this husband of yours. I want to tell him to be sure to bring you to Virginia, where I can guarantee you the time of your lives."

The morning flew by unnoticed. It was as though the three had known each other since childhood, and when the shadow fell across the table, Macha looked up in the middle of laughter and saw her husband.

"Oh, is it time for luncheon already?" she asked easily. "Well, I'm glad you've appeared, because look who I've met, and this is her brand-new husband, Wilbur Schultz."

Wilbur stood up and held out his hand. Richard Withington ignored him and Daisy, who was waiting with an expectant smile. Instead, he glared at his wife with undisguised anger.

"You will oblige me by returning to the hotel within the next five minutes," he grated through stiff lips, turned heel and left the cafe.

Macha was overcome with embarrassment. "I think . . . my husband is . . . indisposed," she muttered.

"I think he does not want you associating with a 'fallen' woman." Daisy fixed a shrewd eye on her.

"Daisy! Honey! No-one's going to insult my wife and get away with it." Wilbur Schultz was furious. "I'll have it out with that fellow and he will apologise to you."

"Leave it, Wilbur." She pulled him down on the seat beside her and stroked his arm. "You'll never understand the English, so don't try."

"I don't think I want to, after this display," he commented, and downed his whisky in an angry gulp.

"I am so dreadfully sorry. I apologise for my husband." Macha was scarlet with shame.

Daisy took her hand in both of hers. "Dear Macha, don't be upset. I know all about it, remember? I lived with it for long enough. Now, take this and don't lose it. One day you may need it, and you will always be welcome."

She gave Macha her card. The Irish girl put it carefully in her purse.

"I'll write," Macha promised. "But please forgive Richard. He does not know the circumstances."

"Nothing to forgive," responded Daisy generously.

As she crossed the street and stepped into the grandeur of the Hotel Kaiserin Elisabeth, Macha felt consumed with violence. She wanted to slap her husband's smug, arrogant face.

"How dare you insult the only reasonable and sincere woman I have ever met in your country?" she was shouting before she had even slammed the door to their suite closed behind her.

"How dare you consort openly with a common American divorcee?" Richard was icy.

"Common!" she shrieked. "Daisy Vanderbilt comes from one of the richest families in the United States of America."

"Poltroons," he sneered. "Rich poltroons."

Macha stared at him, aghast. "Why, Richard Withington, you're nothing but a nasty little snob."

"Lower your voice." He looked down at her with contempt. "I have no wish for the whole world to discover that I am married to a fishwife. Now listen to me very carefully. For several years I have tolerated the embarrassment caused by your uneducated behaviour because I appreciated that with your questionable background you knew no better, but this time you have gone too far. You have put our position of trust with the King in jeopardy."

"Oh, it's the King again, is it? Every time anything shakes your narrow, self-satisfied world, you bring up the King. Well, I happen to think the King is human. He wouldn't mind a jot my talking to Daisy Vanderbilt."

"Then you are wrong, as usual." He bent over her with hard eyes. "I am prepared to condone the fact that you can provide me with no more children, Macha, but your lack of any sense of propriety cannot continue. From now on, you are to change your ways, and furthermore, I forbid you to see that person again."

Her anger was wiped out in confusion. It was as though a stranger were standing berating her in the place of the man she loved. What did he mean, she could provide no more children? Macha stared at him uncomprehending, and as she opened her mouth to ask, he turned and left the room.

The doctor had assured her she had completely recovered from the accident. Surely, he would have told her had there been anything wrong. Perhaps Richard had said this terrible thing out of chagrin, in order to hurt her. Yet she knew in her heart he could never have invented such a lie.

She had been aware of the change in him, especially since her accident. Most English aristocrats, she knew, saw their wives principally as there to bear heirs and run their great houses with grace and efficiency. For companionship, they preferred the company of men. Richard seemed to have become more distant and absorbed in his own interests, the running of the estate and his horses. Macha had attributed this to his upbringing and thought it was perhaps to be expected.

Yet, incidents she had previously ignored came into her mind: the time he had snapped at her for cutting instead of breaking the toast at breakfast; the way he seemed to have become more critical of her clothes; the anxious look she had caught sometimes when her irreverence was making the King chuckle. He had begun to turn down more invitations to Court functions, and she had imagined this was to protect her from strain. Suddenly, it dawned on her that perhaps it had been to protect himself from what he appeared to feel was her unorthodox comportment.

She wished their relationship had not altered; and beneath these reflections, a deep depression was growing over the idea that she could bear no more children. She began to believe it was this which had caused his remoteness from her. Tears fell coldly onto her cheeks.

Macha stayed in their rooms all afternoon, sending only for a pot of tea. As evening drew in, she bathed and dressed for Sir Henry Campbell-Bannerman and his wife, Charlotte, and Frederick Ponsonby, the King's aide, with whom they dined. Richard too appeared to be his usual courteous self, and only she noticed the slight compression of his lips and the deliberate control of his movements.

He stayed over the port with the men for a long time and, finally, slipped surreptitiously into bed beside her in a way which indicated he wished no contact.

At first, Macha pretended to be asleep. Then, as she felt his muscles relax, she asked, unexpectedly, "Is it true?"

"Yes," he replied, without any hint of sympathy.

She thought of her children, of Tom and Molly and Edward.

"At least, we have Edward," she offered, diffidently.

"Yes."

"About this morning . . ." she began.

"What of it?"

"I didn't think there was any harm in it," she said.

"That's your trouble," he retorted. "You seem to imagine you can flout convention with impunity. And it has to stop."

"If you knew the truth of the matter, you might feel differently about this."

"What is that supposed to mean?"

"Daisy Schultz left . . . because . . ." She hesitated, unsure how to express it.

"Daisy Schultz left Lord Bentland because she is thoroughly disreputable," he snapped.

"No!" The injustice made her sit up. "No! He is the one who is disreputable. She left him because he is the same as Oscar Wilde. He loves men."

There was a dreadful silence before he spoke, with a savagery she had never known before:

"What you have just said is the kind of filth from the gutter which I find hard to credit hearing from the mouth of any woman, let alone from my own wife. That you should have listened to such an obscenity is bad enough. That you should have repeated it is beyond belief. This person is obviously a thoroughly evil and corrupting influence, and you are never, in any circumstances, to communicate with her in any form again. Do you understand?"

"But Daisy Schultz is my friend," she protested.

"I will not countenance hearing that woman's name again." His voice was bitter. "Nor do I wish to hear the names of any of your other nefarious friends from the past."

So that was it. With the click of a cog locking into its ratchet, she knew precisely when he had begun to change towards her. During her illness, he had asked about Molloy and about Tom and Molly. His quick eyes must have noted her secretive mien, and she had offered no explanation. He had not asked again, but that evening he had seemed preoccupied; and she realised nothing had been quite the same between them since.

Then, in her agitation, Macha was very stupid.

Leaning over, she put her arm round him and whispered, "Don't be jealous, darling."

"Jealous! Is that what you think?" He jerked away. "My only anxiety had been to save myself any further humiliation brought about by your lack of discretion. Until this moment, I did not appreciate that I had any cause for jealousy."

He flung back the bedclothes and left the room, closing the door behind him with awful control.

Lying appalled in the darkness, she realised she had made the worst mistake in her life.

Throughout the train journey back to England, Macha thought about her marriage. Richard had barely spoken to her since that night, and as the train crossed the frontiers of Europe he spent most of his time in the King's carriage, and so she had plenty of time on her own.

Her love for her husband had grown steadily since their marriage. He was the most gentle man she had ever met. Few other couples were fortunate enough to have the bond their shared interest created between them. He was unstintingly generous, and until recently, had gradually learnt to be more demonstrative. However, this quarrel forced her to understand that the confrontation of his inflexible adherence to tradition by her own natural lack of inhibition must have caused him great inner conflict. In the beginning, he had obviously found attractive the fact that she was so different from the women in his own circle; but he was essentially a very conventional man, who did not care for the unexpected. The novelty had worn off with time and her unpredictability had become merely a strain.

Macha knew she could not have asked for a better husband, or a better life. He was not always right, of course. He was not perfect; but neither was she, and it was up to her to repair the damage, if possible. Looking back, she realised she had been selfish, indulging her own whims at will, and now, if she was to preserve her happiness, she had to compromise. She resolved to change, to try to be more submissive and fit in with Richard's code.

It was not easy. After their return from Austria, she frequently had to bite her tongue when disagreeing with his views. She tried to take up passive occupations, such as embroidery and learning the pianoforte. She forced herself to be more circumspect with their friends. Their house parties included far fewer unorthodox personalities and were, she felt, duller as a result. She gave up smoking, and when fashion raised women's skirts, instead of being a leader in the mode, she waited until the most respectable ankles in Society were revealed before following suit. Even in bed she felt it necessary to be constrained and, for a long time, Richard's lovemaking seemed more of a duty to him than a pleasure.

He remained remote, spending more time alone in the library, where she was rarely encouraged to join him. Their conversation was impersonal, and although she often longed to kiss him impulsively and shake him out of the mood, she did not do so. Her instincts told her the remedy for their problems lay in her self-control. He had to return when he was ready.

In her loneliness, Macha could not even turn to her son, who spent most of his time with his Nanny and for whom a governess had already been hired, although he was only four years old. He had friends of his own age, and each year he was one of the children invited to the annual party given by King Edward and Queen Alexandra for their grandchildren. His development was carrying him away from her.

So she would spend her spare hours overseeing the training of her young horses, or riding over the Downs, imagining herself once more roving freely through Ireland. Her one defiance was a refusal to return to the side-saddle; but, nevertheless, she made sure that her husband was not around when she mounted in her divided skirts and cantered off.

The months rolled by, and Macha, whose optimism had always been so buoyant, began to despair. Her weight dropped and her boundless energy was replaced by lethargy. She began to spend longer in bed, sometimes not rising until midday. At times, she wanted to rush to him and beg for the smallest sign of affection; at others, she thought of running away. Only the thought of losing Edward restrained her. A bottle of Irish whiskey was kept hidden in her room, to which she repaired more and more frequently. Even her horses ceased to interest her, and she no longer had any desire to go out.

When the Epsom meeting came round, Richard had to insist that she accept the royal command to attend. She accompanied him wearing a drab gown and carrying a full flask in her bag.

The travellers' caravans parked on the Epsom Downs opposite the members' enclosure seemed to beckon to her. There were the people she knew and understood, her people, whom she should never have left, she thought. Some might be friends from Ireland. Perhaps even. . . . She did not dare follow that line of thought. But there was no place for her with this cold man, surrounded by preening ladies and superficial chatter. They made her edgy and then angry. Before the first race was run, the flask was half empty. Chewing a peppermint to disguise her breath, she gave a defiant smile and put £500 on Orby.

It was a long time since she had been lucky. In fact, she had given up placing large bets, in deference to her husband; but suddenly, she did not care.

"The odds on that horse are 100–9, Macha. That is a considerable sum of money to risk," he commented now, with heavy disapproval.

"It is." Her eyes, light with anger, turned on him, betraying her feelings for the first time.

Startled, he looked away as the King said, "Let your wife have some fun, Ashreigney. She looks quite peaky. What have you been doing to her? Come and sit beside me, my dear."

The horses were off. They were racing for her future. If Orby did not win, she knew she was going to leave her husband and the high life and the King. She would run from them all and across the course and back to the men of the road and they would never see her again.

The far thunder sounded; the rainbow colours separated into individual silks. There were the growling jockeys and the roaring crowd and the breath of the Thoroughbreds like flames in her ears and Macha was yelling without constraint and Orby shot across her vision like a star. Orby half a length, a length in front. Orby winning by one and a half lengths.

Macha grabbed her husband and kissed him ferociously, not caring any more about the presence of the monarch, the fetters of convention or the gossips, not caring how Richard would react; finally caring only about herself. She loved him. She would show it, and if he rejected that, then she would live her life her own way. No more silences, no more prissy mannerisms and clothes, no more embroidery or bloody piano playing. She kissed him again.

"Bravo!" Edward VII gave a great guffaw. "Lucky man!"

Then, to Macha's amazement, her husband's lips softened just a fraction, but it was enough. He had kissed her back.

That night he came to her room and took her hesitantly at first and then with passion.

"Somehow, I lost you," he murmured afterwards.

"We lost each other," she said. "But it's all right now."

Chapter FOURTEEN

They played croquet across the endless lawns of their country houses. They wined and dined actresses and married American heiresses. Each year they presented their daughters to Their Majesties at Court and revolved round the magic seasonal circle from the Private View at the Royal Academy of Arts to Ascot to Henley and the Eton and Harrow cricket match at Lord's, to Cowes and then to Scotland. The upper-class Edwardians. They raced their horses, shot their pheasants and grouse, hunted their foxes and deer and fished their salmon. They cruised in their yachts, followed the King to Biarritz and gambled in the casino at Deauville.

Their houses were redolent with fleshy flowers—full-blown roses and peonies, gardenias and orchids. Their glasshouses housed exotic fruits—nectarines and grapes and figs; their sideboards groaned under barons of beef. They drove their motor-cars and danced the latest dances—the bunny hug, the chicken scramble, the turkey trot and the tango. Parties, sport, music, theatre, cards and a limitless supply of servants fed their insatiable appetite for pleasure. Their only fear was boredom.

The assassination of the Grand Duke Serge, uncle of the Tsar, in 1905 had caused no more than a *frisson* of gossip. The repeated demands from Ireland for Home Rule were treated with the impatience reserved by the English for Celtic aspirations. The suffragettes fighting for votes for women, chaining themselves to railings and being force-fed in prison, were seen as harpies, or as "emotionally diseased." The warnings by a few writers and politicians of the possibility of German invasion were considered far-fetched. Sir William Harcourt, being asked about the future, replied, "The experiences of a long lifetime have convinced me that nothing ever happens." It was a sentiment shared by almost everyone.

Macha was no different. Lloyd George was a guest at her table and appeared to her as no more than a rather irritating man with roving hands. She skipped H. G. Wells's laboured writings in the *Daily Mail*, preferring the sporting pages, and was more repelled by George Bernard Shaw's goat-like appearance than interested in his mind. Even abroad, she moved in a miniature England, surrounded by familiar friends and staff. The Germans she met were pleasant, if rather stiff, aristocrats in whom she could imagine no danger.

In 1908, Richard Withington's father died, aged 87. Richard and Macha became the Marquess and Marchioness of Bridgemere, second in rank only to the Dukes of the land. Their son, Edward, became the Viscount Ashreigney.

They moved, not without regret, to the palace of Rapsleigh, where the Withingtons had lived for eight centuries, since Richard de Ville was given the lands, formed by an aggregation of manors seized from English families, by William the Conqueror in 1075. It was a vast, sprawling palace, its walls many feet thick, its windows so narrow that all light was restricted. Wings had been added at later dates, and a cluster of smaller buildings lay behind. Three villages and numerous tenant farms were enfolded within its estate.

Richard had no idea how many rooms it contained, and Macha, exploring them over the first few days, was prey to a sense of unreality. The extreme contrast between the two residences seemed to revive memories of her own humble beginnings with a clarity which made her feel like an outsider, almost a usurper.

In the sunlit, airy rooms of Beckworth, with its rosy walls and lush climbing roses and vines, she had belonged. It was not so here. The stern ghosts of a hundred Withington ancestors stalked the passages and corridors and gave her no place. She wanted to tear down the faded brocades and throw out the sombre furniture, paint the walls in the prime colours of her youth—yellow and blue and red—and put her mark on Rapsleigh Palace.

From the far end of a table made to seat eighteen, Richard smiled over dinner at her ideas and shook his head.

"My dear, you may do what you wish with your own rooms, but I don't think Edward, or his children, or his children's children would thank you for disposing of their heritage. I'm afraid the armour and tapestries and all those old paintings are here to stay."

However, when he saw her genuine discomfort, he offered, "Tomorrow, I shall spend the whole day showing you a different Rapsleigh."

So he took her to the attics and opened dusty trunks and boxes, pulling out old uniforms and holding up crinolines against her and telling of bygone battles and balls in which his ancestors had excelled in both battle and love. He put histories to the paintings and showed her his old toys and the slates on which he had made his first childish attempts to write in the schoolroom. They found the cubby-holes where he had played hide-and-seek and the overgrown, tumbledown boathouse, from which he pushed out a boat and rowed her across the lake. In the cellars, he revealed the fine wines laid down by his grandfather. In the stables, the aged pony he had ridden as a boy still browsed in sleepy retirement.

"She must be about twenty-eight years old now," he told her, as the mare nickered and nuzzled at him, with obvious affection.

"As old as me." Macha was awed.

He brought her into his memories and made the palace come alive, and after that day, although she still missed Beckworth, the seat of the Withingtons seemed less forbidding. She had the walls of her boudoir, dressing room and parlour decorated with pale grey and cream silk and furnished them with light modern furniture and so created one corner, at least, which seemed more like home.

Mrs. Wellington was persuaded at last to sell her Chichester house, which she rarely visited now, and to live out the rest of her life with them. Then Richard gave a grand ball to which all the other landowners in the county were invited, many of whom they knew already, that Macha might realise she was among friends.

By the time the new stable blocks and yards were completed, adding to those already there, and the paddocks were reseeded and fenced with smart white posts and rails, and all the stock from the stud and her own horses in training were brought down, she felt much more comfortable and was grateful to her husband for his thoughtfulness.

Her life was charmed, its order seemed immutable. There would always be rich and poor, masters and servants. It had been ever so. It was wrong that the working classes should go hungry and sick without help, but it was up to the masters to be benevolent and protect them. Socialism was a lot of idealistic nonsense, impossible to put into practice.

Women were not encouraged to have opinions and Macha's views were naively simple. Although she certainly believed the English should get out of Ireland, she had the sense to keep this to herself and, while she agreed with the introduction of the payment of old-age pensions in 1909, she felt her husband was right to be annoyed by the gradual increase in income tax from ls 2d in the pound to a scandalous 6s. 0d. For years she was to secretly admire Mrs. Pankhurst and her followers, until one of them threw herself in front of the King's horse, when Macha's concern for the animal and its jockey obliterated her mild sympathy with the cause.

Macha and Richard had established a steady contentment. Perhaps their relationship had not returned to that innocent faith of before the scene in Austria. Part of him was always to remain concealed from her and she, having experienced the painful consequences of his disapproval, was more watchful of her deportment. But they were exceedingly fond of each other.

She became more involved than ever in the breeding, training and racing of her horses and was rewarded by their frequent successes. Richard, in one of his breathtaking gestures of munificence, decided to give half the filly foals born at Beckworth to her. These grew and ran and the best were retired from the Turf to become brood mares and, in turn, produce foals of their own. With his encyclopaedic knowledge of the subject, he remained the respected teacher and she the eager pupil. Each birth became like the birth of a child to them, who could have no more of their own. Each foal was the vessel of fulfilment, hopes and plans and, yes, love. These beautiful creatures were their immortality. Perfect, they would breed perfection on and on down the ages, long after Macha and Richard were gone, maybe even after their own line had ended. They were their legacy to the world.

In fact, the closest Macha came to suspecting fundamental transition was when their dear friend King Edward VII died. He had been a merry monarch, loving pretty women and fine food, sport and good company. Even his childish traits had been engaging—his near obsession with etiquette and correct dress, his taste in naughty theatrical farces and his dislike of losing. They had all known better than to knock his ball off the croquet lawn, and there was a copse at Newmarket from where, in his younger days, he had come galloping out ahead of the field to win races against his cronies.

However, his notorious bark had been much worse than his bite, and his loyalty had even extended on occasion to appearing in court on behalf of his friends. He had swept aside the suffocating restraints of Queen Victoria's reign and brought cosmopolitanism, frivolity and fun into English Society, balancing these with a surprisingly statesmanlike quality on ascending the throne, which had left the crown both secure and popular in the eyes of the people. Macha and Richard attended the funeral, and seeing his beloved little fox terrier, Caesar, following the gun carriage reduced her to tears.

King George V was almost opposite in character to his father, and although they knew him, she was aware their relationship would never be as close and that he was the herald of a different era, one which, somehow, she could not imagine would be so easy and enjoyable. Where the old King had dreamed of restoring Hampton Court to former glory, the new King wanted to pull down Buckingham Palace, sell the gardens and live modestly in Kensington Palace. This seemed an omen of the changes to come.

However, for a few more years the only excitement to disturb Macha's and Richard's quiet ways were the wins of their Thoroughbreds on the Turf, and the nearest their marriage came to a second crisis was when Richard insisted that Edward be sent away to Eton.

It was a struggle against tradition which Macha knew she could not win, and so, although the ache of her son's leaving remained with her like a damaged limb, she kept her sorrow hidden. When the boy returned in the holidays like a stranger, she relieved her grief in long rides over the Cotswolds and accepted what she had really always known: that only her horses, with their courage, their nobility of spirit and their great, forgiving hearts, were worthy of total trust.

By then, the balance of power, both international and domestic, was shifting, and their world was beginning to shake. After the reading of the third Home Rule Bill in the House of Commons, the Irish question had become a crisis with the formation of the Ulster Volunteer Force in the North and the Irish Volunteers in the South. The gun-running of 24,000 rifles and 3 million rounds of ammunition to the northern ports from Germany and the decision of sixty officers at the Curragh Camp to refuse to obey orders if asked to act against

Ulster so preoccupied the politicians and the press that the German threat to Britain was of only vague concern.

When war was declared on 4th August, 1914, Macha reacted with bewilderment.

"War against who?" she asked, automatically thinking that England was about to attack Ireland and experiencing a sudden and shocking rise of patriotism for her own country.

"Germany, of course."

"Oh, them." She was instantly relieved. "What are we fighting them for?"

"Because of the assassination of Archduke Ferdinand of Austria at Sarajevo," Richard explained.

"What's that to do with England?" she wondered, sensibly.

"Well, obviously they have to be stopped," he said. "We have defence-treaty obligations towards Belgium, you know."

That left her even more confused. She really had no inkling of the implications of the news.

"What about Goodwood?" she asked.

He stared at her. "Good God, Macha! What has Goodwood to do with it?"

"We've three horses entered. I wouldn't like anything to interrupt their training."

"Macha, this country is now at war." He sounded quite annoyed with her. "Don't you understand?"

"Arrah! We were at war with the Boers, but life went on as normal," she pointed out.

"This is not the same," he responded heavily. "Still, they say it will all be over by Christmas."

Posters of Lord Kitchener pointing a finger over the slogan "Your Country Needs YOU" suddenly appeared everywhere. The young men in their circle joined the army as officers. The footmen and gardeners became soldiers. They all marched off, grinning with anticipation. It seemed quite an adventure at the time. The elderly and Declan O'Brien, who, like other jockeys, was too light and small to be of use to the armed services, remained behind. Macha was advised to knit socks.

Within a week of war's being declared, the men from the Remount Department of the War Office paid their first visit to Rapsleigh. The army required one million horses. As they talked to her grim-faced husband, Macha hurried to the mares' yard, grasped Macha's Girl by the forelock, tugged her from her loose box and out through a small door by the tack room. At first she thought the gardeners' large shed was locked, but then saw, to her relief, that the padlock was hanging open. She pushed the mare in among the tools and wheelbarrows with a quick slap on her hindquarters.

By the time she returned to the yard, Richard and the government horsemasters were already there. She moved next to her husband as they reached the empty loose box.

"Where's this one, then?" an official asked.

Richard opened his mouth to reply, and she stamped hard on his foot.

"At the knacker's," she put in, as he winced. "Died of colic yesterday."

The two watched miserably as all the carriage pairs and the hunters were lined up and taken to the railway station for the first leg of their journey to France. The shires, which worked the farms, were reprieved, and the best of the racing and breeding stock, being unsuitable for traction or the cavalry, were left behind too, Gold and Gaelic Gold saved only by their false pedigrees.

"Concealing Macha's Girl was quite wrong," Richard chided later.

"I'll see that mare taken over my dead body," she retorted. "She's been with me since I was a child."

"Everyone has to contribute to the War now," he said heavily. "The army needs all the help it can get."

"They won't miss one jade," she snapped back. "Anyway, I notice your pony is still chewing away at his haynet out there."

"The pony is thirty-two years old, Macha."

"And my mare is twenty-two. They're both too old, and you know it."

"Well, we haven't seen the last of the Department. They'll be back before long."

"Why should they? There's nothing left for them," she said.

"There are still the draught animals," he pointed out.

"Yes, we need those for the ploughing," she answered.

"They'll be back" was all he said, too depressed by the day's losses to make an issue of it. The government had paid £50 per animal. In a rare gesture of emotion, he tore up the cheque and threw it on the fire.

One hundred sixty-five thousand horses were impressed during the first twelve days of the War, which did not end at Christmas. The battle of the Marne was decided by an army mounted on taxicab nags from Paris, and as men suffered and died on the battlefields, so did their willing, uncomprehending beasts, left exposed on the line in all weathers, overburdened to collapse with gun carriages and ammunition, mange-ridden, lame and wounded, engulfed in mud, shot and left where they fell when too ill or exhausted to continue. The army began to ship horses and mules in tens of thousands from America and scour Britain again.

When she heard they were returning to Rapsleigh, Macha made her decision, knowing she could not depend on Richard's support this time. That evening, when the remaining staff had retired, she went to Declan O'Brien's estate cottage and they talked for a long time.

"In about half an hour, then," she said, as they parted, and he nodded.

Walking quietly to the stables, she found her little mare browsing by the salt lick. The horse whickered softly and nibbled the pieces of cut carrot from her mistress' open palm, then nudged for more.

Macha rubbed the downy nose playfully and smiled as the mare curled her lip and snorted. It was a game they had always played. She scratched the poll between the alert ears and smoothed the curved, satin neck.

"What a gangling, puny screw you were then," she murmured, thinking back. "And now you're as pretty as a ripe red apple."

She remembered how they had soared together, into the sky it seemed, when fleeing the wrath of the punters at Killarney, and how the filly had hobbled so faithfully behind her, despite her ruined leg, out of the terrible chasm of Dunloe, and then the great Gallinule cantering towards them and Molloy laughing and laughing. She remembered lifting her babies onto the safe, broad back and Macha's Girl carrying them with such consummate care that the flowers beneath her hooves were undamaged.

"The winners came from you. It's your grandson became champion of Europe, and you're not going to any man's war. We loved you, me and Molloy. They're never going to have you for their bloody game," she whispered, pressing her face against the warm skin as the mare mouthed her red hair until it came loose from its pins and tumbled round her shoulders.

They had ridden across England together in that long-ago time, kicked up their heels at the fancy Thoroughbreds on the Sussex Downs and the fancy men out hunting. It was to Macha's Girl that she had told her secrets, confided her triumphs and gone for comfort when their luck was down.

Now she willed her own mind to fill with all the joys of the past they had shared, to transmit love and peace and faith to the other. She breathed softly into the mare's nostrils and let the gentle head drop against her breast as Declan appeared in the doorway.

"Don't stay," he said. "Go back to the house."

"No. We've always been together. I won't leave her, not now."

He stood back as she led her old friend out into the night-black yard, and he waited as they whispered to each other, the woman and the horse, for a moment. Then he raised the gun.

It was as though the bullet had pierced her own heart, the pain was so intense. Macha's Girl gave a gasp and then dropped slowly to the ground, her eyes wide open. Macha stood paralysed, each breath coming in small cries of anguish. Declan, blinded by his own tears, groped to find her with his arms, and they clung to each other, unable to speak, and he stroked her thick red hair as much to console himself as to share her desolation, and when he kissed her, it was out of pity for them both and for the little mare.

"What is this? What is going on here?"

They drew apart, dazed, as Richard's voice sounded harshly in the darkness.

He shone a torch first onto them and then onto the dead horse.

"You've killed her!" Surprise and anger filled his tone. "You've killed that horse!"

"I had to. They'd have taken her for France. I couldn't let them do it," Macha sobbed. "Oh, Richard!"

She stumbled towards him and he stepped to one side.

"How could you be so unpatriotic, so treacherous?" he fumed. "With every woman and child gladly giving up husband and father for their country, you could not even sacrifice a damned horse."

"Not now, man." Declan moved between them with determination. "This is not the time."

"She wasn't just a horse, any horse. She was . . ." Macha wept, unable to explain.

Richard pushed Declan aside and loomed over her. "An Englishman will die at the Front for lack of that bloody horse, and his death will be on your conscience, madam."

"Let her alone! By the blood of Christ, if you say another word to her, I'll beat you to pulp, so I will!"

Declan O'Brien had grabbed the Marquess by the shoulders and was shaking him violently.

"Can't you see she's fit to tear out her own soul with sorrow?"

"You Irish dog! How dare you lay hands on me? You are dismissed! You will leave my property this instant!" The taller man released himself with ease.

"I am employed by your wife, My Lord, and I take my orders from her," Declan responded with dignity, then turned to Macha.

"Go home now, My Lady, and take some rest," he urged, and as she began faltering towards the house, he called out, "Macha!"

She hesitated.

"You have done right, Macha."

They were all much calmer the next morning, and Macha somehow managed to persuade her husband that the responsibility for the episode was entirely hers. Declan O'Brien was permitted to stay on at Rapsleigh, although His Lordship behaved towards him with icy authority thereafter. She did not try to explain again her grief and the place Macha's Girl had held in her life, for she knew Richard would not have understood. Besides, she had grown aware that he himself was deeply troubled by other matters and this explained his reaction of the previous night. She felt he needed her more than he had for many years, and so she concealed her pain deep within herself and turned to care for him.

Richard, at forty-two, was too old to be called up, although he looked much younger. As the villages and land around emptied of able-bodied men, he became increasingly withdrawn, and upon receiving news of the deaths of a nephew and the son of a friend, he shut himself away in the library for several days.

Only the fact that it was in aid of charity persuaded him to accompany Macha to a concert in Bath one evening, and she was greatly pleased to see him relax under the influence of the music for the first time in weeks.

"Does it not seem strange that Man, who commits such terrible deeds, can also create such exquisite harmony?" he murmured, more to himself than to her, as they stepped from the hall to the street.

She squeezed his arm—and at that moment, a well-dressed woman appeared from the shadows and blocked their way.

Glaring at Richard with unmistakable scorn and disgust, she accused, "Are you not ashamed to be malingering here and enjoying yourself while all the real men are fighting and dying in France?"

With that, she thrust something at him and vanished back into the darkness.

Richard stared down at the white feather of cowardice she had pushed into his hand, and his face went grey.

"Take no notice, mavourneen," urged Macha, alarmed by his expression and pulling him towards their motor-car. "It was just a madwoman. They should put people like that away. Take no notice."

He said nothing, and when they reached Rapsleigh, he went straight upstairs and locked his door behind him.

When she turned the handle the next morning, the door opened into an empty bedroom. The elderly butler reported that His Lordship had left the house early, and Macha thanked God for her husband's age, for she guessed at once that he had gone to the recruiting office, and she knew he would be rejected.

"I've joined the Grenadier Guards," he shouted, bounding from the car.

"No! You can't! They only want men between eighteen and thirty-eight." Macha's stomach heaved as he ran across the terrace towards her like a boy. "They'd never take a man of your age."

"Ah, but they have!" he answered in jubilation. "I heard a couple of days ago that Francis Lambton, George's brother, had joined up, and he's older than I."

"What about the estate—and the horses?" She felt sick with dread.

"Macha, you don't need me to run the estate. You're a highly capable woman," he said, smiling. "And you have Declan and several experienced old-timers to help with the horses."

"What of me—and Edward?"

"I shall be fighting to protect you both; and as for Edward, what sort of father would I be in his eyes if I did not seize this chance to defend my country and everything I hold dear?"

"This is all because of that lunatic woman," she stormed. "You are exempt from service. You don't have to go."

"I do have to go. I had already decided before last night." He looked down at her, unwavering, and she saw he was already on his way. "I report to Wellington Barracks on Monday. There are plenty chaps we know there—Cranborne and Chandos and lots of other fellows—so I'll be in the best of company. They're making me a lieutenant."

The Brigade of Guards left for the Front in February, 1915. Macha and Edward travelled to Victoria Station in London to see them off. The three of them stood in a triangle, distanced from each other by Richard's uniform and the need to suppress all emotion. The platform vibrated under marching boots. Men shouted. A whistle blew. Lord Bridgemere shook his son's hand and turned to give his wife a brief embrace.

Macha gripped him to her with all her strength.

"The blessed Virgin watch over you. The blessed Jesus go with you," she whispered hoarsely. "Oh, my Richard, take care."

Then the station filled with steam and he was gone.

His letters home described billets, the food issued from the horse-drawn field kitchens, marches, patrols and how Viscount Chandos was perturbed by the lack of port wine.

"The battalion was given three days' rest last week and we organised some races for ponies up to 14.2 hh, ponies of 14.2 hh to 15.2 hh and horses over 15.2 hh," he wrote once. *"Each entry paid ten francs, and the total went to the winner. It was quite a lark, with Billy Beaumont making book."*

Spring passed and summer came. *"We had a cricket match against the Coldstream Guards last Sunday and won,"* his letter informed her.

He never mentioned the fighting. Very occasionally, he told her a friend had been killed, and once he sent Edward a German helmet. Usually he asked simply about the land and his son and his horses.

Macha too kept much of real importance to herself. Rapsleigh was requisitioned for soldiers recuperating from injuries and subsequent operations. She was completely unprepared for their mutilations and, worse, for their blank eyes. Running entertainments and a canteen and trying to nurse and comfort them, she was filled with a sense of hopelessness. After dark, they screamed of horrors beyond her imagining, and when they were mended, they were sent back to the living hell of their nightmares. None of this went into her letters.

After being halted for a short time (on the ground that it was unseemly for people to enjoy the sport while soldiers were being killed at the Front), horse racing started up again in England, although on a reduced scale. This was mainly to preserve the horse-breeding industry and also because the theatres and music halls and concert halls had remained open. Macha hired some girls to help in the yards and was grateful for something cheerful to write about. She also sent Richard hampers of food, which apparently arrived safely, although she had no idea where he was.

But in their efforts to protect each other from the ugly truths of the Great War, they were doing more harm than good. As neither communicated well on paper, the letters were stilted and artificial, and each was left feeling isolated from the other.

Although of course he was aware that Rapsleigh was now a hospital, when Richard came home on his first leave, the scale of the operation came as a shock. At a time when he most needed the private intimacy of his immediate family, there were strangers in every room. The daily evidence of suffering, which he desperately wanted to leave behind in France, filled his home.

Macha discovered that the husband she had always known as of a rather shy and reserved temperament was now a man irrevocably changed, a man who had lived for months with barbarity and performed atrocities beyond his own conscience, who, to preserve his own sanity, was now locked inside himself by iron bands of self-control. He could not confide in her, and so she could not share the burden. Whatever she said he seemed to find trivial, and he himself rarely spoke at all. Behind a facade of old-fashioned formality, both were tormented by the situation, which neither knew how to alleviate. When his time came to return to the War, they parted in speechless anguish, each feeling personal failure.

The War which was to end at Christmas had reached and passed its second Christmas. The battlefields of Mons, Ypres, Flanders and Verdun had already robbed them of many young relations, friends and the sons of friends. The flower of the nation was being cut down. Word of lost lives arrived daily: villagers, stable lads, gardeners, the boys who had marched off to glory so proudly.

Feeling like an intruder, Macha visited their parents, their wives and their children and was mortified by the humble gratitude which greeted her appearance. It was as though, trapped in the destruction of the fabric of their experience, they read into the fantasy of her title a confirmation of the eventual return to the secure order of the past. Their lord, the noble Marquess of Bridgemere, lived; therefore the clock would turn back in the end. How long, she wondered, would it be before the telegram with his name was delivered to Rapsleigh?

Being so deeply and emotionally involved with the human consequences of the War, it was with a reaction of repudiation that Macha read of the Easter Rising in Dublin that April.

Irish Home Rule had become law a few weeks after the outbreak of war and was, she thought, what her countrymen had always wanted. That some had decided to take arms against England at such a time seemed like treachery and made her ashamed. A few days later, hearing how Sheehy Skeffington, the pacifist writer, and two other innocent civilians had been shot in cold blood in Portobello barracks, she was left not knowing what to make of it all.

Then an unexpected telephone call from Richard Withington, announcing his arrival next morning, put all puzzled reflections on Ireland from her mind.

"What a lovely surprise. I'd no idea you were due leave," she said, tripping across the hall to meet him. "How long have you got?"

His greeting was restrained, and he regarded her a little strangely, but as soldiers were often nervous and suspicious when they came home, she took no notice.

"It's not leave exactly," he said. "You're taking a trip with me. Tell the servants to pack enough for two or three weeks. I want to catch tomorrow's ferry."

"Where to?" she asked, as a patient struggled past them in a wheelchair.

"I thought you might like to go to the Baldoyle Derby," he said. "I don't want to stay here."

"The Baldoyle Derby! But that's run in Ireland," she said, gaping.

"Is there some reason why you do not wish to return to your homeland?" he demanded, almost aggressively.

"No . . . no, of course not, Richard. It's a perfectly splendid idea."

Her reply was automatic, but the truth was that she was overwhelmed by both instant pleasure and trepidation at the scheme. It was twenty years since she had fled from Rosslare, and no contrast could be greater than the life she had left behind with that she now lived. A bombardment of questions about the people and places of that past filled her mind with disorder.

"I shall look at bloodstock while we are there," he went on. "Perhaps we shall even visit Brownstown Stud and buy one of Gallinule's line."

Was there malice in his voice? She decided it could not be, as that sentiment was quite alien to him. Yet there was some kind of threat in the air. He was clearly under stress, and instinct was telling her to be careful.

"I imagine you will wish to see your childhood haunts again, and your old home," he was offering.

"If there is time, it would be a real treat to travel back to Galway," she replied, her easy smile covering her wariness. "Though I doubt if I'll find family there now."

All those months spent so far away and in such degradation, with too much time to think: in such circumstances, men often became twisted by the tricks of their minds; and she knew he had never forgotten the names she had babbled during her illness years before. Perhaps this, together with his passion for unravelling blood lines and pedigrees, had triggered some deep curiosity about her roots.

When he took her that night, she was responsive and loving, but more than relieved when he fell asleep at last.

Dublin was as Macha remembered. Elegant streets of Georgian merchants' houses cut towards the centre, through which the Liffey, thick and sweet as Guinness, curdled darkly. Ryan's, John Mulligan's, the Palace and Kehoe's bars were all doing good business. A light rain was blowing in low flurries across the road. A woman shouted to another, and her voice made Macha's heart leap. Ireland. No place on earth could match it. Ireland was in the air, the stones, the sounds and more. Had she been blind and deaf, she would have known she was home indeed.

They drove towards the copper green dome of the Custom House and the bridge—the bridge lit by lamps set on stone horses with the tails of fishes; the bridge where Molloy had met her on that final afternoon.

"One day you'll be covered in diamonds," he had said.

She touched the diamond spray at her throat and did not hear Richard's voice as her memories went back across the years. Then she saw the ruins—the buildings from Eden Quay to North Earl Street nearly all destroyed and only a shell where the General Post Office had been in O'Connell Street.

"Mother of God!" she gasped.

"Your countrymen thought England would be too ravaged by war to be able to deal with their perfidy," Richard commented with clipped bitterness. "But they were wrong. Unfortunately, it does mean we cannot stay at the Gresham, and apparently they turned the

Shelbourne into some sort of barracks; but the Royal Hibernian is passable."

Impressions from past and present were colliding. A ragged girl stopped to gaze at their motor-car, and Macha saw herself. The shots of only days before became the shot of twenty years ago. Wrecked hopes and happiness from another time seemed to be scattered in the ruins. She became disoriented and displaced.

"Follow me along, M'lady, and I'll show you your sleeping room."

They had arrived at the hotel, and the porter was leading the way, loaded with their luggage.

"I reserved a suite," her husband told the man, with hauteur.

"Sure, a suite's the best thing, Your Honour," agreed the porter, affably.

Macha stifled a hysterical desire to laugh. There were sporting prints along the walls of the corridor, and the porter was reporting a race he had attended the previous day.

". . . the gambled-on horse went nowhere at all. If a big hole had appeared in the racecourse, it wouldn't have caused Horse Two a moment's worry. He won so easily that it defied holy law. Twenty to one the winner, and the crowd giving jeers to Horse Five, the early favourite. God love us!"

The Marquess of Bridgemere's face was a study, and by the time they reached the suite, his wife's accent was as broad as if she had never left the Emerald Isle.

"What I'd give for a taste of poteen," she wished aloud.

"I'll see what can be done, M'lady." The porter gave her a knowing wink.

Richard Withington stuffed a coin into his hand.

"You're a topper, Your Honour." The man touched his cap with classic irreverence and left.

"Poteen! What on earth do you mean by ordering an illegal drink?" her husband rounded on her.

"Now, I don't recall having actually *ordered* it," she corrected. "I just said I'd like a taste of it."

"That man will tell the entire staff and Lord knows who else." He was extraordinarily annoyed.

"Well, that won't be news, since the whole hotel's probably drinking it anyway."

"I did not care for his manner. He was insolent."

"No, Richard. He was not insolent," she retorted firmly. "He was

Irish. And the Irish are not given to kow-towing to the quality in the same way as the English."

He directed another of those odd stares at her.

"I have to go out," he said. "I shall be back in time for dinner. We shall eat here, in the suite."

"Like a honeymoon couple," she smiled, but he did not respond.

At first she sent for some tea, and then left it untouched. She fidgetted with her hair and then washed, paced the rooms and was too nervous to go out. That other time was knocking so hard, she was afraid of what would happen if she opened her memory to it. She gazed from a window at the people outside. Her own people.

The porter tapped on the door.

"Ach! You've not touched your tea, M'lady," he scolded. "But never mind, for I've brought you nothing less than nectar here."

As she thanked him, he put an anonymous bottle on the occasional table.

"Sure, it's a celebration to serve another from the West Coast, like myself," he replied.

"You can tell, then?" She was delighted.

"A Connemara voice never loses its tune," he said. "Have you been across the water for long?"

"Too long," she answered, and made a decision. "Will you hail me a hansom?"

"In a trice, M'lady."

As soon as he had left the room, she put on her coat and hat, took a deep breath and descended to the entrance and the waiting cab.

"It's a long time since I've been home," she told the driver. "So take me around the city for a look."

He spat as he drove her by the Royal Barracks and then again at Dublin Castle. Soldiers swarmed everywhere. He pointed out the landmarks of the Rising—Jacob's Biscuit Factory, St. Stephens Green and the South Dublin Union workhouse, which had been occupied by the Irish Volunteers—and gave an animated report of the fighting.

"Was everyone for the rebellion, would you say?" she asked as they jogged along Grafton Street.

"Some were and some weren't," he replied. "In the beginning, there was a fair bit of confusion, you see, and now there's many waiting to see how the prisoners are treated. But there having been so many executions, I think you could say those who weren't for it when it happened would be all for it if it happened again."

"There's a bit of rough land to the south where folk camp," she said on impulse. "Take me there."

"To the tinks?" He looked surprised, then shrugged and flicked his whip, and the horse set off at an ambling trot in the direction she had indicated.

Within half an hour she was looking at the site where she and Molloy and Macha's Girl had camped in the rain and mud alongside the Connors, the Wards and the Maughams. It was surprisingly deserted; and then she remembered that at this time of year, travellers were always on the road. She felt a little faint—whether from being spared or from disappointment, it was impossible to tell. The sight of a familiar face or a known van would have been irresistible, she knew, and would have led to perilous consequences.

Leaning back against the worn leather seat of the cab, she fanned her face with a handkerchief; and then she saw, camouflaged by the scrub, a small bender tent, and, as she watched, a woman with a baby held against her body by a shawl emerged from it, followed by a short, dark man.

"Drive on! Drive on!" Macha was gripped by sudden panic. "Take me back to the hotel at once!"

Her head ached. Richard had still not returned and, as she closed the door of their suite behind her, she knew she should never have returned to Ireland. Drawing the curtains, she undressed slowly and went to bed and lay in the half-light wishing . . . wishing she were safe at Rapsleigh, wishing the War to end all wars had never started. Years and years had passed since all connection with her homeland had been severed. She had survived and made a wonderful life for herself across the water. She was almost English, and she wanted no ghosts. She wished the past obliterated.

The rain had stopped by next morning, the day of the Baldoyle Derby. The buildings and streets of Dublin were brightly polished with sun, which gave fire to the black opal of the Liffey.

"Do you feel better?" Richard asked, coming into her room with late breakfast on a tray. He had been genuinely worried by her pallor and low spirits the previous evening.

"I do," she answered honestly. "And the fresh air and the races and a good win will increase that a thousandfold. That porter fellow has tipped me a horse, and it's my guess he knows a bit and more."

Frowning slightly, Richard let this pass and waited, reading a newspaper while she dressed. Then he put her cape round her shoulders before shepherding her downstairs to the foyer. While he went to fetch the car, she sat in one of the upholstered chairs there and flicked through a magazine. A few minutes later, the horn sounded.

As the hall porter saw her out of the hotel and Richard left the driver's seat to open the passenger door of the car, a girl ran up to Macha with outstretched hand.

"Your Ladyship! Your Ladyship!"

Macha turned to look. The girl was a tinker, with torn clothes and shoes with holes and tangled, dirty hair; but Macha saw none of this—for as she turned to look, she found herself staring at her own reflection. The same oval face and ivory complexion, the same fine Celtic mouth and most disturbing of all, the same long, silver eyes as her own confronted her. The girl was her image as she had been twenty years before.

"Come along. Ignore the beggar." Richard seized her arm and hustled her into the car.

"But . . ." Macha was so shocked that she did not know how to continue.

"Lady! Lady, wait!" the girl was calling.

"Clear off, tink!" The angry hotel porter was advancing on her, waving his arms.

Richard was starting the car. It rolled forward slowly into the traffic of carts and hansoms and bicycles and trams, and the girl began running after it. Macha's memory gave an unbearable lurch, and the girl became herself running through the pouring rain after the resident magistrate's carriage, mile after mile, out of Mullingar and across the sodden countryside, to plead for Molloy.

"Stop! Let me talk to that traveller," she said to Richard.

"Don't be absurd," he said, accelerating.

"Macha! Macha Molloy!" Her name carried to her ears like the peal of the wind, so loud all Dublin must have heard. "Macha Molloy!"

Wrenching at the handle, she released the door, which swung outward, narrowly missing a boy on a bicycle. The car screeched to a halt, with Richard swearing, and before she had time to get out, the girl caught up with them and stood, panting, beside her.

"Help us, Macha Molloy. For the love of God, come to the aid of your own, now," the girl said.

Hooters and horns and angry drivers blared all around them, and Lord Bridgemere, absolutely livid, was advancing round the bonnet of the car. Macha jumped out onto the street and pushed the girl towards the pavement.

"What is this?" she demanded. "How do you know my name?"

Richard strode up and towered over them. "If you do not stop pestering my wife, I shall call the police and have you arrested. Macha, return to the car at once."

"Save Tom Molloy!" The girl seized her cloak desperately.

"Tom . . . Molloy . . . ?" Macha waved between her husband and the suppliant.

"He's in Richmond Barracks, a prisoner, and no-one can stop them hanging him but you, Macha Molloy." Tears were making clean streaks through the dirt on the other's face.

"Macha! Come away at once!" Richard gripped her shoulders with angry hands and swung her round.

Macha pulled free from his hold and stared at him.

"I cannot," she replied. "I must hear what this girl has to say. Don't you understand?"

"No, I do not understand," he answered, grim-faced. "I do not understand at all, and I insist that you return to the car so that we can be on our way."

"I'm sorry, Richard. That is not possible."

Turning her back on him, she spoke to the other.

"Come with me," she instructed, and led the way back into the hotel. Her husband did not follow.

The two women passed the hall porter, who took a step forward and then thought better of it, leaving them to find their own way to the suite.

"Now, sit down and tell me."

The girl sat gingerly on the edge of the sofa, looking very frightened.

"Tom Molloy took part in the Rising," she began slowly. "He was with the garrison at Jacob's Biscuit Factory and then he was arrested. They say he killed a British soldier and they . . . they are going to hang him. But I swear to you, lady, by the Holy Mother of God, that he never fired a shot."

"How would you know that?"

Since leaving the street, Macha had regained control of herself and was thinking fast. The spectres of yesterday had found her, and her survival was at stake, but she was not going to expose herself further.

"There were not enough guns to go round," the girl was explaining.

"He only had a big stick. That's God's honest truth, lady. I was there, and I swear it by everything holy."

"And what has this to do with me?"

The Marchioness of Bridgemere, who had remained standing, raised her eyebrows haughtily. Her voice was as distant and as English as that of a true born aristocrat. It was a last stand. If the girl could be browbeaten into going away, Macha could still salvage her position with Richard by clever lying and then find an excuse to leave the country for England immediately.

The girl just looked at her with those long silver eyes.

"I suppose you want money." Macha would pay and get rid of her.

The gaze became dangerous and glittered like mercury. It did not waver. Its power forced Macha to drop her eyelids.

"Who are you?" she heard herself ask at last, despite herself, and knowing the answer.

"Molly. . . . I am Molly Molloy."

The past had become the present, with her daughter as its living embodiment. There could never be any going back.

"Your husband is here on a mission. He has brought orders from London to Dublin Castle," Molly Molloy was saying. "Orders they would not trust to the post, orders about the prisoners. He can talk for Tom. You are a great lady now and you can make him stop the hanging."

Macha went over to the girl and stroked her tangled hair.

"Were they good to you?" she shyly asked at last.

"They were."

"And . . . did they tell you? About Molloy? About me?"

"Yes."

"Did you know where I was?"

"Yes. We always knew."

"Yet you did not come."

"No."

"I should have looked for you, found you." The guilt she had suppressed for so many years suffused her like sickness.

"No. You could not." The girl did not react to her touch.

They stayed motionless and wordless.

Then, abruptly the girl stood up and faced her.

"Will you do it?" she demanded. "Will you speak for Tom? Save Tom? We will never come bothering you again. We will leave you to your life."

Oh, it was too late for that.

"Will you do it?"

"I will."

Her daughter started towards the door.

"Don't go yet," said Macha. "Stay a while."

"No."

"Where's your camp? Who are you with?" Macha wanted to know.

"It's better you shouldn't know," Molly Molloy answered.

"You don't trust me," she observed unhappily.

"It's better for your own sake not to know. I'll be at the old south site, waiting, at noon the morning after tomorrow."

With that, her daughter slipped away, unobtrusively and noiselessly as only a traveller can.

Macha could not weep. Swept by emotion, she knew that her life of luxury no longer mattered. The son she had known only as a baby was now a man about to die. The daughter she had mourned for so long would be lost again. She had to act.

"Well?"

Richard, who had returned unnoticed, was standing thunderously before her.

"I think you had better explain yourself."

"I need your help," she said artlessly. "We need your help."

"We?"

"It's a long story. It goes back many years."

"I can imagine." He was glacial. "Sit down."

She began with the death of Jack Sheridan and her refusal to burn the Bow-top after his funeral. She told of travelling alone with her few horses, of begging and going hungry and cold, of the filly with the speed of a cheetah and the race at Killarney, of being lost in the ravine of Dunloe, of meeting Molloy. Molloy, with his blue eyes and black hair. Molloy, with his sorcerous knowledge of horses and his plan.

His expression did not change.

She described the mating of the filly with Gallinule. She reached Tara again and walked through the flowers, surrounded by her attendants, to *Teach Miodchuarta*, the House of Mead Circling. She told of her wedding.

His face maintained its impassive expression.

Even when she confessed to the birth of the twins, he remained like stone. But at the disclosure of Molloy's arrest for gun-running and its aftermath, her husband walked away from her to stare out of the window. She was sobbing by the time she told of leaving her babies and escaping to Wales and how Sian and her husband had nursed her and how she had loved Sian. As she talked, she relived the crossing of England again and the finding of the cottage and meeting Declan O'Brien. Her tears dried as she remembered the growth of her fortunes, the horse dealing, the first win at Salisbury, the training of Gold, Mrs. Wellington's help and James Melbaugh's courtship.

"You know the rest, until today," she concluded quietly. She had held nothing back.

"And what of today?" He sounded like a complete stranger.

"The girl you saw is Molly, my baby, my daughter. My . . . son—Tom, my son—is in terrible trouble, in the jail. Richard, he was in the Rising and she says they are going to kill him."

"Like father, like son," he commented viciously.

"Richard, he did nothing. She's vowed on the Holy Mother that he never fired a shot. He can't die. You can't let my son die. You can stop it. Richard. Richard?"

He kept his back to her, and she stood up, starting to move towards him, when he began to speak.

"So." He turned very slowly, his features so rigid that the words did not seem to be coming from him. "Our marriage has been one long lie."

"No!" she protested. "I've never lied to you, never."

"Never lied. You, a gypsy married to an Irish traitor and the mother of an Irish traitor, have never lied? Woman, your entire life has been a lie."

"No!"

"You set yourself up as a girl of respectable background. You inveigle your way into Society, trick honourable men into giving you their names and position. You betray their families and squander their wealth. You hoodwink the King himself into accepting and trusting you; and now you have the bare face to insist there has been no lie." He was the judge, and she was condemned.

"It was not like that. You know it wasn't. I've told you everything that happened. I had nobody, nothing. Anything I did was only to live. I had to survive."

"Why?" he demanded, with unbearable cruelty. "You would be better dead."

"Don't!" She put her hands to her ears and shut her eyes in horror. "Don't say that to me."

"My God! No wonder Melbaugh behaved as he did." Richard Withington was beyond compassion. "I knew there was something wrong about you from your ravings after that hunting accident. I've known for years, and I've been too afraid of what I might discover if I enquired. I hadn't the guts to investigate. What a fool I've been. What a coward. And now I'm paying for it."

"Richard, forgive me. The saints in heaven know I never meant to do you harm. Help me. Speak for my son, for pity's sake."

"England is at war. The bodies of my dearest friends, men I grew up with, whose families and mine have been one for centuries, are smeared over France, their blood turning the earth to mud, and you dare even to mention the name of a traitor in my presence."

Macha went down on her knees, reaching up to him with her hands. "He's no traitor. I vow he's no traitor. He's just a boy . . . my son."

"The sons of my friends are boys and they are dead." He stepped away from her.

"Richard, I love you. I've always loved you. I'll go out of your life for ever, if that is what you wish, only save my son."

"Don't blackmail me with the word 'love.' You, who have deceived me for the past fourteen years, you, the wife and mother of men who have betrayed England; you know nothing of love." It was as though he found her so repulsive he could no longer look at her. "Yes, you will leave my life. Of that you can be quite certain. From this day, you will never see me again. You are an evil woman."

"Richard!" she screamed.

He closed the door behind him and was gone.

Macha sat in the chair by the fire, and sometime in that anonymous time between three and five o'clock in the night, the fire went out, and still she sat, waiting for him to return. She knew how her story must have appalled him; but he was a humane man, incapable of vindictiveness. In all their years together, she had never known him to say or do anything truly callous. He would think about everything she had told him, and however hard, he would gradually understand. He would be merciful.

Dawn came, and sometime later, after a light knock on the door, a maid entered with her breakfast. A letter addressed to her in Richard's handwriting was propped on the tray. She opened it with shaking hands and read:

By the time you receive this, I shall be on my way back to France. I have arranged for your hotel bill to be sent to me for settlement after you choose to leave. When you return to England, Edward will spend his school holidays with my brother-in-law's family in Northumberland and you may stay on at Rapsleigh until the War is over. At the end of the War, I shall provide you with grounds for divorce and make suitable financial settlement, on condition that you then live abroad and that you make no attempt to contact me from now on. Should either condition be broken, you will receive no financial support and I shall pursue the divorce action myself. The gifts of jewellery, *objets*, clothes and the horses you have received from me in the course of our marriage shall, of course, remain your property.

Bridgemere.

Cold. Cold. She re-read the letter and felt numb with cold. The last sentence was the coldest of all. The masonry of her life was falling about her again. She pulled her satin robe tighter in a futile gesture. Incomplete, inconsequential thoughts tumbled over each other. Edward—would he be allowed . . . ? What would happen to Mrs. Wellington? To Declan O'Brien? Was Ireland "abroad," or did he mean . . . ? She did not really care for Germans. Where would she go? How would she find stabling in a country where she did not speak the language? Surely, he could not mean what he had written. Yes, he did.

Macha felt very tired, too tired to know the rights or wrongs of it all, or whose fault it was; too tired to know what to do. At last, she crept into bed and lay miserably between the cold sheets and then, surprisingly, fell asleep.

Even before she awoke, her limbs and muscles were so heavy that her lungs felt weighed down with depression, and she opened her eyes with a feeling of *déjà vu*. She had been here before, to that place where effort and intention were worthless and existence itself seemed without value. Richard was lost, as Molloy had been lost and the golden fantasy of James Melbaugh. The fragile web of home, constructed with such delicacy and care, was destroyed again. Only yesterday, she had wished the past obliterated. Now she would have sold her soul to turn back the clock one little day.

She arose and dressed like a sleep-walker, drank some poteen and then some more. The fiery taste of Ireland brooks no surrender. It heated her body and sped the blood through her arteries and galvanised her brain and poured back the will to fight. A man was lying in Richmond Barracks; her son. If she could do nothing else, she could fight for him.

Macha walked purposefully from the hotel into a hansom cab and was driven to Dublin Castle.

Chapter FIFTEEN

"Lady Bridgemere, what you are asking is quite impossible."

The official gave that fat, bland smile Englishmen reserve for women and idiots. "While your charitable concern is admirable, I'm afraid this man is a military prisoner and is not permitted visitors."

"Surely members of their families can visit," she pressed.

"Close relations may visit in certain circumstances," he admitted carefully.

Macha took a deep breath. She had hoped the influence of her title would open the cell door, and for Richard's sake, she had not intended to disclose her true connection with Tom Molloy. Now she was forced to change that decision.

"Well, I am a close relation," she said. "There's no closer relation than a mother, and I am Tom Molloy's mother."

The official picked up a pen from the desk and began to fiddle with it.

"Dear lady," he began, looking embarrassed. "I appreciate your distress at my inability to grant your request, and your husband has told me that your visit to Ireland has been rather stressful. Allow me to arrange for someone to escort you back to your hotel to rest."

He did not believe her. In fact, he clearly thought her quite mad.

"What do you mean, my husband talked to you?" she demanded. "He is in England."

"Richard Withington and I have known each other a long time," the man explained. "He told me of your anxiety over these prisoners, and please believe me when I say that in view of your Irish antecedents, I completely understand."

"When? When did he tell you?" Outraged, she realised her husband had outflanked her.

"Why, before he left yesterday. He explained the arrival of orders requiring him to return to France immediately and asked us to look after you during the rest of your stay here. In fact, my wife proposed to call on you later this afternoon."

Macha's heart drooped, but she did not give up.

"Listen! Tom Molloy is innocent. He never even fired a shot during the rebellion. He needs a lawyer to speak for him. He is my son and I demand to see him, and if you won't allow it, I shall go to the general in charge and make him see reason."

"The legal requirements of the prisoners have all been taken care of, rest assured, and I am afraid the military have a great deal on their hands at the moment. It may be some weeks before you are granted an appointment." He regarded her pityingly as he pressed a bell in the desk. "Now, dear Lady Bridgemere, I know my wife would be delighted if you would take tea with her."

A young aide entered the room, and the official stood up.

"Ah, Carrington, tell my wife Lady Bridgemere is here," he said.

"Damn your bloody wife! And damn you!" stormed Macha, and rushed past the two men.

Out in the street, she stumbled through the passers-by choked with tears, hating the English for their smooth imperturbability, hating her husband for having denied her the only chance to see her son in order to protect his own reputation, hating herself for her inadequacy. Somehow, she reached the privacy of the hotel suite and released her misery in solitude.

"You'll forgive me, My Lady, but I let myself in, thinking a drop of whiskey wouldn't come amiss."

It was the porter, standing by her bed with a glass in his hand and a bottle in the other.

"Drink it down, you, now," he instructed, and watched approvingly as she took a gulp and swallowed.

"Finish it off and you'll see things different," he said kindly. Then, taking the empty glass from her, he went on. "My Lady, take my advice and go back to England."

"There is something I have to do," she muttered, still hiccoughing with sobs.

To her amazement, he replied, "It can't be done, My Lady. There's nothing will save Tom Molloy."

"You know about Tom?" She stared at him.

"Sure, doesn't everybody know everything in Dublin. Nothing's secret in this city." He smiled at her naivete. "Leave here, My Lady. Go back to your home and forget about Ireland and her troubles."

"No-one can forget Ireland," she said sadly.

"Well, maybe not, but it's no place for you."

She shook her head as he gestured to the bottle of whiskey again.

"Perhaps the General would listen?" She made one last attempt.

"You'd be martyring yourself to try. If you don't want to be locked up as a traitor alongside the others, take heed of me, My Lady," he warned, with deadly emphasis. "Now I'm going to send up a maid to pack your belongings, and the arrangements will be made. You'll be on tomorrow afternoon's ferryboat with all this behind you before you know it."

Macha accepted that she was defeated.

"Thank you," she said humbly.

"And good luck to you, My Lady," he responded.

So the suitcases were piled ready by the door and Macha, gaunt after a night pacing the floor and two days without food, reached the south Dublin camp site to face her daughter.

The girl came from the bender tent in the scrub and looked into her face and learnt everything.

"I tried," Macha said lamely.

"Yes," confirmed Molly Molloy flatly. "I hear your man went back over the water."

Macha nodded, trying to hide her own misery from one who had far more reason than she to lament.

"Tom . . ." she began, uncertain of whether to continue, "Tom . . . does he look like you?"

"No. They say he's the picture of Molloy the Coper."

"Ah." It was a little sigh, full of recollections. Molloy had been such a sensuously handsome man with his glittering blue eyes and thick black hair. She remembered the line of the artery running down his strong neck and the arrogant tilt of his head, and even after twenty years, her heart shivered. Then there had been that little sound, no louder than a twig cracking underfoot, or an icicle breaking off a windowsill, the sound of the shot which had brought down that dark, tough body, just as now her son would fall. Macha closed her eyes against the spasm of anguish.

"Is this where you're stopping?" she asked at last.

"No. Just friends."

They were awkward with each other, needing to make contact and not knowing how.

"I'm returning to England this afternoon," Macha told her.

The girl made as though to move off.

"Molly! Come with me!" she said on impulse. "I could give you the grand life. Not all your visions of paradise in silver and gold and gems could match it."

The girl regarded her with eyes full of suspicion and shook her head. "I'll be off now."

"Don't go and leave me with nothing," Macha pleaded, stripped of pride. "I'll never see my son; but you're my child too. At least tell me something: the names of the families you travel with."

"I'm to marry Jim McDonagh this year."

"Oh." She was shocked. "Do you want him?"

Molly Molloy shrugged. "The Connors arranged it with the matchmaker after Tom . . ."

"Arrah, girl! The matchmaker! What's a travelling man to offer?" Macha remembered the ways of the road. Her daughter was twenty years old and still unwed because she had no dowry. No Rom or traveller of status within the clans would have offered for her, and now she had no immediate family to protect her. Only the poorest of all would take her.

"*You* married a travelling man," the girl pointed out, sullenly.

Macha could imagine the leaking canvas, the drunken husband, the brood of children, the hunger and insecurity of her future.

"I married a Rom," she retorted. "And you are a Romani *juval* and the McDonaghs are nothing but rough *diddikais.*"

"It's arranged," the girl repeated.

Realising she was growing angry and that more pressure would drive her away, Macha changed tack.

"Take these," she said, producing a handful of bank notes and one of her engraved cards. "That is my name and where I live. Don't let on to the Connors or that McDonagh man about the money. It's for you—enough to travel to me in England, or use as you decide. If you're to stay on the road, I'll give you a dowry, whatever you need; but marry no man you don't want, daughter."

With that, she climbed back into the hansom and was driven off without giving a backward glance. It was the best way. The girl did not know her, did not trust her and needed time to think. She could not be forced; but Macha was gambling on her daughter's taking after herself and that curiosity, if nothing else, would seduce her through the door to the other world just revealed.

England, that other island, rose out of the sea a softer green than the harsh brilliance she had left behind, full-faced and placid where the other was weather-beaten and craggy. The difference symbolised the difference between the two peoples, the one large and formal and narcissistic, the other small and angular and passionate. Ireland brimmed with life and drama, causes and opinion. England lay phlegmatic and lazy, stifled by class and etiquette even in the midst of war. Cushioned for so long by the wealth of other lands, she had never had to struggle. For Ireland, a history of oppression had honed a wild, fanatic race.

Guiltily, Macha realised that it was a relief to escape the insoluble tragedy of Dublin and be driven again through the familiar sprawling park, blond from the heat wave, which wrapped around the mighty defences of Rapsleigh like a fur.

There had been plenty time during the crossing to consider her other troubles, but being essentially an optimist, she had already persuaded herself that time would heal her husband's outrage. He was a man who detested scandal, and the more she thought about it, the more possible it seemed that he might not carry out the threats in his letter in the end. She resolved to live very quietly indeed for the foreseeable future, giving him absolutely no reason for criticism.

After greeting Mrs. Wellington, she asked for Declan O'Brien. When he came into her room, she sat down and told him everything, almost as she had told Richard in Dublin, and the tears ran once more.

As she finished, he sat beside her and put his arms around her.

"Christ of Almighty, but you've not had it easy, Macha," he said. "Why did you never tell me before?"

"There was nothing to be done about the babbies," she pointed out sadly. "I thought I could put it all away from me; and now maybe I'm to lose everything—Richard and Edward and my home; even Molly and Tom all over again. God forgive me, but I can't face it, Declan."

"Now, what sort of thinking's that?" He stroked her hair and cradled her. "You're not the one to quit. Haven't I seen you pick yourself up and fight over and over."

"I'm tired of fighting," she said pathetically. "And anyways, what am I fighting for?"

"Macha, you can't do anything more for Tom Molloy, God rest his soul." He crossed himself as he spoke. "But you've not lost your husband, or your second son, yet, and there's still Molly. And there's yourself. If you give up on all of them, you're giving up on yourself."

"What's the use? Arrah! Declan, Molly doesn't want me; and don't you think I've tried to tell myself Richard won't go through with it? But if you'd seen him, if you'd heard him! He's disgusted with me, and he'll never forgive."

"Listen here, Macha, it's not a fiend you're talking about." Declan gave her a little shake. "The man loves his home and he loves you. I'm certain of it. There he is, far away in the thick of the War, in the presence of death, in some foreign place that would make Hell as lovely as the strand at Cashel. Holy God! What do you imagine's in his mind? He's no different from the rest, woman. He's dreaming of his land in all its beauty, and of his horses and his books and his music. But most of all, he's dreaming of the day he can live at peace again with his darling wife."

"Dear Declan, you're a romantic." She gave a weak smile.

"There's nothing romantic about it," he retorted. "I'm telling you, he wants what every man wants, and the blessed Mary have mercy on me for saying it, but the fact that he's away fighting at the Front is no harm to you."

"What do you mean?"

Declan looked slightly abashed at the expression on her face, but continued, doggedly. "Can you not see that while he's in France, he can take no hasty action against you—and truth to tell, the man doesn't want to go through with it at all?"

"How can you know that?" she demanded. "You weren't there. I'm a traitor to him, and that's something he'll not get over."

"Macha, if Richard had been convinced of what he was saying, you'd not be here now. He'd have had you put out, bag and baggage. Am I not right?"

"I don't know," she muttered miserably. "Honest to God, Declan, I just don't know."

"Aye, well, I do know." He was adamant. "I'm not suggesting it's going to be simple to make him see what's in his own soul; but you're a wily woman and you can win him round."

"How? If he was here, I'd be able to talk to him, but there's a whole ocean between us."

"An ocean! Be jabus! You're on about a little dribble of water you could wade over," he scoffed. "If you were in that man's shoes, wouldn't you want to come round? All you need is a little scheme. And aren't you the one who's invented a few schemes in your day?"

"I have," she agreed.

"Well, invent another. Isn't it as clear as a glass of Jameson's that this is just another competition, another type of race? There's no heat in a wet fire, Macha. You've to work and train to be a winner."

Macha hugged him tightly.

"Arrah! Where would I be without you, Declan?" she asked.

"By dam! I sometimes wonder," he grinned.

After he had gone, Macha went to her bureau which faced the window overlooking the south garden and concentrated on their conversation and then on her situation.

Declan O'Brien's estimation of her husband had been astute. Richard was a deeply home-loving man, and if their relationship was not one of great rapture, she was sure he did love her. Before long, she decided that after allowing a suitable period to elapse, she would write him a series of letters. Picking up the gold fountain pen he had given her one Christmas, she began to draft ideas.

First, she would write of her genuine distress at their estrangement and be penitent for all the sins of her past, saying she understood that she was worthless in his eyes and that his punishment was all she deserved. In this first letter, she would grovel and expect no reply. Laboriously, she worked on the wording until satisfied with the outline. Locking the draft safely in the drawer out of the way of the prying eyes of the servants, she considered the best way to follow it up.

Not only the idea of divorce, with all its consequences, goaded her on. Her worst fear was of being denied her last child, Edward. As she sat, staring unseeing at the dogs playing on the lawn, Tom Molloy and Edward became intertwined in her mind, and she trembled. Whatever happened, nothing must be done to harden her husband's present attitude. Pleading and accusations of inhumanity would only repel him more. Declan was right in believing that he had to be beguiled. There could be no mistake in the plan.

The second letter would tell of how she missed him and recall one or two shared incidents and times of happiness. She would send a little news of his horses and the estate and perhaps even close with some hint of her intention to live the life of a *religieuse* after their parting. Knowing her as he did, she realised, that might appear rather extreme. On the other hand, the ordeal of her predicament could very well have caused such a change in her. She jotted down the idea and left it undecided.

Several weeks would pass after each stage of the correspondence; then probably she would send a parcel or two, with affectionate but non-committal notes enclosed.

Then another letter, this time noting one or two little difficulties arising from her weak position as a woman trying to run the vast estate, problems with staff, or tenants, or in the stables—subtle appeals for his help and protection, indicating how hard she was trying to keep everything in perfect order for his return: a letter to which he would feel bound to reply. This final attempt at reconciliation would be the most important of all. Macha knew that if he did not answer, all would be lost.

What troubled her most about the idea as she worked on it during the days which followed her return from Ireland might have seemed superficial to some, but apart from filling in racing entries and forms and her previous short letters to Richard at the Front, she had written very little. Her handwriting was childish and unformed, half capital and half joined letters. She was afraid it would remind her husband of her origins and of the past so recently uncovered.

Without confiding in Mrs. Wellington, Macha persuaded her to help and spent several hours daily for the next month painstakingly copying out texts from books from the library. In the beginning, she was so ashamed of her efforts she could hardly bear the older woman to see them; and then, quite suddenly, she found her hand flowing over the surface of the paper, and soon, although the writing was far from perfect, it looked quite neat and tidy. At last, she took the draft of the first letter from the drawer, corrected it, copied it out and read it through:

My dear husband,

I know I have done you a monstrous wrong, but I humbly entreat you to read this letter. Although I am prostrated with grief at your decision, I accept that I am not fit to be your wife and I can only implore you to find it in your heart to forgive me one day.

There can be no excuse for the deceptions of my past, but that I was very young when I married Cormac Molloy, no more than fifteen years old, and I vow upon the blessed Virgin that no treacherous thought or deed was ever done by me against England, the country which had been so good to me. It is true that I loved Molloy dearly and his death and the loss of my children were terrible hard to bear. I was only an uneducated travelling girl and made my way as best I could.

It is now my intention to retire from Society and cause you no further distress, Richard, but I shall cherish the years we spent together all the rest of my life, for no woman could have asked for a more gentle and considerate husband than you have been to me. Please do not feel obliged to answer this letter, husband. Indeed, I would not expect it, but I beseech you to pray for me.

Your devoted wife,
Macha Withington.

She read it through again, decided, with a sigh, that it was the best she could do and posted it.

The plan and the practice had had a beneficial side effect. They had kept Macha occupied as Tom Molloy's execution was drawing closer. Had she not forced herself to concentrate on them, there was no question that she would have returned to Dublin and made crazy attempts to reach him. Her inevitable failure might have resulted in her own imprisonment, and news of it would certainly have reached her husband, wrecking all her hopes for ever.

There was no way of finding out the actual date of the fatal event; but when she awoke one morning, she knew her son was dead. With that knowledge, all her resolution crashed and she gave way to hysterical grief, remembering the tiny babe she had left, blaming herself for having made no effort to find him, even when she had been blessed with riches. Her husband was right. She was an evil woman who had caused the sacrifice of one of her own children. Even Molloy, whom she had loved above all others, would have condemned her.

Her conscience gnawed at her, destroying her sense of judgement. The plan to recapture Richard now appeared devious and underhand. He was worth more than to be tricked by the low and immoral woman she began to believe herself to be, a woman who had lied and betrayed him, betrayed everyone she had ever known. Sending that first letter only proved how despicable she was.

It was in the mood of deep depression that she awoke one morning to find Mrs. Wellington standing, white-faced, by her bed. In her hand was a telegram.

Richard Withington, Marquess of Bridgemere, was dead. Killed in action in the battle of the Somme. He had left her unshriven. Alone by the window, Macha was overcome by a profane compulsion to throw herself from it. Watching, as though from outside herself, she could see her body lying smashed on the gravel below. It would be the end of the struggle. The Hereafter could conceal no torments worse than this. She unlatched the sash window and pushed it open. Lifting her skirts, she began to climb onto the sill. A piece of stone broke off and fell to the ground under her weight. She was outside and clinging to the frame behind her. There was no prayer she could make to the unhearing God. She stared at the sunbathed park and meadows with their grazing horses, and it was as though all were covered by a layer of grey ash. Slowly, relaxing her fingers one by one, she released her hold.

An arm seized her round the waist, and screaming, she was dragged back into the room. A man, drawn with consternation, had her restrained in a shackle-like grip.

"Ahh, Declan," she keened, falling against him. "Let me die."

He put her on the bed, pinning her down with his hands, glaring at her, speechless. Whenever she turned her head, his accusing face was before her.

At last, he said, through frozen lips, "Never do such a thing again. Never. Do you want to burn in Hell? Do you want to be condemned by God for all eternity?"

"Richard . . . and Tom . . . ," she started to whisper.

"No!" he interrupted furiously. "I don't want to hear. No reason on this earth is reason enough to destroy the life, the great gift that God has given you. By the blessed Virgin, I'd murder you myself, I'll send myself to Hell, before I'll let you lie in its torture till the end of time."

She wanted to escape, but he would not allow it.

"Macha. Macha. You're not alone." His eyes were gleaming with tears. "Whatever waits in the future, hurt and delight, you're not alone. Hold to that. Hold on to Declan."

For a long, long time they clung to each other and no word was spoken. At last, Macha leant back, wanly, against the pillows.

"How did you know about . . . ?" She indicated the still-open window.

"I didn't," he admitted, his face crumpling slightly again. "This was delivered and I was bringing it to you."

He held out an envelope. It was in Richard's handwriting. Macha could hardly tear it open.

"*My dearest wife,*" she read.

Your letter brought me such joy. I have thought of you constantly and, in this bloody battle, perhaps even because of it, I have grown to understand so much more. How very young you must have been when tragedy overtook you. Here am I, a grown man, bereft and mourning the death of my friends. David and George and Henry and Archie and so many more are all gone—yet how much worse for you, no more than a child yourself then, to have lost husband and children.

Now you write and ask me for pardon, but it is I who beg on my knees for your forgiveness for my own blind wickedness towards you. Thinking of the way I behaved towards you in Ireland, I have been overwhelmed with shame and have not known what to do to try to heal the wounds I must have caused. Shame and the conviction that you must revile me have prevented me from writing, and your own letter to me arrived as the answer to all my many prayers.

My dearest, darling one, can you find it in your heart to absolve me? When this terrible war is over, I vow to spend the rest of my life making you happy.

Write soon, my Macha, and tell me all is right between us again.

For ever your loving husband,
Richard.

"He forgave me, Declan," she whispered, caught between sorrow and ecstasy. "Before he was killed, he forgave me everything."

* * *

The new Marquess of Bridgemere came home from school for his father's memorial service and stood beside her in the village church, stiff with control. Afterwards, as they walked around the wreaths displayed on a grassy mound in the churchyard, she wanted to take him in her arms, but his withdrawn demeanour prevented it.

Later they sat opposite each other in the drawing room, ill at ease. He was at that gawkiest stage of adolescence: somehow too tall for his own frame, all bones and spots, with a voice which gave unexpected squeaks. He looked so like Richard, she thought, yet it was almost like being with a stranger. Eton had long since broken the close bond between them.

"You'll stay a while?" It was more of a question than a statement. "A week or so?"

"I think not, Mother," he replied. "There's a lot on at school at the moment."

"Well, it's not long before half," she said. Perhaps it was best that he keep occupied at such a time. "Do you want to come home then? Or would you rather we went away, perhaps to Scotland?"

"I shall be staying with Uncle Hal in Northumberland," he told her. "Father came to see me at the end of his last leave and told me that was where I was to spend the hols in future."

"Oh, but it's different now," she protested. "He would have wanted you come home now."

"It was his last wish that I should spend the time with my uncle." Edward sounded distant and did not look at her.

"Edward, I need you here. When will I see you?" A sensation of despondency grew in her.

"I expect you'll come down to Eton for St. Andrews Day in September as usual," he replied.

Macha knew that despite his apparent unconcern, he was deeply upset and decided not to insist.

"Well, we'll talk about it later," she said, covering her own feelings with equal control.

When he had gone, she told Declan.

"He's at an awkward age. He wants to be a man, but he's still just a boy," he comforted. "He thinks he should be fighting for his country, but he's too young."

"Mary and Jesus be thanked for that," she breathed, going cold at the idea of Edward's going to France.

"Yes, Macha, but now he's the son of a hero. His father's been killed in action, and he won't only be feeling unhappy; it's my guess he's feeling it's his fault in some way, because he's still at school."

"Oh, Declan, surely not. My poor little boy." She felt she had failed Edward in not recognising this. "What should I do?"

"Let him alone for the moment," he advised. "He's a sensible young fellow and he just needs a little time to himself. He doesn't want you fussing about yet. Now, don't add this to your worries, Macha. You've yourself to look after. Leave him to go to Northumberland for half-term, and nearer Christmas, write to them and explain that you'd like him here. They'll understand and arrange it, never you fear."

Macha moped around the great house and estate, sometimes going for long, solitary rides on Gold and sometimes sitting for hours in her parlour, drawing closer to the fire as the year grew colder.

As Declan had foretold, Edward did come to Rapsleigh for Christmas, but he had altered. Although his mother did her best to create a seasonal atmosphere by having a tall conifer cut and erected in the hall, giving the usual party for the children of the tenants on the estate and presenting him with a pair of marvellously crafted Purdeys, the visit was not a success.

He had grown arrogant and bullying, ordering the servants around with a rudeness which disconcerted her and which Richard would have found unacceptable. He behaved towards her with remote formality which she could not penetrate, and although Mrs. Wellington tried to explain that the boy was only trying to disguise his distress over his father's death, Macha was unconvinced. She felt she no longer knew her own son.

When he had returned to school, she withdrew even further into herself. Her conversations with Mrs. Wellington and Declan, who now dined more frequently with them, were polite, but vague, as though her attention were elsewhere.

Some months later, when the Irishman told her he would be away for a few days, she smiled and wished him success at the opening meeting, not noticing his look of surprise. The flat season had started weeks before, and they had already had two winners.

"I'm going just in time," he told Mrs. Wellington.

"You're sure you're doing the right thing?" she asked anxiously.

"Quite sure," he replied.

Macha wondered absently where he was at evening stables, and it came as news to her that he had gone off. She had completely forgotten their discussion of the previous day.

He arrived back in a motor-car with a companion, a young woman, dressed in plain but tidy clothes, who walked a little clumsily and peered about her from under her brows. The old butler regarded her sniffily.

"I shouldn't have come," she muttered to Declan.

"Yes, you should."

They had reached the door of the drawing room, and he pushed her ahead of him. Macha and Mrs. Wellington looked up and saw a pair of long silver eyes gazing back at them.

"Molly!" Macha leapt from the sofa and ran towards her. "Oh, Molly!"

The girl took a step back, frightened by the vast room and the strangers.

"I thought you wouldn't know me in these fancy clothes," she said defensively.

"Mother of God! Wouldn't I know you disguised as a blackamoor nun, daughter!" Macha laughed, brimming with delight.

The other two tactfully left the room, and Macha and Molly were alone. The girl sat on the edge of her seat snatching glances at the *objets d'art* and paintings and once looking up quickly at the murals which decorated the ceiling overhead. She picked nervously at the tapestry of the chair and was almost squirming with discomfort.

Macha watched her for a few moments and then said, "Come and sit here, by me."

Her daughter did so, full of distrust, like a vixen approaching a farmyard.

"So you didn't wed Jim McDonagh," observed Macha with satisfaction.

"They were as put out over that as if they'd been outbid a pair of matched *batys capalls* by a priest."

"I can well believe. But we'll do better than him for you, just you see," promised her mother, ringing for tea.

Molly went quiet as a uniformed maid brought in a tray of fine bone china, silver teapot, cream jug and sugar bowl, dainty crustless sandwiches and delicious cakes and arranged them on the table. She was too diffident to help herself until urged on by her mother. Then she grabbed at the food and crammed it in with unselfconscious hunger.

"I bought the dress and coat with the money you left," she said, with her mouth full.

Macha, who had already decided that the sooner she put Molly in the hands of Mrs. Wellington and old Mr. Toby Dodds the better, was careful not to criticise.

"You chose well. They're very pretty," she approved.

"No," Molly contradicted. "They're not like yours. They're no good."

She was not a fool, then, thought the other.

"I'll show you around when you've finished eating" was all she said.

As they walked from room to room, between the beds of the ill soldiers and along the galleries and state rooms of the palace, it was difficult to discern whether the sight of the injured or the grandeur of the architecture affected the girl more. Macha covered her silence with light chatter of the family's history and of the way she had chosen the furniture and decoration of her private rooms, deliberately disclosing how out of place she herself had felt at first. Telling of the village and the farms of the estate and of the people who lived in them, she led the way round the garden and to the lake. It was part of her design that they reached the paddocks by the stables last.

The yearlings galloped up in a bunch and skidded to a halt at the gate, and her daughter laughed for the first time, just as she herself had done with Richard at Beckworth. The brood mares put their heads over the bottom doors of their loose boxes in eager expectation of the cut carrots they knew Macha always brought.

"They're more beautiful than the swans of Wexford," breathed her daughter, with shining eyes. "Are they all yours?"

"Quite a few," Macha told her. "The rest belong to your half-brother, Edward."

The stallions were led out, just as they had been for her so long ago.

"Oh!" Molly, confronted for the first time by such magnificence, could only sigh. "Oh!"

Then she added, "The Connors would never let me near the horses. I'd have liked to ride, but that's not for girls."

"What nonsense! There's not a woman in England doesn't ride, and you've horses in your blood. It was a sin to keep you away," commented Macha, annoyed. "If Molloy the Coper had lived, he'd have taught you secrets of breaking and handling and healing and you'd never have been off a horse's back, daughter. But it's not too late, and I'll teach you myself, starting tomorrow."

A groom touched his cap as they passed, and a housemaid bobbed a curtsy as they crossed the hall. In the drawing room, Molly stopped and turned to face her mother.

"What are you going to tell them about me?" she demanded, her face set.

"Tell who?" asked Macha, puzzled.

"You know. All the flunkeys and skivvies and grooms and gardeners and such."

"Nothing," she smiled. "It's not their place to be told anything. Their duty is to look after whoever stays here. Just ask for what you want and they'll do your bidding."

"What about your friends?"

"What about them?"

"What will you say? What will you say?" Her daughter was impatient with anxiety.

"That you're my daughter. What else?" Macha reassured her.

"They'll not think it's right. They'll not like it at all." Molly's voice wavered. "Oh, I'll never fit here. I shouldn't have come."

Macha thought for a moment. She was sick of lies. The lies she had told in the past had caused only trouble in the end. Now that Richard was dead, there was no reason to conceal her own background any longer. Whatever happened now, she was determined to live openly and be herself at last.

"It doesn't matter a tuppenny damn what people think, daughter," she said emphatically. "You're my blood, and I need you more than I've ever needed anyone. Do you imagine I don't understand how all this—the grand mansion and the servants and such riches—are more frightening than a fire in the forest during a drought? I was the same as yourself, remember, just a slip of a travelling girl who'd never slept in better than a Bow-top. Come here and I'll show you there's nothing to fret about."

She took Molly up to her dressing room, opened a closet and took out a gown of pale green wild silk, trimmed with white lace.

"Put this on," she instructed, and noted how thin the girl was as she eased the garment over her upraised arms and closed the hidden hooks down the back. Opening her jewellery box, she took out a five-strand pearl choker and fastened it round her daughter's neck. Then, tilting the cheval looking-glass, she positioned her in front of it.

"See," she said, chuckling over the expression of amazement on the other's face. "You're a lovely girl. A princess."

"Dear Joy! I am so!" Molly Molloy shouted, twirling about, trying to view herself from every angle.

"That's all you need in this world, together with a bit of wit, of which you've plenty," Macha assured her. "For the rest, the fiddling manners and ways of Society, there are people here, good friends, who'll help you."

Molly was no longer listening to her. She was dancing around the room preening, and jumping back in front of the mirror every now and again to catch another sight of herself.

"Bide a minute," said Macha at last, drawing her by the hand into the boudoir and making her sit in a chair.

"Now, Molly. I'm not going to transport you away from Ireland and the life familiar to you without being outspoken. It wouldn't be honest if I didn't admit that there's many a time I've missed the freedoms of the road. The English are a peculiar class of folk, especially the quality, so pernickety about every little thing till they send you half-demented. Learning all their rules and etiquette is no simple matter, and even after so many years, I still make a few gaffes, though mostly it's no bother any more. So, Molly, you're to make your choice. You can stay and try it out, or you can go back and I won't stop you. It's up to you."

The girl stared at the folds of the gown as they fell gracefully around her to the floor.

At last, she asked, "What are they like, really?"

"The English? Holies! There's a question!" Macha giggled. "Well, now, I used to believe they were a cold-hearted lot. They'll cut you off if you flout their code. But then I remembered how the travellers cast me out after my father, Jack Sheridan, died because I broke the taboos. It was just the same. They don't often say what they're thinking, but then look how we play-act among ourselves, speaking one thing when the world and his wife know we mean another.

"Maybe the biggest difference is that they can't seem to let themselves go. They don't get fighting drunk, or rant on at each other, or make much noise. They keep a hold of themselves all the time. For a woman, that's no bad thing. It's not done for husbands to beat their wives. And although before the War a lady's life had little use in it, that's changed now. It's even said we'll be given the vote.

"The English are obliging, Molly. There's more have been good to me than enemies, and they don't often bear grudges. Richard often used to talk of being civilised, and I think that's what they try to be."

"What about the way they treat Ireland?" Molly asked fiercely. "What about Tom? That's not civilised."

"No, daughter, it's not, and there can't be any forgiving them for it," Macha agreed sadly. "The English don't understand Ireland or the Irish and they never will. That has to be part of your choice. If you take this life, you've to accept the past as the past: not to forget, but to put it behind you and start afresh, if you can."

"I don't know."

"Well, there's no haste. Take all the time you need. Stay a while for a look at what's offered and decide when you're ready."

Molly revealed her intention by immersing herself in the nursing of the wounded, working long hours with a skill and devotion which were to leave her exhausted.

After a few weeks, Macha, touched to observe the care she lavished on the soldiers, urged her to take more rest and was abashed at her reply.

"This matters, Mother. Before I came here, I thought it was something if I sold a few pegs or took a copper for reading a palm, but I was only wandering about thinking about the next morsel of food. This work is important," the Irish girl pointed out. "Perhaps I should hate them because they're English, but I can't. These poor souls have been through worse than beasts sent to slaughter, and they want someone to give them a bit of ease and a smile. I think of each one as Tom and do what I can."

Some of the men exchanged bawdy jokes with her; others, in their agony-ridden nights, cried in her arms. They told her of their sweethearts and their mothers. They asked for her when she was not there and visibly brightened when she returned. They loved her.

Nevertheless, Society was not likely to value her qualities with the simplicity of grateful soldiers. She would receive a very different reaction outside the estate unless she was trained to deflect the inevitable criticism.

"You'll be introduced to people who judge by appearances," argued Macha, when Molly protested at the idea of giving up time for such superficialities as elocution and costume fittings.

"Then I can do without them," the girl retorted.

"What about Edward and the rest of the Withington family? They'll turn up here sometime, and I want you to be accepted," Macha went on. "The War has to end one day, and then most things will be as they were before, and believe me, you must be ready."

With great reluctance, her daughter gave way. Confronted by her, even Mr. Toby Dodds gaped for a second, before recovering his usual impeccable courtesy. It was like being faced with the young Macha all over again. As he brought out rolls of sumptuous materials, mysteriously obtained despite the War, the familiar gleam came into his eye at the challenge, and before long, he was scolding this new Irish girl about the state of her hands and deciding the best style for her glowing auburn hair.

Mrs. Wellington took on the pupil with unruffled professionalism, and between them, the designer and the old lady began to effect a transformation that was almost miraculous.

"No! No! Miss Molloy, not 'dress.' 'Frock.' Dresses are for farmers' wives," Macha overheard as she walked in on them one day.

"You are remarkable," Macha told her friend later. "You've not so much as said a word to me about Molly being my daughter. I suppose Declan told you before fetching her from Ireland?"

"He most certainly did not. He would not dream of betraying your confidence to anyone." Mrs. Wellington defended him with asperity. "He merely said he was going to bring back someone important to you."

"But you knew who she was."

"As soon as I set eyes on her. She's exactly as you were at that age," the old lady smiled.

"So you think I'm doing the right thing," probed Macha.

"I see plenty of trouble ahead, my dear. Richard's family are not going to give you or your daughter their blessing—and then there's Edward. . . ." Mrs. Wellington raised her eyebrows expressively. "But yes, Macha. I believe you are right. In fact, I cannot see what else you could do. Molly is your child, and to deny her would be a wickedness."

"The clothes are fine, and I try to learn all that stuff about knives and forks and how to say 'Hello' and 'Good luck to you' in English, to please you; but that's just time-wasting, you know" was Molly's verdict on the business.

Because the lessons irked her, she was forgetful, and as she threw back her head and downed a glass of claret in one noisy swallow after dinner, Macha was not sorry that her son was spending the summer in Northumberland and autumn in Scotland.

On horseback, however, there was a complete contrast. Molly, like her mother and father before her, was a natural equestrian, with the lightest of hands and balance. The first time she sprang from the mounting block into a side-saddle, her seat was perfect, and the response of the horses to her was almost psychic. It gave both women their closest times to ride out together after hours in the stifling wards and sluice. As they hacked through the mote-filled sunbeams which pierced the woods, they came to know each other and grow close.

As another Christmas neared, Macha became increasingly restless and demanding of the household in preparation for Edward's return. She had not taken Mrs. Wellington's advice to let him know by letter of the existence of his half-sister, believing it better he be told by herself in person. Yet during her occasional visits to Eton she had not had the courage to approach the subject, and now was full of dread.

Garlands of holly and swathes of evergreens tied with scarlet ribbon decorated the house, and the giant tree was hung with baubles and candles and presents. The silver glittered and the chandeliers sparkled and the patina on the antique mahogany and oak shone. The smell of wood fires pervaded the atmosphere. Despite still having trouble saying 'th' and having to be nudged when she sprawled, or talked with her mouth full, Molly was much less of a savage than she had been, and her undeniable charm made her uneducated gaucheness seem mere eccentricity.

Edward's train drew into the station. The servants lined up in the hall to greet him. Macha, in her boudoir, primped her hair and tugged at her gown and then at Molly's. Nothing more could be done. Thank God the girl was a beauty.

The Marquess of Bridgemere stalked through the studded oak main door and stared at his tinker sister. Molly lifted her chin and stared back. They hated each other on sight.

Chapter SIXTEEN

"You've always been an embarrassment! Coming to school in those unsuitable clothes and ghastly hats. Showing me up in front of my friends with your stupid Irish accent. Saying all the wrong things to the wrong people at the wrong time and never knowing how to behave. I've always been ashamed of you, ever since I can remember—and now this!"

Edward, as tall as his father, loomed over Macha crimson with rage. She could not believe the loathing in his eyes.

"Even at my father's memorial service you had to make a public display, crying and then reading the message on every single wreath, instead of being driven straight home," he ranted on, saliva showing in the corners of his mouth. "No wonder he wanted to keep me away from you. He told me. He told me the last time he came to Eton. He was going to divorce you. How he must have detested you! Not content with making him look a complete fool for fourteen years, you then had to produce some bastard girl from the bogs."

Macha's open right hand slammed across his face, her left arm swinging back and lunging forward again with closing fist to deliver a second blow, which drew blood in a spurting rush from his nose.

"Silence!" she commanded, as he opened his mouth. "How dare you tarnish your sister's name? How dare you insult your father's and my marriage? There was no question of divorce. Above all, Richard Withington stood for chivalry and decency, and were he ashamed of anyone, it would be of you, his only son and heir, at this moment for having addressed me in such a monstrous manner."

No sooner had she acted and spoken than Macha regretted it. She had wanted to introduce the boy to the idea of his sister gently, but her first words had been inadequate and he had refused to listen. Such a scene had never been intended, and now the damage was done. Edward was holding a handkerchief to his nose. He had gone white and still.

"Ah, son, I'm sorry I raised my hand to you," she apologised. "Let's not quarrel."

She reached out her hand to his and he flinched back as though burnt.

"Stay away from me! Don't touch me!" Even his body was contorted with loathing.

She ran to her desk and took out Richard's last letter.

"You're so wrong about your father and me. He wrote to me just before he was killed," she told him. "Read this and you'll understand more."

"I'll read nothing," he snarled. "You had him so deluded, he probably didn't know what he was doing. In fact, you probably drove him to his death. What man could stand living with the fact that he'd married a slut!"

"Get out!" Macha spat. "I'll take no more of this, boy or no boy. Get out and don't come back until you've returned to your senses."

"Oh, I'll get out, all right, Mother." Edward had regained his flinty self-control. He leaned very slightly towards her. "And I will come back, just as soon as I am of age. I will come back to put you and that bastard of yours out in the streets where you belong."

"The young spalpeen!" exclaimed Declan O'Brien, when she reported the scene. "He'd have got a clout from me, if I'd heard him."

"It was my fault. I didn't manage to tell him right about Molly," she replied, downcast.

"Will you stop blaming yourself for every little thing, Macha?" he retorted. "Edward's old enough to know how to conduct himself, and there's no excuse for today's work. In the name of God, you're his mother! He's always been too much the fine young gentleman and too well breeched for my liking."

"Well, he's gone now and he'll not relent."

"He's a cub trying out his strength. Cock ye up! Tomorrow he'll be over it."

Macha shook her head. Even as a child, Edward had been stubborn, refusing to budge when his mind was made up. Once he had sat a whole morning over a cold breakfast he would not eat. At Richard's insistence, the same food had been placed before him at lunch and then for tea and again the next day. In the end, it was his parents who had had to capitulate. Edward would have starved rather than yield.

It was many years since she had been able to make any real contact with him, although she had tried hard enough and been puzzled and hurt by her failure, attributing it to the influence of the school. Today, Edward himself had told her the reason. He had been ashamed of her. Now he would disown her.

Christmas was full of false gaiety, put on for Molly's sake and the sake of the soldiers. The carols were sung lustily, like bar songs, for few in the great house could retain faith in gentle Jesus, meek and mild. The carnage in France continued relentlessly, the circles on the lake of blood widening beyond physical maiming and destruction to the corruption of love and ideals and souls.

The Northumberland postmark warned Macha of the contents of the letter which arrived on Boxing Day, and she was not mistaken. Lord de Clercy, Richard's brother-in-law, informed her, in terms which had obviously been perused and edited by a lawyer, that the Marquess of Bridgemere had told the family of her scandalous background and that it was his wish that she vacate Rapsleigh upon his twenty-first birthday. Lord de Clercy expressed regret that as Richard had seen fit, against all advice, to make her the sole executor of his Will, it was not possible to eject her earlier.

"Come down to the tack room; I've an idea," Declan said mysteriously. "What's needed round here is a bit of fun."

The smell of hay and leather and saddle soap was evocative of foals' being born on early-spring mornings and blue summers spent training and following her horses round the tracks and autumn exercise on the gallops, misty and brisk. Macha became aware of it for the first time in a long time and drew in an appreciative breath.

"I don't seem to get down to the yard much now," she observed nostalgically. "And I hardly went racing once last year."

"It's time you gave less time to thinking," he commented cryptically. "Try these on for size."

He held out a pair of breeches, a black hunting jacket and boots.

"For heaven's sake, Declan! I can't do that!" she protested.

He gave an impatient snort. "There you are, you see, always arguing, instead of getting on with it. I can remember a time when m'lady wore little else."

"What's all this about?" she demanded.

"All in good time," he said, infuriatingly. "Now do as you're told."

"Someone might come in."

He opened the door and checked the yard, quickly.

"There's no-one about."

"There's you," she pointed out.

"And I've seen you in the altogether more than once," he retorted. "Are you frightened I'll notice how fat you've grown?"

Macha glowered at him, then began struggling with the row of little buttons on her costume. He had the decency to look away, and minutes later he turned to see her dressed in the outfit.

"My, you've not changed," he grinned. "Under all that finery, you're still just a hoyden."

"You'd better have a good reason for this, Declan O'Brien," she warned, feeling ridiculous.

"The best," he assured. "On New Year's Day, they're putting on the first local point-to-point round here since the start of the War, and I've entered old Red Rory. We're lucky that splint kept him from the War. He's a good horse, and he'll show the rest his heels. How would you like the ride?"

"Arrah, Declan. That's quite impossible."

"Be jabus! You've become real starchy, Macha," he said, scornfully.

"And you've gone raving mad," she answered back. "I'm not a girl any longer. Mother of Saint Patrick! I'm a dowager! The dowager Marchioness of Bridgemere. How can I be seen gadding about the country dressed as a man?"

"Oh, I see: you're too old, then," he goaded.

"It's nothing to do with age, and well you know it." She was highly affronted by this suggestion following so soon after the comment that she was too fat. "Apart from anything else, my hair's about three feet long. What am I supposed to do with that?"

"Bob it," he directed. "Isn't that what all you women are doing nowadays?"

"Bob it! Bob my hair?" she screeched. "My lovely hair? Never!"

"Ah, well, maybe you're right," he said, with a philosophic shrug. "The soft living's done for you, and no mistake."

This was too much. Macha drew herself up to her full stately height.

"Right," she said. "I'll show you who's soft. But that horse had better be in top condition, or you're sacked."

"Certainly, My Lady." He touched his cap in mock deference. "And I trust you're perfectly fit yourself after all that Christmas pudding. I wouldn't like to do the horse an injustice."

Macha had flounced back to the house before fully appreciating the commitment she had made. After the briefest of reflection, her immediate thought was to return to the yard and back down. Halfway along the gravel drive, she stopped, recalling the race at Killarney as though it had just taken place. She was urging on Macha's Girl again in her mind—and when she finally returned to her surroundings, her hands were damp with excitement.

To feel as carefree and daring once more, she thought. To bolt over the jumps. To win! That would be one in the eye for Declan O'Brien, one in the eye for everyone and what fun it would be!

Wheeling round, she ran to her room almost laughing aloud with glee. Her riding clothes were ripped off and flung on the bed. Dressed only in a camisole top and wrinkling silk stockings, she bent to touch her toes. She reached them a hundred times before flopping down, breathless.

Then, pulling in her stomach, she examined herself in the cheval glass. What a cheek that man had! She wasn't fat. She hadn't put on an inch in twenty years, and she was fit. Flipping through the pages of her address book and picking up the telephone, she asked for a London number.

"I can be there by four o'clock this afternoon," the man's voice replied to her query.

She asked for a coddled egg and a piece of toast for luncheon, assuring Mrs. Wellington and Molly that she was perfectly well. When they rose from the table, she went for a short, sharp ride over the hills before returning to her room, lying on the floor and bicycling energetically with her legs in the air for fifteen minutes. Then Doris, with much resentful muttering about the war effort, drew a bath, into which her mistress sank gratefully to soak her aching muscles.

By the time the hairdresser arrived off the London train, Macha was sitting rosily in front of her dressing table, her red hair loose down her back.

"Cut it off," she instructed.

"Oh, My Lady, that's a very radical step to take," he demurred. "If you would prefer it off the face, there are many styles I can show you which are both practical and attractively suitable for this busy world of ours."

"Hundreds of women have short hair now," she pointed out.

"Some girls of the lower orders do favour the bob," he remarked snobbishly. "But not ladies. And My Lady's hair is very beautiful—so thick and lustrous; the kind of hair it is possible to do anything with."

"Then it'll make a nice bob, Monsieur Jean, so start chopping," she responded.

He almost closed his eyes as the long tresses fell to the floor, and Macha herself avoided watching in the mirror. At last it was done. Her head felt light and cool. She shook it like a pony which has had its mane hogged and peeped at her reflection at last.

A very up-to-date young woman with an oval face and dazzling wide eyes looked back at her. She had lost years.

"What do you think?" she asked the hairdresser, her satisfied expression betraying her own opinion.

"My Lady looks very . . . modern," he replied with a tight, pained smile. Then, gazing at the floor, he said, "I expect My Lady would like to keep the hair."

"What ever for? To stuff a cushion?" She laughed. "Certainly not. Throw it out."

Declan's beam and Molly's astonished approval of the style compensated for old Mrs. Wellington's bewailing during dinner that evening, of which Macha ate only a few mouthfuls. For the few days left of the year, she dieted and exercised ferociously, relieved that her regular rides on the still-spirited Gold had kept her muscles toned.

On the morning of the point-to-point, pleading a headache, she let the party from the palace leave without her and then changed in the horse box driven by Declan O'Brien. Knowing the whole county would be present at the event, she remained hidden there until the last minute before being given a leg-up on Red Rory and cantering to the start with head bent.

Snow still lay in frills where the hedgerows met the fields; a frost had hardened the going. The spire of Slad church, short and thin, seemed brandished like a knife behind them, the copse by which they would race was as dark as the mouth of a cave, and the first brushwood fence rose like an iron bulwark across their way.

Macha tried to remember that the safest place in a fence is the blackest, but her stomach was churning and her body awkward with expectation, and her mount, sensing the nervousness of his rider, pulled on the reins and bucked. The movement caused her instinctively to sit down in the saddle and lighten her hands. The tension left her, and as she took control, her mind concentrated on the goal ahead, her will fused to that of the horse. The rest of the field, sidling and snorting around them, faded, and the astounded glance which crossed the face of the neighbour who recognised her went unnoticed.

Leaning forward, she whispered in staccato breaths to Red Rory, who flattened his ears and jerked his head as the flag dropped. Up the slope they galloped, Macha keeping calmly in the centre of the bunch, conserving her horse and waiting for the rest to spread out. Jack Hewlett, one of Rapsleigh's tenant farmers, took a fall at the first fence, and the next saw off the young Sir Neville Archer, whose Pride of Paradise had been serious opposition. As they headed over the hill, Macha began to move up stealthily on the front runners. The big hunter took the oxer without breaking stride, and clearing the gate on the far side of a meadow, was in third place. A mile to go and he needed no urging. The powerful muscles of his hindquarters flexed under her as he bounded over a stream, scrambled up the bank and over the post-and-rails at the top.

The last fence was behind them, and Macha rolled in her thighs and gave him his head. The hunger gripped her, stretching her sinews, squeezing her gut: the hunger to win. Red Rory flattened himself past the remaining challenger, and as she lost her top hat, they drew away in a spray of snow.

The steeple of Painswick was glittering, its light as mesmerising as the stone of Tara. With red locks flying, they pelted to its silver sword of victory.

"Mam, Mam! The man of horns couldn't of caught you. You were faster than arrows!" Molly had reached her first, stretching up to pull on her arm, radiant with pride; then Declan, smiling his rare smile, was there, leading in Red Rory. Macha was so full of emotion that she was giggling like a child.

The news of her identity had passed through the crowd faster than the race. Not a few of the men were cheering loudly, and the other riders were running to officials to protest. Macha did not heed and did not care. The wind was still in her hair and the sky in her eyes. No pain, no restraints, no regrets, only triumph. She was free as an eagle.

The silver chalice was being handed to a tall man. It would not be given to a woman, she thought without concern. He turned and walked straight towards her, holding it out, and she saw with delight that he was Sir Freddie Wellington, home from the Front on leave.

"Congratulations, my dear Macha, and well deserved," he said with a conspiratorial wink. "A race of perfection. Gad! I should have dressed you in breeches and put you up on some of my runners years ago. I'd have been a richer man."

That night the whiskey came out, and Macha and Declan and Molly drank freely, and the more they drank, the more the rigid formality which they were all normally forced to exhibit towards each other fell away until they were all roaring at jokes the English would never have appreciated.

"Pat Connor had a pair of horses as alike as peacock butterflies—only one was a roarer . . . " Molly, relaxed and herself at last, began a tale. "Well, he sold the sound one to this fellow in a long coat and then changed them over and delivered the grunter. Only it came out it was a holy father under the coat, and Pat Connor was so heart-scalded with mortal fear of being cursed to hell that there was nothing for it but to switch the two beasts over again before daybreak.

"It was a night as black as a blindfold, and Pat Connor was in more of a lather than a Turk tumbling over a cliff edge. He pushed the one horse into the stall and took the other. And on the way back, doesn't he hear the hooves and burning fires of the Divil himself following, and the faster he goes, the faster comes the Divil behind, till Pat Connor reaches the bender tent about dead with terror and gets a clout in the back that sends him flying. When he looks up, praying to all the saints for mercy, what does he see but the sound horse looking down at him. Sure, the bliddy nag had followed him all the way back."

Macha and Declan sprawled back on the sofa, laughing.

". . . And behind the creature was the poliss—and they put Pat Connor away for six months for horse stealing."

Their screeches must have roused the sleeping servants, and Macha leaned against Declan for support.

"Do you know you've owed me fifty pennies for over twenty years?" he asked her, after they had recovered.

"How's that?" she demanded.

"Because, like the Divil after Pat Connor, didn't I come after you to Killarney races and put the only penny I had to my name on you to win and you did, but they never paid out."

"Arrah! A fool and his money, Declan O'Brien . . ." giggled Macha, and received a playful slap.

He had surprisingly elegant fingers, she thought, catching sight of his weathered hands. It was rare for him to laugh, and she found herself staring at his white and perfect teeth and then into his face. It was lean and creased with the lines which come from riding out in all weathers. Suddenly, Macha realised she had not really looked at him for years. He was so familiar that she had forgotten what an attractive man he was. Recollecting the night, long ago, when she had seen him kissing one of the maids at Ebberly, she wondered about the women in his life. He was intensely private and had never married, but she knew there were women, and, for some reason, the thought was irritating.

"I'm going to bed," she announced, and stood up unsteadily.

"You'll need carrying there by the look of you," Declan grinned.

"Not at all," she retorted with dignity, but did not shake free as he took her arm. He left her at the door of her bedroom, and through bleary eyes she watched him return down the stairs and felt an unexpected craving.

By God, I must be more drunk than I knew, she thought hazily, and fell onto the bed and asleep fully clothed.

The photograph of the presentation of the silver cup to Macha was published in the press and caused an uproar. Letters of outrage were written to *The Times*, ladies of her acquaintance cut her, hunt officials met and were prevented from creating new conditions of entry to prevent such a scandal occurring again only by the influence of the Duke of Portland.

"The sight of ladies hanging head downward from their pommels has come to be considered the most prominent evil in connection with the hunting field," he quoted from Pennell-Elmhirst's *Best Season on Record*. "There has recently been a great outcry on the subject of habit-skirts."

But he could not stop the Jockey Club ensuring that there would be no women jockeys.

The escapade did more than release Macha from some of the weight of her bereavement: it also loosed her from guilt and left her unhindered to review her life with dispassion. Since her arrival in England as a young girl, she had seen Society as the only source of security and success and had genuinely tried to conform to its mores, believing that her dream of owning and racing the finest bloodstock could be achieved only within its protection. To an extent this had been true, but she now began to question the need to continue.

For the first time in many months, she was filled with gaiety. The taste of liberty had been more intoxicating than champagne. She had tried the safe way and found it suffocating. Still only thirty-eight years old, she had as ravenous as ever an appetite for experience. She wanted to take risks and try out the unknown, and the obligation to live out the rest of her days in the staid role of widow and dowager became clearly insupportable.

Although most of the Withington fortune had gone to her son, her late husband, Richard, had set up a trust for her, and he had kept his earliest promise. Half the fillies born at the Rapsleigh Stud since their marriage had automatically become her property. She owned a string of young classic stock and some of the finest brood mares in the land. British aristocracy, wealthy industrialists and Indian princes vied to purchase their progeny. Having ploughed back much of her profits into their improvement and maintenance, she was not rich by most standards, but there was more than enough for her future needs.

As she descended the stairs some weeks after the race, her tangerine dress, with its hem swirling well above her ankles and neckline, bordered by a white lace collar, plunging to display her cleavage, was a blatant statement of her intentions. In throwing out her black weeds, she was also throwing out the past twenty years.

"There's no cure for grief but to put it under your foot and no happiness without an inch of sorrow through it," she summed up her feelings to Declan. "I'm going to get on with it, starting with going hunting again, *my* way, and then we'll enter me and old Rory in another 'chase."

"They'll not let you get away with it," he warned.

"How will they stop me?" she demanded.

"Easy. You're a convivial woman, liking a good crack and company. Where will you dance and dine and show off your wit and your finery when they turn their backs on you?"

"I've friends," she pointed out defensively.

"You'll count them on half a hand," he replied. "Pity the man in a country where there is no-one to take his part, Macha."

"Well, I've you and Molly and Mrs. Wellington and Freddie and I don't give a hoot for the rest. I'm going to do what I like, wear what I like and go where I like."

But a telephone was ringing somewhere in the great house even as she spoke.

The headmaster of Eton sounded quite unperturbed as he gave her the news.

". . . the boy has been rather unsettled . . . death of his father, y'know . . . no need to worry . . . quite capable of looking after himself . . ."

Edward was missing. Macha, in her panic, heard only bits of each phrase.

"What are you doing about it? What have you done?" she demanded. "Have you contacted the police?"

"Oh, I don't think it's necessary to take such drastic measures quite yet." The headmaster was obviously more interested in protecting the school from bad publicity than in her son. ". . . probably turn up at home within an hour or two. . . ."

Macha knew the palace of Rapsleigh was the last place Edward would make for, nor would he go to Northumberland. Running away from school would earn only his uncle's contempt for cowardice.

"The police are to be told at once," she commanded. "And I wish to speak to Edward's friends this afternoon."

"My dear Lady Bridgemere, please calm yourself. There is absolutely no need for you to come down. I have already spoken to some of the senior boys and I can assure you that they know nothing."

"I shall be there after luncheon, and I expect the police at Windsor to have been informed and to meet those boys."

Macha rang off and ran back to her room. Flinging off the tangerine frock, she put on an expensive but plain costume without ringing for Doris. Action concentrated her mind as she reported Edward's disappearance to the local police, ordered the car, climbed into the driving seat herself and sped off, with cans of spare petrol in the boot, which she had always insisted be stored there for emergencies.

Only when she was halfway through her journey did she allow herself to face her own suspicions. Edward looked much older than his age. She prayed that she was wrong.

They gazed at her with deceptive indolence, the four waiting boys, impeccably polite but giving nothing away. In their top hats and short Eton jackets, they looked like old men with young faces.

They were afraid they could not help. Edward had not confided any plan. When she asked if Edward had a special friend, one of them sniggered rather unpleasantly, as though she had made a *gaffe*.

The headmaster stood by, smugly satisfied, as they prepared to leave.

"How old are you?" Macha asked one, suddenly.

"Seventeen," he answered.

"And you?"

"Seventeen," the next replied.

All four were the same age. Edward was only fifteen.

"I want to see all the boys of my son's age from his house," she told the man, with a look which brooked no dissent.

The younger boys were exactly the same as their seniors, courteous but uninformative, and finally, after telephoning home in the faintest hope that Edward might have arrived there during her absence and having this denied, Macha left without hearing a word of the headmaster's platitudes.

As she started the engine and the man turned away, a fair-haired boy appeared by the gates and beckoned.

"I wanted to tell you in there," he began, talking breathlessly and glancing towards the school buildings as she drew up. "Edward was always talking about the War, about going to fight in France. I don't want to sneak, but he might be killed, because I think he's gone to enlist."

Macha's stomach plummetted. This was exactly what she had feared. Thanking him, she set off for home, her emotions jangling with a mixture of impotence, guilt and fear. If she had been warmer, somehow come closer to her son and managed to comfort him . . . If Rapsleigh had been a real home, instead of filled with strangers . . . If only she had not quarrelled with him. . . .

So many young lads ran off, these days, to join the army, and Edward, so tall, would have no difficulty in being accepted. He was clever and would have changed his name and covered his tracks well. His mother did not even know where to start trying to trace him. Images of another official telegram arriving made her tremble.

Declan O'Brien hurried to the police station with a photograph of her son when she returned to the palace with the news, and Freddie Wellington, when she telephoned him, said he would contact the War Cabinet immediately and advised sending them a photograph by special messenger. He rang back, a short time later, with other addresses.

"These boys are usually found," he told her.

"But not always," she pointed out, tearfully.

"Edward has the great advantage over many of being the Marquess of Bridgemere," he responded. "In no time at all, some officer who knows the family will recognise him, you can be sure."

Macha was far from sure. She wrote a letter to the relevant official in London and sent Declan with it to catch the first train. Then she spent all night writing to everyone she knew serving in France, and many she did not know. She wrote to the commanding officers of the main army training camps in Britain. When dawn came, she carried out the worst task of all, steeling herself to telephone Lord de Clercy's number.

"I see," he said icily when she informed him of the situation. And after she had told him what action she had taken, added, "I trust you realise you are entirely responsible for this."

It was what she herself believed, but hearing it from another was like being sentenced.

"You have completely failed in your duty as Richard's widow and Edward's mother," he went on implacably.

She could not argue and was pathetically grateful when he agreed to make enquiries through his own wide circle of influence.

For hours, her distraction was so great that she was unable to think logically. It was only when Declan arrived back from London and insisted that they both sit down and try to approach the crisis constructively that she began to regain control of herself.

"Now, what can he do? There's no doubt he'll try to use his advantage," the Irishman said.

"Oh, he'll not go near any friends, or anyone who knows him." She mistook his meaning. "And he won't dare try to join Richard's regiment."

"No, no. What's he good at?" he explained. "He'll want to use his skills."

"He's done well at school," she offered lamely. "In exams and such."

"And he's a first-class shot," Declan added, with a lack of tact which made her burst into tears again.

"Macha, don't shirk it," he said, not unkindly. "We have to think of everything, anything which could point to the direction he might have taken."

She swallowed and clenched her hands together.

"I know he's a bright chap and good at sport. He can drive a motor-car, and he's cocksure of himself," Declan summarised. "But you're his mother, and you may not have been getting on with him too well lately, but you know what he's best at. What gives him most satisfaction."

There was no hesitation now. "Horses," she replied at once. "He's like his father and me there."

"Then he'll go for the cavalry." Declan was certain. "So we'll contact every regiment."

He put his arm round her shoulders and gave her a hug. Macha's eyes were full of dependence and affection. Since Richard's death, Declan had at last permitted a relaxation of the underlying formality always maintained between them, which had so emphasized their positions as mistress and employee. Now, that was all changed. They spent much time together, dealing with the business of the estate and the horses, and through his unfailing support and unruffled common sense, they had grown close. Even while tormented with worry, Macha reflected that he was usually right and placed all her hopes on his advice. She could not imagine life without him.

Just as Declan had predicted, Edward was found at a camp in the Midlands two weeks later. The hearty C.O. telephoned the news. "We'll send him back to Rapsleigh in the morning. Don't be too hard on him. He's a fine young man, your son, plenty of guts—just the sort we need, Lady Bridgemere," he said. "Of course, we had no idea of his age, but we'd welcome him back when he's a little older. Officer material, y'know."

"I hope to God the War will be over before then and there'll be no need for soldiers," said Macha weakly.

"Oh, there's always a need for soldiers," he laughed. "A young chap like Lord Bridgemere would have a ripping time. Plenty of hunting, shooting, polo, travelling. No better life."

Macha could think of better. As she sat back, limp and exhausted after the conversation, she realised how certain she had been that Edward had reached France. She had pictured him struggling through the mud. She had seen the Hun raise his gun. With a shudder, she turned away physically from her own thoughts.

Somehow, the differences between the boy and herself had to be healed now. Because of his upbringing, they would never be as demonstrative with each other as she would wish, but with her whole heart, she wanted his respect and hoped for his love.

Her dilemma was how to reconcile this with her own dread of the restrictions it would impose upon the rest of her life. Like his father, Edward was extremely conservative, and her plans to live independently and actively would drive him even further away.

At the moment, she knew he would be feeling demoralised and

perhaps even ridiculous. The approach had to come from her, and this was the time to do it.

Sitting up in bed picking at breakfast the next morning, she was so preoccupied with the predicament of making the overture without being repulsed that she ignored the mail on the side of the tray. The curtains were stirring in the breeze, and one of the huge, waxy flowers on the magnolia outside was bobbing into the open window like an incense thurible, filling the room with its citrus-sweet scent. Such a day did not deserve the obscenities of war and enmity. On such a day, it was almost a duty to make peace.

Idly, she began to slit open the envelopes and glanced at a couple of invitations, some race-entry forms and her dressmaker's account. In the middle of the pile, she saw with pleasure an American stamp, a letter from Daisy Schultz.

They had never stopped corresponding, despite the scene so long ago in Bad Ischl. If Richard had been aware of it, he had not mentioned it, and after his death, it was Daisy's letter of condolence which had brought the most consolation. Over the years they had grown into the habit of confiding with each other at length, and despite the distance, Daisy probably knew more about her than anyone else on earth except Declan O'Brien. After winning the point-to-point, Macha had written of her victory and her ideas for the future. This was the reply.

Washington, D.C.
2nd February, 1918

My dearest Macha,

What fun and how energetic of you! How I wish I had been there to cheer you on and see all those aristocratic noses put out of joint by your win. You never change.

The rest of your letter gave me much food for thought. I understand your feelings so well. My own were exactly the same during my unfortunate period in Great Britain. Everything I wanted to do seemed to be *verboten* and all those affected girls with their *dinnares* and *dansares* and *deevies* drove me mad. From what you have told me, nothing has really altered, despite the war.

My dear, to be frank, I cannot imagine your gay schemes will be permitted to flourish, especially now that you are the Dowager Marchioness of Bridgemere. The pressure to conform from Society will be far too great, and you know you are not the sort of woman who could be content in isolation. Also, Molly's position is always going to be very difficult.

Although I have often invited you to the United States, I realise your family commitments made that impossible before, but what is there to stop you now? It is getting on for two years since you were widowed, and from what you say of Edward, he is almost grown and intent on going his own way.

Wilbur and I have talked this over at great length, and nothing would make us happier than for you and your daughter to join us. America is new and hospitable, not hidebound by fossilized old customs. Here, I am convinced, you would find everything you search for, friends and freedom—and, don't forget, our bloodstock can vie with the best in England these days!

Dear Macha, I beg you to consider this move earnestly and come to our wonderful country.

Your affectionate friend,
Daisy.

Their bloodstock could vie with English Thoroughbreds, indeed! Macha grinned to herself and then walked to gaze out over the Cotswolds, hazy in their spring dream. England, with her villages nestling like babes between the breasts of her Downs, her mossy woods and flower-hemmed lanes, her hedgerows of dog roses and honeysuckle, the hypnotic cycle of her seasons, the knifing through the earth of first leaves and the popping buds, the sleepy seductiveness of summer meadows, bronze bracken, golden fruit and silver frost, the deep, white quilt of winter. Could anywhere in the world be more bewitching? She could not believe it.

Yet Daisy's letter had echoed Declan's words. Not all her wilfulness and optimism would defeat the power of this Society. Then, there was Molly. Edward would never come to terms with her existence, and without the protection of his position, she could not be accepted. She was hard-working, with a gift for nursing, but she was far less adaptable than her mother, who accepted the responsibility for having taken the girl away from her roots and who was determined she would have the best.

That afternoon, her son stood before her in the library pink-faced and refusing to meet her eye. She wanted to hold him to her, but the resistance of his stance prevented it.

"Son . . . Edward, you are a fine boy and your father would have been proud of you, and . . . I am proud of you," she began.

He shifted slightly and stared out of the window.

"That you wanted and tried to fight for your country showed great courage, so don't feel you have failed. Don't feel you have let the side down," she went on, gently. "You are almost a man, and your time will come soon."

He thrust his hands into his pockets.

"Tell me"—she changed the subject, knowing he would find it humiliating to give in to emotion—"do you enjoy staying with Uncle Hal?"

"I won't be able to go back there." He looked down at the floor, tight-faced.

"Why not?"

"He won't want me now . . . after this."

"That's where you're wrong, my dear. I spoke to him only this morning and he thinks the world of you. Chip off the old block . . . the young devil . . . credit to the family . . ." She mimicked Lord de Clercy with mischievous accuracy. "I do believe he wishes one of his own boys had had the guts to join up."

Edward gave a tentative and questioning smile.

"You'll hear it from himself, because he's coming to see you." She was glad of the opportunity to reassure him. "So you do like it in Northumberland, well enough?"

He nodded.

"Edward, it is because you have proved you are no longer a child that we should talk as two adults. Maturity is not just a matter of being manly, although that is very important. Maturity is also about understanding many facets of life and accepting them, although some may seem unfair and disappointing."

Macha sat down and beckoned him to do likewise.

"You have grown up at Eton among other boys, and although you all come from similar backgrounds, you must have learnt that each one is different. Sometimes certain people, having been born into privileged positions, look down on those less fortunate than themselves. But they are not gentlemen, Edward. No gentleman ever despises others, whatever their status in life. A gentleman only despises dishonourable behaviour."

Edward was looking confused.

"What I am trying to say is that your father and I were very different, having started out at the opposite ends of society. Some of my ideas were quite foreign to him, and my ways made him raise his eyebrows often, but we had the greatest respect for each other. We were deeply fond of each other, Edward, and happily married for many years. The reason for this was that your father was a gentleman. He was quite incapable of looking down on me, or anyone else, because of their background."

"He didn't know about . . . that girl," Edward said sullenly.

"Molly? No, he did not know. And when he found out, he was very shaken and, yes, angry," she admitted. "But I swear to you by all that is holy, son, that we were not estranged in the end. I want you to read this letter."

Macha handed him the last letter she had received from Richard, and there was a long silence during which her son seemed to read it several times, with eyes which grew red-rimmed. At last he just stood staring at it, and she knew he was trying not to break down.

"Discovering that I had had an earlier marriage was a great shock which your father needed time to think over," she explained, giving the boy time. "But he was a man with the breadth of vision and compassion to understand and to accept. We loved each other to the end."

There was a long pause, and she could see him struggling with a flood of thoughts. Once or twice he started to speak and then stopped.

"Edward, you and I are different and always will be, and although it may not seem so to you, I am not an old woman, and there are things I want to do with the rest of my life which may very well conflict with your ideas. You also may decide upon a future which I might not have chosen for you," she said, eventually. "But that is the point. We each have the right to choose, and nothing would have made your father more unhappy than to know that we were alienated because of our disparity. I want you to consider that seriously. You are our only son."

He looked directly at her for the first time, his expression a mixture of doubt and vulnerability. He wanted to be persuaded, she thought with a little lift of hope.

"I'm glad you enjoy visiting Northumberland. Uncle Hal can be a bit stuffy, but he's a good and quite a wise man. He cannot take the place of your father, of course, but his experience in running a great estate will be invaluable to you in the years to come."

"So will yours, Mother," he said diffidently.

"Ah, son, you'll never know how pleased I am to hear you say that." She beamed at him in delight. "If ever you need anything, you'll only have to write."

"Write?" He looked startled.

"Well, I do understand that you want to make Northumberland your second home," she said, without reproach.

Her son's eyes widened, and then, without warning, his face crumpled and he was in her arms.

"No! No!" he was sobbing, like a little boy. "I want to come home to Rapsleigh. I want it to be like it used to be."

Macha felt happiness free her from the clamp of pain, as though ivy had been cut down from a tree.

"Mmmmm. There, now. There, now. And so it will be." She rocked him, comforting, for a few blessed minutes until, with a bracing of his body, he drew back and became a man again.

Edward did not return to Eton. A tutor was hired, and when not studying, her son threw himself into the management of the estate with Declan O'Brien, went shooting and riding and fishing, and developed a deep interest in the welfare of the tenants and families who worked for the Withingtons. His attitudes towards the workers changed, too, and he behaved towards them with the consideration which had so marked his father.

Each evening he took his place at the head of the table and treated his half-sister, Molly, with a display of impeccable good manners, directing the servants to wait upon her with a mere flicker of his eyes. He made conversation with her, and when she chose lamb and then took mustard with it, he did the same. But his true opinion of her remained masked.

"He makes me feel a fool." Molly furiously plumped herself down on the sofa, after the ladies had retired from the dining room to the drawing room. "Sitting there, high-and-mighty, and giving not the littlest thing away."

"He does everything to avoid making you feel foolish," Macha was forced to point out.

"All that hoity-toity talk about nothing at all." Her daughter was scathing. "Does he think I'm too stupid to understand a good crack?"

"The English don't discuss politics and religion and serious matters in mixed company," Macha tried to explain. "It's considered bad form."

"Well, at least I did everything right tonight." Molly tossed her head. "Except for letting that potato roll off the plate."

"Mustard with mutton is the sign of a glutton," Mrs. Wellington put in before Macha could stop her.

"Holy Mother of God! What does it matter?" Molly leapt back on her feet, outraged. "I like mustard. Why shouldn't I have it with boiled cod, if I want? Anyway, Edward took some too. I saw him."

Mrs. Wellington gave a sigh and announced she was fatigued and would retire early.

"Edward is very young, and I think he is coping rather well," Macha said to her daughter.

"And I'm not, I suppose," Molly retorted, flushed.

"You both do," said Macha, with a tranquility she was far from feeling. Her son was a model of civility towards his half-sister, but equally, he evinced no amicability. "Sure, you'll be as thick as thieves in no time."

Her daughter, unconvinced, flounced after Mrs. Wellington to bed.

It was midnight when Edward came into the room.

"I thought you might still be up," he smiled.

Macha saw he was a little drunk.

"Good man, Declan," he commented, taking another sip from the brandy glass he was carrying. "Sound sort of chap, y'know."

Macha thought about her friend, with his patience and his practicality and that previously unsuspected quirky sense of humour which he so often used to diffuse the family tension, and she nodded.

"He's been the saving of me more than once, son," she confessed.

They sat companionably and without speaking for a while as the ash logs on the great fire cast the flickering light of the flames and the scent of autumn into the room.

"What on earth are you going to do with her, Mother?" he asked at last.

"Do? With Molly?" She was taken aback. "What do you mean?"

"She'll never fit in, never." His words were slightly slurred. "She's not one of us, you see."

"I'm not one of you," she pointed out. "And I don't do too badly."

"You're different."

"No, Edward. I'm the same. I was brought up poor, just like Molly, and I learnt your ways with the help of Mrs. Wellington and others."

He shook his head. "That's not what I mean, Mother."

"What, then?"

He searched for words. "Molly . . . she seems . . . well . . . quite a nice sort of girl. I mean . . . I try to make her . . . comfortable, but I don't think it will work."

"And why not?" Macha felt herself begin to grow annoyed.

Then Edward made an observation so astute that it turned all her ideas upside-down.

"Don't you see? Molly doesn't want what you wanted. She doesn't want our life," he said. "She doesn't like it."

Her daughter's earlier words repeated in Macha's mind. "Holy Mother of God! What does it matter?" What, indeed?

"I feel quite sorry for her," Edward added, and that shocked Macha even more.

She spent a sleepless night thinking about the girl and wondering how she could have been so insensitive. It seemed to be one of her failings. From the day they had first met in that street in Dublin, she had visualised only two options open to her daughter: the continuation of her life as a traveller, or absorption into English Society.

Yet perhaps because he was less involved, Edward had noticed what had not occurred to her. Although Molly had not chosen to return to Ireland, neither had she expressed the slightest wish to conform to the mores Macha was trying to force upon her. She accepted the admonishments of Mrs. Wellington out of deference, but without interest. She was far more concerned with her patients and more curious about the families living on the estate than about other landowners. In conversation, she would often use the expression "real life," as though what Macha was offering were unreal.

Macha, who until then had seen their circumstances as identical, suddenly understood that this was not so. She herself had arrived in England penniless and without family or friends, and had had to make her own way as best she could; but Molly's situation was completely different. Her mother was already rich and established, and that put her in the position of being able to pick what she wanted and decide how she would live.

At Rapsleigh, she had no social company of her own age. The young men were all in France, and when Macha had invited the daughters of their neighbours to the palace once or twice, the occasions had been resounding disasters. Just as their mothers had always done, these well-bred girls talked only of Society events they had attended, the other aristocratic families they knew and visited and the struggle to remain fashionably dressed in these times of shortage.

Molly had managed to behave with mute decorum, but there was no shared experience, and it was clear they thought her peculiar and common. No return invitations had arrived.

Macha contemplated the inevitable end to the War with trepidation. The country would be full of widows, like herself, and it was easy to envisage the scramble which would take place among the girls for the few eligible men to return from the Front. Even with the illustrious name of Bridgemere behind her and overt support from Edward, Molly, with her apparent lack of inclination and outlandish ways, would be left on the shelf.

From the window, she saw her daughter out riding on Red Rory, trotting along the edge of the spinney. The horse was as safe as a rocking chair, but she was gratified by the girl's easy control. Already, she sat with style and confidence.

At that moment, Edward came cantering from behind the trees and accidentally cut right across Molly's path. The Irish girl kicked her mount on and frisked past him in an obvious challenge. Macha caught her breath as the two raced across the park, their bodies balanced, the muscles of their horses shining and rippling and Molly's hair working free as she lost her hat. They looked beautiful. Young and vital and unrestrained, like gods on earth.

They vanished into Halfacre Wood, and minutes later, Edward came riding back full tilt and alone. Macha put her hand to her throat. They had been going far too fast for an inexperienced rider. Her daughter must have fallen. Then, to her surprise, she saw Molly appear from the track which made a short cut to the spinney and brought her out well ahead of her half-brother. Red Rory stopped at last, with flanks heaving, and the girl turned to wait for Edward, who pulled up his horse alongside and glared at her, boot-faced.

Oh, they would never manage to be friends, Macha thought.

Then Molly tossed her long mane of red hair, flung back her head and laughed. Her laughter carried across the grass and in through the open windows of the palace. Unrestrained and infectious, it cheered the soldiers and brightened the vast rooms like sunlight. A look of indecision crossed Edward's face, and then he too began to laugh. They roared and shouted together, jostling in playful attempts to push each other out of the saddle and onto the ground. Macha found herself laughing with them and seeing reflections of herself. Her children, who were more like her than they knew, had discovered each other.

The church bells pealed out on the eleventh hour of the eleventh day of the eleventh month of 1918. The King and Queen made a symbolic drive of celebration. The wounded soldiers shouted and embraced each other and then wept. There were services to give thanks in every church and a surge of balls and parties across the land. Seven hundred thousand young British men had died.

The sick men who had filled Rapsleigh for so long were sent home, or to other hospitals, one by one, and the palace seemed empty and full of echoes without them. As though determined to leave the past years as far behind as possible, Society crammed its calendar with overlapping events and tried to return to life as it had been before the War.

Macha found herself listening to the dated chit-chat of pre-war days, playing endless rubbers of bridge and sitting watching her daughter dance by with one partner after another and an undisguised look of boredom on her face, which was all the more irritating because it so precisely illustrated Macha's own reactions.

"How will I marry you off, if you won't bother with the most basic social graces?" she stormed at Molly, after spending an entire weekend engineering casual garden walks and accidental entrances into rooms so that her daughter could keep bumping into Sir Reginald Hibbert's boy, Reggie, by chance.

"If you mean marry me off to that stuck-up, fat half-wit Reggie Hibbert, then you can't," Molly retorted. "And anyways, who says I want to be married off at all?"

"Well, you've got to marry someone," her mother emphasized.

"No, I've not. You told me in Dublin I shouldn't marry anyone I didn't want!" Molly reminded.

Macha shook her head. "What sort of life would you have as a spinster, child?"

Her daughter flopped into a chair and then straightened her back, moved to the edge of the seat and folded her hands in her lap the way she had been taught. Her reactions were the same as those of a high-spirited young horse which had been overschooled, Macha thought guiltily.

She rang for tea and talked inconsequentially, watching the porcelain cup being lifted by delicate fingers, held at exactly the right angle and its contents sipped with a restraint which left the lips unsullied by a drop. There was a strained atmosphere between them, and she realised Molly was unable to relax in her presence.

How monumentally dull the weekends with the Hibberts had been. How monumentally dull all the weekends were now, peopled with the same old faces, hitting the same balls across the same croquet lawns, listening to the same gossip, with everyone pretending nothing had changed.

Yet everything had changed. The social structure had been turned upside-down; standards of living had dropped; staffs of servants had been decimated and the expectations of the working millions raised. And Macha herself had changed most of all. Once again, the thought of the years to come made her yawn—a wide, aching yawn which she did not attempt to cover with her hand.

Molly leant forward with a jerk.

"Why do we have to stay here?" she demanded. "Why can't we go away?"

Macha misunderstood her. "Do you want to go home to Ireland, then?"

"No." The reply was definite. "But I don't want to stay here, either. Ach, they mean well enough, these English quality, but they're not for me. All these airs and fancies, cocking your pinkie finger and speaking as though your mouth was full when it's as empty as a farmer's promise. You've put up with it, mother, because you had to, but I don't think you like it any more than I do."

"So where were you thinking of going?" Macha humoured her with a smile.

"Anywhere! The world over can't be all the same. We could go to India."

"They drink a lot of tea there," Macha teased.

"Or China."

"They drink a lot of tea there, too."

"We could go to Australia."

"Convicts."

"Arrah, Mother! Will ye be serious! Anywhere! Anywhere!"

"Is it so bad?" Macha stopped being flippant at the note of desperation in the young voice.

Molly dropped her eyes and blushed. "It would be . . . all right . . . if it was just for a while . . . but not for . . . settling."

The settled people. How well Macha remembered gazing at their cabins in Ireland with pity. To be confined between four walls and to an area of a square mile or two had seemed a miserable fate. Yet in a way, the limitations she had been imposing on her daughter were just as bad.

Her friends had all told her the same—Declan and Edward, even Mrs. Wellington and Daisy Schultz—but she had not been listening. Suddenly, Macha realised what had been staring her in the face for months.

"America!" she said. "We'll go to America."

Swearing her daughter to temporary silence, Macha went to her room, gasping at the immensity of the idea. Yet the more she thought of it, the more perfect it seemed. To live in the land free of affectation, the land of hospitality and space and riches—and Thoroughbred racehorses. She re-read all Daisy Schultz's letters, concentrating on every description, every detail she had written of her homeland, and it was as though this huge young country had been especially designed for resourceful women like herself and her girl.

Standing up at the end of the long table at dinner that evening, she drew a deep breath. Mrs. Wellington and Declan and Edward looked up expectantly, and Molly gave a secretive, knowing smile.

"Molly and I have reached perhaps the most important decision we shall ever make," Macha announced. "My darling son and my dear friends, we have decided to leave England. We are going to live in the United States of America."

She held up her hand as their faces froze.

"Now, it's not so far, and I'll return to England and to Rapsleigh often. And you, Edward, will come over there. Every man should see the New World, and what better excuse for the trip than having a mother living there?"

"What about me? It's not right!" He was dumbfounded.

"You'll be in excellent hands with your Uncle Hal to guide you, and in any case, I'm not sailing tomorrow," she pointed out. "By the time I leave, you'll be up at university, having a high old time."

Declan said nothing, and Mrs. Wellington's eyes became watery, and she fanned herself vigorously.

"I know it's a bit sudden," Macha admitted to them. "But it's for the best. I'm not ready to lead the retiring life of a widow, wearing drab gowns and sitting out all the dances. Then, there's Molly to consider. She needs more freedom than England can offer, and although she denies it, she'll want a man of her own before long, and children."

"I . . . I don't know what to say, Mother. What about the horses?"

She grinned. She should have guessed he would give them priority.

"I'm taking my best stock with me. I've read up a lot about the Turf over there. Do you know, there are stallions from some of the finest blood lines and plenty of first-class racecourses. Mind you, it's a bit of a drawback that all the racecourses there are left-handed."

"Are they?"

"Yes—there's not the variety, I must admit."

Suddenly, they were talking about racing and the record of Edward's leading stallion standing at Rapsleigh and the promise of the younger one starting his first season and of the mares she would take with her, and what kind of property she should buy there, and planning his first visit.

In the first rush of excitement, she imagined nothing but the journey, being a traveller again, sailing over the rim of the world and finding another land, new mountains and valleys, new fields and drivers and an endless road. Then, lying restlessly in bed, it occurred to her that she had been picturing three people setting out on this great adventure. But Declan had not spoken a word after her announcement.

If he did not come, what would she do? Who would steady her nerve? Who would keep up her courage? Who would plan races and tactics and work programmes with her and train her horses? Who would turn her dreams into facts? Who would josh her out of her moods and scold her and share it all? Declan had always been there. How could she go on without him? In the heart of the night, Macha wavered.

Macha and Declan O'Brien walked next morning round the stables and picked out the best brood mares and fillies, the ones she would take to America. Gold put his head out of his loose box and nudged her for carrots, just as he did every night.

"How old is he now?" wondered Declan.

"Twenty-two," she replied. "And as wicked as ever—aren't you, lad?"

The horse snorted and knocked impatiently on the wooden door with his hoof, then greedily sank his muzzle into her hand for the tidbits.

"Too old for the trip," Declan commented.

"Not at all." She rounded on him. "He's as fit as a yearling. He kept up with Red Rory for a good quarter-mile the other day. Anyway, if he couldn't come with me, I wouldn't go."

"You know best." Declan still looked doubtful.

"I do."

There was a pause. It was the moment they had avoided all day, each aware of what was in the other's mind and neither wanting to mention it first.

At last, she rubbed her fingers against her mouth and asked, hesitantly, "Have you any plans yourself?"

"Oh, yes," he replied, with an easy smile.

She waited, hoping he would enlighten her, but he just began whistling.

"Would you be staying on here?" she probed.

"No, I won't be doing that."

"So you'll move to another yard?"

"No."

There was a teasing look in his eye, which stung her into irritation.

"Will you stop this shilly-shallying and tell me what you're going to do, Declan O'Brien," she demanded.

"Well, you don't think I'm letting you go off on the high seas with my best horses and that old lag of a stallion, do you?" he retorted. "Someone's got to see them right. I'm coming to America, of course, and I'm bringing Ulick."

"Oh, Declan!" she shrieked, grabbing him tightly to her. "Why didn't you say so? I've been worried sick."

"You didn't ask me," he grinned.

The voyage was booked. The boxes were packed. The palace of Rapsleigh was thrown open for a great ball, with Edward, the young Marquess of Bridgemere, as host. Every mother propelled her daughter towards him, but he danced most with his half-sister, Molly. It was a gesture which moved Macha even more than the presence of royal princes, the cream of Society, the racing world and the whole county, who had come to bid her farewell. Everyone, it seemed, had plans to visit America.

Then it was the morning of the day, and the servants were lined up in the huge hall, old Doris weeping. Declan and Ulick had gone ahead with the horses. Sir Freddie and Mrs. Wellington and Molly were already in the Daimler. Outside on the drive, gardeners and stable lads stood in a group and raised a cheer, and as the car purred slowly through the gates, villagers and tenants crowded to shout and wave goodbye. Macha had never realised she was so loved.

Leaning out of the car and looking back, she saw the ramparts of Rapsleigh rising above the trees to the sky, mighty and permanent like the great family they had housed for so many centuries, dwarfing the momentary part she had played in their history. She gripped her daughter's hand.

The *Aquitania* soared like a floating white castle above them; porters and passengers and seamen buffetted against them, so that they held tightly to each other to avoid being separated. Mrs. Wellington gave way to tears at last, and Macha clung to her.

"Don't worry, old girl. I'll take care of her." Sir Freddie's dear familiar face bent over them as he embraced them both. A siren sounded like a dirge. She was being pulled up the gangway by Molly.

The air was full of streamers, and there was a band playing somewhere. The snowdrop of Mrs. Wellington's white lace handkerchief fluttered.

People, reaching out and crying and shouting and waving, carried her daughter away.

"Oh . . ." sobbed Macha, whirling round, helplessly. "No . . . !"

An arm encircled her and held her tightly.

"That's not the way to the United States," his voice said. "This is the way."

And he parted the throng and led her to the rails and raised her hand in his to wave to their friends.

The mighty liner slid out of the port, past the very spot where she had once stood under the Sussex Downs with her few rough ponies and the great red Thoroughbred stallion who had begun it all, and on into the Solent. The people merged into a tiny ball of colour; the city receded; England became a green jewel in the diamond sea.

"Oh, Declan," she said, tremulously. "Was there ever a time when you weren't by my side?"

"Where else would I be?" he smiled.

"How I love you."

"And have I not loved you since I was a boy, Macha."

"Always?" she wondered.

"Always," he confirmed.

Ahead lay America, the golden land of promise and refuge, offering hope and new life and freedom. They sailed to it together.